*When*
# GRUMPY
*Met*
# SUNSHINE

# *When* GRUMPY *Met* SUNSHINE

## CHARLOTTE STEIN

ST. MARTIN'S
GRIFFIN

NEW YORK

First published in the United States by St. Martin's Griffin, an imprint of St. Martin's Publishing Group

WHEN GRUMPY MET SUNSHINE. Copyright © 2024 by Charlotte Stein. All rights reserved. Printed in the United States of America. For information, address St. Martin's Publishing Group, 120 Broadway, New York, NY 10271.

www.stmartins.com

Library of Congress Cataloging-in-Publication Data

Names: Stein, Charlotte, author.
Title: When grumpy met sunshine / Charlotte Stein.
Description: First edition. | New York : St. Martin's Griffin, 2024.
Identifiers: LCCN 2023033041 | ISBN 9781250867933 (trade paperback) | ISBN 9781250867957 (ebook)
Subjects: LCGFT: Romance fiction. | Novels.
Classification: LCC PR6119.T445 W47 2024 | DDC 823/.92—dc23/ eng/20230724
LC record available at https://lccn.loc.gov/2023033041

Our books may be purchased in bulk for promotional, educational, or business use. Please contact your local bookseller or the Macmillan Corporate and Premium Sales Department at 1-800-221-7945, extension 5442, or by email at MacmillanSpecialMarkets@macmillan.com.

First Edition: 2024

10  9  8  7  6  5  4  3  2

*For my beloved and much-missed Gran,*
*who I would not have survived it without*

Dear Reader,

While this book is very much a lighthearted, hilarious romantic comedy—with a full-on, proper HEA—it does contain some sensitive, heavier topics. These include brief references to parental abuse, childhood poverty, and alcoholism, and an incident that includes fatphobia, plus brief mentions at a few points of the effects that fatphobia can have.

Hopefully, this will help you make an informed choice before reading! I've done my best to handle all topics with sensitivity and love.

Take care of yourselves,
Charlotte

# When
# GRUMPY
# Met
# SUNSHINE

Mabel,

It sounds like the deal is done, pending Harding approving you. Which shouldn't be a problem, being as adorable and talented and funny as you are! As to your question about the rumors you heard from someone in marketing—no, I really don't think he's rejected seventeen other ghostwriters. I think at most it's ten, which I know sounds like a lot but I promise you it isn't. Remember when you worked with that actress from *Emmerdale*? Well, she'd turned down quite a few before she settled on you.

That should tell you something, shouldn't it?

Plus, I have it on good authority that Harding is feeling the pressure to get this sorted after his management arranged that charity thing he requested. All profits go to . . . some food bank, I think it is? So I doubt we're going to be waiting around on this.

And you'll be in Greg Pemberton's capable hands, which have edited a thousand projects like this with far more difficult—not to mention famous—authors and clients. Please, try not to worry too much.

Just be your bright as a button self.

Emmy x

EMMELINE SANDERS
Leafland Literary Agency, Inc.
220 Madison Avenue, Suite 406
New York, NY 10016
leaflandliterary.com
@emmelinesanders

# One

## The Fairy Cakes Were a
## Mistake in Hindsight

*M*abel knew that working with the grumpiest man of all time was going to be tough. She just didn't appreciate *how* tough, until he stalked into the meeting room.

An hour late. With a face like thunder.

And a complete unwillingness to say so much as a word.

No *hello*. No *sorry*. Not even a response when Greg Pemberton introduced them.

"This is Mabel Willicker, the absolutely first-rate writer we've selected for you now," Greg said. And didn't get so much as a grunt as an answer. The grumpiest man to ever live—or Alfie Harding, as he was more commonly known to much of the British public—simply shoved himself deep into the nearest chair.

Then proceeded to glare at everything so hard, she couldn't understand why it didn't all immediately burst into flames. The fairy cakes she'd baked and rather optimistically brought along should have been a melted mess; the glossy oval table between them little more than ash. And when he bothered to look in their direction, good *Lord*. She actually felt the heat peeling off her skin. By the time he looked away, she was sure that she was little more than a skeleton. Only without the benefit of being nothing but bones.

Because at least then she wouldn't have been able to blush.

But blush she did. Her pale face was the color of a ketchup bottle. She knew it was, because she could see it reflected back at her in the polished surface of the table. And any second now, he was going to look back and notice it. Her blazing cheeks, like a sign that said:

*I am never in a million years going to be able to do this.*

Even though she absolutely knew she could.

She was a good writer, damn it.

And great at getting things out of people.

*You just have to find that way in, that little whatever-it-is that someone loves and responds to,* she'd said to Greg, when Greg had suggested that she might not be up to the task. Then she'd seen it on Greg's face: that hint of belief, mixed in with the initial doubt from when her agent had gotten in touch with him about this project.

So it was infuriating that her cheeks were betraying her.

And now Alfie was looking back, and he could see it, and this weird expression just broke all over his face. Like anger, only of a slightly different variety that she wasn't quite familiar with. Which made sense, when she really thought about it, because Alfie Harding was so furious all the time he had probably un-earthed layers of the emotion that nobody else had ever even heard of. He practically had a PhD in Being Really Annoyed. This was just his latest find:

Baffled Contempt.

Or maybe Amazed Disgust.

She couldn't tell for sure.

And before she was able to decipher it, Greg stepped in.

"Now, I know we've had some missteps. And that you're very wary of working with a particular type of person," he started, and honestly in any other circumstance Mabel would have felt relieved. She would have thought that this was definitely the way to go. Do a bit of schmoozing, get them to come around to your point of view.

But with a man like Alfie Harding?

*No,* Mabel thought.

*Abort, abort, abort.*

And when Alfie suddenly snapped to attention, she knew she was right.

Then braced herself for the coming storm. The ten-inch-deep frown, between his black-as-pitch eyebrows. That jaw suddenly clenched so tight you could see every muscle through his stark-as-a-January-sky skin. And finally, that voice—that somewhere-just-past-Manchester voice, familiar to her not only from his numerous surly TV appearances, and that time he'd tried his hand at an acting career, but from her own home. From the places she'd grown up.

From all the pubs and parks teeming with a million men like him.

Because she'd wanted to believe he might be different.

But of course he wasn't at all.

"What do you mean by that, exactly? Are you trying to say something about me?" he barked out, and of course Mabel knew why. Blokes like that always hated being thought of as scared. They never wanted to be wimps in anybody's eyes.

And certainly not in the eyes of some shiny editor.

Or some blushing fool of a writer.

It was obvious—and so much so that Greg clearly knew it now, too. Mabel glanced at him and saw the ripple of realization and discomfort cross his usually never anything but calm, pristine, Patrick Bateman–looking face before he managed to rein it in and smoothly change course. "Oh no, not about you," he said. "I was simply commenting on the process itself. It can be so difficult." And then he gave a little laugh. Threaded his fingers together in that way that seemed to say *if we were shaking hands right now, you would absolutely love it.*

But unfortunately for them both, Alfie wasn't having it.

He folded his arms across his chest.

Like a barricade between him and the two chancers in front of him.

"Didn't seem like that's what you were saying," he said.

"Oh, well, then let me apologize."

"Yeah, but for what though?"

He tilted his head when he asked the question.

*Like a cat*, Mabel thought. *Playing with a mouse.*

Even though Greg was the least mouselike person she'd ever

known. He could silence whole meetings with a look. Almost the whole of Harchester Publishing quaked in his wake. His suits cost more than she paid a month in rent; his license plate declared to the world that he was a Boss.

With an eight, where the O was supposed to go.

Yet to her astonishment, for a second he did actually look cowed.

He seemed to be sweating slightly. And his eyes kept darting to the expensive water someone had laid out on the table. Like his mouth had gone dry, and if he could just wet it a little he could come up with a good explanation for what he meant. Even though it should have been easy. *Just tell him he's a big strong boy and we'll move on*, she thought at him. But he simply couldn't seem to do it.

And now Alfie was starting to look amused.

Smug, almost, it seemed to her, in a way that was just as familiar as his accent and his anger and his overblown macho pride. Give it a second, and he'd be sneering at her the way he was sneering at Greg. Like every boy she'd ever known from high school, or played with in caravan parks on the East Coast, or been insulted by on the number 36 to Ripon.

At which point, she knew.

This wasn't an opportunity.

It was a chance for him to poke fun at people like her.

That was why he'd agreed to this, finally, after years of people trying to nail him down. It wasn't just the charity promise his manager had made, or a chance to prove he was more than a lunkhead, as she'd seen hinted at in various gossip corners of the internet, after that overblown reaction to the supposedly disastrous foreword he'd written to one of his teammate's books.

Oh no, no. He'd probably spotted Greg's massive car and his silly license plate. Or seen the lineup of writers they'd gotten to audition for him like this, as if he were a Broadway show and they were desperate teenagers who'd just gotten off the bus from Idaho. And he must have thought he'd hit the having-a-good-laugh jackpot, when Greg had finally scraped her out of the bottom of the barrel. Mabel Willicker, ghostwriter to such luminaries as some nobody on *Eastenders* and that bloke from *Bake Off* who'd cried so much on his cake he had turned it salty.

It was a contemptuous arsehole's dream come true.

He barely had to do anything to make her look foolish.

Then he could just flounce off, in a huff he could pass off as righteous. And even though it sank her heart to think it, she could tell she had it right. She felt it before he leveled those inky eyes on her, as he answered for Greg.

"Or maybe I should give it a guess: you think I'm a big hairy manimal who's never gonna be able to work well with this here human cupcake," he said. Then just for good measure, he flung a finger in her general direction. As if nobody were going to know that he meant the woman in the pale pink dress with the cherry-covered cardigan to match. Or understand that this was almost definitely a jab about her weight, on top of the rest of this mess.

So really, was it a surprise that she snapped?

Probably, considering she was well known for being the sunniest person on earth. But the thing was—even sunny people had their limits. And apparently, being thought of as a gross joke by a disgruntled ex-footballer was one of them.

"You know what? Actually, now I think about it, Greg, I'm pretty sure this was a mistake," she said. Shakily, it seemed to her. But by god, the words were fully formed. Those were whole and polished sentences that had come out of her. And they sounded almost annoyed, too.

So annoyed, in fact, that she had the satisfaction of seeing his smile drop.

About a second before she swept right out of the room.

Sweetheart,

I know you think that went terribly, but honestly I don't think it sounds that bad at all. Greg seems to think he was a lot nicer to you than all seventeen of the others! I'm sure as soon as we can manage to get ahold of Alfie we can sort all this out. Apparently, he doesn't have email. But Greg has assured me he does have a phone, it's just only turned on sometimes. Tuesdays and Thursdays, I think Greg said, but it was hard to be sure, he sounded extremely busy.

I'll let you know as soon as we hear something!

Emmy x

EMMELINE SANDERS
Leafland Literary Agency, Inc.
220 Madison Avenue, Suite 406
New York, NY 10016
leaflandliterary.com
@emmelinesanders

## Foreword to
## James Dolan's Memoir,
### *It Had to Be Me*

What isn't there to say about James that hasn't already been said? He's a top bloke, never leaves you hanging. No glory-hogging or any of that. No messing you around. Not to get too mushy or anything, but I'd, you know. Shake his hand.

Anyway, enough about me.

Get on with reading this book.

# Two

## How to Accidentally Get a Date with Gary Lineker

*M*abel knew exactly who was trying to call her. After all, she'd just abandoned a meeting with a man Harchester desperately wanted to work with. And most likely he'd taken that as an even greater insult than whatever the other seventeen ghostwriters had done. So there was no way Greg was just going to let her off the hook. At the very least, there were going to be stern emails to Emmy about how she'd never work in this town again.

Even though what she'd done was really the best thing for everybody. She didn't and couldn't work with someone that rude. And even if she could have, Alfie Harding clearly did not want to anyway. It was all just a chance to mess around with people, to him. Or maybe a ploy to get people off his back about writing this thing. She'd heard through the grapevine that he was being pushed by his manager into this deal. In fact, she suspected that was the reason said manager hadn't been in attendance. Too much chance of things being smoothed over. Then next thing you knew, there was no reason not to sign on the dotted line.

No, no, that wasn't what he was looking for. And she should have known it the second she heard that any contract was contingent on him liking whoever he was supposed to work with.

She'd been a fool.

The whole thing would have been a disaster.

A mess of a million scary arguments.

Him, coming up with increasingly horrible insults.

Her, eventually tossing him into the nearest wood chipper.

And she just didn't have easy access to machinery like that.

So it seemed like a good thing to have done what she had done. And she was ready to tell Greg that by the third of what she assumed were his calls. She took a deep breath and hit accept. All of her ready for Greg's slick patter.

And got the deepest depths of the North instead.

"Hello, I am trying to speak with Ms. Mabel Willicker," Alfie Harding said.

As if that made the least bit of sense. Starting with the fact that he was calling her after that whole hullabaloo. And ending with the absolutely baffling words he'd gone with. He sounded like a man attempting to get in touch with customer service.

"I feel like you should already know you're speaking to her," she said in the most sardonic voice she could muster up. Which wasn't very sardonic at all, she had to admit. Truthfully, it was almost as chipper as she usually sounded.

But it didn't shake, at least, and that felt like a triumph all its own.

Not that Alfie Harding was going to acknowledge that fact.

He just made a disgruntled sound. Then said: "Well I'm not just going to assume, all right. I'm bad with calling people." Only he didn't really say it. He shoved the words out from somewhere deep at the back of his throat. It sounded like very churlish gravel being shoved through an extremely sullen cement mixer. But that was fine. Because somehow, it seemed to make her even stronger.

Like his fury took hold of her spine and threaded it through with steel.

*I'll show you who's a human cupcake*, she thought.

Then retorted.

"Because you just do it out of the blue after being really rude to them?"

And oh, the silence that followed was satisfying. She had thrown him, a little. He was on the backfoot now. Probably sitting there in his angry chair in his angry house, stewing angrily over what to say next. Then when he finally came out with something, she didn't think it was what he'd intended.

"No, because I don't understand newfangled phones," he blurted out. Like she'd forced him into honesty, somehow. A lot of honesty, apparently, because suddenly there was more. "I don't know why I can't just stick with my old flip one that has proper buttons on it. Now it's all little pictures that don't tell you what they are, and next thing you know you're sending perfectly normal vegetables to Gary Lineker that somehow everybody else knows means you're wanting to do things to him with your purple penis."

Then it was her turn to be shocked into silence.

She simply stood there in the middle of her tiny kitchen.

Brain whirring, but nothing coming together enough to enable normal words.

And for so long an amount of time, that in the end she just had to confess.

"I have no idea what to say to any of that," she said.

"Yeah, and that's the other problem with doing this."

"You mean because you leave people flummoxed with absolutely preposterous rants about actual national treasure Gary Lineker?"

"It wasn't that weird a rant. And at any rate, this evil phone made me do it."

"Did the evil phone also make you call me a human cupcake?"

She expected another silence for that. After all, her snark was actually getting pretty slick now. In fact, she almost sounded sort of confident about it. Or maybe even amused, in a way she rarely was, when someone was a complete buttface to her. After most insults, she either tried to laugh it off or turned into furious jelly. Her face went red and stayed that way. Every word she said wobbled.

And it only got worse, the more she interacted with the insulter.

Only that wasn't the case, here.

She wasn't the flustered one.

*He* was. "Oh look, I didn't mean all that in the bad way," he burst out almost immediately. Much to her absolute delight. And apparent ongoing ability to tease him to death.

"So there's a *good way* to refer to someone as a generic baked dessert."

"Yes. No. I mean wait. Let me just think for a second, you're going too quick."

*Good lord, who* is *this person*, she found herself thinking.

Because it wasn't just how flummoxed she was making him—a man who once played the entire second half of a game of football after breaking his leg. No, it was the fact that she could hear something in the background. A kind of rustling and shuffling that sounded *really* familiar.

Then the dots connected in her head.

"Are you . . . are you reading from notes right now?" she said, and fully expected to be shot down in some way. Now, she thought, he would come back at her with something good. Something that made sense. Like maybe he'd taken a part-time job in a paper factory. Or was currently reading the script for the sequel to that movie he'd been in about a footballer who gets sent to prison for killing the referee.

Both of which sounded mad, of course.

But less mad than what she'd just floated.

Or so she thought.

Until he answered.

"That is outrageous. I'm offended you'd suggest such a thing," he said.

In the most overblown and obviously lying sort of way that she'd ever heard.

It was all she could do not to laugh. "Alfie, I can hear the pages rustling every time you pause. And I'm pretty sure that you just muttered *I've lost my place now* under your breath."

"Well, you try keeping track of tiny font when you haven't got your glasses."

*Jeepers*, she thought. *He's really doing it. He's just accidentally admitted it.*

Then could not help going further into whatever this was.

"I didn't even know you needed glasses. Is that why you were squinting all the way through one of your appearances on *A Question of Sport?*" she asked.

And didn't know what to expect as an answer. He'd already given her so much weirdness, it seemed impossible that he would go with more. Surely now he would return to the Alfie Harding he had always appeared to be, on the pitch and on telly and in interviews and even while acting: never saying anything above a single syllable, always full of confident swagger, temper flaring in only the most on-the-ball sort of way.

Only he didn't. He did not at all.

That Alfie had flown the coop, apparently.

And this absolutely terrible liar had taken his place.

"No. The studio lights were just very bright."

"But you did it again at that awards ceremony."

"That was only because I was tired."

"So tired that you called Helen Mirren *Helga Muppet?*"

*Okay, that was too far*, her brain immediately informed her. Yet strangely, she didn't feel bad about it. She felt something else, instead. Something that she didn't immediately recognize, after years of never quite knowing how to respond when someone was mean to her. And especially when that person was powerful—which Alfie Harding undoubtedly was.

He was famous, and rich, and used to people kowtowing to him.

Yet here it was, all the same: the sense that she had won.

She knew she had, before he even replied.

And when he did, oh Lord in heaven.

It was glorious.

"See, I knew this would be a mistake. I could tell you'd be all insufferable with me, saying all your cute things until I'm completely turned around. Well, I'm not having it," he said all in a big, angry, frustrated rush. Then he quite clearly tried to slam the phone down on her. Because apparently, he'd forgotten that phones didn't work that way anymore.

## Putting the Boot In

When hardman Griff Mitchell (Manchester United legend Alfie Harding) takes out his rage on the ref during a heated championship match, he winds up with blood on his hands and a stretch in the slammer. He's looking at thirty years hard time in the roughest prison in the country.

But after his cellmate, Little Jim (*Love Island*'s Benny Ormond) is brutally murdered, Mitchell knows it's up to him to get even with the thugs who did it. And now there are no rules to play by, he's going to play to really win. And the score line is about to be drawn . . . in blood.

# Three

## A Fern the Size of a Bus
## Would Probably Do It

*S*he considered telling Greg about the bizarre call from Alfie Harding.

But the problem was: she couldn't even really explain it to herself.

Every time she tried, all she could come up with was:

*I hallucinated the whole thing.*

Because for starters, Alfie Harding shouldn't have had her phone number. And even if by some miracle he had obtained it, there was no reason he would ever have felt the need to call someone like her. Then on top of these two impossible facts, there were the things he had supposedly said. All that mad stuff about penis emojis and wearing glasses she was pretty sure nobody knew he even needed and not wanting to talk anymore because she got him all turned around.

None of which seemed right.

Nothing ever turned him around. And he definitely did not like to reveal anything about himself. She knew he didn't because she had it all in her dossier on him. The one that she'd prepared when her agent had let her know she was up for the job. She had that profile he'd done with *GQ*, where he'd cut the whole thing short because they'd asked him where he got his hair done. Recordings of his post-game interviews, in which he usually responded with nothing but furious grunts. In fact, she remembered Baddiel and Skinner doing a whole series of sketches about it. Until they'd gotten too terrified to carry on.

Because that was the thing about Alfie Harding:

He was genuinely scary.

Which only made this whole business seem even more unreal.

So what exactly was she supposed to say to Greg? She couldn't tell him Alfie had done all that. It would just sound absurd. *Like something a writer in a precarious position would make up to give herself a little boost*, she thought. Then prepared herself to stay silent about the whole business, all the way through the lunch that Greg had invited her out for.

And she was glad she did, too.

Because it didn't really go the way she had thought when Greg had suggested it. She had assumed it was going to be him telling her off, under the guise of advice. *If you want a shot at ghostwriting for bigger names you need to be more accommodating*, she had imagined, as she practiced smiling in a more professional way, in the mirror, and selected her least colorful pair of shoes.

But from the second she sat down, Greg seemed nothing but polite. More than polite, in fact. He urged her to order whatever she liked, on his tab. And told her odd things, like how much she was valued by everyone at Harchester and how much he personally found her cheerful demeanor delightful.

Though it wasn't really what he said that made her wonder if he had gone mad. Or if she had gone mad. Or maybe both of them had gone mad at the same time.

No: it was the way he *looked*. Untidy, she thought, in a way Greg never was. His hair seemed ruffled, and his tie didn't appear to have been straightened that morning. Plus, there was something strange about his face. A sheen to it, as if he felt ever so slightly ill. Or had maybe jogged all the way to the restaurant from home.

It was unsettling.

So much so, in fact, that she sort of wanted to ask.

*Are you feeling okay*, she imagined herself saying.

But couldn't quite bring herself to do it. After all, things had gone well. It seemed foolish to pose questions that might lead them back to Alfie Harding—and especially when he seemed so keen on pretending it all never happened. *They must have finally found someone he could stand*, she thought. *Or gotten stern warnings from Human Resources about angry footballers being rude in boardrooms.*

And she had to say . . . that made some kind of sense.

Not a lot of it. But enough for her to relax.

To sit back in her seat, and smile, and enjoy her soup.

In fact, she had a spoonful of it raised to her lips, when something caught her eye. A flicker of movement from the corner of the room. Only the movement wasn't coming from anything normal, like a waiter handing out drinks or a fish tank full of guppies. No, it was coming courtesy of a *potted plant*.

A violently shaking potted plant. And then she spotted what was making it violently shake. But it didn't make any more sense than it had initially.

Because it was him. It was him. It was only bloody him:

Two-time winner of Footballer of the Year.

Golden Ball recipient.

Alfie fucking Harding.

Just there, grappling with a plant. Like that was a completely normal thing for a man like him to be doing. Even though it absolutely wasn't. He was supposed to be the sort that spent his time in clubs, carousing with babes and chugging pints of beer. He definitely wasn't meant to be hiding behind a fern in a fourth-rate restaurant.

And yet it was happening.

In fact, she suspected it was worse than that.

That he hadn't randomly decided to take up flower arranging.

He had simply stepped behind this plant the second she had glanced his way.

And then panicked when it did a poor job of hiding him.

Even though *everything* would have done a poor job of hiding him. There was hardly anything on earth that could have obscured him from view. He'd been retired for about five years now, but he was still as massive as ever. Heck, if anything, he was even more massive now. His thighs had spread a little bit, and were now roughly the size of carvery roasts. Thick, admittedly delicious-looking carvery roasts, which peeked out from around every bit of greenery. Oh, and then there were those meaty shoulders, named Best of All Time on at least three occasions by *More* magazine, practically framing the quivering fronds. And the sporadic glimpses of his gigantic hands, trying to pretend they weren't doing a bad job of holding the whole thing still.

Though even if she'd somehow missed all that, she couldn't have possibly avoided those eyes of his. They were like spilled ink. Really furious spilled ink.

And there was just no way to mistake that.

A fact that was proven even further, a moment later.

Because despite his best efforts to blend into the scenery, people other than her had also noticed him. She could see the old couple behind him, prodding each other. And the table by the fire exit, with the kids who wouldn't stop throwing spaghetti? They had clocked him, too. In fact, the dad was getting up. With what looked like a pen and a napkin in his hand. Then to her mingled horror and amusement, he sidled up to Alfie Harding.

And asked him for his autograph.

"My kids would be stoked," she heard him say.

Alfie gave him a look best described as rueful resignation.

*Well, I ballsed that whole hiding lark up*, his face seemed to say as he signed his name. Then she sort of wanted to laugh. But she couldn't, because her brain was currently bursting with about seven different unfathomable things about all this.

Starting with what he was doing right now.

And ending with the fact that he was here at all. Because seriously, this could not be a coincidence. He had to be in this restaurant for her, somehow. But then if he was, why had he hidden behind the plant?

There couldn't be a good reason for that. There couldn't be a good reason for *any* of this. It felt too close to something very weird, like being stalked by an incredibly famous ex-footballer. *Probably for the crime of forcing him to confess he wore glasses*, she thought. Which seemed utterly bananas, it did. But no more so than all the rest of this was, she had to admit.

Then had the most appalling urge.

She wanted to go over there. To ask him what on earth everything he had done meant.

And the only reason she didn't was down to one very important detail:

When she looked again, he had gone.

## Alfie Harding *GQ* UK Profile, March 2016

For a man who looms so large in the public consciousness—both in terms of his intimidating presence on the pitch, and his hilariously surly demeanor off it—Alfie Harding appears unassuming in person at first. When we arrive at his local pub, the Fox and Hound, it takes a moment to find him amidst the rabble you'd expect him to be a part of. And then the realization sets in: he's the bloke nursing a beer in the deepest, darkest corner of a place where smoke still lingers in the seat cushions. Drag your gaze across the over-varnished tables and the stained-glass-separated booths too quickly, and you'll miss him.

But once he settles that piercing gaze on you, it's a different story.

Suddenly, the intensity and charisma that captivated football fans and ordinary folk alike is incredibly apparent, and it's easy to see how this has propelled him to an entirely different level of stardom. Whether that stardom sits easy with a man who once listed his hobbies as *not being spoken to*, however, is another matter altogether.

"Enough money to be comfortable, and whatever my manager thought would make me enough money to be comfortable," is his abrupt answer when I ask him why he took the role in the movie—Lionsgate's *Putting the Boot In*, out April 15th—he's currently on a press tour for.

At which point, it becomes very clear why this press tour is, in the words of his publicist, *driving them to drink*. You can count on Alfie Harding to turn up and do the hard graft, but when asked to talk about everything surrounding the hard graft, the man is by turns taciturn, churlish, and often downright annoyed. And though it seems foolish to expect anything else from a man once voted Most Likely to Punch You for Asking Them a Personal Question, it's still quite a shock when he abruptly leaves after we ask him where he got his hair done.

# Four

## Being Followed by a
## Bearded Michael Myers

$S$he tried to tell herself that she was not being followed by an incredibly famous ex-footballer. But the problem with telling herself this? She was almost *definitely* being followed by an incredibly famous ex-footballer. It was obvious she was. Because that was him, over there, pretending to like being in the same Starbucks she had decided to try doing some of her own writing in today.

Even though she could tell he hated it.

Oh god, she'd never seen a man loathe sitting in a coffee shop more than he quite clearly did. He looked like he was being attacked by absolutely everything in the place. Starting with the small water bottle he'd obviously been forced to order, because you couldn't be in here without something. And quite obviously followed by the barista who kept coming over and asking if he was okay, and the man at the table next to him loudly talking about his NFTs, and the toddler who kept running by and standing on Alfie's foot every time he did so.

Though it was the colors that really made him look out of place.

The ones all over the giant mural on the wall behind him.

Because they were incredibly bright in contrast to him. So sitting in their shadow made him look even more conspicuous than he might have otherwise. *Sort of like seeing a funeral director trying to blend in at a child's birthday party*, she thought, and wanted to laugh over how true that seemed. Over that depressing dark suit and that even more depressing dark shirt and that hair of his—so obviously curly as fuck but forever crushed into the most severe-looking side part ever to exist.

But she couldn't even smile in the end.

Because he appeared to be getting to his feet.

And though up until that point he'd pretended not to see her, he did not seem to be doing that now. Instead, he looked directly at her. With bizarre determination, in that blazing black gaze of his. Like maybe the following phase of whatever this was had now ended, and he was about to enter a new, even worse one.

So she gathered her things in a mad scramble.

And bolted for the exit as fast as her legs would carry her. Right down Main Street, until she got to Sykes Avenue. Then when that didn't seem far enough, she turned left, and left again, and finally found herself at what she felt was a good, safe distance from that whole situation.

She even breathed a sigh of relief.

Then realized three things in rapid succession: 1) she was now somehow at least a mile from her home, 2) said mile was very dark and quiet and ran through a park people referred to as "that place where everybody gets murdered," and finally, and most damningly: 3) he was still hot on her trail.

Although the word *hot* was probably something of an exaggeration. Because every time she glanced back at him, he didn't seem to be walking particularly fast. He was just strolling, really. Meandering along behind her in a way that probably shouldn't have been that terrifying.

And yet somehow it was.

In fact, it kind of felt more so—and after five minutes of sweating and frantically checking behind herself and almost stumbling about twenty times, she processed why. She pictured it in her mind, clear as day: this was basically what happened in every slasher movie she'd ever seen. Right now, she was cannon fodder in something featuring a baddie like Michael Myers.

Only it was real, it was very real, and apparently even more relentless and inexorable than any of those movies had ever seemed. *How do they not scream the entire time something horrible follows them*, she found herself thinking. And not just because that seemed a more reasonable response to this. Because she actually wanted to do it. She came within an inch of yelling at about ten different points.

And especially when she saw him getting out his phone.

It looked like he was pulling out a weapon.

He even waved it at her.

Plus, now he was so incredibly close.

Even though she was practically running, and he still barely seemed to be moving at all. He looked like he was out for an evening stroll. She almost could have believed he meant her no ill will at all. That she was driving herself mad for no reason— and then she turned, and saw his hand reaching for her, and that was it. There was no room for half measures, no chance to be reasonable.

She yelped.

And turned.

And pepper sprayed Alfie Harding right in his famous fucking face.

**Alfie Harding's Favorite Things,** *More* magazine,
March 2016

Color: **Black.**

Item of clothing: **Anything dark.**

Time of day: **When it's night.**

Season: **See the last answer.**

Film: **One where you can hardly see anything.**

Song: **That Rolling Stones one.**

Food: **Something burnt.**

App: **I don't even know what that is.**

Emoji: **Are you having a laugh?**

# Five

## The Government of Norway Has Forgiven Him Now

*S*he knew it was a mistake the second she did it. And not in the *Oh god, I've riled the beast and now he's going to murder me* sort of way. No, it was really more of a *Whoops, I think maybe he wasn't trying to chop me into pieces after all* sort of thing. Mostly because his response, when the spray hit his eyes, was not to immediately attempt to stuff her into his murder sack.

No. It was to bellow like an enraged bear, and clutch his probably burning face, and gasp "Why," in the most confused and strangely hurt voice she'd ever heard in her life. As if he genuinely had no idea how things had come to this.

He had thought she was on his side.

And now she had to somehow explain why she wasn't. "Because I thought you were going to bloody do me in," she burst out, before her nerve could make her not. Or at least make her be less furious about things. Then once the fury was out there, she braced herself.

Only to get an answering expression that seemed just as baffled as his one-word question had been. She could see it was, even around the streaming eyes and the fists he was trying to screw into them and his grimace of agony. Though she didn't fully believe or understand it, until he managed to get it together enough to speak.

"You couldn't possibly have thought that. All I did was phone you. Then be in the same restaurant as you. Then watch you from across a crowded coffee place. Then follow you down a street when it's getting dark and there's no one else around and oh okay right yeah I'm seeing it now yep it's dawning on me fuck fuck fuck fuck fuck *fuck*," he said, and honestly she did not know what to marvel over first. Because yeah, watching a realization happen to someone mid-sentence was pretty incredible.

But so was that almost musical use of the word *fuck*. How he built a chain of them, each one slightly louder and more expressive than the last. And the way he added syllables to all of them, until finally, finally, he hit that last one. That three-sentence-long one, with a million sounds in the middle that didn't belong.

Yet felt completely right, anyway.

And that was all before she even got into how he looked as he said this.

That slow collapse of his face from something like surety to complete despair.

Then the way he tried to look to the heavens for inspiration but couldn't.

Because she'd filled his eyeballs with pepper.

It was amazing. So much so that she came very, very close to almost completely letting him off the hook. Maybe even close to apologizing to *him*, as if *she* were the one who'd done something wrong here. But in the end, the several ways he'd fucked up and her thirst to know what the fuck this had all been for won out over her habit of cheerily accepting that everything was fine now. "I have to ask at this point: How did it not dawn on you before?" she asked.

Much to his very obvious discomfort.

"Because I had a very good reason for all those things."

"Like, you have a terrible illness, and following me cures it."

"No, because that's completely ridiculous."

"Well, ridiculous *is* how you see me. So I just thought I'd lean into it."

She shrugged as she said it. Kind of half laughed, like she wasn't being serious. However, he very weirdly seemed to panic the moment she did. Or at least, he panicked as much as a man like him was able. Which mostly meant a lot of angry eyebrows and firm hand gestures and words spat out like gruff bullets. "No, don't lean into it. Lean out of it. Then keep going until you're on my level."

"And what's your level? Super smart and cool and always right about things?"

"Mabel, I'm standing here with pepper spray melting my eyeballs because I failed to grasp how following a woman home in the dark looked. Think it's safe to say my level is several thousand fathoms below smart and cool and right."

Okay, she wasn't expecting *that* response.

Though really, how could she possibly have?

He was supposed to be stabbing her by now. Or at the very least taking some kind of pop at her, for what were—by this point—numerous transgressions. But instead, he appeared to be taking a pop at himself. A hard one, that kind of made her want to be nice to him again. To tell him no, that couldn't be true.

Then he was relieved when good sense won the day. "All right then, what fathom should I be pitching my comments at?"

"Just imagine you're talking to an incredibly serious five-year-old."

"That makes it sound like you think you're a child ghost in a horror movie."

"Because I am. That is the perfect description of me. Miserable, only capable of doing the same thing over and over, and terrifying to absolutely anybody who beholds them. Now let's talk with that in mind," he said, and oh god, he was serious, he was absolutely serious.

He really did think that described him perfectly.

And the worst part was she couldn't even argue.

Because it kind of did fit, once she'd thought about it for a second.

"If we talk with that in my mind I'm likely to end up hiding behind your sofa," she said, and couldn't even stop the wince that definitely darted across her face. Because really, was that the kind of thing she wanted him to know? That she was even more of a soft little scaredy-cat than she already seemed? No, it was not. Now he was definitely going to do her in.

Probably with a scathing insult, she thought.

And got this instead:

"You can't go behind my sofa. I don't even have one."

As if that made sense. Or mattered.

Or didn't seem like another insult aimed in his own direction, somehow.

Because it did. He looked disgusted with himself as he said the words. Then he seemed to tut, and shake his head, as if he couldn't quite believe he was that sort of person. Though what kind of person he thought he was, she couldn't say. All she knew for sure was that she had to find out.

"Oh my gosh, why do you not have a sofa?" she asked.

But he didn't answer her directly. Or at all, really.

"Tell me you didn't use the word *gosh*."

"I will when you answer the question."

He sighed. "I've no idea what the question even is now."

"Don't give me that. I only asked it five seconds ago."

"Yeah, but you've got me all turned around again. Which is especially cruel of you, considering I'm also trying to deal with eyeballs that are about to explode."

He touched them delicately.

Like the fool he was.

"Your eyes are not about to explode. In fact, they should be barely hurting at all, because I got so frightened about blinding someone that most of what's in here is water," she said. Then she held up the can of pepper spray to illustrate.

Like a game show host showing the contestant what they could have won.

But he didn't respond how she expected him to.

He didn't look embarrassed, or rueful.

Instead, he looked almost perturbed.

Which seemed mad for someone like him. And it only got madder from there. "You've got to be kidding," he said. "Listen, right, if some fucker comes out of the darkness at you, you don't worry for one single solitary second about blinding him. Worry about normal things, like where you're going to dump his body after I stab his fucking face out."

And yeah, everything he'd just said made sense.

But god, it was sense that seemed to be coming out of Alfie Harding.

Worse than that: it was sense coming out of him even though he was talking about *himself*. "But the person who came out of the darkness was you," she said. Because honestly, at this point, she was too puzzled to do anything else. Even though she kind of wanted to. In fact, if she was being honest, most of her felt like patting him on the back. But then he said:

"That is technically correct, yes."

And what could she do after that but joke?

"So are you going to stab your own face out?"

"If you must know, I'm seriously considering it."

"Hopefully you're also considering where I should dump you. Because truth be told I'm not very up on the recent developments in body disposal. I'm much more of a *doing children's tapestries* and *baking fun-shaped biscuits* sort of person."

As soon as she'd said that last part, she wished she hadn't.

Mostly because it was the sort of thing that men like him sneered at.

Only, he didn't.

Instead, it was like she'd never said it.

"It's the Thames, you put their dead bodies in the Thames, so people will just think they were drunk and fell in. Though of course now I've said that I feel like I probably shouldn't have to a woman who already believes I'm a maniac. Swear to god, I've never dropped a person in a river," he said.

At which point, she had to concede:

He was a lot more reasonable than she had initially thought.

Or anyone thought, to be honest, because almost nobody seemed to think he was a remotely thoughtful person. She knew they didn't, because not one piece of research she'd done on him had ever revealed anything else. There were interviews out there that described him as the most impossible man ever to live. One of his teammates was asked to use three words to describe him, and all three had been *annoying*. And that made it difficult to know what to make of this.

So she decided it was best to just stick with mild teasing.

"That's good, but now I'm thinking you've dropped an alive one in there," she said, and she was glad she did, too. It kept her looking cool, and he didn't react too angrily. He just seemed frustrated in a way that was surprisingly not that unpleasant to watch. And neither was seeing him scramble for an answer.

"Look, he pushed me first. And I got him back out, you can ask anyone."

"And by *anyone* here do you mean your defense lawyer?"

"I don't have a defense lawyer. He vowed to never work with me again."

He said the words like they were the exact perfect argument to make.

Then seemed to slowly realize that they were not.

"God. Please just stop making me say things," he groaned.

Much to her bemusement. "But you haven't said anything. I still don't know why you don't have a sofa. Or more importantly why the heck you did all this."

"Well, I'm trying to tell you. If you'd give me a second."

"So go ahead then. Start with insulting my size."

"When the fuck did I do that?"

God, he sounded genuinely confused, she thought.

His voice actually went high for a second. Even though she'd thought it couldn't get anywhere above a fucked Ford Fiesta revving its engine. And he threw up his hands, too. Despite clearly hating to make any kind of gesture other than an eyebrow raise or a pointed finger.

So it wasn't a surprise that her response sounded faint.

That it lacked confidence in this whole premise she'd built up.

"You told me I was a cupcake," she said, and sure enough, he snorted in response. Then shot her such a look. A pointed look, like she couldn't be serious.

Before he laid it all out. "Because you seem so sweet I'm afraid of getting sugar poisoning just from looking at you. Not because I'm one of those twats who thinks any woman over a size zero is some kind of personal affront to them," he said, and not even in a smug or swaggering way, either. He was quite patient, all things considered. Quite gentle.

Which of course only made her more embarrassed about it.

Her face was reddening as she responded.

"That is actually a much better answer than I was imagining."

"Too bloody right it is. Now. What other things do you think I did wrong?"

"Probably none, if that one is anything to go by."

"Wouldn't be too sure. I am, after all, a huge shit."

*Are you though*, she wanted to say. But didn't.

There had been far too many times that she'd been sure about something like that—or started to believe that maybe someone was okay—only to be let down when they suddenly revealed their true nature. So it was better not to say it out loud yet. Or at least test the waters more, before she let herself feel safe.

"All right," she tried. "So what about the restaurant?"

"The restaurant was just a coincidence."

"As in you were there anyway and then suddenly we were too."

"Yes. I saw you both come in. I felt awkward after that nightmare of a meeting and the fucking phone call from hell. So I tried to hide. Really badly."

*Okay*, she thought. *Not a bad answer.*

And he looked awkward enough about it that she could believe it was true. Which meant that there was only one thing left now that he'd done wrong. One single, solitary thing, which she was starting to suspect he had a good explanation for, too. But she said it anyway: "You hid much worse in the Starbucks."

Much to his further exasperation.

"I wasn't trying to then."

"So that was on purpose."

"Yes. Sort of. Not the way you're thinking."

"And what way do you think I'm thinking?"

"I don't fucking know, do I," he said. Then after what looked like a second's thought, he came out with this: "The one where I turned up to get revenge on you for forcing me to confess I wear glasses."

Which just about made her heart stop.

Because somehow, he was bang on.

That was exactly what she had thought.

He'd absolutely nailed it. He'd understood precisely what level of absurd he seemed to people. What level of absurd he seemed to *her*, specifically. And there was something so wild about that that she couldn't speak for a moment. She simply stood there, eyes wide, mouth much too open for her liking. And only managed to stop when he started to notice.

He looked up from what he was doing—rubbing at his eyes again, in a way that was only going to make them worse. Then he did a little surprised start. Like her expression wasn't what he was expecting. So she folded it back up, quick.

Then went with a denial. A soft one, of the sort he deserved, really.

"Come on. I never thought you were that weird," she said.

And even though he tried to shrug it off, she got a glimpse of something.

A hint of appreciation, before he sighed and tried to further explain.

"Look, Greg told me you'd be willing to meet up with me in that Starbucks, to let me properly apologize and explain things and then we could work together. So I don't know what wires got crossed or how you thought things would be when you got there. But from my end, you came in and didn't want to sit with me and then when I tried to sit with you, you ran off," he said, quite clearly agonized all the way through the confession, but doing it all the same.

And she'd been right. It was good.

It was very good.

She was already buying it, before she'd even had chance to confirm.

Because it was very like Greg to just not say and hope she'd be okay with it.

And doubly so, when he was as panicked as he obviously had been.

Then Alfie added, almost as a little afterthought:

"And so fast that you left something behind."

As he took what was *definitely* her phone out of his pocket.

Just like he had done on the way here, only very obviously not a threat now.

"Oh my god. Oh my god. Oh my *god*," she said. Because really, what else could she do? She had royally fucked all of this in about seventeen different ways. And top of the royal fucking list was absolutely the fact that she should never have thought he was showing her *his* phone.

Because he'd already told her.

He had a flip one.

That she was guessing did not come in a case with donuts all over it.

"I did try to show you I had it," he said as if she needed to hear anything more when this was already way too much. It made her just a little bit daft. And worse, she now had to explain exactly how daft she had been.

"I thought that was just an odd form of menacing me."

"What? Like, let me follow and murder you or your phone gets it?"

"Well, not that exactly," she said. Then couldn't stomach the lie enough to let it stand. She had to just concede and take her lumps. "But maybe that, exactly."

"Jesus. It's not a baby, Mabel."

"Even though I take it everywhere with me."

"You take lots of things everywhere with you."

"Yeah, but do I also gently cradle them while staring lovingly at their faces?"

"Oh my god, it's a lump of plastic." He snorted. "It does not have a face."

"It does when Oscar Isaac is staring out at me."

"He is not staring out at you. His image is."

Lord, he was so practical about things.

So literal and straight down the line.

*Like somebody's grandad from a mining town where everybody was miserable*, she thought. But weirdly, not in a way that felt mean. She didn't hate that about him, apparently. Instead, she had the thought, and then got a little weird bloom of warmth through her.

As if she was starting to *like* him.

Which, all things considered, sounded like absolute nonsense.

So she shrugged it off, and kept going with whatever this was.

"You don't sound so sure about that," she said, with as much aloofness as she could muster.

"Because I'm not. Technology is a terrifying mystery to me. One time I tried to install a computer update and accidentally committed a massive cybercrime. Next day MI5 were on my doorstep, wanting to know what I had against the government of Norway," he said. And then he seemed to pause. Most likely to give her a chance to take a breath, instead of holding it in the way she was doing. Only then he just stole it, all over again: "So, you know, if you're ever wondering why you can't open any documents I send you, it's because I still use Windows 95."

Because of course she knew what he meant.

But it was so nuts she had to ask anyway.

"And what documents would you be wanting me to open?"

"You know. Book ones. If you agree to do it, that is."

"So you still want to continue with me as your ghostwriter?"

"Of course I bloody do. Isn't that what I just said a second ago?"

"Sure. But it sounded so mad I was sort of worried I'd hallucinated it."

"Well you didn't. It was real. In fact, I've no idea why you'd think it wasn't."

"Because I did a bunch of things that should have put you off ever even wanting to talk to me again. Never mind still wanting me to write your life story. I mean, I stormed out of our first official meeting. And then when the second one happened, I ignored you, ran away, and made your eyes bleed."

She held her breath on the end of that one.

For a different reason, though. A more fear-based one.

Like, *now* he was going to snap. Her list of transgressions demanded it.

Though he didn't seem to know that.

He just grabbed his eyes.

"Oh my god, they're not really bleeding, are they?" he groaned out.

Because he was weird, oh god, he was so weird.

And possibly in a really brilliant way that she didn't know how to cope with.

It made her want to laugh, even though laughing seemed wrong and too much. After all, he wasn't being funny. And she didn't actually feel comfortable enough to giggle at him like the frothy confection he obviously thought she was.

Yet somehow it was really hard to fight.

She had to crush it down hard before she spoke.

And it was still there in the background when she did.

"Of course not. I just said that for dramatic effect," she said in a far too amused-sounding way. Luckily, however, he didn't seem to notice. He just carried on feeling for eye blood, while saying yet more wildly and unintentionally funny things.

"I take it that's a fancy way of saying lies that strike terror into my heart."

"Not exactly. I mean I didn't even think you could feel terror, to be honest."

"Of course I can. And especially over my eyes. I need them to see things."

Oh Lord, but he was testing her now.

And on purpose, she was starting to suspect.

Because even though he said that last part in as deadpan a

way as all the rest, there was a hint of something else there, too. A little twist on the end, like he suspected she was finding him funny. That he had her, somehow.

And he wasn't wrong.

Her laugh was now a wild animal, breaking free of its bars. She had to put a hand over her mouth to keep it in.

Then, just as she was sure she'd succeeded, just as she was certain she'd kept her cool and been as professional and noncupcake-like as possible, in the face of all these ridiculous things they'd both accidentally done, it happened. Words just came out of her, one after the other, each sillier than the last. "Why don't you come back to mine, so I can make sure you carry on having sight?"

And worst of all?

He actually agreed.

Office of the Prime Minister
Oslo, 22 August 2014

Dear Mr. Harding,

I would like to extend my deepest apologies for the misunderstanding that occurred on July 17. I can assure you the Norwegian Government does not believe you are a cybercriminal, and I have personally addressed the issues that led to this unfortunate incident. Needless to say, you will experience no further unpleasantness from any department under my administration.

The people of Norway deeply admire your contribution to football, and we look forward to many more years of your talents both on and off the pitch.

Yours sincerely,
Erna Solberg

# Six

## Googling the Recovery Rates
## for a Broken Bum

She tried not to panic too much, once Alfie fucking Harding was inside her flat. But it was hard not to, when Alfie fucking Harding was inside her flat. Partly because he was Alfie fucking Harding, and in her flat. But mostly because he just looked so jarring and out of place among her things. Like he had in that Starbucks—only worse, because Starbucks had at least seemed somewhat neutral.

But her decor was not.

It was a lot of pastels.

And plump, comfy things.

And all of them were surrounding him, like white cells sensing a terrible disease had entered the body. Now they were going to kill him, before he could infect everything with his aggressively dark clothes and his furious eyebrows and his obvious discomfort at having to be around softness and color.

Which sounded ludicrous.

But only got less so, as time went on.

She put lights on, forgetting that they were mostly just twinkling fairy ones that she'd stuck up one Christmas then not wanted to take down. So now he was standing in the backwash of a bunch of blinking reds and greens and blues and yellows, like a burnt stump of a tree still covered in its gaudy decorations.

Then she went to offer him a drink.

And only realized too late that she didn't have a single thing he could reasonably want. There was no special brew in any of her cupboards. She didn't regularly stock hard liquor. She had a bottle of pink lemonade, and a bunch of different types of hot chocolate.

Oh, and some milk.

Which she felt even sillier offering him than all the rest.

"Sorry, I didn't mean to include that last one," she found herself saying.

But the weirdest part was: he actually took her up on it. She had to pour a bit of semi-skimmed into a mug with Peppa Pig on the front, and then watch him clutching it like it was a pint of booze down the social club, while standing across from her in her kitchen, looking far too big for the space he was in.

And he looked even bigger than that when she offered him a seat. Honestly, she expected her little wooden kitchen chair to splinter the second he tried it. He was probably going to end up breaking his butt on her kitchen floor, because all she apparently had was bloody doll furniture. *Alfie Harding in Need of Intense Ass Surgery Because of Fluffy Fool*, she imagined the headlines reading. Then breathed a sigh of relief when the chair did nothing but creak a bit under his weight.

She was safe from that, at least.

Just not from about eighty other things she'd somehow gotten herself into—such as that promise she'd made to fix his still pretty sore-looking eyes. *Yeah, bravo on that one*, her brain sneered. And she couldn't even fault it for doing so, because now she was processing all the things that promise meant.

She was most likely going to have to touch him.

Kind of a lot, actually. And not even somewhere easy, like his elbow.

No, it was going to be on his face. His big, angry, hairy face, which he was currently using to glare at her over his mug of milk. Like he'd suddenly realized he was furious with her, for all the things that had actually turned out to be at least somewhat her fault. Or maybe for somehow forcing him to be inside somewhere so twee. Or possibly it was just her personality, driving him bananas.

Because she was definitely exhibiting a lot of her not-so-great qualities. Like the fact that she was not a particularly graceful person. So of course when she went to get some water for his eyes, she turned on the tap too far and got it all over the front of her dress. Then, when she'd actually managed to get some of it into the bowl she was trying for, she moved too fast away from the sink. And water sloshed over the sides of it, onto the floor.

While he just watched her steadily.

The way a coach would, on seeing his new recruit fail to even so much as make contact with a football. *This isn't the fricking Premier League*, she kind of wanted to yell at him, by the end of it. But boy was she glad she didn't. Because about two seconds after the thought occurred, she stepped back into the puddle she'd made on the floor. Too hard, and too quick, and in cute little ballet slippers that had zero grip to them.

And her foot just slid right out from under her.

It shot forward, like it was making a bid for freedom.

And Alfie Harding only bloody caught her, before she could go down.

He fully fucking caught her in a way she couldn't even fathom. His hand just shot out, so fast that for a second she thought he was trying to punch her. Then suddenly he had a fistful of her dress. He had a hold on it, tight, and once he did he simply hauled hard, until she was back on her feet. All in one motion, smooth as anything.

She didn't even see him stand in the middle of it.

But he had. Because that was his chest her back was now against. And his hand wasn't bunched in her dress anymore. It was on her waist. *Around* her waist, and kind of splayed over her stomach. All of which she rationally understood. She knew why he had done it. You couldn't stop someone falling on their arse while sitting down. Or just by clutching their dress.

He'd obviously needed to do a few more maneuvers.

But god, other parts of her did not understand at all.

They just panicked. They felt like they were being touched, a *lot*.

And in places she didn't know how to cope with. *He proba-*

*bly isn't even aware a stomach can be anything other than flat*, she found herself thinking frantically. Then even though she had long since learned to love her shape—despite her family's best efforts at making her think there was something wrong with it—she kind of wanted to stop him. To grab his hand and shove it off her, before the uncomfortable feeling it was creating got any worse.

But it was fine, it was okay, it was good.

He apparently wanted off her just as badly.

Because after what felt like the most torturous twenty seconds of bodily contact that she'd ever had to endure, he suddenly broke. He ripped away from her, as fast as he had done all the grabbing and saving. And then he followed this, inexplicably, with one growled word.

"Sorry," he said.

Even though he'd helped her. He'd stopped her falling.

There was nothing about this that needed an apology.

And yet he'd done it, so now she had to somehow make him see that it was ridiculous. Or at least drive home to him that she hadn't hated it, no matter how much discomfort he might have sensed. "No. No. Thank you. Thank you for doing that," she tried. But he wasn't having any of it.

He shook his head, quite clearly furious.

"For doing what? Putting my big hairy hands all over you?" he gruffed out, and with so much conviction it stopped her short for a second. Like she couldn't quite believe he'd said what she thought he had.

Then her brain kicked back into gear.

"But you didn't put your big hairy hands all over me. And anyway, they're not that hairy. In fact, they have what looks like a normal amount of knuckle fur."

"You're kidding, aren't you? Look at them. They belong to the Wolfman."

He held them up for good measure. And yes, all right, they were a little wilder than the average back of a hand. However, they were nowhere near as bad as he was making out. In fact, the effect was actually quite nice. Quite good. Because his hands were big and the hair was very black and she could see it disappearing under his sleeves, all the way up his probably meaty forearms.

Though of course she couldn't say any of that.

Better to go with something that made her feel less weird.

Something jokey, she thought. And it came to her, a second later.

"Yeah, if the Wolfman was inexplicably hairless. There's three strands there."

"Only if three means thirty million to you."

"If there was thirty million of them you wouldn't be able to lift your bloody hands. You'd just have to drag them along the floor like great hair-filled shovels," she said, and didn't think much of it when she did. It wasn't like she was being mean, after all. Heck, she was being the opposite of mean when you really got down to brass tacks. And yet somehow, the second the words were out something weird seemed to happen to his face. The angry eyebrows tried to separate from each other, and his cheeks were doing this weird up-and-down thing, and his *mouth*.

His mouth did not look the way it usually did.

That mean thin line he kept it in was trembling.

It was fighting him somehow, she could see it was.

But before it could win whatever battle he was having with it, he turned his back to her. Fast, like it was of the utmost importance that she did not see the change happen. Even though she already had. She even suspected what it was, but just couldn't quite believe it until he spoke. "Look, just give me your poorly filled bowl of water and I'll sort my eyes," he said, and there it was. Shocking, but undeniable.

Laughter, wavering around underneath his words.

Like he was trying to keep his amusement under wraps just as much as she had. Though of course in his case it was quite a bit weirder that he was even doing it in the first place. After all, she was well known for being a giggler. Her nickname in college had been Champers—because she was bubbly. To this day, some of her friends still called her that, and not always kindly.

But Alfie Harding?

He was not bubbly.

Or even easily amused.

Once during a match he'd kicked the ball and his boot had somehow come off and smacked the goalie in the face. But he hadn't so much as cracked a smile over it. In fact, he'd angrily told everybody to stop laughing about the whole business during his post-game interview. And then threatened the crowd during his next match, because they'd started singing *shoe me the way to go home*.

So this seemed pretty wild.

And weirdly, kind of calming.

Like his practical manner and reassurance had been.

Now it kind of felt a lot more like she could do this.

"Okay, first of all, my bowl of water isn't poorly filled. It has a perfectly reasonable amount inside it, despite my attempts at flinging it everywhere. And second of all, you're not doing your own eyes. You've already poked them so much they're barely able to open. If I let you have a real go at them you'll end up gouging them out. Now sit down, and keep still," she said. Then when he turned, quite obviously startled, she pointed at the chair.

And though he definitely went to protest, he did it.

He sat down, face a picture of grumpy resentment.

Like a kid taking his medicine, she thought—though she didn't take it personally. She knew what he was like. She'd seen him shrug a hand off his shoulder on telly, before today. Even when the hand belonged to his mum.

And he was pretty well known for refusing things like high fives and fist bumps and other even very casual contact-based greetings. Usually he stared angrily at whatever was being of-fered, so she expected the same thing here. Worse than the same thing, really. It seemed likely that he would topple the table the moment she so much as touched her fingertips to his cheeks, to tilt his head toward her.

So she did her best to do said tilting lightly. Like she was hardly doing anything at all. She was just brushing him, with about as much weight as a spider's legs running across his face. He shouldn't have even been able to feel it, her touch was that careful and tentative. But somehow, he did. He quite obviously did.

She saw it happen, almost immediately.

All in one big rush, like he couldn't contain it.

Her hands made contact, and that was it. Every muscle in his face just seemed to melt. The deep line between his eyebrows dissolved; his tightly pressed-together lips parted. And though she could see him fighting to keep his eyes squeezed shut—like this was agony, like it was unbearable, like she was killing him with her fingertips—she could see them started to smooth out.

And it made her bold.

It gave her permission to go further.

To relax her hands on his face, until she was almost cupping that impossibly large jaw and those weirdly pretty pink cheeks of his and that aggressively furry beard—the one that looked like it would feel wiry and rough, but actually didn't. It was soft as sea foam and so luxurious she came fairly close to commenting on it.

To saying something mad like *Oh, that feels good on my fingers.*

Though really, how mad was it, when he was so clearly expressing the same sort of sentiment? His eyes were now wholly unscrunched; his teeth were pretty close to sinking into his lower lip. And when she finally got around to stroking some soaked cotton wool over his eyelids, he seemed to actually make some kind of sound. A kind of strangely long and low and guttural kind of breath, she wanted to call it.

But only because calling it anything else felt impossible.

*It wasn't a groan*, she told herself, over and over.

*He did not groan because I rubbed his face with cotton wool.*

And then he did again.

Louder, this time. Much louder, and so gruff she actually felt it through the hand she had on his face. It ran right up her arm, and kind of rattled around inside her bones, and then somehow, she was blushing. She was really blushing—and without a single good explanation for it. After all, nothing much was actually happening. The fact that he had relaxed didn't mean anything. His groan wasn't that unusual.

And the air in the room definitely hadn't gotten thicker, or hotter.

She was just wearing too many layers, that was the thing.

Plus, what she was doing was very complicated.

It took a lot of effort.

Of course she was sweating.

And if he was sweating too, well.

Maybe he just naturally did that. While sitting down. In totally normal non-stressful situations. *Yeah*, she thought. *That makes all the sense in the world.* And it honestly did, too. Right up to the point where she stopped with the cotton, and asked him how that felt now, and he opened those angry eyes.

Only they weren't angry anymore.

They were completely unguarded, in a way that made him look strange and different. *Calm,* her brain threw up, but that wasn't quite right and she knew it. He looked younger, was the thing. He looked ten years younger suddenly, and all the things that came with it. *Vulnerable,* she thought, *and almost innocent.*

And Mabel just did not know how to cope with that realization.

Though apparently neither did he. The very second he seemed to register that he was doing something a bit weird, he immediately jumped up. And he did it so fast and so violently that he moved the table in front of him. It slid across the cheap linoleum, screeching as it went and sending water sloshing over the sides of the bowl.

*Now who's the clumsy one*, she wanted to say. But she knew why she held her tongue, in the end. He looked stressed enough as it was. She didn't want to make it worse. She just wanted him to do whatever he needed to, to not be bothered by his own accidentally pleased response to a bit of soft contact.

She just didn't expect that *leaving* would be the thing. That he would exit the kitchen, and head for the door without so much as another word.

But he did exactly that.

He marched right to it.

Went right through it.

He didn't even say goodbye.

She went to the top of the stairs outside her flat, just in time to see him disappearing down them two at a time. And kind of thought, as he did, *Well, that's that.* He'd swung away from whatever madness had gripped him when he'd decided that actually she was the one he wanted to work with.

Most likely she would never see or hear from him again.

Then he stopped at the bottom of the stairs, halfway out into the night. He looked up at her.

And he said, "So you'll come round mine tomorrow at ten, then. For the book."

And though she wanted to reply that he was the strangest man she'd ever encountered in her life and she couldn't believe everything that had happened and that probably it was best that neither of them had any more bizarre contact ever again, this was not what came out of her all in rush.

No, what came out of her all in a rush was this:

"Oh god, yeah. I can't wait."

Hey Mabel,

Okay, first of all, I do not know WHAT is going on. But it isn't just you—Greg doesn't seem to be responding to emails at the moment. I can only imagine he's swamped and that's why he overlooked the whole *informing you of a meeting you didn't know you were attending* thing. Although I can't rule out your notion that he's in a bit of hot water and panicked. Don't worry, though, I'll get to the bottom of things.

And in the meantime, if things are looking positive on the Alfie front, maybe just run with it? See where it goes? It sounds like he's of the mind that everything is going ahead, so if you're okay with it I don't see why you shouldn't act as though it is. As long as we can get the contract nailed down soon, and make sure that you're not just wasting your time, I think it's worthwhile to try.

Just let me know if you feel otherwise.

It's a great opportunity, but you know my first priority is you.

Hang in there,

Emmy x

EMMELINE SANDERS
Leafland Literary Agency, Inc.
220 Madison Avenue, Suite 406
New York, NY 10016
leaflandliterary.com
@emmelinesanders

# Seven

## Millennium Falcons Are
## So Last Season

$\mathcal{S}$he didn't really know what to make of the events of the day before.

Most of them seemed like the plot of a movie she adored.

Like when he'd caught her as she fell.

Had he really caught her as she fell?

She was pretty sure he had, because the back of her dress still had the imprint of his fist practically pressed into it. And she definitely hadn't hit the ground, like she would have if he hadn't done anything. No part of her was bruised. She hadn't broken anything. She was fine, totally fine, and that had been his doing.

But gosh, it seemed mad.

Even though it wasn't even in the top five mad things that had happened.

Because there was also the stalking, and the reveal about the stalking, and Greg being fricking nuts, and the pepper spray. Then finally, just when she thought there couldn't be anything more wild—there was his face and the touching and the noise he'd made and oh Jesus, *that look in his eyes.*

What had that look in his eyes been about?

She didn't know. She didn't *want* to know.

Even though wanting to know was now practically her job description.

*You realize you're going to sit in a room with him for hours on end forcing him to say things that'll probably make that eye thing happen all over again*, her brain helpfully informed her. But the worst part was—she couldn't even argue with it. It was right. That was exactly the situation.

And he was going to fucking hate it.

He was going to leap up the very second she pressed him in some soft spot.

Then probably storm out of his own house. She'd have to run after him down the drive, shouting that he lived there. And that wasn't even the worst thing she could imagine happening. After all—it was bad, there was no question about that. But really it was just him, and his own feelings, overreacting to nothing.

It didn't reflect on her in any way.

However, she could imagine ways that it *might*.

Like if he started to think she was enjoying unraveling him.

Because if she was being honest, she kind of had.

And okay, not in a *sexy* way. She didn't fancy him, or anything. God no, he was pretty much the opposite of her type. But she had still enjoyed certain things about him, and he might notice at some point and think more of it than what it was, and oh, that was indisputably worse. It was the sort of misunderstanding she dreaded with a man like him. A famous man, of the sort people generally found very attractive, and who had dated whole supermodels and actresses from actual movies.

After all, chances were high that a man like that would be horrified if he discovered someone who wasn't a size zero had a crush on him. Which, screw him if he did. But even if he didn't, even if he liked that she was curvy, there were other things that bothered him about her.

She was too fluffy for him. Too much like a cupcake.

And that meant a lot of careful consideration of what to wear.

Or at least, a lot of calling friends so *they* could consider what she should wear. Starting with the one she relied on the most, the one who was always there for her and had been since college, the one who even tolerated her using the epithet *bestie*—Connie, oh lovely, good Connie.

"Okay," she started, as soon as her friend picked up. "What exactly would you wear if you wanted to show a man that you're definitely not interested in him in a sexy way. Or that you're trying too hard. Or like you're not just a cute little moppet who's going to annoy the crap out of him. But at the same time, you want to seem like you're ready and able to get down to business."

Because of course she had to be vague. She had to be careful. The contract was very clear about not causing Mr. Harding any embarrassment by revealing that he had hired a ghostwriter.

She just wished she hadn't been *that* vague, once the words were out.

And suddenly all she could hear were screams of delight. "I would say holy shit are you about to get down to some business?" Connie finally managed to say, while Mabel wondered how a) she'd somehow blundered into this suggestion and b) what on earth she was going to do to get out of it.

"Connie. Connie. No. No, oh my gosh, no. The exact opposite."

"So it's someone who is going to get down to business with you?"

"That is not the exact opposite of what I said and you know it."

"I do. But sue me, I got excited about you finally having some sex."

*Finally*, she thought wearily. As if it had been a thousand years!

Which to be fair, in Connie's mind, even a month probably was.

But still. She winced. "Well, you can just put that excitement away, because I'm totally not. I just need advice on my clothes for something kind of important."

"And you're not gonna tell me what this important thing is?"

"I will at some point, you know I will. But just for right now: help."

"Okay," Connie said. Because god bless her, she never made

Mabel regret it when she actually dropped some of that sunny, everything-is-fine disposition a bit, and admitted she was in a spot of bother. "What was the criteria again?"

"Not too try-hard, not too sexy, not too cute."

"So like, a business suit."

"I don't *have* a business suit. And anyway, I think it would seem too slick."

"Right. Then how about something messy? That still says *I get things done.*"

"Tell me what you've got in mind," she said. And Connie did. She spelled out exactly what Mabel should wear, and how she should style herself: from the dungarees that screamed unconcerned about her appearance, but definitely suggested she was a hard worker, to the wild hair she superficially brushed, but didn't tame in the slightest. And as for her makeup?

No pink lip gloss.

No blush.

Just the barest hint of eyebrow gel, then a dab of lip balm, and that was it. The perfect unstudied look.

Even though technically she'd studied harder for this look than she ever had in her whole life. She glanced at her phone and realized she'd been doing this for four hours. Her bedroom was an awful mess from choosing and rejecting twenty-seven outfits. The sink was full of things she'd picked to put on her face, then decided against. And she hadn't even organized her extensive research notes.

She had to do it in a flustered rush, five minutes before she ran out the door. She wasn't even sure if she had them all, as she hurried to the bus stop to get the number 10 to somewhere close to his house.

In fact, she was still checking when she noticed the car.

The one that was following her as she made her way to Crossley Avenue.

Although *following* was probably the wrong word here. It was really more like it had decided to crawl along beside her.

As if the person inside knew her and was just waiting for her to stop and say hello to her oldest friend. Even though she didn't have any friends who owned a car like that. It was roughly the size of a small bus, and so fancy it was sort of hard to look at directly. Like someone would accuse her of stealing just for letting her poor-person eyes alight upon its sleek body, or peer into its hallowed depths.

Not that you actually could.

The windows were too tinted for that.

They were practically blacked out—which had to be illegal, she was pretty sure. But then, rules didn't generally apply to fabulously rich people. Probably the bloke in there was busy snorting coke off an endangered animal steak while smuggling blood diamonds across borders manned by the mafia.

All of which sounded ridiculous, but right.

Until the back window abruptly slid down.

And there was Alfie Harding.

In his ridiculous car.

Driven by an actual *chauffeur*.

Looking at her like *she* was the mad one.

And okay, yeah, technically she was. She should have known as soon as the car started crawling alongside her. But she'd been focused on looking casual, and making sure she had everything, and so she simply hadn't realized.

Which meant she had to endure him being all incredulous and annoying.

"Are you getting in or what?" he wanted to know.

And the answer was, of course, yes.

* * *

*S*he tried not to be too impressed by the car.

But it was hard to be anything else when the car was so impressive.

The back was partitioned off from the driver, and so big it had two sets of seats facing each other. Plus, they were all made of the most unbelievable leather. It felt like sitting on a slippery cloud. She sank into it so deeply, her feet stopped touching the floor. And almost everything in the thing was heated.

Her butt was lightly toasted within moments.

Then somehow her boobs were, too.

Even though the only thing touching them was the seat belt.

Apparently, it had filaments in it—which if she was being honest, seemed both nuts and mildly dangerous to her. But really, what did she know? The car she'd spent the most amount of time in was her dad's Ford Cortina, and the fanciest thing that had had was a sunroof. And even *sunroof* was massively stretching it. Really, her dad had just driven it drunk under a bridge too low for it and peeled part of the roof off. Then he'd attached a latch, so you could fasten it down or take it off, depending on the weather.

Not that it really mattered much when it rained.

It pissed in regardless. She still remembered how everything smelled in there.

Like mold and sodden material and alcohol, always alcohol.

Or in other words: the exact opposite of the scent currently surrounding her.

Here, it was like an angel had farted. She had to stop herself from taking deep breaths, just in case the perfumed air wasn't some fancy car diffuser. Because even though it seemed absurd, she was starting to suspect it wasn't. That it was coming from him, somehow, despite how sweet and light and airy it was.

*He's supposed to smell like engine oil and old turnips*, her brain groaned.

But there was nothing she could do for it.

She just had to lean away and breathe normally, so he would never know that she liked getting big whiffs of him. After all, that would definitely count against her on the *letting him think she liked him* front. And it was even more of an imperative that this did not happen now while she was here in his ridiculous car, on seats that felt like heaven, while he sat across from her looking almost absurdly polished.

His hair seemed newly trimmed.

She suspected he'd brushed his beard.

Or that someone had brushed his beard.

Most likely a barber who cost more than she spent on rent per month.

And his suit. Jesus Christ, what kind of suit even was that? She glimpsed it out of the corner of her eye, and sort of wanted to cry a little bit—it was that beautiful. Every line of it was as crisp and sharp as a facet of a diamond. Yet somehow at the same time it looked soft. Like it was made out of wool.

*Or fuzzy felt*, her brain supplied.

Which felt both ridiculously *I have been poor and obsessed with arts and crafts all my life* of her and absolutely accurate at the same time. Because sure, she didn't have the language for any of this. But she did have the language for what it looked like from the perspective of someone who had never had a single bean. And that felt kind of valid if she was being honest about it.

So she kept on with it.

She applied it to his shoes, which gleamed and glowed like the most perfect conkers on the playground. And his cuff links— his actual cuff links—that looked as if they were made out of platinum, or some other fancy metal.

And then finally there was his house, which apparently sat on the end of a driveway so long she thought they'd gotten lost down some country road. *I think we should have gotten off at that last junction*, she came pretty close to saying. Then there it was: this great big squares-piled-on-rectangles-piled-on-squares thing, looming up like something out of a terrible dystopian future she didn't want to be in.

*It's like a house from an episode of* Black Mirror, she found herself thinking, as they exited the car and made their way up to it. And though that seemed wild and rude of her, it did.

The whole thing was white, completely white, in a way that had to be impossible to maintain without the help of some frightening futuristic device. And though there were a lot of windows, you couldn't see through any of them. Which made sense, considering how much he probably didn't want people peering in at him.

But at the same time, it was creepy as fuck. It made her think of all the weird things that could happen in there without anybody ever knowing. Like if it turned out he was into smearing spaghetti all over himself and slipping and sliding through the halls, he could totally do it, and nobody would ever be the wiser.

Though she couldn't imagine he was. The place was just too pristine to ever manage to conceal the mess you'd make. You could wipe forever and never get these slick white walls and polished wooden floors clean—both because of the immaculate look of them, and the sheer amount of such surfaces there seemed to be. They went on endlessly, gleaming away as far as the eye could see.

Like she had somehow found herself in a museum.

That for some inexplicable reason had no art.

*Does a human being actually live here*, she found herself thinking.

And then felt kind of afraid to move, just in case her presence as a person set off some kind of alarm. She just stood in the massive hallway, trying not to sweat or seem alarmed or anything of the sort. Oh, and she definitely couldn't take off her coat now. Because if she took it off, she'd reveal her disastrous outfit underneath. And though said outfit had seemed like a good idea when Connie had suggested it, it didn't now, in this gosh darn palace.

It just looked like she was trying too little.

Way, way, way too little.

To an embarrassing degree.

So she kept her coat on as she followed him into what looked like a *second* hallway, dominated by an enormous staircase. Then just as she was trying not to gawp at that, he turned abruptly and stared, and she knew. She absolutely wasn't going to get away with the coat thing. There had been a fancy hanging apparatus back there that he'd put his on. And quite obviously, he had expected her to do the same.

But she hadn't.

Much to his thankfully misguided distress.

"Look, I know it seems like it's gonna be really cold in here. But I can actually make it so boiling hot you'll think you've stepped onto the surface of the sun, if you like. And not just from above. From below, too. Because the floors heat up," he said.

Though weirdly, he didn't seem proud about that fact once he'd said it.

He winced instead. Like all those facts embarrassed him, somehow.

Or made him uncomfortable.

And she could kind of see why that might be the case. After all, it was entirely possible he wasn't that okay with all this excess. He had grown up in effing Watford. The most widely shared anecdote about his childhood was that he'd had no bed as a kid and had to sleep on the floor in a sleeping bag. Ten years into his career he'd still been living in a one-bedroom flat a mile from the club. *That way I can walk to work*, he'd told a reporter.

So this had to be at least somewhat weird to him, too.

And especially when he was with someone who didn't look on it with cynical eyes. Or even taking-it-in-their-stride eyes. Hers were as big as moons, and he was clearly clocking it. He clearly understood what was going on. It was the reason, she thought, that he didn't volunteer any further information.

Instead, she had to ask. Even though she didn't want to, she had to.

Because Lord, the living room was even more ridiculous than the two halls.

It was just a big, hyper-polished box. Like the kind of place where an event was about to be held before people turned up with the chairs and tables and tasteful decorations. Literally its only feature was a sunken middle bit, which you had to step down into. But there was nothing in the step-down bit. Just more glossy wooden flooring without so much as a stitch on it. Not even a rug, or a mat of some kind.

Which she supposed made the heating thing more reasonable. *This place would ice through three-inch flipping slippers*, she thought.

Then couldn't stop herself saying something about it.

"Where is all your furniture?" she blurted out.

And got about the amount of distress she'd been expecting.

He practically squirmed. And he wouldn't look at her when he answered.

"I hired someone, all right. Because I know fuck all about decorating."

"But whoever you hired hasn't actually decorated anything."

"Of course they have. It's called minimalism, look it up."

"I would, but I'm pretty sure it's not going to say 'a style of decor that people do when they want to take rich ex-footballers for a ride.' Which is totally what's happened here. I mean, what did letting someone do absolutely nothing cost?"

"It was very reasonable, actually. Almost cheap, in fact."

"So a small fortune then."

She saw him break before he spoke.

That faux-confident expression slid away.

The wince came back with reinforcements.

And then he just went ahead and gave in:

"My hand shook as I signed the check," he said. Much to her delight. Because it *was* delightful, watching him fight his urge to be honest. Not to mention kind of cool to know that honesty and being straight down the line obviously meant a lot to him. Though naturally, she couldn't tell him that.

All she could do was carry on ribbing him.

But in a slightly more gentle way than before. "That was your hand trying to tell you not to be an easy mark," she said, and he sighed heavily in response.

"Well I know that now, don't I? But at the time they were

saying a lot of very important fancy-sounding things, and then they hated my wicker chair and my coffee table shaped like the *Millennium Falcon* and Christ, I don't know what happened."

"They saw you coming a mile off, is what happened," she noted, and as she did she looked around. A little theatrically, it had to be said. But it did serve a purpose. It drove something shocking home to her that she couldn't help commenting on. "And now I'm realizing that oh my good golly you don't have a TV. There is no television in here. Is there actually no television anywhere in here?"

"I want to plead the Fifth on that."

"Alfie nooooo you didn't. You didn't let them take your telly."

"They said having one was not in season at the moment."

"But you don't even have a good phone. How are you watching things?"

She turned to him then, just in time to see him crack again. And this one was worse, this was one was really despairing. Like he couldn't quite believe he'd let all this happen and it was really bringing him down. Then he explained why.

"I'm so behind on *Repair Shop*," he said.

And what was she supposed to do at that point? She couldn't just carry on exclaiming about it and teasing him over it. Not when he'd admitted that this situation was bad, and that he didn't like it, and most importantly: that he loved a gentle show about carefully fixing people's broken family treasures.

It was just too adorable for her soft little heart to take. She couldn't even maintain the casual-but-professional stance she'd vowed to hold on to. She had to care. So she got out her phone and started scrolling through options.

Much to his perturbation. "What are you doing now?" he wanted to know.

As if what she was doing might be deadly to him.

And she had a history of doing said deadly things.

Which to be fair to him, she somehow kind of did.

Just not this time. "Ordering you a TV from Amazon," she said.

He still reacted like she'd threatened him with poisonous spiders, however.

"You can't do that," he said, in his grumpiest, most indignant voice.

Even though he was wrong and ridiculous.

"Of course I can."

"But I don't even have an account."

"Oh my gosh, really? I am stunned by that incredible revelation."

"You sassy little bugger. I'm not as bad as you're making out, all right."

"Uh-huh. So when I ask you for an email address to make the account, you're going to be able to give me one, then. I don't have to make it for you."

She flicked her gaze up from her phone, just in time to see him start to struggle with the desire to say no, and the need to be honest about things. And she was glad she did, too, because Lord, was it a sight. He looked like he was trying to swallow something enormous and terrible and couldn't quite manage it. His entire face was one big grimace; his eyes were almost watering. And when he finally managed, it almost seemed like a relief to him.

"Just go ahead and create one," he said in one big *thank fuck for that* rush.

He needn't have bothered, however. For one very good reason.

"Already did. I went with alfiehardingisaluddite at gmail dot com," she said.

Which was a bit too mean in one way. But good in another.

Because it bounced him back quickly from having to swallow a bad thing.

"Okay, I know what *Luddite* means. And I'm not best pleased with you calling me that. In fact I think it's outrageous of you, considering I picked you up in an electric car and brought you to a house with a shower you can turn on from all the way across the bloody country."

"Yes, but can *you* turn it on from across the bloody country?"

"Of course I can."

"Great. Show me, then."

"I bloody well will do."

"Awesome, I can't wait. In fact, I think I'll just take a seat right here on the floor, seeing as how you got conned out of having any chairs," she said as she did just that. She settled down on what *was* actually pretty freezing hardwood and folded her legs together in front of her. "And now I'll watch you use your probably analog flip phone to turn on your shower. Should be easy, considering we're not even as far away as down the road. We're just in the next room. Right?"

She looked up at him after she'd asked, expecting the same struggle as before. But there was much less there this time. He didn't look like he was fighting his honesty, at least. He looked a little resigned, and just a touch chagrined.

Like he was getting used to whatever this was now.

He was starting to go with it.

"You already know it's not going to work no matter what I do, don't you," he conceded.

"Of course I do. But if I say that, then I won't get to watch you try."

He shook his head and blew out a breath. "You're sadistic, you are. Like a really evil Mary Poppins."

"I'm trying not to be. But you just make it so easy and fun."

"And I want to be furious with you for that, I do. Only I can't be."

"Why can't you be?"

"Because it is," he said.

And now it was her turn to be the one thrown.

Because she knew what he meant. He was suggesting that this was easy and fun for him, too. Or at least, that he was starting to find it so. Something about it was beginning to appeal to him, amid his irritation and struggling and impatience.

All of which sounded right.

But she couldn't quite believe it, until he suddenly tossed her his wallet.

One-handed, as he said something that removed pretty much all doubt.

"Now. Here's my credit card. Get that fucking TV ordered, will you."

## CLEAN LINES DESIGN

We specialize in decluttering, de-emphasizing, and creating an understatement. It is our belief that a home should be about more than comfort and functionality. It should be a space in which your mind can expand endlessly without encountering frivolities and fuss. *No hinderances or encumbrances* is our ethos, our watchword, and we will work tirelessly to ensure your home achieves this vision.

Our services include:

- Floor smoothening
- Cupboard handle removal
- Sourcing unobtrusive beds
- Creating an abundance of flow
- Erasing problematic corners

For further details, contact
Bracken and Firth St. Vickersby-Smythe at
cleanlines@cleanlinesdesign.com

We are here to help you unlock your minimalist dreams.

# Eight

## Her Superheroine Name
## Would Be "The Persuader"

*S*he wasn't sure how things had shifted between them. Or even to what extent they really had. But she knew it was happening, at the very least, because when he suggested she *take her bloody coat off for fuck's sake*, she didn't hesitate. She let him take it and hang it up on the special hanging thing.

And it didn't even bother her when he turned back and saw what she was wearing and had this to say: "By Christ, what look were you going for there then? *Blue Peter* presenter from 1987? Are you about to show me how to make a spaceship out of a toilet roll tube without getting my good clothes messy?"

Despite how much it should have.

It should have made her feel like she'd failed at looking like anything but bright and cute and fluffy. But instead, she just felt a little rueful. And kind of relieved.

And after a moment, she realized why:

It was the fact that he was gruff, and often irritated, and they squabbled constantly. But he'd yet to say a single truly cutting thing to her. In fact, this was probably the closest he'd come—and somehow, it still wasn't that mean. He hadn't said she looked poor or slovenly or a million other things he could have gone with.

He'd gone with something that maintained his blunt, cranky persona.

But wasn't cruel in the least. It didn't hurt her.

And that felt so strange and new she didn't quite know how to process it at first. She wasn't used to men—and in particular, men like him—being whatever this way was. She was used to getting shanked in the back when she was at her most vulnerable. Which she indisputably should have been, here.

She was inside a fancy museum with its attractive owner.

But she still felt pretty comfortable. She felt okay being that *Blue Peter* presenter. She even let herself get out the biscuits she'd baked the night before and vowed to eat only when he wasn't there. The ones that were shaped like bunnies, and always broke the ice for her when she was sort of nervous.

And when she offered him one, he grumbled and groused.

But she could see him eyeing them.

In fact, he only stopped when she sat down, and crossed her legs, and started getting out her pens, and her notepad, and her research files, and her phone, to record him. Most likely because all this made him realize that the *getting comfortable with each other* part was now over.

And they were into the *tell me all your secrets* part.

Even though he very clearly did not want to tell her any secrets.

It was the reason he was currently stalking around as she got sorted. As if he were never going to settle into this. So when she finally did ask something, she considered what had kept things light and easy before. What had given him space to talk freely with her.

And tried to go with the same thing again.

To be a little bit cheeky with him, a little bit silly.

But in a way that would never really hurt him. That she knew didn't really matter to him, or even that he'd said to her himself. "So. Alfie. We've established that you're an easily conned Luddite who may actually be the ghost of a Victorian child who died down the mines," she said, with her tongue just ever so slightly in her cheek. Then got her reward: he stopped stalking.

And she could see it all over his face again.

He was trying not to seem amused. Even as he acted put out.

"Oh god. You're not really going to put that in the book, are you?"

"That depends entirely on you."

"Yeah, but depending on me is a recipe for disaster."

"Not if you're willing to share other things I could put in instead."

"And you know full well I'm not. So Christ knows what this is going to be."

He rolled his eyes on the end of that.

But she noticed he sat down as he did it.

Same as her—backside on top of the step down, feet on the bottom.

Like she was giving him the same comfortable feeling as he had given her.

Or at least she was starting to give it to him, with just the right levels of being silly. "I was thinking something like me putting my knee on your chest. You know, to get some leverage when I really have to yank to get things out," she said, and got his eyes actually sparking with laughter in response.

Though he shook his head. "You're not thinking that."

"How do you know?"

"Because you're not a yanker."

"So tell me what I am, then."

She leaned back on her elbows, waiting for what she knew he'd already gotten.

And sure enough, here it was: "A tricksy little shit who gets you all turned around. Then next thing you know you've shared seventeen of your most painful life stories and that terrible thing you did when you were twelve and swore you'd take to your sodding grave," he said—because he was perceptive.

A quality he didn't always let show to much of the public.

Or even had to her, for much of their time together.

But he was. He did. He caught things easily.

And that should have made her careful.

Yet somehow it didn't.

She just went with it.

"Sounds like I'm pretty good at my job then, hmm," she said, and when she did he showed her exactly why she didn't try to deny it with him: because she knew he wouldn't really hold it against her. Or if he did, he wasn't going to act like it was the worst thing in the world that she was decent at something and said so.

Though even knowing this, she didn't expect what she got.

"You're excruciatingly good at your job. Better than I ever was at football," he said. Almost wearily, too. Like he was telling her something annoying instead of giving her an outrageous compliment.

"That's ridiculous. You're one of the greatest flipping footballers of all time."

"All right, steady on. I was decent. And you're a lot better than decent."

"But I've barely done anything to deserve being deemed as such."

"You don't need to do things to deserve it—like getting out that little notepad and jotting things down and trying to wrangle me around to revealing things. You just do it naturally when I'm least expecting it. Like a superpower you don't know you have and didn't really mean to use."

*Fucking hell*, she thought.

Though she stayed calm about it.

Because sure, that was a cool thing to say.

But she couldn't let herself get too gooey and excitable over something cool, the way she usually did back in the nonprofessional portion of her life. That would have been a complete novice mistake at this stage of the game. Especially when he was possibly only gushing about her to throw her off guard and make her go soft on the questions. Which she absolutely was not going to do. She couldn't do it, no matter how kind he was to her. She had to go in a certain way, from particular angles, or she wasn't going to get what she needed.

And she intended to get what she needed.

"So. You somehow think you were only a decent footballer," she said while he was still probably waiting for her to react to that nice thing he'd tried. Then got the reaction she was looking for. He was on the backfoot again, just like that.

"I *know* I was only a decent footballer."

"Think a lot of people would disagree there."

"Yeah, well they're all full of rubbish, aren't they. Whoever they are."

"You at least know they exist, then. The people who sing your praises."

"I know that saying people sing my praises is a little strong."

"Are you sure about that? Because I've got about a million quotes here, somewhere. And I can easily read them out to you. It'll take me until sometime next century, but I'm willing to do it."

She made a show then of riffling through her notes.

Though the truth was—she did actually have what she was describing.

There was a whole file among everything she'd researched and collected about him, full of superlatives used to describe his form, his speed, his power on the pitch. And the compliments didn't stop there, either. On *Match of the Day*, Alan Shearer had once referred to him as the greatest team player the sport had ever known. People had given whole speeches about his legendary status during actual award ceremonies where he'd been the main recipient.

And all his coaches felt the same way about his work ethic: above and beyond, exemplary, always willing to go the extra mile.

The only problem really was his temper, his grumpiness. Though even that had rarely gotten in the way of his game. It had affected everything else, everything outside it—like deals that he soured by not knowing how to schmooze. Press tours that he couldn't properly participate in because every inane question made him furious. All of which the public loved him for, of course. He went viral all the time, for some hilariously surly response to something.

But it did make her wonder if this was the reason he'd finally agreed to the memoir business. She'd gotten the impression that he'd burned a lot of bridges, and this had been a *last chance saloon* sort of thing, job opportunity–wise. Or even maybe a way for him to set the record straight about who he was underneath the gruff persona. And if that was the case, well, she was there to help with that.

She was ready to point out the truth of him.

But just as she was about to do so, she realized something.

He was watching her as she searched and arranged her things.

Steadily, like it fascinated him.

But maybe also unsettled him at the same time.

"So you've done your research, then," he said after a moment.

Like maybe he'd thought he might fool her on some things.

But now knew with deadly certainty that he couldn't.

"Of course I have," she said. "You know I have if you really think I'm good at my job."

"I do think you are. But not because you've compiled a dossier on me."

"I would hardly call this a dossier."

He made a scoffing noise. "Why on earth not?"

"Because it makes me sound much cooler than I am. Like a spy who's infiltrated your shadowy organization. And now I'm going to take it down from the inside, as revenge for something terrible that you did to me."

She wasn't sure what to expect in response to that. Usually when she constructed some absurd premise like that, she got confusion. And it seemed likely that she would get the same from him. He was, after all, eminently practical and pragmatic. He didn't suffer fools and flights of fancy gladly.

And it did look like it was going that way.

He frowned immediately after she'd said it.

Then looked like he was gearing up to tell her off.

Which he did. Just not in the way he was supposed to.

"Now hang on," he said. "I haven't done a single terrible thing to you."

Because apparently, he was practical and pragmatic and all that.

But he could be all those things in service of a ridiculous scenario, too.

And oh, he did it so well. Like the scenario was completely real.

So it was easy to act like it was real back.

"Except insult my clothing."

"That isn't a good reason to destroy my terrible empire."

"Yeah, but the fact that you just admitted your empire is terrible probably is."

"I only called it that so I was in keeping with the framework you'd established," he said, because he was just admitting it now. He was admitting that he had gone with her weird thing. And oh god, that was so good.

Even if she couldn't admit it. "Despite the fact that the framework I'd established is total nonsense I made up just to drive you round the bend."

"Especially because it is. Otherwise, it's just chaos."

"I think it might be chaos anyway, to be honest."

"Yeah, I know. But I'm frantically trying to pretend otherwise."

"You don't look frantic, though."

"How do I look, then?"

*Like you're enjoying yourself again*, she thought.

But knew she had to pretend otherwise. "Really annoyed," she said.

Because the thing of it was: this was the truth. He *did* look annoyed.

It was just that he had so many flavors of annoyed that she was starting to see that some of them were less meant than others. Some of them were faintly amused, or almost relaxed. And he knew it. He accepted it.

Or at least, accepted it in his own inimitable way.

"That's just my default expression," he said.

"So you're not actually, I take it."

"Maybe. Maybe not."

"There's no *maybe* about your own emotions."

"There is when everything makes you so mad it's hard to tell when something does the opposite," he said, then only seemed to realize exactly what he'd told her after it was out. A bit of gut-wrenching emotional truth, she thought, of the sort that he very plainly hadn't processed that much before.

And it threw him a bit.

His eyes went briefly wide.

She saw him mouth the word *fuck*.

Then he passed a hand over his face. As if that might make the feelings he was clearly having go away. Or at least hide them from her. Even though he had to know he didn't need to do anything of the kind. And if he didn't know it, she was going to make sure he learned.

Through the medium of lighthearted encouragement.

"Well, maybe we could test it out. You tell me a thing that got your back up, in the past. And we'll compare how you feel when you talk about it to how you feel when you play daft games with me about how I'm a spy who's mad about dungarees," she said, with what she hoped was the right amount of sly humor. And his expression said that she'd gotten it right.

He almost smiled in a rueful sort of way.

"You think I don't know what you're doing, don't you," he said.

Then they were off again, like minor emotional devastation hadn't happened.

"No, I know you will. But I reckon my cheek might get you to say it anyway."

"Fuck's sake. That's amazing. You're absolutely right it will. I want to do it."

"So go on, then. Something that made you really mad."

He seemed to consider for a second.

Head tilted to one side, eyes dark and faraway.

Though she suspected it was less about dredging up some memory and more about wondering if he should go with the memory he wanted to. If it was too much to reveal, maybe. But then he came back to her, he focused on her face, and the second he did he just came out with it. Like he hadn't hesitated at all.

"My dad dragging me down the pub," he said.

To which she couldn't help making a guess.

Even though she knew what he meant, she had to do it.

"And you hated it because it made him a bad dad," she said.

Then got the exact shocking explanation she'd imagined.

"No, I hated it because I fucking hate the pub."

"As in there was a particular one you disliked?"

"I think you know that's not what I'm saying, Mabel."

"Yeah, I do. But it sounds bananas, so I'm checking before I write it down."

He shrugged. Like it was no big deal that a huge chunk of his whole persona was built on absolute bullshit. Or that it wasn't a big deal that he was telling her, even though it really was. In fact, this felt like more of a revelation than the *angry all the time* thing—even if he didn't seem to think so. He didn't seem the least bit bothered about saying it. As if some part of him liked that he was this way.

Or at least liked sharing it with her.

Which probably explained why he simply carried on.

"I've never liked going down the boozer. It's not my thing, despite what people think of me. Usually on a night out I just stand there, like a lemon, pretending I'm enjoying ten pints of lager that aren't really lager at all," he said, so matter-of-fact about it that she couldn't doubt it was true.

Though she still had questions.

Lots of half-marveling questions.

Which had nothing to do with writing his memoir.

"What are the pints then, if not lager?"

"Mostly shandy. Sometimes I get away with fizzy apple juice."

"But surely someone can tell that you don't stink of booze if you do this."

"Nah. You just swill a bit of proper stuff round your gob and splash a bit on yourself and you're golden. Nobody is ever any the wiser."

Another shrug. Though this one seemed just a touch more defensive.

Like he could fend off her questions about that with his shoulders.

Even though he had to know he absolutely could not.

"But why don't you want anybody to be the wiser?" she asked before she could even think about stopping herself. And got the pained reaction that made her sort of wish she had.

"Because it's embarrassing. Footballers are meant to be a certain way."

"So massive arseholes who start drunken fights in nightclubs, then."

"Well, when you put it like that of course I'm gonna sound more normal."

"That might be because you are normal. Just a thought for you there."

"Yeah, but it's a thought that only someone like you might have."

His eyes flicked up to her, a second after the words were out.

And then he held her gaze for what felt like a long, long time.

Or at least, long enough for her to understand what she hadn't before:

He didn't mind sharing this with her because he was starting to guess that she wouldn't care. That all that was meaningless to her in a way he obviously hadn't encountered much before. A fact that he then confirmed when he said in this amused sort of way: "You don't even think it's weird that I don't like a drink, do you."

"Honestly, that was the most relatable part to me."

"So you don't like it, either, then."

"Most of it tastes like piss."

"Christ, doesn't it, though."

"Give me a nice Mr Slush any day."

"Fuck yeah. That blue flavor? Second to none," he said.

But there was something underneath it, she suspected.

Something else they were saying without really saying it.

About alcoholic fathers, and the effect they could have on you.

Sometimes they turned you to the drink.

And sometimes you went the other way.

Even if you couldn't quite admit that was what did it to you. Not to yourself. Not to someone just like you. Not to anyone.

"You know you can't put any of this in the book," he said after a moment.

With regret, she thought. With real regret, and reluctance.

And it was the regret and reluctance that made her answer him.

"Even though you just told me all of it, and I'm supposed to then put the things you tell me into your book about you in words you think sound good. And also: it's *exactly* what you should be putting into said book."

"What? So people can think it's about some completely different weirdo?"

"You're not a weirdo for feeling that way. And anyone who says otherwise is, frankly, a jerk. A huge one, who doesn't understand anything at all, really."

"Mabel, you just don't know what it's like. You don't know."

"I know that you shouldn't have to pretend to be something you're not, just because people are used to the idea of you as some hardman who loves boozing. You're still normal if you enjoy other things, Alfie. You're still a bloke, even if you're the sort of bloke who enjoys watching *Repair Shop*, and likes confessing things to *Blue Peter* presenters, and prefers drinking sweet things before getting home at a reasonable hour to have a shower that he turned on by swizzling the knob."

He looked away at that.

At some distant idea of the sort he wasn't allowed to have.

"God, that sort of bloke sounds so happy," he said, and oh man, he just sounded so wistful. So despairing about this thing that seemed small to her but obviously loomed large for him. *Trapped by your own persona*, she thought.

And no matter how much she wanted to pretend she didn't care, she couldn't.

It made her heart pound weirdly, just thinking about that fact.

She honestly felt a bit sick for him.

So couldn't help saying heartfelt words to him.

"Maybe you could be, too. If you admitted you liked those things," she said.

Then he met her gaze, and oh god. A lot of stuff happened when he did. Intense stuff, which kind of made her wish she'd not gone down this path or had sounded more calm when she'd said what she'd said or just something, anything that didn't lead to this. But it had now, and there was nothing she could do. She just had to hope it didn't cause some terrible explosion.

Because god knew, that was what he looked on the brink of.

*Surely we're on the brink of something*, she thought.

Then just as suddenly as it happened, he shrugged.

"I'm gonna go make a cuppa. Want one?" he asked.

And thank god, thank god, that was the end of that.

"He was nothing less than professional, always early, always prepared, never skipped training, never complained about the rain or the heat or even injuries. But he was also, indisputably, the surliest and most annoying man I ever worked with."

—Roy Tattersley, Coaching Assistant 2009–2010

"Three months we were there, and we only learned on leaving that he'd not been able to ever watch the telly in his swank hotel room because he hadn't known how to use the voice activation to turn it on. Swear to god if you didn't know time travel doesn't exist you'd think he had blipped here from 1972."

—Jack Bonsaro, teammate 2007–2010

"One time I woke up and he was standing over my bed, fully dressed, with his suitcase next to him. Like he was going to pack me into it if I went one second over the time we were supposed to be out of there."

—Jack Bonsaro, teammate 2007–2010

"He could have done it, too, because he always had hardly anything in his suitcases. Two tracksuits, always black. No spare shoes, he always just took whatever he had on his feet. People always used to say he got his hair that black because he dyed it but I knew he never did. Because he never had anything except a toothbrush in his wash bag."

—Jack Bonsaro, teammate 2007–2010

"The wash bag thing isn't true, Jack's lying. My client is well known for taking a bottle of Hugo Boss Macho wherever he goes. Macho, for the man on the move."

—Geoff Haswell, manager 2005–Present

# Nine

## Pretty Sure Kate Bush Never Wore Dungarees

It didn't surprise her that he knew how to make a good brew.

Especially after the roller coaster of revelations they'd just gone through.

But still she found herself thinking *Damn* the second she sipped from the mug he handed her. Because said mug was a proper one with a big body and a sturdy handle, and the liquid inside was the color of oak tree bark, and the whole thing was so hot it burned her tongue a bit on the way down.

Oh, and he'd obviously used the right brand.

Tetley's, she suspected.

And it was good. It was better than good.

She'd drunk the whole thing down before he'd even gotten halfway with his, much to his amusement.

"Liked that, did you?" he asked as she set the mug next to her on the step she still sat on. And what was she supposed to say—no? The evidence that she had was right there in front of him. Though honestly even if it hadn't been, she wasn't sure she would have lied. He'd given plenty of concessions to her. He'd admitted secret things about himself, and not held back on certain things. So she could do more, too.

"You bet your sweet bippy I did," she said.

And she was well rewarded for it, too.

He almost *smiled*. Sparks briefly lit up his gaze.

Before he remembered he was supposed to be stoic and shut it down.

Though even that wasn't completely a thing. He was a little less closed shut than before. And when she suggested they go back to the topic they were discussing, he didn't refuse. Or at least, he didn't refuse entirely. "As long as I get a say-so on what goes in the book we can talk about whatever you want," he said, and when he did she thought for the second time that day:

*Because he likes doing this.*

*Just not if anyone else is going to hear.*

"I'm only going to put in what you approve."

"Then why are you scribbling everything down?"

"Just in case you change your mind about pretending to be what you're not," she said. And yes, she was being a little cheeky. Sure, she wasn't exactly serious. But even so, she saw something flash across his gaze. A flicker of reaching light, a hint of relaxation to his features. Like he was letting himself think, for just a moment, that something along the lines of what she was describing could actually be that easy.

Before he remembered he was a tight little clam. And tried to seal himself up.

"Well, I'm not going to. So don't," he said.

"Should I stop recording you, too?"

"Oh my Christ, you're not recording this."

"Of course I am. How else am I supposed to capture your voice?"

"I don't know. Watch some interviews where I talk a lot."

He spread his hands, like that was self-evident.

Even though he bloody well knew.

He knew, the little shit. And now she was going to prod him about it. "You understand full well that there are no interviews where you talk a lot. People stopped even having you on the radio because it meant a good half an hour of dead air every time. Even when the chat was only supposed to be ten minutes long."

"That's some bloody exaggeration right there."

"Are you sure? Because you know I have the one you did with Chris Moyles here in my phone. And I could just play it now, so we can compare what I'm saying to what actually happened. You know, in case I really am being unfair."

*That* got him. She could even see him going over the very thing she was talking about in his head. Remembering it, in all its excruciating detail. Because it had been excruciating, that was for sure.

And it was probably why he then blanched.

"Actually, you know what? It's fine," he said. "We don't have to do that."

To which she couldn't resist holding up her phone.

"But it wouldn't be any trouble. Look. I can just press play."

"No, don't press play. Just put it down."

"I want to," she said. "It's just that it's hard when the person you're with is a big exaggerator. You being that way makes my fingers really heavy, and so once I start moving them toward something I can't really get them to stop."

"None of that's even a real thing."

"And yet I'm still doing this."

"Because you're an arsehole."

"And sadly, being an arsehole makes heavy-finger syndrome even worse."

She let her hand tremble, then. As if it really were holding up something that weighed about a thousand pounds. And she made a good show of looking distressed, too. Like a funny dad, pretending to pinwheel over some steep drop for his kids.

*Absurd,* she thought. *Ridiculous.*

But he sagged anyway.

"Fine. Fine, I take it back. You're not any of those things. You're a nice person who never describes things as way more ridiculous than they actually were. Happy now?" he burst out. Mostly angry, she thought, mostly irritated seeming.

But with that hint of amusement that he couldn't quite hide.

She couldn't say yes to his question, however, for one very good reason:

"To be honest, no. I was looking forward to hearing Chris sweat again."

And now his amusement was more sixty/forty than ninety/ten.

Most probably because he was remembering exactly what she'd described.

"Christ, it was rolling off him. I'd have been sorry if he wasn't such a twat."

"I mean, fair. Considering he cracks a joke about living up north that'd put a posh playwright from the eighties to shame, five seconds into the interview."

"Well, what can you expect from a softie southern bastard?"

"Nowt much, seems like," she said, and let her accent go as thick as it could when she did. At which point his amusement went directly to a hundred percent.

Though maybe amusement wasn't quite the right word.

It was more like a flash of recognition.

The simple pleasure of hearing something so familiar, when you'd had to exist for a long time among people who weren't. People who were so well-to-do that the accent had gone, or were just from so far away that everything they said sounded different to you. No *nowts*, no *seems likes*, none of those things.

*Must be lonely*, she found herself thinking of him.

Even though the situation was exactly the same for her.

She couldn't remember the last time someone had talked to her like this.

Or heard something in her accent that they liked and wanted to talk about.

Even Connie sounded posher than she did, and she hadn't grown up that far from where Mabel had. And that made it extra nice to hear it all from him.

"Whereabouts you from?" he asked with genuine interest in his voice.

And she answered with just as much interest in hers.

"I doubt you really have to ask that."

"Leeds, then. Probably round Kirkstall."

"We were about five minutes from it."

"Your dad go down the Brudenell?"

*God*, she thought. *He even knows that.*

*He knows the local pubs.*

And he was right about her dad, too.

"He did. Couple of times a week."

"And the rest."

"Yeah. And the rest."

"Thought as much."

*So you did guess then*, she thought. About a second before he nodded, like *Yeah. I saw it in you and you see it in me—that hole left in you by fathers who go boozing every night of the week and piss away your lunch money and do awful things like sell your kiddie diary to keep them in pints for the foreseeable future.*

Because his dad had done that last one to him in particular, she knew.

She had seen the things people had said about it, even though she hadn't been able to bring herself to read the excerpts. It had felt like too much of an invasion. Too much like rewarding a scumbag for hurting him. Hell, it hurt to even think about it.

So she did her best to make things a little lighter.

"It did strike me that our backstories had some similarities when I was investigating your criminal organization in a slinky red dress while smoking a cigarette in a holder," she said.

And was pleased when it worked.

"So suddenly you're Jessica Rabbit."

"Maybe not quite that."

"But not far off."

*What does that mean*, her brain kicked up.

But he didn't so much as almost look down at her boobs.

There was zero impression that he meant it as a compliment.

So she ignored it, and carried on. "Yes. Except with alky fathers and soft mums and schools where someone got stabbed or trapped under collapsing ceilings. Once a week. Until everybody was suspended or in hospital except you."

"Assemblies sure were weird with just one person."

"Oh god, yeah. If there were any questions asked, it had to be you that answered."

"True," he agreed. "But at least we won all the awards. I mean, I skived for a whole term and still got best attendance."

"Three years in a row I got neatest in my year, and just look at me."

She waved a hand at herself. At the dungarees, mostly.

But he immediately looked at something else on her.

Then pointed, just for good measure.

"That incredibly wild hair should have disqualified you, for starters. You look like you've been running over the moors, crying for Heathcliff for the last week. Put you in a black dress and get you dancing around and you'd be Kate Bush," he said, and okay, this time she couldn't help wondering if he meant it *that* way. The you-look-like-a-very-beautiful-woman way.

Because Cathy and Kate indisputably were.

There was no getting around that.

But the thing was: she kind of wanted to get around it.

It felt like there must be a way to get around it, somehow.

*Supermodels*, she thought, *he dates supermodels, not mad-haired cuties in rainbow-print blouses*. Then tried to focus on the other part of what he'd said. The part that made more sense. "Honestly I'm kind of scared to tame it at this point," she said. And was thankful when he didn't seem to think anything of it.

"You don't need to be scared. You just need to go careful."

"Know a lot about the subject, do you?"

He shrugged. "Used to do it for my little sister."

"Because you were her real parent."

"Pretty much that, yeah. They'd let it go to the dogs, so I'd sort it."

He shrugged then, like it was no big deal. Even though it was. All this kind of was, if she was being honest. The thing about Jessica Rabbit, and Kate Bush, and then her hair, and him being weirdly complimentary about it, and now somehow, she'd led them to this. Then to cap it off, he said, "Can sort yours for you now, if you want."

And she just didn't know how to respond. She pretended to jot something down for a second, just so she wouldn't blurt out the wrong answer. Which definitely felt like a yes. *Don't say yes,* she told herself. *Just fob him off, somehow.*

But god, she didn't sound convincing when she did.

"Oh no. I don't want to trouble you."

"It's not any trouble. I like doing it."

She raised an eyebrow. "You *like* doing it?"

"Yeah. It's soothing. In fact, you'll probably find it soothing, too."

"I seriously doubt that," she said. Though very likely not for the reasons he was thinking. He chuffed at her, as if she were saying he didn't have the skill. But honestly, right at that moment in time, she was more worried that he *did.* That he was going to be super amazing at touching something on her, just as she was feeling complimented by him and inexplicably happy about that fact.

None of which seemed like a good thing.

In truth, it seemed like a very dangerous thing.

But it wasn't like she could just say no.

That would look even weirder.

So she agreed.

And tried to take comfort from the fact that he didn't seem the least bit concerned about the whole thing. "Good stuff," he said, then he slapped his knees like some old boy getting ready to strike a deal, and stood, and went off to find what she assumed was just a (hopefully) very powerful hairbrush.

Which it was.

But he had other things, too.

Some kind of product that you put in floofy hair, and one of those fancy combs hairdressers always had with a spike on one end, and a whole hairdryer with attachments that she couldn't imagine he would ever need to use. His hair was obviously thicker and curlier than he ever let it seem, but it was fairly short.

So what did he need all this for?

Did he regularly have women over and end up doing their hair?

It was hard to say, and she definitely intended to ask. After all, asking was her job. But then he started actually rolling up his sleeves—like someone about to really get something done here—and she could see those forearms, which were in fact as hairy and meaty as she had imagined, and finally he said "Budge up" and she realized:

He wasn't going to sit next to her.

He was going to sit *behind* her.

With his legs on either side of her body.

And after that all her questions just kind of dried up.

She simply did as he'd indicated, and shifted forward, and let him move behind her.

Even though letting him move behind her was easily one of the weirdest and most nerve-racking things she'd ever done. She could feel herself going all hot before he'd even sat down. Then he did, and he slid around her, and something brushed against her butt and her back and oh god, his *thighs*.

Oh no, oh fuck, his thighs.

His thighs were really big.

And they were surrounding her, like meaty prison bars.

If meaty prison bars could somehow be a great thing at the same time as being stupendously awful and agonizing. Because Lord, they were all the things. They looked incredible, every time she dared glance to either side of herself. And they felt incredible, whenever he shifted and they sort of brushed bits of her.

Heck, they even smelled good.

Like that scent she'd noticed in the car.

That light, expensive scent—the one that made her want to take big breaths.

But also felt as if she were being plunged into hell. This was *hell*.

And it wasn't about to get any better, either, because now he was telling her "Just relax." He was saying "I'm gonna touch you now." Then he did, he touched her head, and his hand felt so enormous it should really have made her scream. But it didn't, it didn't. It couldn't, because oh Lord in heaven was he ever gentle.

It was like being handled by a cloud.

She almost started crying, it was that soft and good.

And it didn't stop there, with him cradling her head and making it tilt.

It was the same when he started on the hair. She felt him part a section of it, smooth and efficient as a professional, and then there was this warm sensation and this stroking sensation and a slight tugging sensation, and she realized he was doing it. He was brushing through the bit he'd separated out.

But instead of it feeling like agony, it somehow felt like she was being massaged. Slowly, yet firmly. Over and over, until she wanted to do something absolutely deranged. Like moan, fucking hell she wanted to *moan* over it. As if his hands were having sex with her head.

When really they were hardly doing anything at all.

*He's just brushing your hair*, she tried to tell herself.

But unfortunately her body just didn't want to listen.

It was too busy trying to lean into him in a way that would look even weirder than making sex sounds about it. After all, people groaned all the time over head massages. And there was a strong chance she'd be able to disguise it as a cough, if one leaked out. But if she started rubbing her head into his hands and putting her body right against his body, how would that look?

Like she'd gone out of her mind.

Or was really horny for him.

Or both.

Even though neither was true. She was fine, she was calm, she was totally normal. And then for some unaccountable reason she felt him push his entire hand deep into her hair at the back, like right into it with all his fingers, and honestly the only thing she could do to stop herself from pushing right back into that absolutely glorious sensation was shoot her own hands out and grab something, hard.

She just wished the things she'd grabbed weren't his fucking *thighs*.

Because yep, that was exactly what she had done.

She had gotten ahold of him.

Really high up.

In the worst possible place.

And apparently she had done it so hard that he made a noise when she did.

A loud one that sounded half shocked and half annoyed and all something else, something familiar that she didn't want to name or even think about, but she found herself doing so anyway. *It was the kind of noise someone makes when you suddenly give them a blow job they weren't expecting*, her mind helpfully informed her.

Then she vowed from that moment on never to let her mind talk again.

*You are a dipshit*, she told it.

And she was right to do it, too.

Because he did not seem to be feeling the least bit sexy at all.

"Mabel, you appear to have latched on to me like a frightened cat," he said after what felt like the longest thirty seconds of her life. Then even more horrifying: "So if you could tell me what it was I did that induced this state in you, I would be grateful. Because then I can stop doing it, and you can hopefully relax your fingers enough to detach them from my thighs."

At which point she had two choices:

She could tell him he'd given her a sexy feeling.

Or she could say something that would not mortify her to the end of her days.

Though really, when you thought about it, that was no choice at all.

"I think you just snagged some hair," she said.

Then held her breath.

Waiting to see if he would buy it.

Kind of sure that he wouldn't.

Until he did.

"Yeah, sorry about that," he said lightly. "Think I went in too deep."

And now instead of feeling relieved, she had to think about *that* phrasing for the next hour. While he carried on doing her hair in just as excruciating a way as he'd gone about it before. Only now she wasn't allowed to grab anything. Because if she did, the thing she grabbed might be his thighs.

So she just had to resist the leaning, somehow.

She had to hold on as he brushed and stroked and fussed.

And finally, plaited. Because he did that too. Deftly, like he'd done it a thousand times before. Then she felt him fasten the braid back with pins she hadn't even known he had, in a way that felt familiar even as he was doing it. Though it took until he was finished for her to uncover what he had done.

She put her hand to it, and there it was.

A circle at the back of her head.

*Like Princess Leia in* Empire, she thought, and was so surprised and delighted that she turned without thinking. She looked at him, one hand on this thing he'd done, and with a question finally on her lips. After all the ones she'd fought back and de-cided against, finally there was one here that she could actually let out.

And then she saw him.

His startled expression on seeing her.

The way his eyes seemed to search all over her face as if he'd never properly seen it before. Which of course he hadn't. She'd been hiding it from him behind the maze of her big, bouncy mess of hair. And now that it was there, it was all really there, and it clearly wasn't what he expected. It was weirder, or bigger-boned, she suspected.

*Broad faced*, her dad used to say. Though none of those things really explained the way he lifted his hand. How he let it hang in the air, a millimeter from her cheek.

Before he seemed to realize that he was being weird, and let it drop.

"There," he said gruffly. "Much better."

But somehow, she didn't think it was.

She thought that perhaps it was a lot worse.

And in a way that she had no idea how to ever fix.

In fact, she was still thinking about how to fix it when he escorted her to the car, sometime later. Then just as she was getting in, he put out a hand. And without even thinking about it, she took it. She let him guide her in.

As if they were something else altogether.

Instead of exactly what they were.

## QUESTIONS TO ASK/THINGS TO CLARIFY

- Do you really only carry a toothbrush when you go anywhere?

- Your manager claims you use the cologne you briefly advertised, but I am pretty sure it's Davidoff Cool Water you smell like. (Maybe take out the Davidoff Cool Water—you only think that because it reminds you of high school, only matters that it's definitely not Macho.)

- Actually important things like describe where you grew up, instead of stuff that is just swirling around your head thanks to eight million absurd quotes from his teammates, his manager, and people who just think they know him.

- Suggest he adds some of his own words to this, he's got such a turn of phrase. Wonder if he ever wanted to do anything with that? Something's there. Dig deeper.

- Come on, Mabel. Ghostwriting might not be your dream writing gig, but you're good at it. You're getting somewhere. You can do this!

## ANSWERS FOR YOU, YOU BLOODY NOSY PARKER

- Yes, I only take a toothbrush with me. But that tosspot is saying it like it's a bad thing, instead of all you need when them hotels always had everything else. Tiny soaps, shampoo, conditioner, moisturizer—they had the works, so why would I pay for my own? You seen how much Palmolive costs these days?

- It is Davidoff Cool Water. Because how was I to know you were only supposed to use that stuff in 1997? I liked the smell, and always wanted some, and so when I could afford it, I bought some and stuck with it. End of.

- Don't tell Hugo Boss this but I hated Macho.

- I told you, I grew up in Manchester. Weren't you listening?

- Stop letting things people said about me swirl around your head. There's already enough swirling in there from all the things you forced out of my gob. You're still fucking forcing it out now, look at me here scribbling away on this piece of paper you meant to throw away.

- Don't you bloody dare dig deeper!

P.S. Next time you want to make up some daft questions and toss them before I can see or hear how daft they are, make sure you actually aim well. I found this scrunched up in one of my shoes, even though it was bloody miles away from the bin.

P.P.S. I knew it, I knew you were after more than ghostwriting, I bet there's a million amazing stories in that weird head of yours.

## Ten

$S$he decided the best approach to the whole weird *leg grabbing* and *face almost touching* and *hands briefly grazing* thing was to just pretend it all never happened. She had never dug her nails into his thighs about an inch from his groin. Really, it had been a mile away from the danger zone, and she'd barely brushed him. And he had definitely never nearly caressed her cheek. Probably he'd just seen an errant hair and wanted to brush it away. He was, after all, a well-known perfectionist.

He strived for the best, always.

So why wouldn't he have with that?

Yeah, that made sense. Or at least, it made enough sense that she could focus on her actual job here. Instead of focusing on intense weirdness that made her want to scream into a pillow. And she did focus on it, too. She started organizing her notes and typing up the things she knew he'd let her include.

Which wasn't much when she really got down to it.

Because no matter how good he thought she was at getting things out of him, he was undoubtedly better at evading. He led her down the garden path so many times she lost count. And to such a degree she actually found herself just listening to his bizarre tangents. She found herself *laughing* over them.

Seeing as she could now that she was alone.

She was allowed when he couldn't see her finding him funny and fascinating.

And weirdly, it seemed to help. Because when she tried actually getting something down, when she wrote an opening for this memoir—just on a whim to see if she could do it—she found she could. In fact, it felt easy. Like she could already hear his voice in her head. She could feel it, deep in her chest.

It was a part of her, somehow.

As second nature as her own self.

*He's the other kid with you in the assembly*, her mind said, about an hour in.

And though that was an unsettling thought, she couldn't deny it was true. It felt to her as if she'd always known him. As if she'd once been friends with him, years ago, and now they'd been reunited somehow. They had seen each other on Facebook, or heard about a divorce one of them had had via a brother-in-law of somebody's cousin.

Something like that.

And now they were catching up.

They were talking about *Repair Shop* and *Wuthering Heights* and bad dads, like nothing had ever happened. All of which was good, it was a very good thing, she knew it was a very good thing. She was not going to see it as anything but a good thing. And especially when Greg was suddenly calling her, in the middle of the afternoon. Now, she thought, she had great news to report.

*Progress has been made*, she imagined herself saying.

But unfortunately, she didn't get that far.

Because it wasn't Greg.

It was his number, his name that showed up on her phone. However, it was definitely someone else who immediately started talking. Clearly it was, because they sounded so different from Greg in every single way that she wanted to whack her phone to make sure it hadn't just malfunctioned. And possibly started sending her messages from the lead in a production of *Oklahoma!*

Considering the guy who was talking started this conversation with the word *howdy*. Then he just launched right into loads more absurd talking, without even giving her a chance to process that first thing.

"Real sorry for calling you at whatever time I am calling you at. I think it's a reasonable hour but I can't be sure, seeing as I'm jet-lagged as all get out and not quite sure what hour it actually is. Anyhoot, you're probably wondering why the heck this fella is calling you. Well, here's the thing: ole' Greg decided what was best for him was to take a leave of absence. And by leave of absence there I mean a polite way of saying he fled in the night for no reason anyone can think of. So I threw my name into the hat to help out with this whole mess, and here we are."

She could practically hear him spreading his hands on those last words.

Hell, she could practically see him. His voice was so quick and expressive and full of character that he was easy to picture. Most likely he wore bow ties; she'd bet anything he had lines pressed down each leg of his jeans. And if he didn't have a jaunty mustache she was a monkey's uncle.

In fact, she almost said it to him.

*You have hair on your upper lip, don't you.*

But then he was off again, like a rocket made of rainbows.

"And now you're probably thinking hold your horses there, buddy, before we get to the mess we need to be properly introduced. Which, well, you'd sure be right about. So the name's Henry Samuel Beckett, though folks generally call me Beck. And I believe you are Mabel—any nickname there I should know about?"

She managed a no, and not much more. Partly because he was still clearly brimming with things to say. And partly because she was starting to get a sinking feeling about those brimming things.

"Well, that's great. So Mabel, lemme just start out by asking you: Have you by any chance recently perused social media of any kind? Because I may have noticed a thing or two this morning that I felt might be good to bring to your attention. You know, just so I could be a little soft landing for you on that, if you're in need of one."

*Soft landing*, she thought. Then had to force herself to bring up Twitter, as Henry Samuel Beckett kept right on talking. "I sense that you're probably looking right now as we speak, so I'll just go ahead and reassure you: I personally have no problems with people believing you are a new mystery woman spending time with one Alfred Harding. You need have no fear that we here at Harchester Publishing Incorporated are not behind you one hundred percent."

And that was nice of him, she thought. But honestly by that point she was already not listening. She was clicking through her socials on her iMac with what felt like a combination of terror and intense confusion.

Because she hadn't done anything.

Nothing remotely weird had happened.

She had just gone to his house, that was all.

*People must go to his house all the time*, she thought, but even as she was doing so she was remembering that article in the *Daily Mail* about him. The one that insinuated things about him never having anybody over. Or how about the piece in some magazine about him never touching anybody.

Yet he'd touched her.

And so of course there was now a blurry picture of her doing so going around social media. And okay, yes, the social media accounts were minor. Plus, they weren't picking up a lot of traction. But still, that was her in her dungarees with her hair all sorted and her expression incredulous over what was happening, walking out to Alfie Harding's car. Followed by their hands touching, like something out of *Pride and* fricking *Prejudice*.

None of which felt normal, or good, or like something she could laugh off.

Especially when Henry Samuel Beckett was currently rattling on in her ear about how if any potential relationship should develop between them, she need not worry about conflicts of interest or Alfie exploiting her. "After all, he isn't your boss. We are. And I will personally see to it that you are fully protected from any legal issues, or hinky power dynamics, or anything of the kind. All you need to do is say the word and I will make it my personal business to see you are safe and secure in all matters."

Even though nothing of the sort had even entered her head.

First, because she couldn't imagine Alfie *ever* being that kind of dude.

And second, because it wasn't actually happening. It would never happen. It was not a thing. So now she had to somehow reassure this near stranger that something nonexistent that wasn't even possible hadn't caused her any kind of emotional or legal damage.

Which went about as well as she suspected it would. In the end she panicked and told him she had to go and feed a cat she didn't have, just so she could calm herself down. So she could strip off the jumper she was sweating through, and fan herself with a file marked ANECDOTES FROM COLLEAGUES, and have a long drink of something she wished was whisky but was actually just pink lemonade.

She felt better after she'd done all this, however.

Even though she was a maniac dripping lemonade while standing in the kitchen in just her bra and sweatpants, she felt more sane. After all, when she thought about it objectively, it was clear that things were not that bad. It was just a small bit of attention. Nobody was really talking about it.

And it didn't seem like anyone even knew who she was.

She was safe. She was fine.

Until about five minutes from now.

When Alfie Harding was going to be picking her up in his car again.

*Oh god oh god oh god*, her brain panted as she tried to call him. Just to tell him to maybe wait around the corner, so she could go to him. Sneakily, possibly while wearing a disguise.

Only he wasn't answering, and he didn't have voicemail for some inexplicable reason, and texting was almost certainly even more futile than either of those two options. If she tried, he'd probably respond by setting his phone on fire.

So now it was purely a matter of getting to him first.

Even though she was half dressed and sweaty as fuck.

With pink lemonade all down her front.

*And he was already having his driver hammer on the fucking horn.*

Because god, that was definitely what that constant wailing sound was. She'd somehow panicked herself into being ten minutes late, and now there was a constant siren drawing attention to itself right outside her flipping door. Probably her entire street was now looking out their windows with their phones at the ready. That Instagram influencer who was trying to make this whole thing go viral was going to have a blooming field day.

And that was before she heard the other thing going on. The less loud, but indisputably more terrible thing. The thing she couldn't believe was actually happening until she went to her window, and there it was: Alfie Harding, yelling up at her flat.

While standing.

In his car.

*With half his body only out the fucking sunroof.*

That was his entire face and shoulders and upper body she could see.

Just right there bold as brass, where anybody could clock him.

And then just in case that wasn't bad enough, the thing he was shouting was her *name*. It was her whole entire fucking name. "*Mabel Willicker,*" he yelled up at her. "*How long you gonna keep me waiting out here like a doorknob?*"

To which the answer was, of course:

*Until I think of a way to murder you.*

Though she couldn't say it. She couldn't say anything. If she opened her window and yelled back it would be bedlam, it would be hell, she didn't know what would happen. Her only option was to somehow get down there if she wanted this to stop. So that was what she focused on. She wiped herself all over with a soapy sponge and threw on her clothes and stuffed crap into her bag, and then pelted down her stairs so fast she felt her teeth clack together at the bottom.

She almost bit through her fucking tongue.

But honestly it wouldn't have mattered if she had.

He took one look at her as she burst from her door like a wild-haired confetti bomb sent from somewhere south of wherever the Care Bears lived, and immediately stopped his hollering. *Shit*, his face said. *I'm in for it now.* And he was right, too, he was. Because her tongue was still intact, and now he was going to get fricking told. "For the love of heck, stop bellowing after me like some hairy Richard Gere in the ten-pence version of *Pretty Woman*. Things are bad enough as it is," she hissed the very second she was within a reasonable distance of his daft-arse self. And she didn't regret it once she had, either. Not even when she processed that she'd just referred to them in a slightly romantical fashion.

Because he didn't care about that. He didn't see things that way.

Things were not that way between them, and never would be.

And that just left the current disaster to go over.

Though she got him into the car first. She made him sit down and then climbed in and sealed them both safely inside. And only then did she let him say what she knew he'd been saving since she'd held up a hand to tell him to stop and get in the bloody car. "How do you mean things are bad enough as it is?" he asked. Though his face said it all.

He knew it was not going to be something he wanted to hear.

Or even something he was likely to understand on any level whatsoever. And he was right about that. "So you've not seen Twitter, then," she said, and got the exact answer she expected— his face turning into a maze of confused lines.

And then this:

"I don't know. Is Twitter the one that's ruining democracy?"

She couldn't laugh, however. It wasn't a laughing matter.

"They're *all* the ones that are ruining democracy. That's not the point."

"Then tell me what the point is. Quickly. Before I start to panic."

*How to explain*, she thought, *to a man who still has a flip phone.*

Then tried to break it down into chunks as manageable as she could.

"There are pictures of me at your house going round," she said.

But even that wasn't enough, apparently. He just shrugged.

"Yeah, I'm not seeing the problem. That's what happened."

"Right. But people aren't just taking events literally, the way you do."

"There's no other way to take them. Nothing else happened. Or at least, nothing else that was visible to them. They couldn't have possibly seen me plaiting your hair. And even if they did, so fucking what, it didn't mean anything," he said in a way she thought he intended to sound scornful and sure.

But to her horror, it didn't come out that way.

It came out jittery and weird.

Like he'd gotten lost down some dirt track on the way to making his point.

And then he'd said that thing on the end. About it not meaning anything. Even though he had no reason to say that at all. Because of course it hadn't meant anything, of course it hadn't, why on earth did he feel he had to make it a thing?

She didn't know. She didn't *want* to know.

She just wanted to focus on the problem at hand.

"Alfie, calm the flip down. Obviously, it didn't. *We* know that. But the problem is, the general public do not. In fact, the general public tend to think—much as they do with any lusted-after famous man who has a vaguely mysterious sex life—that any person within a ten-foot radius of you is getting the living daylights doinked out of them by your Duracell Bunny penis," she said.

And it felt good when she did it.

Then she saw his eyebrows hit his hairline and realized.

Though of course it was too late to do anything about it now.

She just had to deal with the fact that she'd talked about his cock.

And that he was going to give her what for about it.

"Shitting hell, how do you even *know* someone once called my penis that?" he said in a voice so ripe with incredulity and indignation she couldn't help feeling embarrassed.

Even though she hadn't really looked into it that deeply.

Like with the diaries, she'd pretty much steered clear.

It was just that with this, you couldn't really keep yourself clean.

"You say that like you don't know it's one of the few relationship details of yours that ever made it to the papers. And by *relationship details* I of course mean a one-night stand that led to a kiss-and-tell which contained one particular funny thing about you being able to go for hours that totally caught on with your fans."

"They barely chanted it, all right."

"And I suppose no panel shows mentioned it repeatedly."

"If they did I do not recall," he said. But she could tell he already knew that wasn't convincing. She saw his expression go from faux innocence to exasperation before it finally landed on what looked like weary acceptance as he conceded the point. "Probably because I worked hard to repress the memory of Jimmy Carr saying the words *on and on and on* about my cock."

*That honesty of his*, she thought. It was a real killer.

Hell, it almost killed her, too. Because now she had to think about that very thing against her will. "We've all worked hard to repress that memory, Alfie," she said finally, as Carr's laugh rattled around in her head.

Though it at least seemed to galvanize him.

He clapped his hands together—like a really angry TV presenter trying to get a show back on track after it went badly awry. "Right, here's what we're going to do. From now on, I will only pick you up from that post office round the corner. And whenever we get to mine, we'll drive round the back and you can slip in through the second kitchen door," he said. And it made sense, it all made sense. She even wanted to say that it did. But somehow went with this instead:

"You have a *second* kitchen door?"

Though oddly, it helped that she did.

It took everything further away from that thing he'd said about plaiting her hair.

And the thing she'd said about his nethers. And all the mess they were in.

Now they had a plan in place, and they could go right back to their bizarre banter.

"You're saying that like you've not seen my house." He snorted.

And she fired right back, without even thinking about it.

"In my defense, it was hard to notice anything but the lack of furniture."

"Well, I've got some now so you can stop your complaining."

She raised an eyebrow. "The TV came then, did it."

"And some other things."

"So you used Amazon by yourself?"

"No, I got my assistant to do it for me."

She saw him grimace after he said it.

Like he knew he shouldn't have.

But he was wrong to think so.

Because now she had another completely harmless thing to rib him about.

"I can't believe you've got an assistant," she said with just enough withering disdain and eye rolling to get him to bite. To get him to throw up his hands and try to come up with some kind of reasonable defense.

That was not in the least bit reasonable at all.

"All rich people have one. It's like the rules," he said.

But it made the conversation even funnier, and that was the main thing.

"Because money makes you forget how to wipe your own bum?"

"All right, smart-arse. She doesn't do owt like that for me. She just, you know, makes sure I'm going to the right places for meetings I don't want to be at while wearing the right fancy suits because apparently you can't just buy them at Burton."

He shook his head, like he was disgusted.

And now things weren't just much easier.

She was almost laughing. *Burton*, she thought.

Cheap, silly old Burton, where every lad she'd ever known bought their clothes. She had to bite her lip and look away while she came up with a retort to that. And when it did come, it was a lot warmer toward him than she strictly intended. "To be fair, that suit you were wearing yesterday was hecking amazing," she said, and as soon as she did she knew what she was going to get.

That spark in his eyes. One eyebrow lifting.

A slightly softer, more wry twist to his voice.

"Was that a compliment? Steady on, mate. I might think you like me," he teased. And okay, he didn't mean it. He wasn't saying she really did. But still, she felt the urge to cover for herself. To give herself an alibi on the *something about you produced a complimentary feeling in me* front.

"No, I like whoever bought it."

"Of course. Should have realized."

"You should. I mean, whoever it is sounds much more amazing than you."

"I'll pass these kind regards on to Daisy. She'll be thrilled to find another person she can have a good laugh with about me behind my bloody back."

"I wouldn't laugh about you behind your back."

"Yeah, you don't mind doing it to my face. Hairy Richard Gere, you cheeky little sod," he said. Though here was the thing: it felt good when he did it. Because she could see he was almost laughing, and not even trying to hide it. And he clearly hadn't taken it in a weird way. He'd taken it as intended:

As a joke, as just a bit of teasing, of the kind he seemed to quite enjoy.

Which meant that everything was okay now. Order had been restored.

No one was taking things the wrong way and they'd nipped

the whole *mystery woman* thing in the bud and now they were going to have a good, productive day. And they did. Everything was fine. It went smooth as silk, and she went to bed that night with only one thought in her perfectly calm head:

*Crisis averted.*

**Tweets**, March 23, 2022

**AlfieHardingsRightBoot**
@beardaddict
Okay but was that an actual woman coming out of his house

**WagInTraining** @sparklebeard
Replying to @beardaddict
where are you seeing this all I got was the blurred splotch
abby had

**AlfieHardingsRightBoot** @beardaddict
the queen had it I think go look it's some weirdo in
dungarees, personally I don't think he actually touches
her hand if you embiggen the picture it looks like he's just
nudging her wrist

**BootScoot** @bootscooting
Replying to @beardaddict
Why would he be nudging her wrist, no he's totally touching
her hand. But I think that's his sister.

**Watchingthefootie** @tuesdaygirl
ARE YOU SERIOUS THAT ISNT EDITH IT LOOKS NOTHING
LIKE HER, IVE SEEN HER stop ruining THEPRIDE AND
PREJUDICE MOMENT

**AlfieHardingsRightBoot** @beardaddict
yeah pride and prejudice if it was made by channel five
now shut up the lot of you I'm blocking anybody who brings it
up again

EXCLUSIVE: Who is Alfie's mystery lady? Harding spotted emerging from his luxury five-million-pound bachelor pad with new woman who affectionately brushes his sleeve as they make their way through the grounds—just weeks after his breakup with model/actress Veronica Taylor.

**Footballer Harding was pictured outside home with mystery woman**

**As they walked down the driveway, she brushed his sleeve**

**The new pictures come just weeks after his breakup with Veronica**

**Harding is notorious for guarding his privacy and guests are rarely seen at his bachelor pad**

Footballing legend Harding left his luxury five-million-pound bachelor pad accompanied by a mystery woman in a black dress this past Thursday.

As they walked down the driveway, the woman grew closer to the Manchester United superstar, and affectionately brushed his sleeve.

It's not clear who the mystery woman is, or if Harding has begun dating again after the disastrous end to his brief relationship with Veronica Taylor, 27. Taylor indicated in the kiss-and-tell exclusive we published earlier this year that Harding "never wanted to talk" and "always scowled at everything."

But those problems all seem to be in the past for Alfie as he appeared with his new lady love looking dapper in a black suit which he layered over a black shirt. He wore his hair in his trademark severe side part, and his beard had been neatly trimmed. Sources tell us wedding bells might be in the air, though when we reached out to his publicist for comment the response was "What are you talking about, that was a Jehovah's Witness he was directing back to the motorway."

# Eleven

## Local Nobody Might Be
## Engaged to Famous Werewolf

$\mathcal{S}$he wasn't sure when the banging started. Her alarm clock told her it was eight thirty when she first woke, but there had been a lot of dreaming about loud noises before that. In one of them, someone had been stealing her bin lids.

So it seemed likely that this had been going on for a while.

Still though, she didn't imagine it was anything weird.

Probably just her downstairs neighbor forgetting his keys again. In a second, Mrs. Porter from the other flat down there would bustle out in a fury and let him in. Then there would be peace again, in which she would get at least another hour's kip before she had to get ready for the car that would be here at ten.

*Yep, that checks out*, she thought.

Only somehow it wasn't checking out.

It just kept going and going and Mrs. Porter wasn't doing anything, and now somehow there was shouting, too. Loud shouting, of the sort that usually happened when the bailiffs came round to repossess the possessions of a man who'd died without anyone knowing three weeks ago.

*We know you're in there*, she was pretty sure she heard.

And she had no choice, after that. She had to go check it out.

She'd never forgive herself if she just stayed in bed while her dead downstairs neighbor got burst in on by burly men looking for a Bluetooth speaker that didn't actually work. *It only plays the beat, you can never hear the lyrics*, she thought of saying to them, as she thundered down the stairs that led out from her flat and threw open the front door.

Though god, she wished she'd considered it a bit more before she did.

At the very least she would have put on something other than her pajamas.

And maybe she might have brushed her hair, too, because Christ, Alfie was just gonna go spare when he saw the state it was in. *I only did it the other day*, he'd say, upon seeing it splashed across the sixth page of some third-rate newspaper.

Then she had to wonder why the fuck it was his outrage she was focusing on.

And not the fucking newspaper part, the newspaper part, oh god, there were newspaper people on her front doorstep. *Paparazzi*, her brain screamed at her. That was exactly what they were, quite obviously. They all looked like her dad after an all-night bender, and every one of them had a camera they were jabbing at her aggressively, and when they shouted all she could think of was a bunch of dogs barking.

Before she realized *what* they were shouting.

*Mabel*, they said. *Mabel Willicker.*

Because apparently, they didn't just know where she lived. They knew who she was. And it seemed like they were intent on shouting about it really loudly, for reasons she just couldn't fathom. It didn't make any sense—because even if they'd heard Alfie shouting her name yesterday, they shouldn't have been here bellowing it at her on her doorstep. They didn't even do that for actually famous people.

Unless the famous people had murdered someone, of course. *Oh god, did I accidentally murder someone while I was sleeping*, she found herself thinking as she slammed the door on them, and took the stairs two at a time, and stuck a charger into her poor dead phone after what felt like seven shaky attempts.

And saw what she would have done much sooner, if she weren't a huge dipshit who let her phone die while in the middle of all this madness:

Her voicemail inbox was full of messages.

Most of which were just incoherent screaming from almost

everyone she knew. And even the ones that didn't do that were incredibly disturbing. Connie's husky voice had gone so high it sounded as if she'd been sucking helium. *What is going on, my Instagram feed is jammed with I-told-you-sos about you and then some stuff about Richard Gere from someone called Gossip Queen?* she yelled at one point.

And the message from her other bestie, Berinder, didn't sound any better. It was just a lot of questions, so rapidly asked they sounded like one word. *Like, I knew you were secretive about anything that actually super matters to you but oh my god he's been in actual* movies, *Mabie, how on earth did you even meet him,* she finished.

But the worst part was: she couldn't answer either of them.

She couldn't immediately jump into group chat and at least share *something*.

And not just because she was the friend people came to with their complicated problems, rather than the friend who had complicated ones she knew how to share. No, there was also the fact that everything she could share would betray Alfie. Not to mention blow her years-long carefully constructed cone of secrecy around her ghostwriting, and break the NDA she'd signed for Harchester. So now she was even more isolated, deep feelings–wise, than she usually forced herself to be. She just had to smile and winky face at them.

Even as she went through everything else she was being bombarded with.

Like the other messages.

From other friends.

Friends she barely spoke to.

Hell, she even heard her sister among it all, and her sister hadn't been in touch for *years*. And all that was before she even got to Henry Samuel Beckett, sounding just as chipper as he had the other day but now with just a hint of panic. And her agent with twenty missed calls and three emails that ended on a simple bold-lettered WHERE ARE YOU.

Then finally, there was Alfie.

Alfie, who hated using phones.

But had somehow left her ten voice messages.

And a grand and unbelievable total of thirty-seven texts.

Then when he'd obviously not been able to get hold of her, he'd done something even more astonishing. Something that made her groan in horror the second she saw it. She had to put her phone down for a second and take several deep breaths. Because Lord in heaven, he'd only gone and joined Twitter. He had joined it, and put his face on it, and written a bio and everything.

*Do not talk to me I am here to talk to Mabel,* it said.

And it was true, he was. The first thing he'd done was attempt to DM her. It was there in her inbox when she looked: **MABEL YOU HAVE DRIVEN ME TO DO SOCIAL MEDIA ANSWER IMMEDIATELY BEFORE SOMETHING MUCH WORSE HAPPENS,** he had put, as if he thought his difficulties with contacting her were purely down to using the wrong method.

Instead of imagining it could be literally anything else. Or at least, something that wouldn't have led him to make the worst move in the world. Because of course the first thing people had done was go absolutely nuts that Alfie Harding was on Twitter. Then once they'd finished being nuts about that, they'd gone absolutely nuts about the fact that he referred to her in his bio.

And then once she'd seen them going nuts about that, she unearthed exactly what had started all this. She scrolled through the news section after someone linked to something, and it was like opening the seventh fucking seal. Literally there was just tweet after tweet quoting the same twenty articles and Instagram posts from names she actually recognized, and every single one of them was about Alfie Harding and the fight he had apparently had the night before. Some of them joking and using his old game names and such (*Alfred the Great at It Again* and *Duracell Bunny Brawls Outside Bar*), some serious (*Alfie Harding Attacks Reporter On Street*), and all, without exception, absolutely hideous.

And not because he'd been fighting.

No. Mostly it was what he'd been fighting *about*.

Right there, in black and white, on something that wasn't even the middle of *The Bumfuck Bulletin*. It was dead center on the front fucking page. Of a national newspaper. Under a garish red headline about his fisticuffs, and a picture of him looking like an apoplectic werewolf on the verge of eating someone.

*Harding yelled the words "How dare you say Mabel Willicker is too fat to be dating me,"* she read with what felt like the most amount of mounting horror she'd ever experienced in her life. And then somehow, somehow, it got even worse than that. Because he hadn't stopped there, apparently. He'd kept going, directly into a bunch of even more terrible things. Like punching whoever had leveled this accusation. And headbutting the man who'd agreed.

And finally, oh god, finally he'd said the words:

*True* and *she's* and *love* and *my*.

In an order that made her stomach drop right out of her butt.

Honestly she screamed the second they sank into her brain.

Even though the reporters were still on the other side of the door and would definitely hear such a sound of panic from her flat. In fact, they'd probably be recording it, ready to send it to TMZ. *True Love of Maniac Footballer Bellows in Horror,* she imagined wildly. And couldn't even make it not make sense.

Because it made plenty, compared to all the rest of this shitshow.

He'd punched someone. And headbutted someone else.

Then declared her to be his true love.

*Dear god in heaven why did he declare me to be his true love*, she groaned silently to herself. But she had no good answers to that. It was inexplicable and preposterous, and not just because of the circumstances. Because it was him doing it. It was Alfie Harding, a man who never revealed his feelings about anything. Who had never so much as revealed a single detail about any relationship he'd ever been in. Heck, she wasn't even sure what kind of relationships he'd had, aside from one-night stands and brief things with a series of glossy famous women.

Yet somehow, he'd done this.

And he didn't even have a good explanation for it. *What else was I supposed to tell them*, he actually had the nerve to say in one of his messages.

Even though she could think of at least fifty things right then and there, off the top of her head, while sweating buckets into her pajamas and being hounded by the paparazzi on her doorstep. *You could have told them they're fatphobic wankers, or that you weren't at liberty to discuss your private life, or Christ, even just say we've been on one date and you find my body hot as balls*, she thought.

But no, no. He had to go and say something that inescapable and ridiculous.

Now they were practically a grand romance. Next thing you knew, people were gonna start speculating about their impending nuptials. Or not even next thing you knew, because Instagram and Facebook and Twitter were already full of people wanting to know if they were engaged. *There's a ring on her finger in that video of her leaving his house*, someone with three hundred thousand followers was saying.

Then they'd shared enhanced photos.

She had to spend the next hour examining gigantic pictures of her own hand, while trying not to absolutely lose her everloving mind. Or text Alfie to tell him she was going to punt him into the bloody sun. Or answer her phone, which was now ringing almost constantly. Courtesy of numbers she did not know.

And when she googled them, the news wasn't good.

It was bad, it was real bad, she was in a lot of trouble.

Trouble that was about to get worse.

Because judging by the sounds outside, the car was there. And now she had to go get in it, while pretending getting in it meant nothing at all.

## ALFRED THE GREAT AT IT AGAIN

Alfie Harding got himself into yet another explosive fight outside an East End pub on Tuesday night after what appears to be a stern exchange of words with paparazzi.

Harding allegedly threw the first punch in reaction to a series of insults aimed at the new woman in his life. The woman, who wasn't present, had to date been unidentified. But Harding was heard yelling "How dare you say Mabel Willicker is too fat to be dating me," clearing up the short-lived mystery.

Willicker, 33, is a freelance writer and reportedly a lifestyle guru. When we contacted her agent for comment, we were told "Oh my god, I have no idea what you're talking about." Friends appeared similarly mystified by this development, though secrecy around Harding's love life has been the standard throughout his illustrious career.

This made it all the more surprising when bystanders reported that Harding had also bellowed "She is my true love," after delivering a thorough headbutting to a man who had claimed otherwise.

"He was like a wild animal," one anonymous pub patron noted.

Police have released a statement, suggesting no charges have been filed about the incident, and they consider the matter closed.

# Twelve

## I Know, I Can't Believe
## He Doesn't Like Sausages, Either

*S*he did her best to look more normal when she next opened her front door.

Or at least, normal enough that ten thousand people wouldn't scream *Is she wearing fucking* My Little Pony *pajamas* at her for five hours, as they had upon seeing the last shots the gaggle of paparazzi/influencers/god only knew what else outside had taken. But the problem was: nothing could ever be normal enough now. She stepped out in something she felt looked nice—a green swing dress covered in little folksy animals paired with red low-heeled shoes that looked like old-fashioned telephones—and what felt like everybody on Instagram and Twitter wanted to know if she'd intended to look like a Christmas tree.

Immediately, like they were all across the street watching her every move. She had to somehow walk to the car while glued to the screen, just so she could correct anything else she did that seemed weird.

Only it wasn't really possible to correct the rest of what they were talking about.

Alfie must have gone mad, a lot of them seemed to agree.

But even the ones that didn't were kind of unnerving to her. Many were a dab hand in grudging or backhanded compliments, like: *She's cute as a button I can't believe she's thirty-three I thought she was twenty-five*. And: *Those shoes are so cool they really distract from her chunky ankles*. And though she could dismiss a lot of it as Alfie's stans, who she already knew got mad and passive-aggressive about anyone he dated, though she could compartmentalize and push stuff to the back burner in her head, there was some stuff she couldn't.

Some stuff she wasn't even sure she wanted to shove aside.

The truly kind stuff that had her all mixed up within seconds of reading it. *I'm so glad someone like us has scored a major hottie,* one said. *She deserves,* another person had tweeted. *Yessssss my new cute curvy overlord rule over him with a benevolent hand,* a third had said, while doing a whole dance on TikTok about it.

And it was cool. It was good. She'd never felt so buoyed in her life.

But at the same time, it was something else. Something that made her feel like she could never live up to whatever they were saying. She didn't know how to be that person they were imagining. Heck, she *wasn't* that person they were imagining.

She was good enough for them to believe she was dating a very famous, very beloved ex-footballer. But she wasn't actually doing it. It was all just nonsense. It was made-up stuff that was making her all hot and prickly and excited and terrified at the same time.

So she decided:

Her best bet was just to turn off her phone.

And then maybe pretend she didn't have one.

*Alfie has the right idea,* she found herself thinking. Then immediately took it back before he could see her and guess that she had ever thought for even one second that he was correct about a single flipping thing. No, she wanted him to only know that he was quite possibly the most ridiculous person alive.

Especially when she got to the car.

And he got out. And tried to *fight* the few *paparazzi that were still trailing after her.*

*Again.* "You leave her alone, you dirty great fuckface," he yelled as he launched himself at the one who almost had hold of her arm. She actually had to put her hands on his chest to get him to calm down. She had to touch him, even though she absolutely didn't want to. But even more shocking:

Somehow, against all odds, it *worked.*

He stopped, like she'd put a bullet in his gut.

And that furious expression? It melted away, as fast as it had arrived.

Now he was just looking at her, all soft and weird and oh Christ, she had to get them in the car immediately. They were taking *pictures* of him looking at her like that. Someone cooed "Aw, look at the lovebirds." A girl in the background screamed "It *is* like *Pride and Prejudice*."

So she opened the door, somehow, and shoved Alfie in.

Before he could say anything more or do anything else.

Though somehow, he still found time to fuck things up.

Because he grabbed her when he realized what she was doing. He hauled her in after him. So now she was sprawled on top of him in the back seat of the car with the door still open, and a bunch of people snapping away at them.

*"Alfie Harding Bonks Fiancée in Front of Reporters" is going to be the headline tomorrow*, her brain moaned. But there was nothing she could do. She was too busy trying to clamber off her alleged fiancé without accidentally flashing her arse at any of them. Because yes, the dress she was wearing was longish, but when she'd fallen on top of him it had definitely ridden up.

She could feel air on her bare legs.

Maybe even her bare thighs.

And her bum was really massively in the air.

It was right up there, directly in their faces, and she had no idea how much material was covering things. She had to reach back and check before she could do anything. Only when she tried, Alfie seemed to understand what was going on. He saw her pull at her dress and clocked them snapping away.

And then decided that the best course of action was to shield her from sight.

By putting his hands.

Over the thing.

They were taking pictures of.

At which point, she felt pretty sure she blacked out.

Only without the benefit of unconsciousness. She was still

somehow fully aware as a small crowd took photographic evidence of Alfie Harding holding her butt in his hands. And
couldn't do a thing about it. She couldn't breathe, or move, or
even tell him to stop.

When she tried, all that came was a sound only dogs could
hear.

So she just had to rely on him to get her out of this.

And of course he was doing a terrible job.

He tried to turn her so they couldn't see her anymore. Or
maybe so he could get to the door and shut it. But when he did,
he somehow wound up squeezing what he was holding. Then
he seemed to realize he was squeezing and panicked. He said
"Sorry sorry sorry" and got her around the waist instead.

Though quite honestly, that was just as bad—if not worse.

Because he was strong, he was really strong, and someone
being that strong wasn't something she was really used to. She
wasn't used to someone actually bodily lifting her. So the second
he did she kind of panicked, and clung to him. Her arm went
around his back and her legs seemed to almost clamp around
him, and though she absolutely did not intend any of it she
knew exactly what it looked like:

He had decided to flip her over, mid-fuck. And she had apparently appreciated that so much she was now digging her
heels into his arse.

Much to even *his* consternation.

"Mabel," he gasped out.

As if she had done it on purpose.

As if she wanted any of this to happen.

*This is all your fault*, she wanted to yell at him. But as he
was currently between her legs, she still couldn't manage much
beyond a furious expression. Which he fortunately seemed to
understand meant *get the fucking door closed now.*

Then it was done, and they were safe, they were safe.

Or at least, *she* was safe. *He* was a whole different matter.

"I think I might have to destroy you now," she said the
second it was just them. And she was pleased with herself for

doing it, too, considering she was still sprawled across the seats like someone recently fucked—dress up around her thighs, legs spread around him, face so red someone could have seen it from the moon.

Not to mention the fact that he was kneeling over her, breathing hard.

Like he was the one who'd just done the majority of the work.

Really, it should have been impossible for her to say anything to him ever again. But she had, she'd done it, and she'd gone hard on him, too. So hard, in fact, that he didn't seem to know what to say for a second.

Then he seemed to shrug with his face.

*Fair point*, she thought the expression suggested.

Before he added, just for an underline probably: "I'd argue, but it definitely feels like I deserve to be demolished for my crimes."

And that was a good start, it was. But not good enough to let him off.

"You do. Especially when you factor in that one of these crimes was grabbing my butt in front of a million people, some of whom make their living by selling pictures to papers. Good god, Alfie, why did you grab my butt in front of a million people who make their living by selling pictures to papers? Why?"

"You can't possibly think I've got a good answer for that."

"Then you lifted me. You turned me over, like . . . like . . ." she said, and flapped her hands to try to indicate what she couldn't spell out. Which he thankfully seemed to understand.

"I know what it was like, all right. I know what I did."

"And that's before we even get into the other stuff."

"Oh god, not the other stuff. Please, can we just not talk about the other stuff right now? I'm traumatized enough as it is without having to get into all that," he said, at which point she had to say: she was glad she hadn't let him off.

Because now he was really going to get it.

"*You're* traumatized enough? Alfie, I ghostwrite books for a living. I see maybe three people a month, and one of them is my postie. I am well known in my pretty tiny friend circle for being only at my bubbly best in small groups, and I'm pretty sure part of the reason I chose this career path was my terror of being seen as a fool by potentially millions of people. And yet now, because of you, I have to somehow cope with the fact that I am currently plastered all over the *Daily Mail* online, looking like a toddler with a shocking amount of very poorly brushed hair," she burst out. All in one big go, like lancing a boil.

She even let out a groan of relief at the end of it.

Only to get *this* in response:

"I did show you how to get the tangles out."

Though to his credit, he cursed himself once he'd said it.

Like he'd done so without thinking, and now regretted it.

Not that it mattered to her. "Holy crapola, did you actually just say that?"

"No. I never. You've fallen asleep and me saying that is just a horrible nightmare. In a second I'm going to wake you up by telling you something completely normal, like you looked like a soft rabbit."

"But that isn't completely normal either, Alfie."

"I know," he groaned. "I heard myself saying it and my brain just started yelling."

"Well, it obviously needs to get faster. So it grabs you before you do it."

"And what are the chances of that? You've seen how I am. Stuck in the past, slower than an old man sucking a toffee. It's a fucking miracle I can even keep up with you at all, conversation-wise. Never mind saying things that make sense."

Now it was his turn to let out a kind of sound of relief.

She didn't know why, however.

He'd hardly helped himself with that.

"So that's your excuse for doing this, then." She snorted.

But surprisingly, he shook his head. He sagged and sat back on his heels.

And then he just said: "I don't have an excuse for doing this."

At which point, she couldn't help it.

She had to go a little bit softer.

"Well, at least tell me why you did it."

"As if I have the first fucking clue. Mabel, I don't know why I do anything. A fact that you well know after the meeting debacle. And the phone call debacle. And the restaurant debacle. And the Starbucks debacle."

She rolled her eyes. "I get it. You have a lot of debacles."

"Yet you're surprised this happened."

"Well, this is a lot worse than the others."

"How is it any worse than me looking like a stalker?"

She sighed. God, he could be such a fool sometimes.

So straight down the line and single-minded. "Because I was the only person who even remotely thought you were, you great lummox. It took ten seconds to work things out and make things right. But we are never going to be able to make this right, because you're about to be on *Look North* screaming that you love me while trying to murder two people for daring to deny it."

And then here it was again: that focus on all the wrong things.

"Hold your horses there, I never tried to murder anybody," he said.

So now she had to patiently explain. She had to sit up, and slide out from between his bloody legs, and spell it out. Quite possibly using hand gestures. "But you did do the other thing, Alfie. You did the other thing. The thing that is even madder than murdering people."

"Oh, come off it, loving someone is way less mad than that."

"Yes, you're right, it is. But not if it's impossible that love could ever happen with that person. If love between you and them is less likely than a billionaire actually doing something useful for humanity. Then it's just bloody bonkers."

That got him, she thought. She saw it go in, just as he was about to say something. And it stopped him cold. His mouth closed back up again; his gaze turned inward. Then that line between his eyebrows deepened, as he seemed to wrestle with what she'd said. To maybe deny it a bit before he accepted it as true. Though even after he had, she could see he still wanted to fight.

Just a little bit, and on a different point.

But he had to say it. "Well, what was I supposed to do? They were being really horrible about you, Mabel," he gruffed out. "You didn't hear them, they were a right pair of fucking bastards. And I just snapped, I lost it, and next thing I know I'm saying things you think are ridiculous."

"Because they *are* ridiculous."

"Well, I know you believe that now."

"So then you're going to think of a way fix it."

"I've tried, love. God knows I've tried. I was up all night going over possible ways to resolve this mess, and all I could come up with was joining a site I hate so I could message you in all caps and then not be able to delete it while thousands of people yelled at me that I was the worst person in the world for flubbing that sitter against Argentina fifteen fucking years ago. Even though it wasn't my fucking flub at all," he said. And honestly, she wasn't sure what she liked best.

The rising panic and incredulity in his voice, as he went over his own ridiculous actions. Or the way he got to the end of it all, voice almost hoarse from trying to force all that absurdity out, and then just seemed to collapse from the effort. He put his face in his hands and made a sound of such frustration.

And so of course she couldn't carry on anymore.

She couldn't be mad at him.

He hadn't meant to do any of this.

It had all just happened, and he'd tried to sort it.

Plus, he clearly massively regretted it all, anyway.

So she sighed, and let things fall into silence. And when she finally did say something, it wasn't about the point. It was about the other thing he'd said, the ridiculous thing that he clearly had no understanding of at all: when you're famous on social media people will say completely irrelevant nonsense to you all the time.

Even if said nonsense isn't fair in the slightest.

"Yeah, Pendleton really should have passed to you sooner," she said.

And it worked, too. He dropped his hands, and as he sat back in his usual place—across from her, on the diagonal—he answered in a huffy but still obviously relieved to be talking about something else sort of way. "He sat on that fucking ball for half an hour, dithering fuck."

"It was his whole problem, not being decisive enough."

He made a derisive sound. "If you asked him if he needed the loo he'd say *not sure*."

"Which was probably why he pissed himself over them penalties."

"Never seen anyone knock out a fan in the crowd before or since."

He shook his head on the end of that. Clearly remembering, in a way that relaxed him even further. And it did something else, too. Because suddenly he seemed to be turning something over in his head. Then after he had, he gave her this long look. This assessing look, that said he'd figured something out.

Something she hadn't meant to reveal.

But was obvious after all the specifics she'd just gone into.

"You like football, then," he said, and okay, he wasn't exactly right.

However, he wasn't exactly wrong, either. "It was mostly just because of my dad," she said, and when she did she thought about it. She thought about Euro '96, screaming at the telly when Spain scored. Chanting *We Are Leeds* on the terraces; him telling her that Sheffield Wednesday were a set of bastards. Him drunk, her trying to drag him down Elland Road in the dark—and then after that not wanting to watch it anymore. *Too good for it, are you now*, he'd said to her.

Then she looked away from the past, and at Alfie Harding. Alfie Harding, who believed he was nothing but was actually everything. Legendary center forward, one of the finest footballers in the game, a man her father had once grudgingly called all right for a fucking Mancunian.

And Alfie Harding said this:

"Yeah. Same."

At which point, she knew.

She knew. But she couldn't believe it enough not to ask.

"You only got into football because your dad made you?"

Then he nodded. He nodded. He actually *nodded*.

Half amused, she thought, to see her shock.

But half something else at the same time.

Something that made his voice a little hoarse when he replied.

"He had to drag me to practice at one point. Gave me a clip if I said no."

*Fucking hell*, she thought. Then couldn't even rein it in for her response.

"That's horrible. That's the worst thing I've ever heard."

"Any worse than what you had to deal with?"

"No. But then I wasn't forced to play it for a living."

He sighed. "You get used to things you don't really enjoy. After a while."

"After a while you should have stopped. You could have stopped, Alfie."

"Yeah, but I think you know why I didn't. In fact, I'm betting it's one of the reasons you settled for writing a memoir for some annoying pillock instead of writing your own stuff. Counting every penny, always worried about the wolves at the door—even when you don't really have to be anymore," he said.

To which she sort of wanted to reply no.

No, that wasn't one of the reasons why she never went after more.

This was just what she was comfortable with. What she was good at.

She didn't have deep unexamined issues having to do with money.

It was fine doing this. It was fine. It was absolutely okay.

*Tell him it's okay*, her brain said.

But somehow *this* came out instead:

"I still do the calculator when I go round the shops."

And got a sound of recognition and a rueful nod.

"Caught myself doing it at the takeaway the other day. Some bloke asked me why I was adding stuff up, when I was Alfie fucking Harding. Had to tell him it was for tax purposes. Couldn't face explaining all that when it's been over twenty fucking years since I last had to survive on salad cream fucking sandwiches."

"For us it was crisps, for a sandwich filling. My dad used to get big cheap boxes of them on offer from Kwiksave. Horrible, like little shards of plastic. But it was better than just bread and margarine, so we didn't complain."

"Complaining never got you anywhere anyway."

"No. Often times it would just make things worse."

"You'd wind up with a clip round the ear."

"Yeah, or maybe the belt."

She regretted it as soon as she said it.

Partly because she didn't know how she had said it, considering she usually hated to reveal a thing about the less fun aspects of her past. But mainly because she saw him react the second she did so. Like someone had walked over his grave, she thought it looked like. His shoulders went stiff; all the cords in his neck stood out; the hands he had on his knees suddenly clenched into fists. And he didn't sound calm when he finally got some words out.

"Your dad still around, by any chance?" he asked.

Then he cracked his knuckles, one hand over the other, in a way she understood. She understood all of what was happening, even before she told him, in a voice that sounded too hopeful about something she wasn't supposed to want:

"He died about ten years ago."

And then he just went ahead and spelled it out.

"Good. Now I don't have to kill him with my bare hands," he said.

While her heart tried to beat right out of her chest.

And she couldn't even fault it for that, either.

Because yeah, you weren't supposed to want violence. But god, sometimes it was good to know someone thought it should happen on her behalf. That she wasn't just weak or nuts or exaggerating. Someone who didn't just deserve pity, or whatever else she usually feared she would get, if she dropped some of her Bubbly Girl armor. It was bad, and he would do things about it, if he could.

Things that made her want to do good by him, in return.

"I wouldn't have let you even if he was alive."

"Because you loved him, despite it all."

"No. Because friends don't let friends serve seven to ten in Broadmoor."

She saw him register that word: *friends*. She didn't regret it, however.

It was okay now. And he didn't make it otherwise, either.

He gave her a half smile instead.

"I'd have been all right. Like I told you, you just roll them into the Thames."

She nodded. "Ah, should have remembered that."

"Well, you know now. So it's safe to let me do anything like this."

"Okay. I will let you go back in time and murder my dad for giving me the belt. But you've got to let me go back in time to murder yours for giving you clips and making you be a footballer," she said. Then couldn't help trying for it, just a little bit. "Instead of whatever you really wanted to be."

But he was onto her immediately. He made an amused sound and shook his head. "You're not going to get me to tell you what my dream job was that easy."

And now she was calm and easy, too. She almost laughed, in fact.

"Oh, come on. I thought that was a good attempt. It almost worked."

"To be fair to you, it did. It was on the tip of my tongue, then."

"So just let it out."

"I can't. You'll put it in the book."

"I've told you I won't if you don't want me to."

"Then what exactly would I be telling you for?"

"Same reason you've been telling me all the rest, I'm guessing."

*Because I trap you into it*, she answered for him in her head.

Only that wasn't what his expression suggested when he met her gaze.

It was something else, something less wary, less guarded. And then he said:

"So because it feels okay to with you."

And oh, that was nice. That was good.

It made her glad she'd said that thing about friends.

And fully understand why she dared to share things with him.

They created some kind of strange space for each other—the thought of which made her soft in her response to him. "Yeah. Do it just because it feels okay."

"This one wouldn't, though. It's embarrassing."

"You've told me embarrassing things before."

"No, but they weren't really embarrassing things. Or at least they wouldn't read as embarrassing things to someone like you. You don't fucking care if a bloke like me watches *Repair Shop* or isn't into football. But this one . . . this one maybe you would care about. It might seem like I'm making fun."

*Of what*, she thought.

But she couldn't imagine what on earth it could be.

So she went with the only possible answer to it.

"I wouldn't think that, Alfie."

"Maybe you wouldn't. But still, I'd rather not."

"All right. So we'll talk about something else."

He sighed. Heavily. "Is something else gonna be the mess I made?"

"I think it might have to be, to be honest, friendo. Not many ways around it."

"Christ. Caught between a rock and a hard place."

"Well really, it's more like a rock and a thing we have to do."

"I don't see why. We could just pretend the whole thing never happened."

"And I would agree if it was just between you and me. But you said it to the whole world. So you've got to set the record straight."

Now it wasn't just a sigh in response. It was a full-on groan. "And how am I supposed to do that? Just tell everyone I was lying?" he asked as if that was the most ridiculous tactic anyone could come up with.

Instead of being completely reasonable.

"Yes. Yes, that is exactly what you tell everyone."

"But then they'll think you *are* too hideous for me to date."

"Well, so fucking what if they do. It's not like it's hugely untrue. I mean I don't think I'm hideous. But I'm obviously not much above cute."

*Nope, shouldn't have said that*, she thought, the second it was out. But oh, it was too late now. He already had a face like thunder about it. He snapped it to her like she'd thrown a switch. And *god*, the growl his voice reached.

"You fucking what? Jesus Christ, you take that back right now, Mabel."

"I will not. Mostly because you won't headbutt *me* for saying it."

"No, but I will call the *Daily Mail* and tell them we're married now."

Now it was her turn to snap a look at him.

She didn't growl, however.

Her voice went high instead.

"Alfie, you wouldn't. Say you wouldn't, immediately."

"Not until you disavow that shitty thing you just said."

"But it wasn't even that shitty."

"Of course it was. It was shitty in about eighty different ways."

"Really? Because I'd be amazed if you could come out with one."

He gave her an irritated glare for that. And he sounded impatient when he spoke. "You know why I can't come out with one, all right. I know you know."

"I really don't. Maybe you should explain."

"Oh, stop playing silly beggars."

"I swear I'm not."

Now she got a sigh.

A heavy one, too.

Though she could tell it was because he believed her.

And knew he had to explain. Awkwardly, slowly, like he was pulling his own teeth out. But he had to, and he did. "If I start talking about how nice you look, if I give examples and all that, you might think it means more than it does. You'll think I'm trying to cop off with you," he said. Then he had the nerve to also give her this scrunched-up look, like *Fuck, I don't know what you're going to think of this*.

He should have known, though, really.

Because it was nuts to imagine anything else. "Alfie, I am *never* going to think that. The very idea is impossible for so many reasons, starting with the type of women you usually date and ending with the fact that we are oil and water. Honestly, you could say to me directly that you want to fuck my face with your cock, and I'd just assume it was code," she said, and yeah, obviously she immediately regretted going with *fuck* and *face* and *cock*.

But it was necessary to drive the point home.

He was being absurd.

And it worked.

His awkward look vanished.

Then was replaced by confusion.

"What the fuck would that be code for?" he asked.

"I dunno. Maybe you want me to eat some sausages you cooked."

"That makes no sense. I would never cook sausages. They're horrible."

"Yeah, I don't think that's the problem with what I'm saying."

"I don't, either. But I've forgotten what the point was, so I went with it."

"You haven't forgotten. You just can't say it because it's not true. And that's okay, because not everybody has to be gorgeous in the way you have to be gorgeous to date a footballer. I'm perfectly happy being the way I am. A little bit plain, with a massive bum, and a lot of very unmanageable hair."

She saw him close his eyes about midway through what she'd said.

Like it was causing him pain. Though she couldn't have said why.

Or what made him suddenly spit out: "Fucking hell, I hate you so much for making me say this. So when I do you had bloody better erase it immediately from your mind. Got it?" But he was fierce about it, so she simply nodded.

She made a sign, like Scout's honor. Two fingers up.

*I do solemnly swear.*

And then he nodded, satisfied.

About a second before he looked away and started speaking.

"You are lovely, Mabel. And not just lovely in your soul, neither. No, I mean lovely like a painting of someone important from a long time ago, reclining on some fancy thing with their thighs all soft and their shoulders all round and everything so plush it makes you ache to touch it. Lovely like the bit of moorland I used to go to near me, all wild and free, with that tangle of hair down your back and those eyes that sometimes seem brown and sometimes seem green and always, always feel like they see right into you. Sharp as a knife, but so soft you hardly care if it goes in. You want it to go in. You say thank you when it does. Because Lord, it feels so good."

And in the ringing silence that followed, she thought two things:

That this was quite possibly the best compliment anyone had ever paid her.

Then, more importantly: what it meant, in a way she had to say out loud.

She couldn't stop herself. There was no way to hold it back. It was just there and it was obvious and it needed to be out.

"Oh my god," she said. "You wanted to be a writer."

**Tweets,** March 27, 2022

**Watchingthefootie**
@tuesdaygirl
WHAT DO YOU THINK OF ME NOW, BITCHES
THAT WASNT JUST A HAND TOUCH
THAT WAS A BUTT GROPE

**StickingYourBootIn** @ontheterraces
Replying to @tuesdaygirl
lmao pride and prejuduce 2: electric buttaloo

**SwiftieForLife** @mattygorgeous
Replying to @tuesdaygirl
vindication.gif

**OarsCores** @annannann
Replying to @tuesdaygirl
. . . . . . . . . . . . . . . . . . . .
. . . . . . . . . . . . . . .
god I wish he'd grope my butt like that

**Watchingthefootie** @tuesdaygirl
Maybe if you grow one he will
OBVIOUSLY HES INTO THE BIG GALS

# Thirteen

## While You Were Sleeping on Independence Day

$S$he tried several times to say something to him about the things he'd said in the car. But the problem with doing any of that was: oh god, she just really did not want to. Even though it was important, even though she needed to know stuff about it to the very depths of her soul, even though her fucking livelihood depended on it . . .

She couldn't think of anything worse than asking.

Or even hearing what he had to say.

Because what if she said *Do you really think I look like that*, and he laughed and took it all back? Hell, what if she said *Do you really think I look like that,* and he *didn't* laugh and take it all back? What if he just looked at her with those dark eyes of his and said *Yep, I meant every word, you are a painting of a wild stretch of moors?*

She would die. She was already dying.

It was too much to deal with all at once.

And that was *before* she even factored in the other thing: Alfie Harding, one of the greatest footballers of all time, who had played for decades and was an acknowledged expert on all things having to do with the game, who had won multiple awards because of it and was currently having her write a memoir entitled *My Life in Football*, had not actually wanted to be a footballer at all.

He had wanted to be a writer.

She knew he had.

His expression had confirmed her guess.

He'd looked at her like she'd slapped him.

Then walked into the house seeming shell-shocked.

And of course that wasn't the only reason it rang so true. There were other hints. Like how publicly hurt he'd seemed over the reaction to that foreword he'd written. Or the answers to the questions he'd written down that she hadn't intended to give him. How much he'd appeared to enjoy writing them; how smart and funny his words had seemed. The way he'd had such trouble settling on a ghostwriter—once just evidence of his crotchetiness, now suggesting something more. Something like shame about hiring someone, or maybe even a repressed sense that he could do better himself.

So it just felt terrible to press him on it now. *You shouldn't have guessed out loud*, she chided herself. But really, how could she have done otherwise after that? He was good. There was no way to get around the fact that he was good. That he would be good if he tried his hand at it.

Considering how it had made her feel.

So now she had to deal with the fact that he had longed for something.

Something he could have had quite easily, under different circumstances.

But he hadn't had those circumstances. So instead, he had thrown it all away.

Buried it down deep, never told a soul about it.

Been just like her, without even the benefit of the consolation prize she'd taken. *No wonder he's angry all the time*, she thought. He had every reason in the world to be angry. If anything, he should have been even more furious than he already was. Or at the very least, not as kind as he often revealed himself to be. Like when he had threatened to murder her dead dad. And defended her against the paparazzi and internet insults.

Oh, and then there was the fact that he had bought her things.

Because the second she stepped into his house and saw the furniture he had purchased, she knew that was what he'd done. And she knew why he had done it, too. It wasn't for himself, or even to save face in her eyes. It couldn't possibly be when there wasn't a thing there that he could use to either sit on, or make himself seem more normal. There was no couch or coffee table or anything of that kind.

No. There was just something for her.

Something that would make *her* comfortable.

And so obviously that she couldn't even doubt it.

He'd bought her a squishy, pastel love seat, of the exact kind she had in her own place. Then just in case that wasn't enough, he'd put a little table next to it. A really fancy table, with compartments for putting things in, and holders for pens and drinks, and then she touched it and saw what else it did.

It swung out, over the chair.

Like the sort of thing you found in universities.

*So you can take notes with ease*, her brain reminded her.

But of course it didn't need to. She was already feeling that purpose, right up to the roots of her hair. It was honestly all she could to not scream something ridiculous at him, like *This is the nicest thing anyone has ever bought for me*. She had to keep her back turned to him and squeeze hard until the only thing that came out was "thank" and "you." Though even that didn't go well.

Her voice sounded real shaky.

And kind of a little breathless.

She couldn't blame herself, however. She was still recovering from all the rest of it, and now there was this to contend with. Of course she was going to be all weird. She just hoped he wouldn't notice.

Then was surprised when he didn't.

He just said "No problem," and by the time she'd managed to turn around again and face him, he'd gone to make them both a cup of tea. She could hear him in the kitchen, rattling spoons and mugs and probably whatever futuristic device he used to boil the water. *I bet he's got one of them taps where it comes out scalding hot*, she thought. And then felt a bit calmer about things.

Or at least calm enough that she could enjoy what he'd gotten her.

She sat down in the chair and organized her things all over the table.

And when he brought her the tea she put it in the cup holder.

All of which he looked dead pleased about.

"There," he said, as he brought his mug to his lips. "Sorted."

But it wasn't. Because he then sat across from her on the bloody floor.

"You should have gotten yourself something, you daftie," she said.

And got the kind of brush-off she expected in response.

"I'm fine like this. Nowt wrong with this here step."

"Apart from the fact that it will aggravate all the injuries you know I know about. Like the back problems and the repetitive strain to your hip flexors and those pins you had to have in your lower leg that still give you trouble but you won't have removed because it's not strictly necessary and you hate hospitals too much to—" she started to say. But he cut her off before she could finish. He held his hands up.

Like he couldn't stand to hear another second.

"Yeah, all right, all right," he said. "Christ, you make me sound like a complete broken-down old knacker. I guess just get the glue factory on the horn, have them come round to pick me up tomorrow, eh? I'll be sticking your little arts and crafts projects together by the end of the month, no problem."

She wasn't sorry, however.

Because he was being a plonker.

"You could still run rings around just about anyone in the country, and you know it. That's not the point. Me sitting up here like lady muck while you gradually erode the bones of your arse is. Now at least have some cushions," she said, then tossed him the assorted ones he'd arranged on her chair.

And he took them, too.

Grudgingly, but he did it.

So now there was just one thing left to do:

Talk about how the fuck they were going resolve this mess.

A fact that they both realized to their great dismay.

"Fuck," he said. "You still want me to come up with a solution, don't you."

And what exactly was she supposed to say to that?

*Nah, it's fine, I'm sure it'll all go away on its own?*

She couldn't.

She'd already glimpsed the latest photos circulating on social media.

There was absolutely no way out of this but through.

"I was kind of hoping that would be the case, yeah."

"Well, the good news is, I've got one."

"Great. Fabulous. Let's have it, then."

"Even though you're not gonna like it."

A heavy silence fell, then. Mostly because she was going through all the horrendous possibilities in her head. And if his expression was anything to go by, said possibilities were very horrendous indeed. He looked like they were punching him from the inside out. There was actual pain in his eyes.

Pain, and more terribly, hope.

Like he was willing her to go with whatever he was about to suggest.

Even though she already knew that wasn't going to be a thing. She was sweating before he'd even said it. She had to wipe her palms on her thighs as she worked up to telling him to go ahead. And then she did, and still somehow got something she could never have imagined in her worst nightmares.

"We're going to have to lean in to it," he said.

Matter-of-factly, too.

As if it weren't the most ridiculous thing ever to be spoken aloud.

"You've got to be having me on. Alfie, tell me you're having me on."

"I can't, love. I wish I could, but there's just nothing else to be done."

"Of course there is," she sighed. "And you can start by not going stark raving."

"Oh, see, I knew you'd be like this. It's why I didn't say it in the car."

"You thought this up in the car? You've had this in your head for hours?"

"I've had this in my head since I landed us in the shit. And believe me, I haven't enjoyed it. But the simple truth is: it's the only fucking option."

She rubbed a hand over her face at that. Mostly to give herself a second to really think about what he was saying. To see if any part of it made sense. But nope. No. It truly and absolutely did not.

"Okay, so let's just be clear on this," she said. "What you're proposing is that we pretend that we actually are a couple. Even though people are already finding it difficult to believe that we are a couple. And neither of us is good at being couples with anyone, even on our best days while with someone who adores us."

"I've never been with anyone who adores me, so that hardly matters."

"Okay, a) that's not the point, and b) what the heck, Alfie, Jesus *Christ*, is that true? Please tell me that's not true. You were with that lass from that girl band, weren't you, the redheaded one, she was mad for you, I'm sure she was."

"She broke up with me because my laugh annoyed her."

Immediately, she thought of him holding his amusement in.

Always, constantly, holding his amusement in.

Never going beyond a smile, or a spark in his eyes.

"Oh my *god*, is that why you never laugh at anything now?" she asked, and the worst part was, he didn't even fucking hesitate. He just plunged right into his answer as if it took no time at all to consider or admit. As if it were nothing.

"Yes. Yes, that is exactly why. Now please continue telling me how nobody is ever going to believe that a woman who barely tolerates my presence could ever be dating me."

"I'm trying, but I've sort of forgotten how to say things."

"Well, I don't know why. You've seen what I'm like. It can't be that wild to you that people find it hard to get on with me. That things about me annoy them. In fact, it's weirder that you have trouble than me," he said. Then he gestured and nodded in her direction as if she would somehow not know whom he meant. Or that she would try to deny it if he didn't give it an underline.

And to be fair to him, he was right about that.

The first thing that popped into her head to say was this:

"Maybe I'm hard to get along with, too."

Much to his disgruntlement.

"Like fuck you are. You're the warmest chatterbox I've ever met."

"Yeah, but sometimes people don't like that. They find it annoying. Or they figure out things about me underneath that aren't so fun, and then aren't as interested in being my friend. Both of which should really apply to you. Honestly, I don't know why they haven't yet."

"Probably because that all sounds daft. I mean, fuck's sake. You're a little bit annoying, sure. But not in a bad way annoying. More like in some other way annoying. A kind of funny way that's entertaining. And as for the other thing—why the fuck don't people appreciate someone like you trusting them enough to tell them their scary things? That sounds grand to me." He paused then, considering. Or at least, she thought he was considering. But then he suddenly finished with this: "Plus, you know. When you tease me it doesn't feel like shit. And that's always something I appreciate."

And after he had, she knew.

He hadn't wanted to confess that. But he'd done it anyway.

So now she was going to confess something, too.

"Well, just so you know, I thought the same of you, not long ago."

"What, that I'm soft and funny? Are you having a laugh? I'm like fucking concrete. Humorless concrete. Encased in a vibranium box, buried six feet down."

"Alfie, the very fact that you just put it like that proves you're hilarious. And anyway, that's not what I was talking about. It was the other thing, the thing about not teasing someone in a way that feels like shit. You do it, but it doesn't hurt."

"Yeah, but that's just because it would be terrible to. It would be terrible to crush someone as sweet as you. Like trampling a gentle talking mouse from a story about them triumphing over adversity," he said, and all the way through he didn't even look at her. He was busy fussing with his cuff link, like this wasn't a cool thing he'd said. So it was only after a moment of silence that he seemed to realize his words had had an effect of some kind.

At which point he looked up.

And saw her astonished expression.

And got completely the wrong impression about it.

"Sorry. I didn't mean to call you a gentle talking mouse," he said.

Because he was a fool who didn't understand a single thing about himself.

He didn't know he was kind. That he was the sort of person who hated the thought of ever punching down. Or maybe even that this was a wonderful thing in him. It was all just there, casually, instinctively, while he went on, oblivious.

And she kind of didn't want him to be.

She kind of wanted him to know.

"It's all right. To be honest, I thought it was really lovely," she tried, and though he chuffed and called her a bloody great weirdo in response, she knew she'd hit the mark. She could see the blush creeping over his face.

And just called it like she saw it.

"Trying to undercut being a softie with me now, are you," she said.

And to his credit, he didn't try to deny it.

"Yeah. Is it working, by any chance?"

"Not even remotely."

"*Fuck.*"

More silence followed, then.

It was of the more comfortable type, however.

Like they'd joked themselves out of the various discomforting things that had come at them all at once and could now take a brief breather. A few moments of quiet tea drinking, and maybe a bit of amusement, followed by some measure of resignation when it came to their predicament.

Because as much she was still fully against leaning in, she could feel herself starting to debate it in her head. To think about things like what people would surmise if she didn't. And not just the bad people, not just his stans, merrily insulting her all over social media. The people who were currently cheering her on.

She checked her mentions while they were in this lull in the conversation, and there were fifty times the amount that had been there before. And some of them seemed so young, so impressionable, so pleased that some plump lass from nowhere had made good in this way. *Like a curvy Yorkshire Cinderella*, one of them had written.

And it was meant in a slightly jokey manner.

But then Mabel saw this same girl talking to her friends, and it wasn't quite as tongue-in-cheek. It was something else. Something warm, that at the same time filled her with the weight of expectation. *Would it be so bad to just do it for a little while until it's reasonable that we dump each other*, she asked herself. *Just so lasses like this don't have to wake up to a knew-it-would-turn-out-to-be-a-disappointment kind of thing?*

And her brain actually answered *Maybe*.

Though she couldn't quite bring herself to go with it to Alfie.

"So are you seriously suggesting we pretend? That's what you want to do?" she asked instead. In a scornful way, too.

A way that made him sigh heavily.

"It's not that I want to, Mabel. It's that the other options are all so foul they make me want to sick up. And I didn't even do that when Michael Henrique went for my legs and turned my right ankle into spaghetti." He shook his head, clearly remembering the incident in question. "Bone was poking out and everything. Three of my teammates started crying. One of them had to have therapy. But I didn't even so much as burp my dinner into my mouth."

And now *she* was remembering it.

Much to her extreme discomfort.

"I know. I've seen the footage."

"So you get it, then."

"I get that." She pointed one way. Then the other. "I don't get this."

"But why don't you, though?"

"Because there are worse things than being thought of as too hideous to date a football player," she said. And it felt good when she did it. It was a solid point. Plus, she hadn't taken on any of their sentiments, or gone with any of the specifics. So the specifics weren't there to make him mad all over again.

Only somehow, he still looked mad anyway.

Or at least, more mad than usual.

And just a little bit pained, too, in a way she didn't understand. Until he said: "Maybe. But there aren't many worse than knowing you're terrible at the one thing you've always wanted to do, mostly due to being humiliated by a lot of people. Then hoping that maybe hiring a ghostwriter would at least put you back to square one, help you open up and get used to sharing things, only to have to tell all the people who took the piss that you hired one."

Then suddenly she was mad and pained, too.

Because he'd said it out loud, he'd admitted it.

And not in a way she could just gently receive and reassure him about.

In a horrible way that she couldn't even deny was the case. The whole situation would seem like that, she knew it would. It would hurt him to have to do it, and even if it didn't—nobody was supposed to know. They weren't supposed to tell anyone. Heck, she'd signed an NDA that *demanded* she never tell anyone. She could be sued into the middle of the next century just for vaguely trying to explain what the real situation was. And sure, Alfie would probably try to stop it.

But Alfie wasn't the only one involved.

Harchester and her agent and his manager were all in the mix.

So where did that leave her? *In jail, wracked with guilt over causing him some terrible blow to his emotional well-being and sense of self,* she thought. Then winced so hard at the idea it was a struggle to get words out.

"Okay, in my defense that did not occur to me," she said.

To which he did a good job of pretending it wasn't a big deal.

"Why would it? You only guessed about five minutes ago."

"Yeah, but I should have realized straight away. I mean, it's obvious."

"It doesn't feel obvious. Feels absolutely bonkers that I thought I could ever."

"Well, actually, I've been thinking how not bonkers it is. Considering how good you are with words. And how cool that thing you said was," she said, and silence followed. An uncomfortable one, which she kind of wished she hadn't prompted. After all, it had only been five minutes since she'd vowed never to mention his description of her. And with good reason, because now here it was, in the room, making a mess of them both.

She felt as if she was bracing hard enough to hold herself in a roller coaster without a seat belt. He looked like he wanted to die rather than have this conversation. Plainly, at the very least, he regretted saying the things he had. Or wished he'd gone less hard about it. Even though it was okay, it was fine—she understood it hadn't meant anything. That he was simply being nice.

Or, as he then pointed out, that honesty about certain passable things about her had gotten the better of him. "It was just a factual description of you, Mabel," he said. And she was glad he did. Because now she got to be as plain speaking about it.

"Yeah, but the point is: the factual description was really excellent, mate."

"You don't have to say that. I'm fine about it, all right? Writing isn't for me and that's okay. I just don't want it rubbed in my face, that's all. I don't want everybody to know I'm rubbish at my dream job. And the fastest way for everybody not to know is this fucking foolish idea."

"Well, at least you concede it's foolish."

"Of course I fucking do. It's like the plot of a romantic comedy. Bill Pullman has to pretend he's married to Sandra Bullock so nobody finds out that he is secretly really terrible at being the one thing he always wanted. Like, I dunno. Becoming a president who saves the planet from a massive alien invasion."

He rolled his eyes at himself, then. And with good reason, too. It *was* an absurd thing that he was proposing, after all. Even if it was slightly less absurd than it had been ten minutes ago.

However, she couldn't really focus on that right now.

Because of the example he'd used to show how absurd it was.

"All right, there are two things here that we need to extensively go over," she said, and could tell immediately that he knew he'd gone with the wrong thing. He closed one eye in a kind of half wince. Then braced himself.

"And I'm guessing I'm not going to want to hear either of them."

"You are really, really not."

"Go on then. Hit me with them."

She held out a finger, ready to tick items off on it. "Okay, well, firstly: I seem to be Sandra Bullock in this scenario."

"It was just an example. And off the top of my head, no less."

"Which I will accept. So that means we can move on to the other thing."

Now his whole face was a wince. In fact, the wince was so intense he couldn't take a drink when he tried. His teeth were gritted too hard.

Though she couldn't show him any mercy.

She wanted to know about this too badly.

"You like romantic comedies?" she asked.

And he spread his hands.

He just spread his hands.

"Honestly, who doesn't," he said.

But oh, there was no chance she was going to let him get away with that. Because okay, it wasn't as disturbing as being a footballer who hated football. Or even as astonishing as a dude with a reputation for liking a drink not actually liking a drink at all. However, it was still pretty wild.

And on the end of what was now a long list of wild things.

So what could she do but point that out?

"Typically, footballers who headbutt people."

"I told you I didn't mean to do that."

"How on earth did you not mean to?"

"Me neck just slipped."

*God, the way he puts things sometimes*, she thought. The *me* instead of *my*, the use of the word *neck* there, the idea of such a thing happening because you slipped—it was all so good. And so hard not to laugh at. In fact, she was no longer sure why she was even bothering resisting. It seemed silly, after all this.

Though she wound up glad she'd done it, anyway.

Because it felt more like a reassuring sort of moment.

"Well, it doesn't matter. It's shocking that you like them, but cool."

"You don't really think it's cool. You're just saying that to get me to talk more."

"If you never said another word about it, I'd still say the same," she said, and she meant it, too. The fact that it got him anyway was just a happy side effect. Now she got to watch him taking that in, and enjoying it way too much for his own liking, before finally, finally, his gaze went inward, and she knew what was coming.

A memory of some kind.

And sure enough:

"I wasn't allowed to watch them—usually because me dad wanted some other fucking shit on like *Top Gear*, and thought they were softie bollocks only girls were meant to like. But some of them were on sometimes late at night, after everybody had gone to bed. So I used to creep into the front room once they were all tucked up, and watch them with the sound turned down and my ear almost pressed against the speaker bit of the telly," he said in this low rumbly way that made her really feel it. Though even without that, she knew she would have.

Because the thing was—he didn't just like romantic movies. He'd apparently *always* liked them. He'd always liked them so much that he'd pinched these small, secretive moments with them. And that was a lot more to take in than she'd thought. It almost bumped it up the list of ways in which he wasn't the man he had always seemed to everybody, and not just because of what it said about him.

No, it was because of how it felt to her.

How familiar it was, in a way that made her ache.

She thought of a thousand daft things she'd loved.

Then all the ways she'd been denied them, again and again. All the shows she couldn't watch, because her dad wanted the darts on instead. All the books she couldn't read, because books were for people who thought they were better than him. And finally, there was the one the most like his.

The movies that she'd just *longed* for.

God, she couldn't stop herself telling him about the movies she'd longed for.

"I used to save up every fifty pence my mum sometimes slipped me, until I had enough to go to Blockbuster. Then I'd rent one and watch it on the DVD player we had that barely worked because my dad got it out of the bins round the back of Argos. Sometimes you could hardly make out a thing. But I loved those bits of Julia Roberts and Robert Downey Jr. and Jennifer Lopez that you could see, around the parts that were breaking up and freezing and falling apart," she said.

And oh, the look all over his face once she'd gotten it out.

It wasn't even the kind of tune out she was used to from blokes like him.

It was sheer investment.

Pleasure, even.

Like he wanted to talk about this quite badly.

And already knew just what he wanted to say.

"Sometimes the freezing and falling apart saved you. I mean, who wants to know that Drew Barrymore is actually thirty posing as seventeen in *Never Been Kissed*? Traumatized I'd have been as a teenager, if our bullshit TV and DVD player had let me see more than half of the movie."

"Oh shush. You saw enough of it to know."

"Of course I did. But it was funnier to pretend."

"It was. Plus, that movie is a load of cobblers."

"Yeah, not one of my favorites."

*Favorites*, her brain yelled.

As if this was more thrilling than the writing thing.

Which it wasn't. But it was close. Not to mention easier to talk about.

"What were they, then?" she asked. And he didn't even flinch.

Or take a second to think.

"Any with Sandy in it."

"Because you fancied her."

"I just liked the warmth she brought to everything." He paused. But then saw her raised eyebrow, and broke. "And yeah, all right, I wouldn't have said no if she had decided I needed to help her infiltrate a beauty pageant by giving her a snog."

"Pretty sure that's not the plot of it."

"Well, it was in my head after I watched it."

She nodded. "The actual one is pretty janky, to be fair."

"A lot of them are. But fun. And full of love."

"So that's what you like about them, then. That they're full of love."

She bit her lip when she said it. So he would know that she was teasing him.

But weirdly, he didn't seem to react to that. He didn't tell her to fuck off.

He just looked away at nothing. Like he was really considering the question.

Because none of this was a joke to him, not really.

It was lighter to talk about. But it meant the same.

And he was full of a million things about it that he'd never been able to say.

So he did now. Slowly, a little hesitantly. But he did. "I like them because sometimes things are really bad in them. Things are bad and wrong and so lonely your heart could crack in two over it. But even when they are, you know all of it is gonna turn out all right. That Sandy will be okay, in the end, that she will be all right and someone will take care of her and she will be loved, she will be deeply loved in a way that just never happens in real life. Real life is the other way around. You hope to be loved like that, and then no matter what you do you're just left on your own."

And when he was done, he let the silence spool out.

Until he seemed to realize said silence was going on for a long time.

He seemed to register that she was quiet, very quiet, and he looked at her.

Then saw what she was doing before she could hide it.

"Mabel, what you crying for?"

"I'm not crying. My eyes are just annoyed."

"Well, tell them not to be before I panic because emotions are happening."

"There's no need to panic. They're going to stop in a minute."

They were, too, she was going to make them. Because she hadn't meant for this to happen—she'd just wanted to talk about something familiar and fun. And now it wasn't familiar and fun, it was this: her with tears streaming down her face for reasons she couldn't understand, while he didn't seem to know what to do.

And then he did seem to know. He got up.

He started coming toward her.

Which was undoubtedly worse.

*No*, she thought at him. *No no no.*

But she couldn't say it out loud, so he just carried on.

He crouched in front of her. And *gave her* his fucking *handkerchief.*

"Come on now," he said. "Things aren't that bad."

But the point was: they were. And he knew it. He felt it, too—that longing for more than whatever this was. For more than relationships that turned out terribly and loneliness that ate you alive, and always, always settling for something less. So why, she thought, shouldn't they at least have this? Some low-stakes and sort of silly version of what they would probably never actually have?

At the very least, she'd get almost all the fun of it, with absolutely none of the risk. Some glamour, some sense of what it would be like to be wooed and loved just like in the movies, with that safety at the end that Sandy and Julia and Reese always enjoyed. And even if it wasn't the rom-com fantasy she was currently imagining, he was right. This would get them out of the situation with a minimum of fuss. Her professional reputation would remain intact; his secrets would stay kept.

*It'll be fine*, she told herself. Then somehow, she was just saying it. She told him: "I suppose it wouldn't be so hard to pretend that we're a couple." And in that moment, with him suddenly looking at her with such pleasure all over his face, she truly believed that this would be the case.

Hey guys, so today we're going to have to get into what we are now all officially referring to as the butt incident. And it's a long one, so I thought I'd try out the new ColourPop palette as we chat, give you guys a bit of a feeling for these pastels which are TO DIE FOR. So you can either grab yourself a latte, snuggle down into your fave oversized hoodie, and vegetate through this gossip moment, or you can, I dunno, get ready with me while we dish?

Your choice completely. You do you, boos.

So I'm just going to start by priming the eyes with a little bit of—you guessed it—some Tarte Shape Tape. I mean, what else would I use? And while I do that, let's just go over the timeline we have and what we know so far.

Okay, so everybody's favorite surly bearded bastard, Alfie Harding, appeared to have given up on dating altogether. Then suddenly he's seen with what can only be described as a mystery lady. I know, I know, I sound like the *Daily Fail*. But there's no other way to describe her, she comes out of nowhere, she's already in the inner sanctum of his actual freaking house somehow, and oh, guess what?

She's not a skinny supermodel.

And so obviously all the WAG wannabes and his stans and the gossip channels are going nuts trying to figure this gal out. Which I was, too, because I mean. She can't possibly be one of us, right? I'm not even getting into it, because I know if I start celebrating the victory that's when it's all going to turn out to be a Jehovah's Witness again.

Ha, you guys remember that?

Anyway, but then. Then, my babies.

Omg.

He gropes. Her butt.

And so of course it's time to call it. The fat and fabulous girls have bagged one!

*Maxim* magazine, February 2010

## ALFIE HARDING'S TOP FIVE ALL-TIME BRUISING MOVIES

### 1. *Bloodsport*
Can't remember the plot for the life of me but loads of bones get shattered so it must be up there.

### 2. *Rocky*
I hate the romance obviously but the fights are good.

### 3. *Rambo*
The next ones in the series are probably harder, but they're shit.

### 4. *Commando*
I mean you've got to include summat with Schwarzenegger, haven't you?

### 5. *Die Hard*
Apart from the stuff about him getting over himself and loving his wife for who she has become instead of trying to hold her back it's a ten on the bruise scale, especially when his feet get all fucked up.

# Fourteen

## Apparently, a Shoe
## Being Tied Can Be Sexy

*S*he knew within about an hour of saying it wasn't going to be hard that it was going to be very hard indeed. Mainly because of things like her agent, who upon being told it was true wanted to start talking about selling the rights to her story. And then there was her sister, the one she hadn't seen for years, asking if they could go on a double date. *To somewhere fancy*, she added, *that he can pay for.*

And she wasn't the only one suggesting such a thing.

The girl who used to bully her in high school had the same idea. *You could both come round for a cup of tea*, she'd written, with a P.S. on the end that wanted to know about a possible signed number eleven shirt. Which was bad, it was definitely bad. But somehow still didn't quite reach the heights of saying *yes* to the question *are you actually dating Alfie Harding* on Twitter.

Just via DM, she thought.

To a few more friends than Connie and Berinder—most of whom were cool about it. They thought she was secretive, but that wasn't new. And they were excited, though not in a bad way. In fact, she felt better about things after sharing with other people. Even if it was just in this small way, which kept things as light and throwaway as she usually liked conversations to be. *See*, she told herself. *You can open up sometimes. You can be real.*

*You don't always have to joke and smile and be sunny.*

And then she checked her timeline and discovered that one of these friends had screencapped her messages, and sent them out to literally everyone in the entire world. Or at least, literally everyone in the entire world was the way it felt. Because thirty seconds after the tweet went out, it had twenty-seven thousand responses.

And all of them were even more intense than any she'd received over mostly speculation. Some people were absolutely furious that she was daring to date Alfie Harding. Especially the ones who thought they were communing with him on the astral plane. And the other contingent—the ones who seemed to be supporting her—were still being kind. They were saying things like *do it for the big babes.*

But it felt even more uncomfortable than it had before. Like she was just a body. Or holding up a trophy for a race she hadn't even agreed to enter. *I won a man people think of as much more normal than me*, she thought, and then kind of wanted to stab her own brain out.

And not just because that idea was gross about her.

There was also the fact that it was gross about *him.*

It made him a thing, a prize, an object.

All of which she would have hated if he was just a bloke to her.

But she especially hated it now when she was starting to suspect that he wasn't. That in fact, it could well be that she considered him a good friend. And definitely more of one than the dude who'd just sold her out for likes and clicks. *Oh, come on*, he had messaged her, right after posting her private confessions to the entire internet. *Are you really saying you're not loving the attention?*

As if all attention was equal, and everybody felt the same way about it.

Instead of what she actually felt right now:

Like she had made a grave mistake.

And apparently, Alfie pretty much thought the same way.

Or at the very least, he did not enjoy any of this type of attention. He seemed absolutely baffled and furious when she explained what was happening on social media. And even after she'd calmed him down, he was wary of telling anyone he knew. She had to seriously persuade him to tell the two people who definitely needed to know he was dating someone—his assistant, Daisy, and his sister, Edith.

And both of the calls he eventually made were incredibly short.

*Will I get to meet her*, she heard Edith say.

Then he replied *absolutely not*. And that was the end of that.

As if he was scared of making things worse somehow, it seemed to her.

So even though this had been his idea, she couldn't help feeling for him. He clearly hadn't imagined all this—her being insulted and him being seen as some gold tick in her dating column. And it made her want to reassure him, in weird ways.

*Even if we were really dating you'd be more to me than that*, she thought.

But then she felt embarrassed about even briefly imagining this as real, and had to think about something else for a long time, until it went away. Which took a good deal more time than she really wanted it to. In fact, it lingered, all the way through everything else they had to do that day. She showed him the notes she'd taken and the sort of start she'd made, and he seemed pleased. Then she suggested that perhaps he should try writing some of it himself, considering he definitely could. And he seemed markedly less pleased by that.

Though he did help her fill in some blanks.

He got into it a little more after she'd warmed him up.

But regardless, all the way through there it was:

This unsettled feeling. This *will he think I think this is something* feeling.

And how on earth she was going to avoid that when they were supposed to be pretending to do the opposite. *I will just have to let him take the lead on everything*, she thought—which seemed like a good plan. It made sense in her head as they got ready to leave his place to get her back to hers.

Then they stepped outside.

And he did the usual things:

He locked the house, nodded to his driver.

Put his keys in his pocket, checked he had his wallet.

Oh, and as they walked to the car he reached out.

And took *hold* of her fucking *hand*.

Just like that.

Like it was nothing.

Like he was grabbing his phone.

He didn't even look at her when he did it, that was how casual the move was.

Even though she'd never experienced anything less casual feeling in her whole life. It was honestly like getting struck by lightning. Like he'd suddenly become Storm from the *X-Men*, and had accidentally set his weather-creating abilities on maximum before making contact. She almost screamed at him to turn it down. And she couldn't even stop the other reaction from happening.

Her whole body just tried to yank away from him automatically. Hard, too. Really hard, in a way that should have worked. It should have detached them, immediately—and then most likely given anyone watching a right weird eyeful of their completely not real relationship. But they were saved by one simple fact: pulling away from Alfie Harding, when Alfie Harding was quite clearly not expecting it, was apparently a very difficult thing indeed.

*More* than a very difficult thing.

It was impossible. Insurmountable. Like she'd somehow accidentally sunk her hand into a concrete block. For a second she truly thought she might have dislocated her own shoulder trying to get away.

And that wasn't even so wild a thought.

Because he clearly thought the same, the second they were in the car.

He was immediately on her, like he'd accidentally cut her arm off with a chain saw. She had to stop him pulling off her jacket, to check it was still attached to her body. And he kept pressing it, and saying *does that hurt, does this hurt, are you all right, can you move it*. Then he made her lift it, just to make sure.

Before he finally sat back on his side of the car and sighed.

"I'm sorry. I just really wasn't expecting you to yank away like that. I didn't think about it. But I should have done. I should have known," he said. She didn't know in what way, however. As far as she could see, she was the one who messed up.

"Why should you? It was silly as heck. I don't even know why I did it."

"You did it because I touched you without your say so."

"But I did say so," she said. "In the house."

"No, you never. You said we could go ahead and pretend to be a couple. You didn't sign off on all the things that might involve. Like me grabbing you when you haven't told me I can. And now look, you're injured because of it."

He gestured at her arm. But he didn't look at her.

Which was a good thing, too, considering her face was a picture.

Because okay, it was kind of the bare minimum to ask for permission before you touched someone. And also: she'd kind of known he was like this, from various reports of his behavior over the years. He smacked unasked-for hands off butts if other men did it in front of him. It was him who'd gotten Robbie Jenkins booted from the team after stuff surfaced about the women he'd groped.

And even though she'd never read the kiss-and-tells about him, she knew what was in them. She knew that he'd flabbergasted at least two separate women by stopping the second they'd said stop. So it wasn't a shock.

Yet still somehow it rocked her a bit to hear him spell it out.

It made her heart start beating a bit too hard; suddenly she felt oddly hot.

And she had to take a second before she could say anything. Just in case what she said was something weird and gushing, like *God, that's such a cool thing to come out with*. Then finally, once she was calm, she spoke. "All right. So why don't you lay out for me exactly what you might want to do."

And thankfully, he didn't seem to notice her voice shook when she did.

He just started at the top of his apparently very practical list.

"Well, you've seen *take your hand when we go outside.*"

"Yep," she said. "And you should know I'm okay with that from now on."

"Good, because I reckon that'll be a convincing one. And I've done it before. But there's also a bunch of little things, probably annoying things, that I can see on you right now and I'd definitely want to do them if we were together."

*Do them*, she thought, with a little jolt.

But she was pretty sure he wasn't trying to say anything sexual.

So she did her best to act like she'd never gotten that impression at all.

"You can see them on me? That sounds ominous."

"It isn't. Or maybe it is. I don't know. I think you're going to hate it."

"Just say it then, before it makes my guts churn the last thing I ate into butter," she said, and she could see he didn't like that idea. He didn't enjoy making her nervous. Yet somehow, he couldn't quite seem to let it out. He still hesitated.

And when he finally broke, it was only to nod at her shoulder.

"Half your collar is tucked into your jacket," he said.

Exasperatedly, she thought. Like it was obvious.

Then when it clearly wasn't, he just seemed to break.

"Do you really not get it? Okay look, if I was your boyfriend, I wouldn't be able to stand that. I would see it when we were out and want to sort it. I wouldn't be able to help myself. And it's not the only thing I wouldn't be able to stop doing, either. There's also that you haven't buttoned the jacket right. You've missed one and it's puckering. Oh, and your shoelace is undone—which to be honest is something that drives me mad even as someone who isn't pretending to be your boyfriend. All I can see is *shoelace shoelace shoelace* and all I can think of is you tripping over it and so if you could either fix it or quickly tell me how you feel about me doing these things so I can fix it, that would be a weight off my apparently bonkers mind," he said.

He needn't have worried about doing it, however.

All she could think after he had was:

*Why the fuck are you not up to your eyeballs in amazing relationships?*

Because god, she could hardly imagine having someone who cared so much about you that they noticed your fucking shoelaces. It seemed like a myth. A thing up there with fricking Bigfoot. She almost wanted to ask him if he'd ever had John Lithgow yell at him to go back to the forests.

Then tried to respond in a more normal way.

"I feel fine about them. You can if you want," she said.

And watched him blow out a big, relieved breath. Then gesture at her foot.

"Oh, thank Christ for that. Come on, let's have it, then," he said. So she did, unthinking. After all, what was there to think about? He was only going to be touching her through shiny red leather. There was about three inches of the stuff—not to mention the fake phone receivers on either side of the heels. So it wasn't going to be like the hand hold, or the hair thing, or when she'd touched his chest.

This was a super boring, near contactless kind of touch.

Or at least that was what she thought.

Until his fingers were suddenly on the back of her ankle.

On that arch, she thought, that seemed both sturdy and delicate.

Then after that she didn't know what to think. It was hard to, really, when you could see someone cradling you in his massive hands. Gently, so gently, like they weren't really massive at all—which she supposed was the real killer.

It was that contrast between how he looked and how he was.

That brutishness of him, as he moved like she was made of glass.

It made her go all rigid, in ways she didn't really understand. Then just as she was at the maximum possible level of tension she could feel, just as she was holding her breath, he ran one stroking, smooth-as-silk finger around the inside rim of her boot. Like he was trying to make sure the thing was sitting right on her, she thought. Like he was trying to make the leather lay flush against her skin.

Just a simple action, really.

Though of course it didn't feel like that.

It felt like he'd somehow managed to make love to her ankle with his hand. She actually bit her lip over it, then had to force herself to stop so he wouldn't see. Or ever know that having her laces tied was inexplicably giving her a lot of inappropriate feelings. *What the fuck is wrong with you*, she imagined him saying, and that helped. She managed not to squirm as he pulled the laces taut.

But god, it was a close thing.

He just did it so firmly.

So forcefully.

The way people did when they were lacing up far sexier things, like corsets or saucy underwear or maybe some kind of kinky device that she didn't want to really think about right now. *He's just doing it professionally, like how he probably did his boots before going onto the pitch*, she told herself.

Not that this helped.

Now he was highly competent, on top of all the rest of it.

And really her only consolation was that he appeared to be finished. He set her foot down, and sat back, satisfied with his handiwork. "Job done," he said, and she was home clear. Or at least, she was home clear until she realized: now they were going to have to discuss other things. Lots of other things.

And the other things weren't just hand-holding.

"All right. So on to the big stuff," he said.

Just as she had almost gotten her red face under control.

"I don't think we need to go much bigger than shoe tying, do we?"

"Well, not in my estimation, no. But it might be in yours, is the thing."

"Okay, so start by telling me what your estimation of a little more than this is."

He shrugged. "Going on dates with you. To fancy restaurants and that."

"That doesn't sound so bad. I like fancy restaurants."

"And when we're in them, I might say nice things to you."

She shrugged. "Who doesn't like someone saying nice things to them?"

"Then when we're outside, I might put my arm around your waist."

"I think I can handle an arm in that particular place."

"Oh, and I might possibly have to sometimes occasionally snog your face off on your doorstep. Or on my doorstep. Or, you know, whoever's doorstep we happen to be on because that's usually where I get papped snogging, for some reason."

He said it like all the rest, was the thing. As if it were on the same level as mild hugging or polite eating of food. When of course it very decidedly was not. In fact, the second she heard the word *snog*, she was right back to hair prickles and squirming and a face that felt much too hot. And this time, he noticed.

Just not in the bad way, fortunately.

"And I see I've reached your limit," he said.

"Limit would be one way to put it, yeah."

"Would the other way be that I just gave you a glimpse of hell?"

"Hell is a bit extreme. But probably a bit closer than the other thing."

He seemed to consider. "All right. So maybe we can fake the snogging part."

"You can't fake snogging, Alfie."

"Course you can. Watch, I'll show you."

*No, don't*, she thought at him, and almost actually jerked back. She had to glance at him to check she hadn't. To make sure he wasn't looking at her like she was mad. Even though it wouldn't have been, in her estimation. Anyone would be scared at the thought of him suddenly kissing her. And how was she to know that he wasn't about to do anything of the kind?

He certainly moved toward her like he was.

Then at the last second he turned. For some reason he put his back to her. And his arms went around his own body. And suddenly she knew, she knew before he did it what he was doing. He was going to do the whole *my hands are somebody rubbing my back while I kiss them* thing. At which point, she just couldn't help it. She burst into giggles before she could even think about how dangerous it was.

Though she understood why, of course.

Because he was trying to make her relax.

So it felt okay to just go ahead. To give it to him.

And he didn't make her regret it.

"Well, that got you laughing," he said.

"I'm as surprised as you are by that fact."

"I dunno about that. I thought I'd never crack you."

"You've been cracking me for ages. I just pretended otherwise."

*In for a penny*, she thought. *In for a pound*. And oh, the reaction it got.

He actually threw his hands up the heavens. "Oh, I fucking *knew* it," he growled out. "I knew you were holding out. You little *demon*."

"*I'm* a demon? What about you—you've been doing the same exact thing."

"Yeah, but you know why I do. You know I've got good bloody reason."

"Well, maybe I do, too."

"All right then. Let's hear it."

He folded his arms. But his face didn't match the body language. It wasn't annoyed or defensive—it was open and waiting. Almost eager, it seemed like. But of course she couldn't give him the whole truth. She couldn't tell him about fat girls and even remotely attractive men and what happened when you seemed too giggly with them. When you laughed at their jokes, like you fancied them.

He wouldn't understand. And then she'd have to explain

the whole bullshit thing, and it was annoying and embarrassing enough having those memories of a million handsome dudes treating her like that in her own head, without having to explain it to him.

He'd probably think she held him in the same contempt as she held those pillocks. Or find it all baffling in a way that she'd never be able to make him understand.

And she couldn't afford that now, with everything that stretched in front of them. So she simply said this, instead: "I just don't want to seem too silly in front of someone so stoic." And it worked. He didn't look the least bit perturbed.

In fact, he shook his head. And his eyes seemed to go all soft.

Like he thought she was wrong to feel that way. But it kind of hurt him that she did. And then he said, "You could never seem too silly because you laughed, Mabel. I want you to laugh. I want you to be happy. Or at least, as happy as you can be, when you're hanging around with a grumpy arse like me."

And oh, oh, oh. That hit her hard in the feels.

So hard, in fact, that she simply had to set him straight.

"I *am* happy, hanging around with a grumpy arse like you. Because you're not that. You're sweet, and kind, and most of all, I trust you. So you know what? If we have to kiss, we have to kiss. I know it'll be all right. I always know everything will be all right when I'm with you," she said.

And in that moment, she didn't regret it.

She really believed it was true.

Hey Mabel,

So oh my god? What is going on? I've been absolutely swamped with calls and emails and god knows what else. Are you okay? Why didn't you tell me what was happening? I mean I know you said you were getting along well with him but I had no idea you meant *this* well.

Obviously, I'm most concerned with your well-being, and how we're going to handle all this attention—I thought maybe it was all just to do with the brawling and the headbutting and the declarations of love, but it seems to be feeding on itself a bit and spreading across social media as a Thing.

Which might be taking a toll on you, but also could be something of an opportunity? I know you've always been reluctant to branch out a bit beyond the ghostwriting and such, but this could be the springboard you always felt you needed. I can put out some feelers, especially now that you've got this new super-enthusiastic editor.

I think he's hinted at something we could put together?

Let me know how you're feeling, what you're thinking.

And hey—I'm happy for you, sweetheart.

Big hugs,

Emmy x

EMMELINE SANDERS
Leafland Literary Agency, Inc.
220 Madison Avenue, Suite 406
New York, NY 10016
leaflandliterary.com
@emmelinesanders

On the first day on set I was . . . now you fill in this part!

Mabel, I'm not doing that much, I've told you. You can't just give me a one-sentence prompt like I'm doing a creative writing assignment in school. Though I've gotta be honest, I used to bloody love them things. You know, when some substitute comes in and they never knew what they were doing and so they'd just go "Okay, everybody, give me a two-page story based on the prompt: you've found a monkey in your toilet" or summat like that.

And everybody else used to moan and groan because filling two whole pages was a lot. But I never thought it was, I always thought that was nothing at all. I'd get to the end of the second one in my exercise book and realize the monkey wasn't even out of the toilet yet. My main character was still constructing his elaborate winch-like device to extract him.

I could never go on, though. It was already weird that everybody else in class had scratched out one sentence while I'd crammed in seven thousand of them in my tiniest handwriting to make it all fit. I'd have to tear the page out and claim I'd written swears all over it, so the teacher would let me throw it out.

Still, I'd be thinking about that monkey all day.

Eventually I nicked exercise books from the supply cupboard, so I had a fake one that I wrote bollocks in, and a real one that I kept to myself. Twenty-seven pages I ended up with on getting that winch working. Then the boy and the monkey became best friends, and fought an invading army of aliens, from the movie <u>Aliens</u>.

You remember that?

Best bit is when he teaches her how to use his gun.

P.S. Actually, you can't include any of this.

# Fifteen

## Natasha Denona Probably
## Never Forgets How to Eat Cereal

$S$he felt moderately calm about things, when it came time to do something a little more flashy than going round to his to write his book. Mostly because he did just as he had in the car that afternoon. He spelled it all out, nice and clearly, with predetermined boundaries in place. *I will come and pick you up at six, we will have dinner at seven at somewhere fancy enough for people to see us, during which time I shall touch your hand, and maybe your knee, and probably do something sickening like feed you something from my plate, and then I shall bring you back to yours, and kiss you at the door while pretending no fucking massive wanker is across the street snapping our picture*, he'd told her.

So she was fine about all that.

But what she wasn't fine about was the one thing she hadn't thought of while panicking about weird hot reactions to nothing, and worrying that touching him and kissing him would make her break her own bones. She was going to be out on the town with Alfie Harding. Alfie Harding, who regularly wore suits last seen in a Bond movie, and had girlfriends who didn't just *use* products by Natasha Denona.

They posed in *adverts* for Natasha Denona.

Natasha Denona was somehow their best mate.

Heck, for all she knew some of them *were* Natasha Denona.

Whereas she didn't even really know who Natasha Denona was. She just popped up when Mabel searched "eyeshadow that a footballer's girlfriend would wear." Alongside about seven thousand pictures of eyelids that looked as if Michelangelo had done all of them as some kind of sequel to the Sistine Chapel.

Which, needless to say, put her own attempts at makeup to shame. Even though her attempts weren't that half bad, really. In fact, most of the things she did, style-wise, weren't half bad. A good proportion of social media seemed to think she looked great, and wanted her shoes, and liked her dresses.

But that wasn't the point.

The point was:

She was a mid-level cute sort of stylish.

The people he dated were professional-tier elegant.

So really, was it any wonder that she was beside herself by the time he arrived? She didn't think so. She thought it was perfectly understandable to have one leg in a pair of tights, two odd shoes on her feet, and a dress on backward when he showed up. But of course he had other ideas about that.

"What in the fucking fuck are my eyes beholding here, then?" he wanted to know as soon as he stepped into her flat. And she didn't think it was just about the absolute state of her, either. No, she thought it was very possibly about everything she had just done to every room in the place.

Because she'd made a mess.

A really big, horrendous mess.

That he was currently marveling at.

"Did your wardrobe explode, by any chance?" he asked. But at this point she was far too desperate and frustrated to react well to something like that. Instead, *she* practically exploded, before she could contain herself. She actually threw what was in her hand at him—a pair of socks that she couldn't even remember grabbing.

And words pretty much fizzed out of her mouth.

"Just shut up, Alfie. Shut up and help me," she said.

Then got him, shaking his head faux sadly.

"Helping whatever this is is beyond my powers I'm afraid, love. I mean, last I checked I'm not a wizard. And even if I was,

I reckon it would end the world if I attempted a spell that sets this to rights."

"Oh, give over. It's not that bad."

"Not that bad? You have a pair of knickers dangling from a lighting fixture."

He pointed up at the offending article: her Pusheen-covered underpants, snagged on the rainbow-striped lampshade above them. Which she then tried to snatch back down, even though snatching them back down was never going to be a thing for her. She was five foot two.

She couldn't even jump that high.

Though she tried. She hopped and stretched.

And when she failed, he just stepped forward and snagged them.

Because he was tall, apparently; he was tall, and in a way she hadn't really noticed before. Even though a) she had read the words *six foot one* in his bio a million times before and b) she always noticed, with men. She didn't like being loomed over, and so always found herself seeing it, and moving away.

But with him she hadn't, weirdly.

Like he'd never done it to her.

Like he stayed away, she thought.

Or seemed different somehow, even when he was close.

"Here you go, weirdo," he said as he handed them to her.

And even then there was no sense of that overwhelming height.

There was just embarrassment over what she'd done.

Followed by the urge to defend herself.

"Don't call me a weirdo, you great turnip. I didn't intend to do it. They just made me mad, so I threw them. And the lighting fixture happened to be in the way. It was purely collateral damage in my pursuit of justice. So I'm not sorry," she said. And just like that all the tall-man weirdness was gone.

Only to be replaced by more of him, pointing at other mad things.

"Are you sorry about the millions of bras spilling out of that bin?"

"No. No, I'm not. None of them fit me right. They deserve to be in there."

"All right. But surely you at least regret the cereal all over every surface."

He made circles in the air, over said cereal-covered surfaces.

You know, to really emphasize exactly how much there was.

And okay, he wasn't wrong. But she had her reasons, damn it.

"I was hungry, all right," she said. "Stress meant I forgot to eat for ten hours."

"And I think you'll find there's two problems with that: one, you better be fucking joking about not eating for ten hours; we are going to have a serious talk if that's true, and two, when you are half starved you insert the food *into* your mouth, Mabel. You do not spray it all over your flat to such a degree that I am now almost beside myself with the need to get out the vacuum cleaner."

"But I don't *have* a vacuum cleaner," she said.

And oh god, the look on his face. It was like she'd told him a dog had become prime minister. He seemed both absolutely furious and completely astonished. As if he could take all the rest—but this? This was a step too far.

He couldn't even speak about it for a second.

Then he did, and good fucking *Lord*.

"Right, that's it. I'm calling the police," he said.

And somehow it just happened again. She laughed.

She laughed loud, and long, and helplessly. To the point where he did it, too. He let out a little sound that probably could have passed for a laugh in the right light. Even though it immediately broke the deadpan affect he'd attempted with his joke. It made it not serious. It made *him* briefly not serious.

And apparently, he didn't mind at all.

He was obviously starting to enjoy that he could do that with her.

Or even that he could use it to break any tension or dispel stress.

"Are you calm enough to tell me what's happening now?" he

asked once they were through nigh on giggling. And she nodded, even though she had caveats.

"I am. But you're not going to like it. In fact, it's going to make you mad."

"Nothing is going to make me more mad than the news that you do not own a vac. You've already hit the peak with that on its own. So you may as well just tell me. There's no harm in it now."

"All right. Here is a picture of your last girlfriend."

She turned the laptop she had open on her dining table, and he dutifully peered at her googled selection of images. Before raising an eyebrow. "Think *girlfriend* is putting it a bit strongly there, mate."

"So how would you put it, then?"

"She pretended to like me for a bit."

He spread his hands, like *what are you gonna do.*

So then she had to try to not look like she'd been stabbed.

*Act like it's not a big deal,* she told herself.

But the best she could do was say this:

"Goodness, that's rough."

While not looking directly at him.

It was fine, however. His focus was elsewhere.

"Probably not as rough as what you're about to say."

"What I'm going to say isn't rough at all. It's just the truth."

"I highly doubt that. But come on, then. Let's have it out of you."

She looked at the pictures after he'd said it.

At the beautiful woman in all of them.

Who looked the way people expected a footballer's girlfriend to look.

"She's very glamorous. And I am really massively not glamorous."

"Well, that's not as bad as I thought it was going to be. But still not great."

"How is it not great? Just look at her. She's like a posh Christmas decoration."

"She is. But you don't have to be that. I've dated other types of women."

He turned his face away from her as he spoke. But she caught the reason why. She saw the side of his face quirk up, and knew he was scrunching one eye. That he was wincing, in the way that suggested he knew he wasn't going to get away with that.

And of course he was correct on that score.

In fact, he got a snort of derision.

A loud one, which rang right through her scornful words.

"Like heck you have. They are all glorious glossy goddesses. Every one of them is accomplished and polished and pretty and rich. I mean Lord, look at this one's eyebrows. They're so sleek and tidy. You could fit five of hers into one of mine," she said, and then measured them with her fingers. She pinched them around the photographic evidence and applied said pinching to her own.

And now it was his turn to be derisive.

"Okay, first of all, that's a ridiculous way to back up your claim. And second of all it doesn't even matter, because I like big eyebrows as much as I like small ones. More actually, because I've got a bit of a thing about hairy women that we're not going to go into." He held up a finger when she tried. *Don't you dare*, it said. Then she had no choice but to let him continue. "But what we *are* going to get into is the fact that none of this fucking matters, seeing as not a one of them could stand me for more than five minutes. We were not compatible, we were never compatible, compatibility is never a thing that happens to me. So who gives a fuck?"

*I give a fuck*, she thought at him. But as the thought was about his yawning loneliness and not about the point, she did her best to steer away from it. "Alfie, what you think about eyebrows and compatibility issues just doesn't count here. What looks right to other people is what counts. And if I go out to the place we're going to, exactly as ordinary as I am, I won't look convincing to these other people as your date."

To which he clearly did not want to agree.

But had to, grudgingly. And annoyingly.

"Well probably not with your dress on backward, no."

"It's not my fault that it's on backward. I couldn't undo the zip."

"Yeah, that was my top guess, love. Want me to help you out of it?"

"No. I want you to come back tomorrow, after I've maxed out my credit cards at Monsoon and cleared out the L'Oréal stand in Boots," she said, and sighed. She even sank down into a chair that wasn't covered in crap.

But he had no good news for her.

He just gave her some gritted teeth.

And a shake of his head.

"You don't want Monsoon and L'Oréal."

"Oh Jesus. Because they're not even good enough?"

"They're fine. You'd be fine in them. You'd be fine in anything, honestly. You always look amazing. But if what you're wanting is super polished, we can achieve that very easily. Just give me an hour and try to pretend you don't mind a single thing I now say," he said. But he was being ridiculous because what else was she going to do? Scroll Twitter? Twitter hadn't stopped asking her if Alfie Harding could really go for hours, for the last week. She now had ten thousand followers, and they had separated into two factions. Those who hated her, and so had a snide comment about everything she said. And those who loved her, and now cheered on everything she said.

And both of these made her unable to log on.

Though even if she could have, she wouldn't have.

Because she knew what he was going to do. And she was going to stop him, no matter how much he tried to block her efforts. Which he blatantly did—he walked away and turned his back before he got out his phone. Then he put out a hand when she got close, as if to hold her at bay.

And that would have worked.

If her fury at what he was doing hadn't won over her fear of being too touchy-feely with him. But apparently it did because she did it without a second thought.

She got hold of his sleeve and tugged in a way that shocked him enough to turn. He looked at her with what could only be described as pride at her nerve all over his face, just as whoever he was calling answered. "Daisy?" he said as Mabel carried on trying to reel him in enough to get the phone. "Yeah, it's me. Sorry to be calling so late but— Yes, I know that's what I pay you for. Yes, I know I never ask you for anything and you feel like you're robbing me. No, I'm not going to pay you less money— Can you just. Daisy, I need your help."

*In more ways than one*, she thought.

Then stood on tiptoe and almost got the blasted thing.

He had to whip away quick and tilt his head up and to one side.

But that wasn't going to work for long, and he obviously knew it.

It was the reason he started talking fast, around what definitely sounded like an almost laugh. "Okay, so here's the thing. I am trying to take my new girlfriend out, but we need an outfit, and some high-end makeup, and a vacuum cleaner. Don't ask me why, I can't explain any of it without making her get all agitated. Let's just say her zipper flew off and she ran out of lipstick and her vac backed up when she tried to suck up three feet deep of Rice Krispies."

And now he was definitely laughing, the little shit.

So she stood on his shoes, and *yes*.

She had hold of his phone hand.

Though god, he was strong. Not to mention good at carrying on a conversation with a plump little kitten hanging off him. "Yeah, that was her in those photos. And yeah, that sounds absolutely right. Fucking hell, you're good. Think her shoes might be smaller though, she's a five, not a six. I know, the telephones make her feet look bigger but they're weirdly small. Think that's why she's always falling over. All that hair makes her top heavy," he said.

Because apparently his last goad hadn't been enough.

He had to really go for it, and for reasons that made her feel just a bit gleeful. *He's enjoying you messing with him like this*, her brain informed her. And she couldn't even deny this was true. She'd never seen him laugh the way he was doing—breathlessly, in between words. "I've got to go, she's trying to murder me," he said.

Then he ended the call with one hand.

And *lifted her off her feet with the other.*

"Right, madam," he said as he practically turned her upside down.

Like she really was a kitten, being cheeky as fuck with him.

And okay, then she got it. Then she understood why he liked it.

And why it wasn't bothering her, either.

Because they were being big kids.

Just a pair of big kids on the playground.

So of course it wasn't triggering any anxiety, of course it wasn't.

This was fun, it was just fun, of the sort that could never be weird. Not even when he set her down on her feet, and for just a second his hand lingered on her waist, and she was looking up into his face and he was looking down into hers and they were both breathing super hard.

Like they'd really exerted themselves.

Even though she couldn't remember when that happened.

She didn't want to remember, really.

So she stepped away before she could.

"I can't believe you just did that," she said airily.

And he took a second, but he answered airily, too.

"What? Turning you upside down, or the Daisy thing?"

"Both. All of it. But especially the Daisy thing."

"See, I knew you would hate me calling her."

"And can you blame me? You just sent your assistant out in the middle of the night to buy clothes and makeup and a vacuum cleaner I can't afford from shops that will probably all be closed anyway," she said with as much incredulity as she should muster. However, said incredulity had no effect on him.

He was already toppling it with a pointed, weary look.

Then he started counting off on his fingers how she was wrong.

"Okay, first of all, to her this is like, four in the afternoon. She's used to having to deal with stuff like shit-faced men who need picking up in the early hours of the morning. Second of all, I am absurdly wealthy, this is like buying a pack of peanuts to me, so I don't wanna hear any more about it. And thirdly, there's no such thing as opening hours for the places she's going to go to. She'll be at somewhere like *Vogue*, riffling through their winter collection," he said.

And all she could think when he did was *fucking hell*.

Because now it was believable, but astonishing.

"She never will," she gasped.

"I'm telling you."

"That's absolutely mad."

"I know. Different world when you've got some coin, love."

He rubbed his fingers together on the end of that statement. Almost sneering, like he didn't much like this state of affairs. But that was all right. Because she didn't like it, either.

"That doesn't mean I want it flashing around on my behalf."

"What else am I gonna flash it around on behalf of? I've no fucking clue what to do with it all. I saved and invested every penny while I was on the pitch because I thought that was smart and once my back was fucked I'd be like Gazza, penniless and desperate—and you know how I feel about that." He shook his head, clearly thinking about it. And clearly wanting to not. Before he plowed on. "Thing was, though, all it did was give me this mountain of money that I can't even give away fast enough to make a dent. I dump it on some charity, turn around and there's somehow twice as much as there was before."

Then he was quiet. And she was the one thinking about things.

Like how he'd forced those food banks not to mention him.

But they had anyway. They had told her.

*Someone should know*, they'd confessed.

"So you do give most of it away, then," she said.

"Not most. Enough that I can sleep at night."

"I think the amount you drop should have you out like a light."

"Still buy fancy things and have my fancy car and fancy house, don't I."

Now it was himself he was sneering at, quite obviously. Even though he was being daft. "You had that one-bedroom flat in Manchester until people started climbing the walls and hiding under your bed. Fame made you do this, and you know it. You know it made you need a fortress and a well-protected car someone else drives and a few nice suits. So don't try coming the raw prawn with me, old son," she said.

And he gave into it. She saw it happen with a snort over *raw prawn*.

Then a long breath out at the end her sentence.

"I'd argue, but *fuck*, I miss living like a normal person."

"Yeah, I know you do, mate. I know you do. I would, too."

"Then I'm sorry I'm dragging you into it all."

"You're not dragging me into it all. I'm scared right now, not gonna lie. But for me it's just temporary. Playing dress up. Kind of fun for a couple of months, then I get to set it aside. But you never will. You're Alfie fucking Harding."

He had been looking at nothing, but now he looked at her. And for just a second, just a brief moment, his eyes were as vulnerable as they had seemed that day when she'd touched his face. Then it passed, so fast she could almost believe it had never been there at all. There was just him, making it seem like nothing, really. "Well. At least Alfie fucking Harding has some furniture now," he said with a shrug. And of course, she couldn't help going with it. It made her too gleeful to do anything else.

"Been enjoying it, have you?"

"Other day I fell asleep in your chair while watching telly."

"Ah, that's the stuff. That's the life right there."

"Yeah," he said. "Thanks to you. Talking some sense into me."

"It's not that hard. Your number-one quality is sensible."

It was, she thought. Though maybe not in the way he thought. He immediately searched the heavens for some escape from this condemnation. Spat out the words: "*Christ*. That sounds so boring."

But that hadn't been what she meant.

He needed to know that wasn't what she meant.

"It isn't, though."

"So what is it, then?"

He raised an eyebrow.

Waiting, she thought, for the terrible verdict.

But the only verdict was this:

"Like being constantly comforted, by something I've never known."

**Tweets,** March 31, 2022

**MabieBabie**
@mabelwillicker
Phew, exhausting day today.

**StickingYourBootIn** @ontheterraces
Replying to @mabelwillicker
Lmao total confirmation that he can go all night

**doug** @doug353425637
Replying to @mabelwillicker
fat slut

**IWillFightYou** @ConnieBoBonny
Oh look it's first name bunch of numbers here to bless us
with their wisdom

**BusyRugMaking** @BerinderSutanpal
They say fat and slut like they're insults

**BigLad** @alanparker23
Replying to @ontheterraces
How would she know if he can go for hours she's making it
all up

**IWillFightYou** @ConnieBoBonny
Replying to @alanparker23
I'm gonna make YOU up you POS

# Sixteen

## Milk Can Get You Drunk
## if You Just Believe

Mabel didn't know what to expect from Alfie's assistant, Daisy. From the glimpses she'd gotten of her in various photographs and the information she'd gleaned thanks to social media, she knew the woman was pink-cheeked and had hair like Bettie Page. That she had a penchant for wide-legged pants that made her big round butt look amazing, and was sharp and funny and always ready to solve problems.

But that didn't say anything about how she'd react to this. To Mabel, now in a bathrobe, hiding behind Alfie to as great a degree as she could while Alfie was busy trying to force her into letting him tidy up. "Just at least allow me to fold some clothes, please, I'm going out of my mind," he was saying as Daisy swept into the flat.

So she couldn't imagine this was going to go great.

And it was their first test, too.

Their first chance to see how convincing they could be.

Which made it doubly terrifying. She almost didn't manage to step forward and greet the woman. He had to urge her with his hands. And say embarrassing things like: "Daisy, this is Mabel. Mabel, this is Daisy. Come on, come out from around me, you can say hello, she's not going to bite you."

Luckily, however, Daisy did not seem to care in the slightest. She didn't laugh. Or look at them both like they were bonkers. She just dropped everything she was carrying onto the couch. Then scooped Mabel into a hug. "Hello, at last," she said.

Followed by more, there was more, there was *loads* more all tumbling out of her. "Do you know how amazing it is to see him finally with someone he's actually bananas about? He will not stop talking about you. Mabel did this, Mabel did that, Mabel is driving me round the bend. I had to stop him wittering on about you the other day, when usually I can't get a word out of him about anything. The first time he ever asked me for a suit it took him three weeks to confess his collar size."

She said that last from behind her hand.

Like it was just them, whispering about him conspiratorially.

Though Mabel didn't know how to be conspiratorial back.

She was too busy asking herself why on earth he talked about her so much.

And then reminding herself that he had probably been seeding this for a bit now. Most likely he had started right away, and that was why he seemed calm and wasn't looking at her and decided to focus on something completely different. "Look, I told you I have a very thick neck. I'm sensitive about it, all right. And you guessed it anyway, so I don't know why you're telling her all that. Just trying to show me up in front of my new lass, you are," he said.

But Daisy just laughed. "Yes. But I wasn't trying to do it with the collar thing. I was trying to do it with the revelation that you do nothing but rave about her all the livelong day."

"Well, she's my girlfriend, isn't she? Course I'm going to rave about her."

"It doesn't look like she knows that."

"Well, I don't know why. I tell her all the things I told you."

"So you've said to her that she makes your knees weak, then."

*What the fuck*, Mabel thought. And had to shoot Daisy a look.

Like maybe she could tell if Daisy was lying simply by studying her face.

Which she could not. Daisy just grinned, like she'd won the game.

Because now Alfie was very inadvisably furious.

"I never said that," he growled out from between gritted teeth.

Even though really, there was no reason he shouldn't have.

It was a perfectly normal thing to say about your girlfriend. Or even a perfectly normal thing to say if you were propping up a phony one. So what he was doing here was anybody's guess. Heck, even he didn't seem to know.

He just looked hot and uncomfortable now.

But thankfully Daisy didn't seem to register it as fake.

She seemed to register it as emotionally stunted. "Don't let him get away with that, he adores you," she said. Then just as Mabel was busy blushing and floundering and trying not to look like this was completely throwing her, too, she said this: "Now, to the matter of outfits. I brought several options, all of them of course exquisite, complete with shoes and underwear—which is going to look spectacular on everything you have, I might add, you can thank me later with some flowers, Alfie."

And oh god knew what was going to happen at that point.

She could practically feel Alfie vibrating next to her.

Like he was trying to stop himself from saying anything silly.

Then Daisy held up something flimsy, swathed in tissue, and said:

"I bet he's already picturing your boobs in this."

And there was just nothing to be done.

It was over, it was all over.

"Shut up, Daisy, I am not," Alfie snapped out.

Helplessly, Mabel thought. Like someone being drowned by their own feelings and an incredibly bizarre and complicated situation. And now Daisy was looking at them curiously.

So she had to do it.

She had to step in.

With probably the worst confession in the world.

"He hasn't seen me naked yet," she said.

As if that were ever going to be a real and possible thing.

He was a footballer. He practically fucked people for a living.

Though it helped that Alfie immediately seized on what she'd said.

"Right. Exactly. No nakedness as of this moment," he said.

And then it was just a matter of driving it home.

"We're taking it slow. Really slow. Almost glacial, in fact."

"What she said. Glacial," Alfie agreed. "Like an ice age, in our pants."

"Even though we definitely want to."

"Christ, do I fucking ever. Just want to roast her right now."

She didn't mean to shoot him a look. Or let her eyes go wide.

It just happened, the second he said it, and the only thing that saved them was how much the actual sentiment seemed to satisfy Daisy. She nodded, like that made all the sense in the world, and started riffling through the pile of outfits again. So she pretty much missed Mabel gawping at Alfie, while Alfie did his best not to acknowledge that any gawping was happening.

He just stared straight ahead.

Like what he'd said was normal.

Which she supposed it was, really.

It was the way things were meant to be with him—a fact Daisy confirmed.

"Well, roasting someone right now does sound more like you," she said, so it was fine, it was fine, it all made sense. They were in the clear.

It was just that she didn't *feel* like they were in the clear.

She felt all weird and wobbly and sweaty.

And apparently, so did Alfie.

His face was glossed with perspiration.

She could see him actually vibrating, minutely.

"You can go now, Daisy," he said through gritted teeth.

Though somehow it didn't feel any better once she had. She waltzed out, with a wink, leaving them in what felt like the aftermath of an alien invasion. She immediately wanted to hide

in a cupboard, or start screaming, or maybe sink to the ground.
Every one of her muscles had apparently turned to soup; she
was incapable of speech for a full minute.

And Alfie was no better.

He went directly to the fridge.

Got out her four-pinter of milk.

Then chugged it straight from the bottle.

"I'm sorry," he said when he was done downing a dairy product like it was hard liquor. "I had to drink something. My mouth
feels like I just ate fifty cream crackers all at once. I'm honestly
afraid I may never experience saliva again."

"It's all right. Because I'm going to take it off you and do the
same."

She did, too. Without even caring that he'd just had his
mouth around it.

Although she did think about it quite a bit once she'd done it.

Mainly because he stared at her as she did.

Thankfully, however, he didn't say anything about the fact
that they'd just kissed via the medium of a large plastic bottle of
milk. He sank into a kitchen chair instead and blew out a long,
agonized breath. "Well, that was fucking hell on earth."

"I think I passed out standing up."

"My entire soul is sweating."

"You said so many things," she moaned. "So many."

"I know. And I regret every single one of them."

"You should. You almost fucked us about ten times."

"Yeah, and even when I didn't, I made a fucking mess. I
mean that roasting thing, oh god, I said I'd roast you, why did
I say *roast*? I could have just said make love, but oh no. I had
to let that come out of me, like a horny demon with no control
over himself." He put his head in his hands. Then finished in
a voice muffled by the embarrassment barrier they provided,
"What must you think of me?"

He was being daft, however.

There was nothing *to* think of him.

He'd done what he had to do, and in this at least, he'd been convincing.

"That you're a footballer, trying to act like I'm your girlfriend," she said softly, reassuringly. She even sat down with him. Knees almost touching his, hand near his elbow on the table. And she was rewarded with one fewer hand on his face.

"Yeah. But how would you want to be my fake girlfriend if I'm like that?"

"Well, mostly because there isn't anything wrong with roasting. Unless roasting means you put your penis in my ear. Then I suppose I might have objections about having pretend sex with you."

He gave her a withering look. "Your earhole is safe from my cock. It's just another word for fucking. That I wish I hadn't said. Because now it looks like I have no idea how to treat soft little beans like you, who are probably used to gentle progression toward being seduced in a suite full of candles and rose petals."

"Alfie, I don't think I've ever been seduced in my entire life."

"All right. But you have had the slow progression."

"I guess. I don't really need it, though."

"So what do you need, then?"

"Just wanting someone so much it feels like I might burst if I don't have them hard and fast and probably up against a fucking wall. And knowing that they want to have me in exactly the same way."

The words were out before she could stop them.

And they were bad, she knew they were bad.

She'd said things about *having*, and *walls*. So it wasn't a surprise when his face seemed to drop about three feet. Or that he couldn't seem to say anything, for a second. He just sat there, mouth open, with no words coming out. While she frantically googled *how do you take words back* in her head.

And came up with nothing, obviously.

She just had to ride it out. To wait, until her confessing that she wanted to be done hard faded. Which it did. It did. He recovered, eventually. "Right, well," he said. "Good to know. Excellent

information to have. For when we're pretending to be an item."
Then he dusted off his hands and stood, and she realized.

All that was left now was doing just that.

For months and months.

In public.

While dressed in the sexy clothes his assistant had brought.

Text Messages, January 2014

**Daisy 12:03 p.m.**
Hey Alfie, so I'm going to need your collar size.

**Grumpy Bastard 1:27 p.m.**
Who is this and how do you have my number?

**Daisy 1:28 p.m.**
It's me, the assistant you hired.

**Grumpy Bastard 5:10 p.m.**
Then why are you asking me for my personal information? I'm onto you, you're one of them scammers trying to get my bank details.

**Daisy 5:12 p.m.**
Because collar size is the key to doing that?

**Grumpy Bastard 5:33 p.m.**
How the bloody hell should I know, I'm not a scamming expert.

**Daisy 5:34 p.m.**
Or a phone expert, judging by the picture of your finger you sent me.

**Grumpy Bastard 7:04 p.m.**
Well if you'd stopped texting me so fast maybe I could take a minute to get it right. How do you even press the little buttons so quick?

**Daisy 7:04 p.m.**
I use my scamming powers.

## Seventeen

## All Missions Now Done with Closed Eyes, NASA Announces

$S$he knew she was taking far too long to get into the clothes Daisy had brought. But in her defense, all of them were a terrifying nightmare. Starting with the underwear that was just as outrageous and complicated as Daisy had promised. She had to actually climb into it, like she was getting ready to parachute out of an airplane. It took twenty minutes just to work out where everything went.

And once it was all on, she could kind of see what Daisy had meant.

She glimpsed herself in her dressing table mirror, and almost lost it.

She had to put on one of the dresses, quick, before she started getting turned on by herself. But it didn't help. Because now she was encased in a deep blue velvety thing that felt like fucking heaven and hiked her tits up to somewhere around her fucking *neck*. She actually found herself double-checking that they were inside the material to the correct extent. As if she'd somehow left them dangling out.

But nope. They were where they were supposed to be.

You couldn't see nipple.

There was just so, *so* much pushed-up boob.

It was honestly kind of obscene. And to the point where she didn't know what to say.

Alfie had to knock on her bedroom door after she spent too long sitting on her bed, forlorn. "Mabel, what is going on in there? You've been an hour now. I've had to rearrange dinner twice.

I'm not even sure if this last slot I've got is when the restaurant is actually open. I think they might just be doing it because I'm me," he called through the wood. So now she had to explain.

Even though explaining was impossible.

"I know, and I'm sorry. But things aren't exactly what I expected."

He paused, then: "So none of it fits right, then? She got it wrong?"

"No, she didn't get it wrong. I'm in a dress."

"If you're in one, I don't see the problem."

"That's because you aren't looking at it," she sighed.

"Come out then, so I can."

"I don't want to. And you can't make me."

"No, I can't. But I can tell you that nothing on you could horrify me."

He was lying, though; she knew he was. He sounded horrified already.

Still, though, she didn't expect the aghast look on his face when she gingerly opened the door. Or the way he said "Bleeding hell fire" in a voice that sounded like he'd just come out of a working men's club, circa 1987. Oh, and he staggered back, too. Sort of like she'd punched him.

*And then shielded his eyes with his hand.*

So that was all super cool.

"You said you wouldn't think it was awful."

"I don't think it's awful," he said. Then right as she was starting to calm, he couldn't seem to help adding: "I just don't know what to do when tits attack my face."

Because he was an arsehole; he was a big, ridiculous arsehole.

"Oh shush. They are not attacking your face. They are being very calm, in fact. They just also appear to have gained about five hundred percent extra boob somehow when I wasn't looking."

"Only five hundred?"

*Damn you*, she thought.

Even though he a point. "All right, a thousand."

"Got to be. It's literally all I can see, and I'm not even looking."

"You can look if you want," she said. "I'm not going to think you're doing wrong."

"Yeah, you might not, but I will. Good god, it feels like I'm violating you with my eyes when I so much as catch a glimpse. You're fully dressed, and yet somehow at the same time I've never seen anyone so naked in my life."

"So you agree then that I can't go out like this."

She waved her hands at herself.

She didn't know why, though.

He still had his hands cupped around his eyes.

"Well, not unless you want every person in the world calling you for a date."

"Every person in the world would not want a date because of *boobs*."

"They would when the boobs are that fucking bananas. You could probably get an alien who doesn't even know what boobs are on side with those fucking weapons of mass destruction. That wall is turning its head right now, and it neither has a head nor is capable of turning. It's an inanimate structure, made from mostly brick," he said, all in a big angry go. Then the anger dissipated, like it always did, and he seemed to realize he'd met-aphorically blown out her brains with his imaginary gun. "See, and now I'm talking way too much about your tits again."

*And in far too complimentary a way for me to cope with*, she thought.

But of course could not say. She had to stick with joking around.

"In your defense I want to, too. Even though they're mine."

"Yeah, but when you do it, it's cute. When I do it, I'm a per-vert."

"You're not a pervert for noticing something that can be seen from space."

"Gonna go knock some astronauts the fuck out in a second for ogling you."

She cracked up laughing almost before he'd finished speaking. And she did it loudly, and for a long amount of time. So long, in fact, that he broke, too. She heard him doing it behind his hands—like he found it too infectious when she did it, or even hadn't quite realized just how hilarious what he'd said was.

Because she'd noticed: that was a thing with him.

He didn't seem to expect people to get the joke.

Or find him funny.

Even though he was. God, he was.

He almost made her forget the dilemma, he was that good.

She had to take a few breaths and refocus on what mattered.

"Seriously, what am I going to do, Alfie?"

"Well, the rest of the dress is good. So maybe we could try a nice wrap."

"I don't have a nice wrap. I have a lot of colorful cardigans and things I've crocheted myself."

"There must be something among the stuff she brought. She'd never send you out in just that." He dropped his shielding hands, but kept his eyes turned away. Then he walked toward her bedroom. "Here, let me look. I'll find something."

Which he did. He came out with a blue wrap-looking thing, as soft as silk with an artfully rough-looking fringe all around it. And even though he refused to so much as dart a glimpse at her, even though he kept his face turned away and his eyes on the fucking ceiling, he managed to kind of drape it over her. He arranged it, carefully, in a way a posh lady would probably have it, across her décolletage.

And it worked. It truly did.

She honestly didn't know why he still looked like she was thumping him in the face, when he finally looked again. Though it passed as soon as it had come, so maybe it hadn't happened. Maybe things were okay now, she thought.

As he held out an elbow to her.

And she realized something, in a rush:

She was going to have to hold on to him, for the rest of the night.

# THE WINTER GARDEN

## TWO-MICHELIN-STARRED FINE DINING

### Our Story

The Winter Garden opened in 1972, and at the time
was only the second French restaurant of its kind
in the country. It offered, and still does today, an
unparalleled experience of classical French cuisine,
with the very highest attention to detail with regard
to food, wine, and service. Under the careful guidance
of Head Chef Garrison Bearing, The Winter Garden
has steadily maintained its status as one of the best
restaurants in Europe. We welcome you to join us on a
culinary journey.*

### MENUS
A La Carte
Lunch Menu
Menu Gold
Menu Silver
Wines

*Bookings may only be made six months in advance with a
£300 deposit, unless you are a VIP patron.

## Eighteen

### Falling into Fondling a Beard
### Is Totally a Thing

The restaurant was everything she expected it to be.

Which was to say that it looked like a diamond, if a diamond could somehow serve you a meal. It almost made her want to press her face against the glass, like the Dickensian orphan she knew she was by contrast. And once inside, this feeling did not abate. It intensified. She barely wanted to touch anything, in case her grubby hands sullied it. Suddenly, all she could imagine was the manager—who most likely moonlighted as the Duke of Durham—telling her she owed the restaurant five hundred grand for melting a table with her poor-person fingerprints.

And if she couldn't pay, she was going to debtor's prison. Which she was willing to bet now only existed to punish people for crimes against this specific place.

"You look like you're walking through a minefield made of ice. On stilts," Alfie whispered to her as they were steered toward their table by the poshest person she'd ever encountered. She couldn't do anything about it, however. She was too busy trying not to breathe in case her breath set off an alarm.

Not to mention all the walking in sky-high heels she was having to do.

She almost wobbled over at least twice.

The second time he had to actually do something to stop her going down. Though he did it with as much agility and skill as he had when she'd almost slipped in the kitchen. He just sort of tightened his biceps around the arm she had through his. Then he tilted his body, and oh holy fuck, suddenly she was almost off her feet. She was lifted right out of the stumble she was about to go into.

And then set back down as if nothing had happened.

Which probably seemed like the case for everybody there. The whole thing had taken him seconds, and almost no movement at all. He hadn't even looked at her while he did it. She wasn't even sure if she'd just imagined it, in the aftermath. So what was there for anybody to see?

Nothing, quite clearly.

And that was good.

Because literally everyone in there was staring.

"Why are they all looking at us?" she whispered the second the posh escort left them. She wished she'd hadn't, however. Because he slid closer in the plush booth they'd been given to hear her better.

"Go again, this ear's fucked," he said.

So now they were almost wedged together, facing out onto a sea of eyes that were all turned in their direction. While talking so closely they could have licked each other, no problem, and so low it had to seem like they were saying something bad.

Instead of just panicking about being gawped at.

"I think I must look wrong," she said. "They're onto me."

"You don't look wrong. You look spectacular."

"But check him over there. His eyes are practically popping out."

He reached for the water on the table and poured her a glass. Almost like he was ignoring what she was saying. Then just as she was about to panic he said, "Which one? Old man with his child bride, or Tory wanker?" And she understood, clearly: he hadn't made that move to brush her off.

He'd done it so he could surreptitiously look.

And she could now finger the culprit.

"Tory wanker. Though how we know he is one I don't know."

"It's called growing up in communities left to rot by an

enemy you can now sense from fifty paces. Now if you'll excuse me, I have to go batter said enemy for trying to undress you with his eyes."

"He is not trying to—" she started to say.

But Alfie was actually *getting up*.

So instead of doing that, she had to grab his arm. She had to grab it, and do it hard, and then yank, and even then he didn't wholly give up the ghost. He struggled against her grip, just a little bit. And he looked completely indignant about her attempts at restraining him. "Mabel, stop holding on to me. It's not fair when you know I can't do anything to stop you."

"The fact that you can't is why I'm going to do it more, until you see sense."

"My sense is perfect. That twat needs a beating. He's laughing now."

"Yeah, probably because he knows he's got Alfie Harding riled."

"So he's doing it on purpose?" He cracked his knuckles. "Even fucking worse. I'll kill him."

"You're not going to kill anyone for not even doing anything."

"He did do something. He leered at you. Like you're a piece of meat."

"I'm not even the type of meat he'd want to leer at, Alfie, sit down."

He didn't, though. He just seethed and twisted in his seat, agitated.

So she grabbed the lapel of his jacket and pulled until he was looking at her—mostly to give him a piece of her mind in a more effective manner. *You are being a massive fool*, she imagined herself saying. Only she didn't have to.

He stopped the second he met her gaze.

Like her gaze was some kind of sedative.

It dropped his shoulders. His fists unclenched.

All the tension went out of his face. And when he finally spoke, he sounded weird. Hoarse, and strained, and like he wasn't quite sure what he was telling her. But had to do it anyway. "You just don't get it. You don't get how you seem to other people. How dazzling you are, the way you walk into a room and light it up," he said. At which point she wasn't quite sure what happened.

She only knew that somehow her hand was no longer on his lapel.

That it was on his face. That she was touching his beard.

And she was saying his name. *Alfie*, she said. *Alfie*.

As if the other more normal words were all stuck. But it was all right because he didn't seem to mind. Or notice that anything was weird. He just held her gaze in his for what felt like a long, long time, eyes all soft and warm like they had been that first time she'd touched him here. And even after that gentle light in them died, and he turned away, it wasn't a bad thing. Because he gruffed out under his breath:

"That was really convincing affection. Good job."

Then they carried on with dinner like nothing had happened.

* * *

The rest of the dinner went pretty smoothly after that. Or at least he didn't threaten to beat anyone else up. Or get hypnotized by her. Or make her touch his face until everything got real unsettling. Instead, they ate delicious food, and did things like clink their glasses. As if they were celebrating some nonexistent anniversary for a relationship they didn't have. That they would never have. Because he said as they got into the car: "Considering we have zero sexy feelings for each other we did a good job of looking like we're two people who have sexy feelings for each other."

So that was all settled.

No matter how weird things felt.

Because she had to admit: they *did* feel weird.

It was kind of why she wanted to scream *no*, when he asked her if it was okay to do the thing on the doorstep. *What if I accidentally put a hand on his beard again*, she found herself thinking.

Then didn't know exactly what was wrong with putting a hand on his beard. After all, it hadn't meant anything.

She hadn't done it in a sexy way.

It had just been an abrupt overflow of affection. Most likely brought on by him trying to defend her honor, or some daft nonsense like that, and he had obviously known that. Though of course she couldn't help thinking: maybe he wouldn't know it if she did it a second time. He might think she had a real thing for the beard touching. That she was mad for it.

And what then?

Heck knew.

But it was too late to back out now. They were getting out of the car, and he had his hand on her back, and the hand was kind of burning a hole through her dress. It felt very hot, and very big. And then they were there. Standing in the low glow of the light over the door to her building. Every part of her wanting to think about whoever might be taking their picture right now.

But none of her thinking of that at all.

Instead, she was just trying not to seem like she didn't like looking at his face too much. While having to pretend that she liked looking at his face a lot. All of which was hell, it was a mess, honestly they should never have done this.

"Ready?" he whispered, and she came so close to saying *Absolutely not*.

So close. Just not close enough.

Because he was already leaning.

And if she pulled away now, anyone watching would know it was all just a bunch of bullshit. They probably already did, because she couldn't seem to stop herself from stiffening up. Like he'd turned her to stone just by being too close and letting his warm breath stir against her face. And then he did it, he touched his mouth to hers, and oh, it got so much worse. She could actually feel her nails biting too deep into her palms; she held her breath so hard it hurt something inside her chest.

And not just because it was Alfie doing this.

Or because she was afraid of all her own reactions.

No, no. It was how he did it that really hit her hard. It was the sweetness of it, the gentleness, the unexpected softness of his lips. She'd always thought they looked mean beneath the tangle of his beard. But they weren't, they weren't—they were plush and tender and warm, like the curve of a peach that had just been plucked.

And god, it was making her go funny.

Now her eyes had gone all wide, she knew they had.

They felt like a set of saucers someone had stuffed into her head.

And that would have been bad, probably. Only he was looking at her like that right back. She could actually see the white all the way around his eyes. If he'd been anyone else in the world, she would have said he was terrified. But he wasn't, he was Alfie Harding, and Alfie Harding wasn't afraid of anything.

So probably it was just disgust.

Or maybe horror.

Yeah, she thought.

He was horrified by how she felt.

And that was why he ripped away and went, without even saying good night.

***Makeup Babe Golden Glam* YouTube Transcript, April 4, 2022**

Okay, so we're going to be looking at the long-awaited Golden Glam palette from Natasha Denona. And I thought we'd do something a little different today, because if you've been following the whole *butt-groping, headbutting, big, beautiful babe on Alfie Harding's arm* drama, you may be interested to know that this is the exact palette that his new gal used to achieve that dynamite look at The Winter Garden the other night.

Honestly, I have no idea why he couldn't muster up any enthusiasm for that kiss everybody is talking about when her eyelids looked like that. Maybe he hates warm bronze tones, I don't know. Possibly the whole thing is phony, I have no idea. As you know, I stay out of the gossiping and sniping on social media.

This is a no-sniping zone, folks!

But I do think that she looked banging regardless, and probably deserves better than that hairy asshole, and so we're going to go ahead and start out with a little primer and then we're going to dip into Sultry Nights, this pale beige in the top left.

# Nineteen

## The View from That House's Window
## Must Be Spectacular

*M*abel didn't want to think that he'd found her that repulsive.

But it was hard not to when everybody else in the world seemed to think so, too. There were whole articles and posts and TikToks with titles like *Disgusted Man Gives Woman Awkward Peck* and *Somebody Help a Kiss Has Given Me Lethal Levels Of Secondhand Embarrassment*. The two factions in her Twitter mentions were torn between the idea that he was only doing this for publicity in order to get a role in some prestige TV show, and a theory that the pictures were sabotage to prove nobody could ever love a fat woman.

So really, what was she supposed to think?

There weren't very many options.

He had done it and found it horrible.

And now they were in even deeper shit than they'd been before.

Which probably explained why her doorbell was suddenly ringing over and over and over like somebody was just wailing on it—and she knew the someone was Alfie. She knew he'd just been sitting in his car, stewing away about this nonsense, and when she'd taken too long—because of course she had to take this long, now that she needed to look like a glamour model every time she so much as set a toe out of her door—he'd blatantly decided to come to her.

And sure enough, there he was on her doorstep. Surrounded on all sides by what now looked like people with banners saying they supported true love.

Holding what looked like a *printout* of *web pages* in his fist.

"Oh good god, how do you have a printout of web pages?" she asked the second they were safely inside and away from prying eyes. Though she sort of wished she still had those prying eyes, now that he was in front of her. They would have made sure that she didn't have to get into any of this, ever.

With what looked like the most furious man ever to live.

Seriously, she'd never seen him look so incensed.

And she'd once pepper sprayed him in the face.

"Don't act like it's weird, Mabel. Daisy wouldn't stop yammering at me down the phone about it, so I made her do me copies of all this bullshit and then fax them to me. The way that normal people do all the time," he said because he was ridiculous, oh god, he was the most ridiculous man she'd ever met.

"Yeah. If by normal people you mean being from 1985."

"I have no idea what that even means."

"It means how the flip do you have a *fax machine*?"

"Because I've had it so long it's technically classified as an antique. That fella off *Roadshow* told me it was worth fifteen grand. What do you think I'm going to do, piss money down the lav? Fuck no, I kept hold of it. And look, I was right to. Because now I know that the interwebs thinks I find you repellent and am suddenly incapable of kissing in an exciting way."

He thrust the papers at her on the last word.

She didn't take them, however.

Mainly because a) she knew what they said.

And b) what the fucking fuck, he had a fax machine worth fifteen grand?

"I honestly cannot tell what part of that is a joke and what part is real," she said.

"I wish *none* of this was fucking real. It's like a nightmare I can't wake up from. Yesterday I almost murdered a man for ogling you. One of my only friends thinks me getting a rollicking online is hilarious. And this morning that Henry Samuel whatever the fuck from Harchester sent me fucking *flowers. Don't listen to people saying you're a terrible kisser, I'm sure you're great,* the card said."

She did her very best not to laugh.

God, it was hard going, though.

Her face actually ached from the strain.

"Yeah, just to be clear he probably really meant it," she admitted."The first conversation we ever had, he used the word *anyhoot.* With a *T* on the end. And he keeps sending me emails that say things like *Hang in there, I know you two crazy kids can make it, reckon I'm going to wear a blue tuxedo to your wedding.*"

"A blue fucking tuxedo. To our *wedding.*"

"Apparently, he believes in true love."

"There *is* no true love. A fact that I proved by kissing you so poorly that someone called LivingInsideAlfieHardingsUnderpants said they had known all along that I could never feel anything for a woman with a bum like yours. So now I have to go murder someone for a) looking at your bum, b) disparaging my taste in bums, and c) apparently having a house right next to my cock without me knowing it."

Okay, now she did laugh. And she suspected that he almost did, too, when he saw her trying to hide it. His face wavered, and he had to fight to maintain his six-foot-deep frown.

"Stop it, Mabel, this isn't funny."

"You look like you think it is."

"Yeah, but I'm trying not to. Because seriously, what are we gonna do?"

She sat down on the arm of her couch before she answered.

Mostly because what she had to say wasn't going to be easy.

It made her stomach churn like whoa just thinking about it. In fact, for a moment she considered going with something else, instead. Something like *Let's just forget all this, it's bonkers, it's never going to work, and we're both going to end up doing completely humiliating things.* But he just seemed so agitated about it, and so determined, and her brain automatically went to those little lasses outside with banners, and in the end she couldn't.

She had to go with a solution instead.

"It's obvious what we're going to do. Next time you kiss me, you will do your level best not to look like you're being repulsed by a massive hideous monster," she said. Much to his utter fuming disgust. He actually made a snarling noise about it.

"What have I said to you about repeating what they say like it's true?"

"That I should do it even more to really annoy you."

"You know full well that wasn't it, you little liar."

"I do. But if I lie we don't have to get into this."

She got an even more annoyed noise for that.

And oh, now the jacket was coming off.

"Well, we are getting into it. Because I'm not having you think I was turned into an old man who can't kiss by the sight of your annoyingly nice mug. And especially not when the actual reason was just me seeing you gawping at me like you were about to have your face eaten off by an inexplicably bearded shark."

"Okay, first of all, never talk about sharks with beards again."

"I know, as soon as I said it I wished I hadn't." He rubbed a hand over his face wearily. "I'm gonna have some nightmares tonight, I tell you what. *Jaws* completely fucked me up as a kid. I had to pretend I was bored by that Statham movie not long ago, because I was shitting bloody bricks."

"I don't blame you. One time I couldn't stop bingeing stuff on the Discovery Channel that said the gigantic prehistoric ones are still alive in big ocean holes, and now I can never go on a boat. If part of fake dating is going to be doing stuff on a yacht we are boned. You'll have to tranquillize me just to get me onboard, and then all the headlines will be *Angry Man Has to Sedate Terrified Weirdo Before She Will Allow His Face to Come Anywhere Near Her.*"

He shot her some angry eyebrows.

Though she could see there was laughter in his eyes.

And she knew why, too—because he had her. He had her. "So you do actually believe me, then," he said. "About your terror throwing me off."

"Well, you know. It sounds somewhat plausible, I suppose."

"You cheeky mare. It's not just fucking plausible, it's the truth."

"Fine, it's the truth. But honestly I don't know why it was that way. You understand my brain is okay with it, no matter what daft thing my face is doing. So just, you know, get in there. Do what you would usually do."

He sighed and shook his head. "It's not that easy, Mabel love."

"Explain why it isn't."

"Because it's not something you want. You've made that clear. And all I could think when I went to do it was *No no she hates your big hairy demonic face stop now you disgusting pervert or else I'll call the fucking police.*"

*What the fuck*, she thought. And answered accordingly.

"I don't think your face is big and demonic and hairy."

"Yeah, but you do, though. You said so. I know you did."

"What? When? I bloody never. Someone's having you on. It's bullshit."

"Well, it didn't look like bullshit when EatingButthole234356 showed me."

He started riffling through his fax papers on his last word. He needn't have bothered, however. She knew what was coming. She saw it behind his eyes, the second he mentioned a name that ridiculous. He was talking about Twitter, something on Twitter—and sure enough, there it was. Her replying to Connie after Connie had suggested that Alfie Harding was actually really hot.

And apparently, she had not agreed.

Which was good on the *convincing him she wasn't gaga for his face* front.

But bad on the *hurting his feelings* front. And the latter won out. Of course it did. She couldn't let that stand. "Alfie, that was four years ago," she said, even though she knew it was going to make things worse for her. And it did.

"I know. But you must have meant it."

"Even if I did, it's not necessarily a bad thing."

"Of course it is. You make me sound like the fucking Beast of Bodmin."

"Yeah, but men who look like the Beast of Bodmin are—"

Don't finish that sentence, she warned herself.

Because there was reassuring him.

And then there was reassuring him so much that she collapsed her whole house of cards. So she took a second and went with something other than just telling him she found him attractive: "—appealing to most women. And you know it. So stop talking daft," she said, and it solved one problem. But apparently not the other.

"It's not daft when you looked so frightened."

"I looked frightened because I was being gawked at."

"Oh. Right. Yeah. I forgot about that."

"Plus, I haven't been kissed in a while."

He paused to take that in. "Well, how long is a while, exactly?"

"Too long for me to tell a footballer about."

"Now hang on, this footballer hasn't had a go in ages."

"Yeah, and unless by ages you mean five years . . ."

She knew as soon as she said it that she shouldn't have. Though in her defense, it had seemed like a good way to really drive home that he wasn't repulsive. And in a way that kept her safe.

She just hadn't seen the way it wouldn't help at all.

Until his eyebrows hit his hairline.

"Five fucking years?" he cried. "Oh my Christ, I'm kissing someone whose virginity has probably started to somehow grow back. Give it another week and I'll be deflowering you, this is a nightmare. I'm never gonna be able to do this now."

He was being daft, though. He had to know he was being daft.

And if he didn't she was going to tell him. "Of course you are, because virginity is just a load of made-up cobblers."

"Yeah, I know it is. But having someone you don't like that

way being your first proper snog in half a decade isn't. You should be getting it from someone you're wild for, at the very least. Someone you really want to do this to you."

"I don't have to really want it. I just have to convince you I do."

"Oh, and you think you're gonna be able to achieve that, do you?"

It was the scoff in his voice that made her say it. "Of course I am," she said.

And once she'd gone with it, there was no way to take it back. She didn't *want* to take it back, if she was being honest. She wanted him to know that this wasn't some awful, unpleasant thing for her. And doubly so, when they playacted her saying goodbye to him on her doorstep a moment later.

Because when he turned to face her, he just looked so . . . pained.

Like he was foisting something awful on her.

He was the Beast of Bodmin, forcing a kiss virgin into a snog.

Even though nothing could have been further from the truth. She didn't feel forced at all, and he didn't look like a beast to her, and oh god, she regretted writing that daft tweet. She hadn't even meant it then. She'd just wanted Connie not to fall for horrible footballers who did things like spike her drinks, even though the truth was: she'd always felt that he seemed like one of the good ones. He *was* one of the good ones. And that was why she took hold of his lapels, and yanked him all the way down, until he was within easy kissing distance.

Then she just did it. She pressed her mouth to his, good and firm. And not even in a closed and mealy sort of way, either. No, she did it with her lips parted. So he could get a little bit of heat and slickness, so he could know she meant business.

And it worked. It proved her point.

Because he made a sound into her mouth. He let out a little astonished grunt—like he couldn't believe she'd done this. Though she didn't really get a chance to savor the victory. It took him all of ten seconds to recover from the shock of her hands in his hair and her mouth all hot on his. And the moment he did, he didn't react with disgust or horror or anything of the kind.

Instead, the light seemed to shift in his eyes.

They went funny. They went sort of foggy.

And the lids dropped so low she could hardly see the black beyond. Almost like he was drifting off to sleep, she thought— only she knew he wasn't doing anything of the kind. It was obvious he wasn't because he made another sound. A thicker, heavier, oddly helpless sound, which seemed to reverberate through her.

Then suddenly he was pressing back against her.

And oh god, the way he went about it.

He just sort of slanted his mouth over hers, in this incredibly firm but rolling way. Like she'd seen people do in movies but had never experienced in real life. She hadn't even thought it *existed* in real life, if she was being honest. It had just seemed like one of those things people did to look on good on camera.

Only somehow it wasn't.

It was an actual kissing technique that someone could just do to you. They could just rock their mouths against yours, over and over, in these long, languid strokes that she didn't *want* to admit felt good. She didn't want to enjoy them. It seemed absolutely ridiculous to enjoy them in these circumstances.

There were people by her gate gawking at them.

And yet it was happening all the same.

She almost made a whole sound, about thirty seconds in. And the hand she had in his hair wanted to tighten. It wanted to clutch at him, desperately—like he was somehow drowning her. Like this was all she had to hold on to before she went under. And then, oh god then, she felt a hot wet flicker against her lips. She felt something slick and good stroke her there and knew.

That was his tongue. He was kissing her with his tongue.

And not even in the usual way that almost never felt good.

No, this was hot. Even she could admit it was hot.

It made her think of other things, lewder things, like some-one licking her pussy. And of course the second she thought such a thing, her whole body just went boneless. He had to ac-tually stop her sagging with an arm around her waist. Which of course only made things worse. Now she was just being cradled in big strong arms, while someone kissed her like he was trying to make her come.

And honestly, she couldn't be sure that was impossible.

What he was doing felt more pleasurable than actual sex she'd had.

By the time he pulled away she was almost beside herself.

And that was bad, oh, it was so bad, because for just a second she came close to doing something ridiculous—like pulling him back to her by his lapels, again. Only this time, she kind of sus-pected she really meant it. That it wasn't just to prove he wasn't hideous to her, or something daft like that. It was all him, and how he'd made her feel. And just as she was reckoning with that, he nodded.

Like he was saying *job done*.

Then he breezed away without a second glance.

**Tweets,** July 2018

**BeingThirstTrapped**
@ConnieBoBonny
Am I just in a dry spell or is Alfie Harding hotter than he's ever been

**MabieBabie** @mabelwillicker
Replying to @ConnieBoBonny
Friend, what are you talking about he's hair with eyes

**BeingThirstTrapped** @ConnieBoBonny
Yeah that's what's good about him, the hairier he gets the hotter he is

**MabieBabie** @mabelwillicker
Okay maybe you have a point about the hair, but what about all the mauling people that he does oh wait wait let me back up I think I'm just making him sound even more like a sexy werewolf

**BeingThirstTrapped** @ConnieBoBonny
Stop, mercy, I'm horny enough as it is

# Twenty

### Yeah, if the MCU Ever Allowed Hot Snogging

The good news was: people *definitely* seemed more impressed by their second kiss than they had been by their first. In fact, it was voted Best Use of Tongue in a Twitter poll about Alfie's various doorstep snogs over the years. *I honestly had to make sure you definitely can't get pregnant just by looking at a picture*, one person said.

But the bad news was: literally everything else about it.

Starting with the fact that she had fucking loved it, that it had been the best kiss of her life, that she had come incredibly close to dragging him back for more like a complete saddo. And ending with the certain knowledge that he had not experienced anything of the kind. To him, it had been the equivalent of doing his fucking laundry. He'd pulled away like he'd just finished folding and now got to have a nice sit down. Even though this was all the opposite of what she'd intended.

She'd wanted him to feel good about this.

And instead, she'd briefly become one of his stans.

Next thing she knew she was gonna be contacting him via the astral plane.

It was maddening, utterly maddening. She didn't even know what to make of it. *You were just coming off a kiss drought*, she told herself. But that didn't feel wholly convincing. Nor did the idea that he'd shocked her into it, with all that sudden tongue action. So where did that leave her?

She didn't know.

It made no sense.

The only thing she could think was: *He's just that good at kissing.*

But even that didn't really help her. Because now she had to be around him, while knowing that he was. And she felt pretty sure that this knowledge was going to show on her face at some point. *You're going to look at him and think about his incredible tongue-kissing skills, and when you do your eyes will light up like a pinball machine,* her brain informed her. Then even more horrible, it added: *and he'll know why. He will guess that you're massively into it.*

At which point, all she could do was pray.

*Please, Alfie, just do not ever guess,* she thought at him as she climbed into the car for their latest date. And to her relief, it did actually seem like he might not. Or at least, like he hadn't so far. He was just his usual self: occasionally annoyed, often indignant about something she'd said, and frequently hilarious.

Not to mention just as fussy as he'd said he would be. He smoothed down the collar of her dress before she even knew it was sticking up. And when her wrap slid off her shoulders, he stopped it from hitting the ground. He slid it back on for her.

All of which was good for easing her mind on the *does he know I liked kissing him* front. But maybe not quite as good at preventing her from ever liking it again. Because try as she might, she couldn't quite tell herself that she wasn't now enjoying him touching her just a little bit more than she had.

And she was already sure that she'd enjoyed it to a greater extent than she'd maybe thought. Or ever let herself admit. Though really, could anyone fault her for that? *When no man has ever made you feel good it hits you hard the moment one does,* she told herself. Yet somehow it didn't seem to help. She just felt unsettled and strange and like she should be even more cautious than she had been before.

Even though now, of course, they were in a situation where she couldn't be cautious at all. She'd gone for it once. She couldn't suddenly *not* go for it a second time. Not even when he said the following words, as they were leaving yet another fancy restaurant: *I was thinking, since this is technically our third date, that we should probably kiss like something is going to happen. Like maybe I'm coming in with you for more than tea and crumpets if you catch my drift.*

And Lord, did she ever want to put the brakes on, then.

Her first instinct was to say *Oh dear god no.*

But what would he think if she did?

He might guess the reason why.

Though even if he didn't, the other options were not exactly palatable. She didn't want him to think she was terrified again. And especially not when they were making all this progress. A few more of these things, a little more work on his book, and she could safely suggest a phony breakup.

At which point, they would be in the clear.

They could pretend they were going to be just good friends.

Then actually *be* just good friends—or so she hoped.

Because that was the other thing:

She didn't want to just let him go, after all this. She wanted to see him, even after his memoir was all done. And to get to that, they had to go through this. Despite how much this was making her squirm and scream into her pillow at night and kind of want to throw herself out of the nearest window.

So she decided, right then:

She was going to be cool.

She was going to be calm.

Or at the very least, she was going to react a normal amount to him kissing her. No almost groans, no wanting to grab, no weakness in the knees, she told herself, all the way through dinner. And she could feel herself internalizing it. It felt pretty ingrained by the time they got to the short path up to her door.

Like it was something she could really do.

And then she got out her keys.

And went to put one in the lock.

And as she did she felt him lean down, and *kiss* her *fucking* neck.

Just straight up kissed her neck, like that was a normal thing people did all the time as they were trying to get indoors. Instead of something she was pretty sure she'd never even seen happen to Julia Roberts in eighty movies about people being really horny for Julia Roberts. There were whole erotic novels she'd read that didn't hit whatever this goddamn thing was.

But apparently, he was just doing it anyway.

And so much so that she was starting to fail pretty badly at the task at hand.

She kept missing the lock with the key. At one point, she was fairly sure she tried to insert it into the letterbox. Then just as she thought she had some sort of handle on it, he put his whole hand on her face. He took hold of her jaw and turned her head until she was looking back at him. Until she was gazing into his eyes, and he was gazing into hers, and oh god, she knew what was coming.

She knew but was absolutely powerless to stop it.

And not just because her dignity relied on it.

Or the scam they were pulling demanded this of her.

No. It was because he'd turned every bone in her body to molten lava.

She couldn't have moved if she tried. She just had to stand there, face turned up to his, keys and door and lock completely forgotten. And then she got to watch as he leaned down slow as warm syrup and claimed her mouth. *Softly,* she thought, *so softly,* and no different from how he'd done it before.

In fact, if anything this was a good deal more tender.

But Lord, it did not register as tender to her body.

It registered like complete filth. And when it did, she couldn't help reacting just a little. Just with a hand on his arm, to sort of steady herself. And maybe a tiny bit of turning, so it was easier to do this. Nothing major, she told herself. But oh man, he did not seem to think so. No, he seemed to think it was now open season.

She'd given the green light to more.

And more was him making a sound into her mouth.

One that was so convincingly like a moan she could have sworn it was.

Then he pushed her back. He pushed her all the way back, until she was pressed against the door. And Lord in heaven, did he fucking kiss her. His hand actually went into her hair all the way in right up to the roots; his mouth was a fucking fever over hers. All she could feel was the heat of it, the slickness of it, the way he insinuated himself greedily against her. As if he wanted it, it seemed like. As if he truly couldn't get enough of doing this.

And it all conspired to make her lose it, just a little bit.

A sound like a sob actually rose in her throat.

She had to get the door open before the sound could break out of her. And she did, too—she managed to get the key in the lock and push her way inside. But the problem was, now they weren't just kissing. They were stumbling into her building *while* kissing. As if they were actually going to fuck, somehow.

Even though she knew that couldn't be the case. This was all just fake, it was phony, it wasn't the least bit real. It just didn't feel *the least bit real*, now that their legs were tangling together and his tongue was doing obscene things to the insides of her mouth and his hands were in some absolutely bonkers places. Like on the nape of her neck. And somewhere incredibly low down on her back.

*That's actually just your butt*, her brain said.

And if she was being honest, it kind of was.

He was pretty much grazing it with his fingertips. And even wilder, she had this feeling—this incredibly compelling and completely impossible feeling—that he kind of wanted to just do it. He *wanted* to fully grope her there.

Though of course she knew that couldn't be true.

How could it possibly when he had to know:

He could have done whatever he fucking liked. He could have just gone ahead, and she wouldn't have faulted him for it. She wouldn't have faulted him for anything. Her whole body was now so ripe and aching he could have shoved her dress up to do it. Just got it around her hips and slid a hand over her underwear-covered backside.

Or more.

Or worse.

*Oh Jesus, just put your hand inside*, her mind moaned.

And she knew that her mind wasn't talking about getting under her outfit.

It was talking about these little knickers she was wearing. It was talking about him pushing his hand inside them and squeezing and stroking whatever he found there. First the curve of her ass. Then other things, hotter things, wetter things, things that were actually not great to be thinking about right now.

Because suddenly the door was closed.

And he was pulling away.

And okay, yeah, he seemed reluctant about it. But *reluctant* didn't really help her. She still wound up in a dimly lit vestibule, with a head full of horny thoughts about a man she was only supposed to pretend to want, while the man in question was right in front of her.

So now she had to somehow pretend she wasn't affected at all.

While being more affected by anything than she'd ever been in her life.

It was honestly all she could do to stay on her feet—and she didn't even do that well. She could feel herself sort of sliding sideways along the hallway wall. He had to shoot out a hand and haul her back to something like standing. And the rest of her was faring no better. Her face was on fire. She felt flushed all the way to her toes.

It probably looked like she'd been punched.

In fact, she knew it did, because he looked pretty despairing about the state she was in. "Oh Christ, that was too much, wasn't it. I went too far," he said the second he managed to meet her gaze. Which was very fast, all things considered. He didn't even seem to need to catch his breath.

Whereas she . . . well.

She knew she sounded like she'd just run up a mountain.

It took her what felt like half an hour to get words out.

And that didn't help when the words she wanted to get out were these:

"You didn't go too far, Alfie. I'm totally fine," she said, but not only had she taken this long to do so, she also sounded like a broken set of bagpipes when she did. So it wasn't a surprise when he gave her his most incredulous look.

"Does *fine* now mean looking like you've been clobbered?"

"I don't look clobbered," she protested. "I look normal. Ordinary. Boring even."

"If you did I don't think you'd still be sliding sideways down a wall."

"Give over, I'm not doing anything of the sort. And even if I am it's just because of these shoes. They're making me stand funny," she said, then pointed, for good measure. As if perfectly stable flats were going to prove anything at all, other than the fact that she was a liar trying to cover her own tracks.

Because he was right: she did currently look like she couldn't stand up straight. And that wasn't even the only thing she was doing wrong—as he was only too happy to point out. "Are they also making you breathe like you've just wrestled a shark?" he asked. But she wasn't about to concede just yet.

No, she was going to be inadvisably mad instead. "I swear to god if you mention sharks one more time I'm going to kill you."

"That doesn't seem like much of a threat, coming from someone so weak they can barely stand up under their own power," he said, then glanced at her face. "And who is also apparently dying of what looks like extreme sunburn."

"Oh, don't exaggerate. My cheeks are not that red."

"Mabel, they are glowing. I can feel the heat from here."

"Well, maybe you shouldn't have almost grabbed my bum."

She wanted to take it back the second she said it.

Mostly because it acknowledged that his actions had had an effect.

But also for the thing it did to his face. This flash of horror just ripped across it before he could smuggle it down to a more reasonable reaction. And the reasonable reaction he eventually settled on was also not particularly great. It was pure disappointment in himself, top to bottom. And his words backed that assessment up: "I know I shouldn't have almost grabbed your bum. That's my whole point. I went too hard, for reasons that completely escape me, and now you're all traumatized. Seriously, I'm five seconds away from calling the police on myself."

"You don't have to call the police, that's not what I'm saying."

"Then what are you saying? That it's more of a civil matter?"

"No, Alfie. I'm not going to sue you."

"Right. So you're just going to never speak to me again."

God, he was insufferable sometimes. Because of course she couldn't let that stand. She had to correct him. And she was agitated when she did it, too, so it all spilled out of her in a big angry rush. "I don't think I could ever not speak to you again now, you great jerk. And especially not over this. This wasn't anything bad. You didn't do anything wrong. I'm just not used to being kissed by someone who's this actually blooming good at it," she burst out.

Then had to slowly grasp the contents of what she had said. Not the worst thing. Not *I'm massively into your super-hot self*, or something like that. But not the best thing, either. Because apparently, she'd told him he was some kind of kiss wizard. And he couldn't seem to help the surprised pleasure that immediately dawned all over face. His eyes gleamed; she saw his tongue curl up and touch his upper teeth. Like a cat who'd accidentally gotten hold of a canary.

Only to discover the canary actually somehow *liked* being there.

Because she did. She had. And now there was no escaping.

Of course there wasn't. He was leaning forward now, voice low and just a little bit amused. "Are you saying you enjoyed that?" he asked, and she couldn't fault him for it.

But oh god, how she wanted to.

"No. I did not say that. You're imagining things."

"I don't think I am. I think you just admitted my moves are grand."

"Well, I didn't. And even if I did, don't talk like you don't know they are, all right. Like it's a shock that someone might mildly enjoy them."

"It's not a shock that someone might. It is a shock that *you* do."

He nodded at her, on *you*. And pointed, too. As if somehow, she wouldn't know who he meant. He had to finger the guilty party, so the horny cops would know who to arrest. Though how they would need extra evidence, she did not know. She couldn't even get words out without sounding like a hairdryer set on high.

"Well, I've no idea why," she tried. "I've got the same business as everybody else you've ever snogged. In fact, my business is probably worse off than most, considering nobody has messed around with it for a very long time."

It didn't do her any good, however.

His eyebrows shot up the second she used that euphemism.

"Okay, I have to ask: by *business* here do you mean—"

"You know what I mean, Alfie. Don't make me say it."

"Think I'm gonna have to, love. It's blowing my mind too much to not."

"What about it's blowing your mind? You just fucked my mouth with your tongue. For the second time, I might add. And I handled that first one like a pro, so I reckon you can give me just a small break on not coping very well here."

"Oh, I'll give you a break about it. While being gleeful as fuck."

He did look gleeful, too, she thought. He was practically grinning, the little shit. She could actually see all his teeth, for the first time ever.

Not that she really understood why.

"Why the fuck are you gleeful? It's not an achievement, making a woman who hasn't had any in years get a bit turned on. That's like being proud because you won a race against someone whose only race experience was stumbling through the woods once in high school after an annoying man claimed it would be good for you," she said.

But all that got her was this:

"I want to punch this annoying man."

"Great. Focus on that."

"Yeah, but I can't. Because you also said you were turned on."

*Damn, did I*, she asked herself. And was dismayed to find she had.

It was fine, though. She knew how to mitigate the damage.

"I said I was a bit turned on. As in a really tiny amount."

"It doesn't look like a tiny amount. It looks like a lot."

She scoffed. "A second ago you couldn't even tell that it wasn't disgust."

"Yeah, because I never in a million years thought I could do anything that would get you going. Partly because you've actually *told* me so, you've tweeted as much, but also just because I'm the opposite of everything a woman like you *should* want. You should want Steve fucking Rogers, charging in like a golden glowing sunbeam to tell you how great everything is gonna be now he's here. But I'm not that at all, and yet somehow I've managed this. I can tell I have because it's all over you. You're all flushed and trembly and breathless," he said while gesturing at her again. Only this gesture was a lot more than a pointing finger. It was his splayed hand, stirring the air over her face and body. And right after those words, too.

Those actually delighted-sounding words.

So it wasn't a surprise that she sounded breathless when she responded.

"You make it sound like a good thing."

"Well, it's not a bad one."

"Of course it is. It's humiliating."

"I don't see why. Nowt wrong with being horny, love."

"Yeah, but there is summat wrong with being horny in front of you."

"Why? We're both adults. You've told me what made it happen. The thing that made it happen isn't weird or gross. As far as

I'm concerned, you can be like this until the fucking cows come home. Be as riled as you want for as long as you want."

He shrugged and spread his hands. Like he was talking about something ordinary, like getting stuck into an all-you-can-eat buffet. And okay, it kind of did sound pretty straightforward and practical, when he put it that way. Especially when he made that point about them both being adults. But even so, it still didn't sit right with her. It couldn't, because now she knew he truly bought what she'd made him believe. He truly thought she wanted something else.

She was safe from him ever thinking she wanted him.

And she didn't want that unravelling.

Not while the image of the kind of woman he went for danced in her head.

So finally, she said, "I don't want to be riled. And definitely not for a long amount of time." And he seemed to get it. Even if he got it while highly amused.

"All right. So what do you need to do to cool off? Take a cold shower?"

"Yeah, I'm not sure that cold showers are really a thing."

"So maybe we should watch something really unsexy."

"If we watch something really unsexy my mind will drift."

"And what exactly is it going to be drifting to?"

"I'm not going to keep saying, Alfie."

She snapped the words out, fully exasperated now.

Especially since she had almost gathered herself back to-gether again. She'd managed to straighten up—or at least not lean so violently to the left. Plus, her face felt quite a bit cooler. There was really no need for him to keep pressing her buttons about it. Though apparently, he had other ideas about that. His mischievous expression told her so—and to such an extent she braced herself.

And sure enough, here it was: "Not even if I like it when you do," he said.

Because apparently, he'd progressed from little shit to full-blown bastard.

"You don't like it. You're just mocking me."

"What would make you think I was mocking you?"

"Your entire face right now, you annoying arse."

"My face isn't doing anything right now."

"You look like you're trying not to laugh while really wanting me to know that you're laughing at me," she said, and could immediately tell she had him there. He had the decency to look a little sheepish about it. He scratched his beard, at least, and looked away. But then he looked back, and oh no, oh no.

His eyes were still gleaming.

Something worse was coming, she thought.

But could never have imagined how right she was about that.

"Well, yeah, all right, I am laughing a bit. But that doesn't mean I'm not into what's going on. That I'm feeling nothing. I want to be aboveboard and by the book; I'm not suddenly immune to hot kissing and really turned-on women. In fact, really turned-on women are kind of my kink. It's why I can only get into porn that really convinces me she's having a fucking whale of a time," he said, and honestly she didn't know where to begin:

With the fact that he'd said he was feeling it, too.

Or with that kink he'd just thrown in there, like a goddamn grenade.

Truly, it just about knocked her off her feet—never mind that sliding-sideways business. She had to steady herself on the banister beside her. And even after she'd calmed down, she didn't really return to anything like normality. Because now that one concept was going round and round in her head.

"Yes, but did you have to tell me that?"

"I'm trying not to, but it just keeps coming out of me."

"Well, put it back again before I absolutely lose my mind," she insisted.

"There's no need to lose it. I mean, there's a simple solution to all this."

"If there is I have to wonder why you didn't tell me it five minutes ago."

"Because it felt bad to. But now we've broken the *what I masturbate to* ice, it doesn't quite feel the same way. In fact, I honestly think you're thinking the same thing but feel embarrassed about it. So I'm just gonna tell you—you should feel free to go right ahead and take care of yourself," he said.

And looked pleased with himself about it, too.

Even though he definitely meant that she should masturbate.

He was 100 percent absolutely saying that she should masturbate.

Worse, in fact: he meant that she should masturbate while he was, at the very most, just a single wall away from her. Because he was supposed to come up to her flat now and pretend to be doing sex stuff. So how was this going to fucking work? "Alfie, there is absolutely no way I can do that. You're going to be with me for the next however long it takes for you to screw someone."

"So all night then. And maybe some of tomorrow, too."

*Fucking show-off,* her brain yelled at him.

But all she could actually manage was putting her face in her hands.

"Oh my *god*, you can't possibly need all that time."

"You've got that dossier on me, love. You know full well I do."

"Yeah, but you could make an exception in this case."

"What?" he chuffed, quite clearly outraged. "So the papers can tell me tomorrow that I couldn't go the distance with you? Or worse—imagine that I couldn't get it up? I'm not having that. I'll endure a million years of sweltering away in a tiny flat with you before I'll let anything of the kind happen. No, this is what we have to do."

*Let them think whatever they like,* she wanted to tell him then.

Only he'd said something else in that diabolical point he'd just made.

Something that didn't just send her mind spinning. It sent electricity up her spine. She almost swooned because of it. And so of course she just had to say something about the whole business, even if she couldn't do anything but gasp the words breathlessly. "*We*? So *you're* going to do it, *too*?"

"Well, I was considering it, yeah."

"But you're not even in a state."

"You say that like I didn't just tell you what cranks my motor. Right before we extensively talked about the kind of stuff that cranks my motor. While you're massively looking like all the things that crank my motor."

She saw his gaze flicker over her face as he said it.

And then for just a second, just the barest moment, said gaze went down.

It moved over other things in a way she understood perfectly— before he seemed to get a handle on his manners again. Or at least, the manners *he* thought he should have. Right now, she couldn't have cared less if he had suddenly decided to have no manners at all. *Go on and search all over me for signs of arousal*, she thought at him. Even though she still didn't know where they stood right now.

"Yeah, but there's cranking your motor a bit, and needing to get off."

"And which one of those two things do you think I am?"

"The one where you look calm and relaxed."

He did, too. Even when she factored in that look he'd given her, he did. In fact, the only sign of that *motor cranking* thing he'd said was his flushed face. The rest of him was as tidy and composed as a man about to step onto some red carpet.

His suit was crisp; his hair looked completely unruffled.

And his voice, when he spoke, didn't so much as waver.

"Only reason I do is I'm good at keeping a lid on that sort of thing."

"It would show in other ways, though. Very noticeable ways."

"Not if you wear five pairs of underpants."

"And by *that sort of thing* I'm assuming you mean—"

"That my hard cock can't really be contained by just one."

This time, it was her who looked down. Though in her defense, he had just basically said he had an erection. And not even a reasonably sized erection, either. No, apparently, he had an erection so huge it had to be leashed, like an enormous and really excited dog. All of which she kind of had some idea about, considering what several kiss-and-tells had said with regard to his whole situation.

But still.

It was something else entirely to have it spelled out.

And especially in the casual way he'd just done it.

She couldn't even tell him off for bragging.

He didn't seem to register that it was a big deal.

He was just being honest, and practical, and oh god, the way that made everything so much worse. "Did you really have to put it like that?" she moaned, but honestly she should have known not to.

Now he looked even more devilish than he had before. Like he hadn't really understood he could push her buttons before. But as it was at this point clear that he could, all he wanted to do was jam his fist down on them. "Honestly, that was the tame version. I was going to tell you that I'm just aching for a good, long fuck. But then I thought maybe you'd think I meant that I want to fuck you really badly, and so changed my mind at the last second," he said.

And boy was that maddening for so many reasons.

*Both making me want it and denying it to me at the same time,* she thought.

Then she kind of hated him just a little bit for it. Especially when it was already so clear to her. "I'm never going to leap to the idea of you wanting to fuck me, you giant dillhole—any more than you think I want anyone other than Steve Rogers. I mean, you typically date the opposite of me in every way, and even if you didn't I'd be hard-pressed to imagine you with anyone other than a German supermodel whose idea of conversation is you grunting when she asks you her yearly question. And so now I've got to hold that notion in my head, while also somehow reckoning with the fact that you said *aching* and *good* and *fuck*. So thanks for that. It's really helping me out," she burst out.

But he didn't even have the decency to be remorseful.

"I should say it is. Considering my goal is to get you to do yourself."

"Even though that's absolutely silly as a goal to have."

"No sillier than standing there, all heated and trembly and probably slick between your legs but refusing to go see to it because you're afraid I might notice you're doing a totally normal, basic thing that means absolutely nothing."

"It does mean something, though."

"Oh? And what might that something be?"

He raised an eyebrow on the end of that. Then waited for an answer he had to know she couldn't give. She couldn't say it was more than what he was describing. That it was a whole sticky, complicated thing to her. Because what would he think then? *That you're absolutely wild for him*, her mind supplied. And really, that only left her with one choice.

One absolutely bonkers, ridiculous choice.

She gave in. She started up the stairs.

Even though he immediately yelled after her.

"Attagirl," he said. "You know it makes sense."

And it was infuriating, it was. But he was right. It did. It was a physical thing that she could fix. A simple matter that she could resolve. No thoughts about it, no feelings, no more arguing with him until it sent her round the twist. Just her leaning against her bathroom wall with a hand between her legs.

And if she thought about him out there, doing the same thing, well, that was all right wasn't it? It was just more of that boiling-it-all-down-to-basics stuff—sensations and chemical reactions and X leading to Y. It wasn't that she desperately wanted him in particular. It was just that she wanted *something*.

In the exact same way he did.

Because he did want a part of this.

She was sure he did.

Until she exited the bathroom, still flushed and half-lust fucked, feeling more relaxed but somewhat ashamed at the same time, and found him in her kitchen, looking cool as a summer breeze, eating her fucking food. "I made myself a sandwich," he had the absolute temerity to say.

Like that was all he'd been doing this whole time.

Like it hadn't really affected him that much at all.

Then all she could do was smile.

While trying not to die.

**Gossip Queen Insta Reels Transcript, April 5, 2022**

So I'm just going to very quickly clear the air and by clear the air I mean suck it, you doubters and haters, he stayed over at hers ALL NIGHT and you know how I know this? I camped out on the other side of the street. Check out my sweet tent, losers!

# Twenty-One
## Thank God for Soundproofing

$S$he decided that the best course of action was just to tell him that they should cool off now. That they had done enough to convince the world this was a real thing—if the tabloids and comments on the latest post from Gossip Queen on Instagram were anything to go by. So maybe they could just skip the doorstep kisses and such. And just possibly occasionally look like they were hanging out now. At very tame and easy-to-cope-with venues where nothing even needed to happen to make them look convincing.

Like, say, at a Beyoncé concert that Daisy had somehow managed to get tickets to. *So you can give Mabel a reason to stick with your grumpy arse*, the note read.

And Mabel seized on it immediately. Because what better activity to do than be at a concert together? Concerts were loud, and they were bright, and they surrounded you on all sides with seething people. There was nothing less sexy and intimate than that. Nobody could possibly expect them to start snogging under those circumstances.

Then they got there, and she very quickly grasped:

The tickets weren't for some mosh pit where the only possibly sexy thing that could happen was getting a bit of an icon's sweat on you. No, they were for some sort of VIP box, which seemed to be so far away from the crowds you could barely even tell they were there. She had to keep going to the glass and looking down, just to make sure they really were. And that was the least of her problems.

Because the box itself looked like a fucking bedroom.

The walls were made out of what appeared to be red silk; the lighting was so dim she could barely see her hand in front of her face. And there was an actual couch that seemed closer to a bed than something you perched on to watch a concert. She sat down and immediately sank so far back she didn't even have to look up to see the ceiling. Then of course he just sat right next to her.

So now they were practically lying down.

In what could only be described as darkness.

While Beyoncé crooned about doing it all night.

It was abominable. She almost wanted to cry. *I think this might be starting to destroy me*, she thought of saying to him. But the problem was: she didn't know what was doing the destroying. She had no idea why this was coming over her in such intense waves. It never had before—not even with people who were her exact type, whom she was actually dating, and who absolutely found her attractive.

It was just happening, no matter what she did to curb it.

And she knew this because when he turned to look at her, there it was.

It just rose up through her body, like some kind of inescapable tsunami.

Even though he wasn't doing anything. He was just gazing at her and gazing at her in this weird heavy-lidded way, and things seemed very hot and very tense suddenly, and then somehow, against all her better judgment and every bit of sense in her head, she found herself actually leaning toward him. Like you did when you wanted to kiss someone. Even though that couldn't possibly be the case. There was no reason on earth for this to happen. No paps waiting to snap them, no stans or haters wanting to watch this little play they were trying to put on.

It was just them.

And this.

And one inescapable fact: she wanted to. Somehow, he made her want to, and he did it so hard and so strongly she couldn't seem to fight it. All she could think about was getting that mouth on hers again, no matter what the cost would be. And she knew the cost was going to be sky high. She could already see his eyes widening; he seemed to tense all over.

Like he couldn't believe she was really doing what it looked like.

But that was fine because she couldn't believe it, either. *It's like you've warped my brain with your ludicrously hot kissing*, she wanted to yell at him. And the only thing that stopped her was him, leaning right back. Just a little, but he definitely did it. She felt the air stir between them, and the light in his eyes shifted. Now it wasn't just surprise. It was something else.

Something soft and foggy, like before. Like at her door.

And when she made contact, he didn't pull away. Quite the contrary—he made a sound, all long and low. The way people did when they sank into a warm bath, she thought.

Which seemed wild, it really did.

But not as wild as the hand he immediately slid over the nape of her neck.

Tenderly, it seemed to her. However, it also felt firm—as if he wanted to hold her there. As if he wanted to make sure there was even more contact than she was giving, and for a good amount of time. Though if she was being honest, she could understand that. After all, she didn't think he'd lied about liking horny women.

And she couldn't deny that she was very horny indeed.

Somehow, she had pushed herself right up against him. Her breasts were tight to his chest, and one of her thighs was almost over his. Then he shifted, and *almost* suddenly became *absolutely*. Now they were sitting with their legs all tangled together to the point where the bits in between were getting very close. In fact, a couple of times she was sure she felt something.

Something thick, and hard.

Like he really was affected this time.

And what was she supposed to do after that?

She couldn't put the brakes on. Her body immediately forgot what brakes even were. All it wanted to do was squirm and wriggle and kiss in an increasingly lewd way, until finally she was just doing it in the hottest, wettest sort of manner she knew. But it was fine, it was good.

Because he didn't seem to mind in the slightest.

She heard him groan again, and this one wasn't open to interpretation. It wasn't *Okay that was quite nice but now I'm going to make a sandwich* levels of whatever. It was thick and deep and gravelly in a way that reverberated through her. She actually felt it pulse between her legs—and that was before he seemed to decide that he had had enough of her pushing him back into the couch.

And pushed back.

Oh god, he pushed back.

He urged himself against her until she was almost sprawled over the arm, mouth working over hers so quick and hard and greedy it made her gasp. *Fuck, that's too much*, her mind threw out. But the rest of her didn't think so. No, the rest of her seemed to be begging for more. She arched up into him; one of her hands had gripped the back of his jacket. If she held on any tighter she was likely to rip it.

And that was before she felt where his hand was.

Because this time, it didn't just graze her ass.

It touched her there.

Fully touched her in a way he didn't seem to want to do.

But couldn't seem to help doing, all the same.

And oh, that was good. It was great. It might even have been the hottest thing she'd ever experienced. She didn't ever want it to stop—just that feeling of someone wanting to squeeze her there that much, even if it was all just an extreme kink for complete horniness that was making them.

But it had to stop.

Considering the concert was somehow now, inexplicably, over.

*How fucking long were we making out*, her mind marveled. But her body already knew the answer—way, way too long. Far too long. Just an absolutely ridiculous amount of length. Because god, every single part of her was now spaghetti. She couldn't even stand up under own power. She had to use the couch to get into something like an upright position, and even then she did an absolutely terrible job of it. She almost just slumped right back down again, like she was drunk. He had to get her by the waist and keep her on her feet.

Which of course only made things worse.

Now she was a thrumming aroused mess, with a hot man's arm around her. And okay, yeah, it wasn't anywhere near as bad as it been a second ago. He wasn't groping her arse. But by this point everything felt so oversensitized and sort of primed that even that felt like being fucking fondled.

And it made her react accordingly.

A little startled breath left her lips; she went weak in the knees all over again. Ten seconds more of this and he was going to have to carry her, it felt like, and she was only spared by the slap of the night air and the sense of where they were headed. *Soon we will be in the car,* she told herself, *and then after that a short journey and not even a doorstep kiss to endure and I can go do myself until I die.*

But then they got there, and two horrifying problems immediately dawned on her. Like Ripley in *Aliens* realizing the terrible thing is in the bloody ceiling. One: absolutely nobody on earth ever got home fast from a concert thrown by the most famous woman on Earth. And two: especially not when their car suddenly won't start.

"Oh noooooooooooooo," she moaned, the second their driver, Phil, sweatily confirmed. "I'm so sorry, Mr. Harding," he babbled. As if Alfie were ever going to be mad about something like this. It was just one of those things. An unfortunate accident. A twist of fate. An absolute kick in her fucking vagina.

That there was no real way to rectify. Because Phil said he knew a bloke who knew a bloke who could find them a mechanic. But five minutes after he disappeared in the direction of the arena, they got a text from him: just waiting for him might be an hour.

And there was no way to get a lift any other way. Nobody was going to be able to get through thousands of people trying to leave.

So that just left one option:

Being trapped in the same situation she'd been in with him the other day, only in a much smaller space, after a far more heated encounter, with even higher stakes than there'd been before. Because the issue was: now she knew full well how easy it was to make a fool of herself. But for some reason, her body didn't seem to care.

Like it knew something she didn't.

And that was all just too high risk for her.

"Maybe we could walk home," she found herself suggesting.

And for just a second it really looked like Alfie was considering it. Like he didn't want to have to do this, either, and was desperate enough to entertain a twenty-mile hike in the dark with a woman in heels and a dress made of spun sugar. Not to mention about a hundred of his fans and her cheer squad following them all the way.

But then he seemed to process that and resigned himself to their fate.

"It'll be all right," he said.

Then helped her get in.

And got in himself.

And sealed them shut in a too-dark and completely sound-proof bubble.

"I've got a torch," he said, though god she wished he hadn't. Now she had to either say *No, don't put it on*, and explain why, or *Yes, go ahead* and endure him actually seeing her in this state.

Because it *did* feel like a state.

She couldn't seem to stop squirming, or biting her lip, or breathing hard. And of course every time she did, that ridiculous underwear she had on just seemed to slide over everything she least wanted it to slide against. It felt like she was being caressed every five seconds by the silkiest hands in the world.

All of which was definitely making everything worse.

She almost wanted to put her hands or arms over her chest just in case the situation going on there was remotely visible. But then how would that look if she did? Probably like she was desperately trying to hide something, instead of just being a normal person doing normal things.

*You're fine, you're fine, you seem fine,* she tried to tell herself.

About twenty seconds before Alfie suddenly gruffed out:

"If you want, I can get out of the car so you can do something about this."

As if all he wanted was a replay of the whole thing in the hall.

Even though this time, there was absolutely no way she could let him get it.

She was going to be the one with the sandwich at the end, here, even if she had to lie even harder than she had the first time he'd clocked her losing it. "I have no idea what you're talking about. I am totally okay," she said.

Convincingly, too, it seemed to her.

Not that it mattered in the slightest.

"Mabel, you look like you're about to die of terminal horniness."

"How would you know? You can't even see me. It's pitch-black in here."

"Not sure it being pitch-black really matters at this point. In fact, I reckon we could be down a fucking coal mine at the end of time and I'd be able to clock this, love. You're practically glowing. It's like being opposite a radioactive furnace."

She tried not to wince over that.

Mostly so she could sound confident when she responded.

"Oh, don't exaggerate. I'm barely warm," she said as breezily as possible.

But he wasn't having it. Of course he wasn't. "If you were barely warm you would have wrapped yourself in your coat by now. Yet somehow you haven't."

"Well, maybe it was just too hot in the arena. And too hot in here."

"Possibly. But then that wouldn't explain why your nipples look that fucking obscene, would it? So could be you want to pretend it's freezing if you would prefer to have that particular base covered. And I'm guessing you would, judging by the way you keep trying to cover them without actually making any contact whatsoever."

"Jesus Christ, do you have eyes made out of night vision goggles?"

"Mabel, I'm pretty much a mole, as you well know. Not to mention completely against copping a look from unsuspecting women. You're just so turned on that your diamond-hard nipples are capable of leaping directly into my eyes."

She couldn't argue with that. Mostly because arguing was apparently really difficult when you were this embarrassed and turned on and also kind of wanting to laugh at some bastard's funny turn of phrase. But also, just because it was impossible to, when that same bastard had you bang to rights.

So now she had to come up with something like an excuse.

"Well, I told you what your kissing does to me," she tried.

And it worked about as well as she imagined it would.

"But you started it this time," he said, plainly outraged at her nerve. His voice even went high on the end. She couldn't give in, however. She was already ten goals behind in the game of not giving away that you really want to fuck your friend way more than he would ever want to fuck you.

"Only because you looked at me."

"Oh, that's a weak fucking excuse."

"I know it is. But the other reason is ridiculous, so I'm going with it."

"You're bloody not. You tell me right now why you went for me, or else."

*He's got nothing, call his bluff,* her brain suggested.

And foolishly, she listened.

"Or else *what?*" she sneered at him.

Then got pretty much what she deserved for poking the bear.

"I'll kiss you again."

"Alfie, you wouldn't."

"You better believe I would. And I'll make it twice as dirty, too."

"I refuse to accept there even is such a thing. People would combust."

"So you'd better explain then, hadn't you. And quick, the clock is on."

She heard him actually tap his watch. Like a crime boss, giving her sixty seconds to consider his diabolical deal. Though the weirdest part was: it really did work. She didn't even make it to ten before she cracked like an egg. "Fine. I did it because I wanted to feel that way again," she blurted out.

Then braced herself for the no doubt terrible repercussions of admitting this.

And got complete bemusement instead:

"But you seem to *hate* feeling this way," he said.

Even though he had to understand, really. He had to know that she wasn't just disgusted by him, or something like that. *Surely you know*, she thought, but as the silenced deepened, she realized. He truly didn't. He needed her to actually explain.

"Yeah, but not because it's horrible, Alfie."

"Well, if it's not horrible, then why exactly?"

"It's just embarrassing to me. To be all overwhelmed like this."

More silence, then. And this time it was nerve-racking enough that she tried to glance at him, through the darkness. Just to catch a glimpse of his expression, maybe, so she could take a guess as to what response he was cooking up. But all she could make out was the pale curve of his turned-away face, the gleam of his cuff links, a hint of his fist where it lay on what could have been his thigh.

So she had to wait for what felt like an agonizingly long time.

Before he finally, finally spoke.

"You've got nothing to feel embarrassed about, love. I want you to enjoy yourself," he said. Then just in case that wasn't wild enough, he added: "In fact, if I'm being honest, I might be slightly encouraging that state of affairs."

And when he did she thought two things:

That it was completely unhinged of him to do this.

But that it also explained a lot of things.

"So *that's* why you groped my arse."

"Oh yeah. Definitely why. No question about that."

"Well, good job. Now I'm dying of being turned on."

"Then you had better do something about it, hadn't you. Because I'm telling you now for nothing, I'm not rolling you into the Thames after you've died. I like you too much to do anything but get you a proper funeral, even if it means being sentenced to thirty years in Broadmoor for murdering you with my incredible snogging technique."

She went to scoff at that last bit. Only no sound came out when she tried.

And she knew why, too.

Because he was starting to convince her.

Somehow, he was starting to convince her, *again*. Even after all the ways it had been embarrassing to be so beside herself while he seemingly felt so little, even after that fucking *sandwich*—it was still happening. In fact, it took her a full thirty seconds to refuse. "It was bad enough in the bathroom. There's no way I can while you're right there," she said.

And even then, she could feel herself listening to him.

"I'll get out of the car, then. Go for a walk in the car park," he said, and still she hesitated. Before seeing sense and trying to shut him down.

"Yeah, and what are you going to say when people ask you what the fuck you're doing? Well, officer, my fake girlfriend really needed a wank, so I politely offered to go for a stroll? Or worse—people out there notice it's Alfie fucking Harding wandering around after a Beyoncé concert, and decide to mob, mug, or molest him. Or possibly all three. At the same time. Just because I was horny."

"So I'll look away. Like really away."

"No amount of looking away is going to spare you this."

"Yeah, but if it's only me you're worried about sparing there isn't a problem."

She shot a look at him for that. But even though she knew he could feel her eyes on him, he didn't turn to face her. He kept on staring out the window in a way that pretty much confirmed that he was saying what she thought he was. That he was telling her he wanted to hear, and wanted to see.

Even though it was too wild for her to actually swallow.

It made her heart pound harder than it already was.

And all she could manage to gasp out was:

"You don't mean that. Alfie, say you don't mean that."

But incredibly, he did not seem to want to oblige.

He actually let out a little snort of derision. Like she was being ridiculous.

"I want to. But you know how I feel about lying," he said.

And now she found herself in the weird position of kind of needing him to.

"Well, couldn't you try this once, for me."

"All right. Yes, please protect me from the sights and sounds of a woman greedily doing herself three feet away from me. That seems abominable and would definitely not almost make me come in my pants like a fucking teenager."

"Now you're just *trying* to make it sound unconvincing."

"I'm really not. It's just that fucking ridiculous."

"Well, you didn't seem that bothered last time I did myself."

"Yeah, aside from frantically wanking, I was a picture of cool."

This time she didn't just shoot a look at him.

She about fell out of her seat.

Though to be fair, it was hard to stay in said seat when your brain was suddenly screaming at you. *OH MY FUCKING GOD I TOLD YOU HE WAS INTO THIS*, it bellowed. Even though it was a little fucking liar. It hadn't said anything of the sort. In fact, all it had said since the whole thing had happened was *Well, lady, you really embarrassed yourself there*. So as far as she was concerned, her brain could fuck right off while she figured out exactly what was going on here.

"So you actually did it. You jerked off," she said.

Then waited, with bated breath, for him to say no.

And got nothing but him being withering with her.

"Of course I fucking did. I was beside myself."

"You say that like you think I should just know that."

"Because you should. I made it pretty fucking clear."

"Mate, you were not fucking clear. In fact, you're the most incredible hider of sexual arousal I've ever seen. It's like nothing at all is happening to you. Or you can just turn it off at the drop of a hat. You probably shag women, they blink, and you're fully dressed at the door waiting to escort them to a funeral."

"Yeah, and that's true. However, I think you'll find I did also *tell* you I felt that way," he said, and okay, yeah, he had mentioned something to that effect. But what was she supposed to make of that when actions didn't match up with words?

There was only one explanation she could come up with:

"I thought you were just mostly lying."

"What the fuck would I lie for?"

"To make me feel better about doing it."

"If that's what you need to feel better you're going to feel fucking fantastic when I describe how desperate I am to get off right now. Honestly never been this hard in my fucking *life*. My cock is aching, actually aching—I think it might burst if I don't do something about it soon. And it wouldn't take much, either. Just lick my hand and rub over it once, while thinking about the woman three feet away from me, with her hand in her knickers. Like I did then, back at your flat, right before I came all over myself."

*Hard, aching, lick*, she thought. *He said* hard, *and* aching, *and* lick.

And then couldn't seem to think about anything else. As if her mind had gotten stuck in some kind of feedback loop, and said feedback loop was too exciting to bear. She almost couldn't speak because of it, and when she finally did, she did not sound normal. "Did you really think about me doing that?" she asked, and heard her own voice going up and down like a boat on choppy waters.

It was okay, though. He sounded just as bad as her.

Only his version of it was hoarse.

Like he'd swallowed a bunch of extremely horny sandpaper.

"If you hate that, the answer is I swear I'll never do it again."

"I don't hate it, Alfie. In fact, maybe you could tell me more about it."

"Love, I'll tell you anything you like, if it'll get you where you need to be."

"Just what's true. Say true things to me only," she said, which sounded mad as she blurted it out, she knew. But he didn't say anything about it. As if he understood now. He could see just how skeptical she was about all this.

And exactly how hard he needed to go to convince her it was true.

Which was apparently even harder than he'd gone before. "So I should tell you how slick my cock feels right now?" he asked, all low and soft and matter-of-fact. For maximum impact, she suspected. And maximum impact was definitely what it had. She felt it go right through her, like someone had licked the length of her spine. And though she wanted to be calm in response, she couldn't be.

Telling her how hard he was had been too much, on its own.

Saying something this lewd about sent her over the edge.

"Oh my god. Oh my god, yes. You should say things like that," she burst out.

But he didn't seem to mind at all.

He just carried right on being the filthiest fucker she had ever known.

"Feels like I've already come, it's that much of a fucking mess," he said, and after she'd finished feeling the words run right over her clit, she managed to respond with the incredulity he fully deserved.

"Jesus Christ, that's so far gone. How are you this far gone, over *nothing*?"

"Probably because I don't consider everything you just did nothing. You licked into my fucking mouth, love. All hot and quick and greedy, too, just like I like it. And then you rubbed your body up against mine, and got hold of my jacket, and made hot little noises like you were fucking loving it. You were *loving* me doing it hot and hard back at you, as if nothing else in the fucking world mattered."

"It doesn't when things feel that good," she said.

But she didn't realize how true that was, until he replied.

"So I should probably go on, then," he said.

And all she could think was: *Yes.*

*Yes, make me feel more of whatever this is.*

*Make that lightning happen along the length of my spine.*

*Make me squirm and sigh and press my thighs against this ache.*

Though the actual words came out a little more ungainly than that.

"Uh-huh. Go on. Go on. Say more," she gasped. And he did. He *did.*

"All right. I'll tell you what else got me this fucked up."

"Please do. In as much great and vivid detail as you like."

"It was how you looked when we got in the car. Like a horny little slut, desperate to come. Flushed, ripe, those tight nipples pushing against the material of that maddeningly flimsy dress. Lips all slick and flushed and wet, like you were just waiting for something to ease between them. A finger maybe, when someone wants you to get it all nice and slippery before they slide it into your cunt. Or maybe more than that, maybe you want more, do you want more, love?" he asked.

Like it was just that easy to talk dirty to someone.

And to make you want to talk dirty back at them.

Because somehow, she didn't even hesitate.

"Yes. Yes, if you mean a cock, yes."

"I do," he said. "Now, do you want to hear the rest?"

"Honestly, I want to hear whatever you would like to say."

"Then I'll tell you I'd go slow, so slow and easy until you're eager for it, until you're begging for it, until you want me in your mouth so much you'll just take all of it, without even thinking twice," he murmured, and all she could think about when he did was what he'd said in the hall about what he had in his trousers. And what she'd felt on that couch. Then imagine the long, slow slide of it, past her lips.

"Ohhh fucking hell, Alfie."

"Too much?"

"Yes. No. I don't know."

"Gonna need a definitive answer before I continue."

"So then you'd just stop right now if I said. Even though it feels like this."

*Like everything is just one long, sweet ache*, she thought. *Like all that exists is the thrum of your pulse between your legs, and the greed for whatever comes next, and his low voice coming out of the darkness at you, telling you all the things you never knew could make you feel this way.*

*And yet they do, all the same.*

"It could feel like I was about to come in your cunt and I would," he said.

And somehow it was this that made her break. Just that idea of him being so willing to never go beyond what she wanted, and with words that made her want to go further than she ever thought she could. Because she couldn't stop herself now. She had to put a hand between her legs, she had to.

Even if he knew exactly what she was doing, the moment she did.

"Oh, Christ you're doing it, aren't you," he groaned. And what was she supposed to do, deny it? There was no way to. The sound of her sliding her dress up was loud enough, on its own. Then she stroked over herself, and oh god, somehow that rang out even louder.

It was all she could hear.

And probably all he could, too.

Though he didn't seem to mind.

When she apologized, his reply was this:

"Why be sorry? You know I want you to."

And oh holy fuck, the sweet sensation that sent through her. It made her beg before she even knew she was willing to.

"God yeah, tell me that. Tell me you do."

"I will, if you tell me exactly what you're doing."

"I'm rubbing myself through my underwear."

"And that feels good?"

"It feels slick."

"*Fuck*, you filthy little thing," he burst out.

At which point, she knew she should have felt embarrassed. This was definitely where that emotion was supposed to go. But here was the thing: nothing was happening.

It couldn't happen when she could hear what he was doing, too.

He was breathing too hard, and that was definitely the sound of a hand on expensive material, and then after thirty seconds of this torture chamber of frantic, fumbling noises he came out with this: "Oh fuck, I gotta do something, too. You all right if I do something, too? Because I'm fucking losing it here, listening to you touching yourself in ways I can pretty much make out without even looking."

And though all she did was groan helplessly in reply, and nod in a way he probably couldn't see, she knew it was enough. She heard him fighting with his belt, and then with his zipper, and finally she got what she wanted the most:

The slide of his hand over his slick cock.

Slowly, she thought, slowly.

Though that didn't seem to last long.

Most likely because she wasn't holding back anymore, and he fucking knew it. "You're fingering your cunt now, aren't you," he moaned, like he just couldn't help it at this point. He had to let out his filthiest possible thoughts. But that was fine by her. Because a) he was absolutely right.

And b) the words went through her like fucking lightning.

She heard him say *cunt* and all she could do was go harder.

To sink right into that heated wetness, over and over.

Which of course, in turn, made him so much worse.

It made him groan and fill the car with the slickest sounds.

And urge her on in ways that made her go round the bend.

"That's it, baby," he said. "That's it, get yourself off."

So she did. She did. She worked herself until she was right there, right on the edge, back and forth in that greedy, grasping little hole, with her thumb on her oh-so-swollen clit. Barely brushing it, because even that felt like too much. Wanting to do more, but waiting, waiting, waiting. And she knew exactly what she was waiting for.

For him to win the game of who wanted it more.

Though honestly, she didn't expect him to actually do it.

In her head, he was still the one who stood apart from all this. Like it was all just an average Saturday night to him. He didn't care, he wasn't bothered, it didn't matter. He would do it all again tomorrow, with some woman she could never hope to be. And then just as she thought this, just as she felt it, it was there. The sound of him calling out her name into the stifling air.

"Mabel," he groaned. "Oh god, Mabel, I'm coming, I'm coming."

And after that what could she do, but follow him down?

I was at the Beyoncé concert last night

And I can tell you all that something weird is going on with those two. I don't know how this fits with him actually hating her, but I didn't even see them in that VIP box and I climbed up as far as the scaffolding would let me. Plus, I'm sure that it was her who had me booted by security, I didn't even do anything wrong.

It doesn't matter though because then when I was outside in the parking lot i saw them arguing. They were both red faced and looked like they could hardly stand up so I bet they'd been fighting a lot before too. And then they got in the car and they didn't even go anywhere? I reckon that she was being awkward wanting to go somewhere else or something, what do you all think?

I didn't get to see anything else because her fans were there (how does she have fans, she doesn't even do anything, she's not even a lifestyle guru I don't know where that came from) and they shouted at me to leave her alone. And called me fatphobic! Me! Everybody knows I have LOADS of fat friends, so how can I be fatphobic? My boyfriend defended me though, he thinks she's rotten too, he says he's lost all respect for Alfie.

I told him our theory that she's brainwashing him and he thinks we're onto something. KIND REPLIES ONLY PLEASE I AM JUST SHARING INFORMATION.

## Twenty-Two

### And Now the Sequel to
### Only One Back Seat of a Car

$\mathcal{S}$he didn't know what to say to Alfie on the drive to his place.

Partly because she had never done anything as wild as that in her whole life.

But mostly because the drive home involved being in the back of Daisy's car.

So really, what could they do? There was no way to have an intense, probably awkward conversation about the fact that they'd just wanked while not once looking at each other, with Daisy right there in the driver's seat. Though if she was being honest, there didn't feel like there was much of a way to have said conversation even when Daisy finally and blessedly dropped them off.

Instead, they just watched her drive away in silence.

Probably in part because he was now realizing, like her, that they had let Daisy leave them both here at three in the morning, with no way to go anywhere else. And yeah, okay, even if they'd thought about it for five seconds they would have been forced to allow it to play out. There wasn't a good explanation they could have offered for why he needed to be left here and she needed to be driven home.

But still.

It felt bad.

It felt real bad.

And doubly so after he suddenly said, into the darkness left by Daisy's retreating car: "You know I've only got the one bed, right." Because of course he did, of course. His house was still pretty much the place that furniture forgot. He didn't even have a couch—so that was out as something to sleep on. *I'm gonna have to try to get some shut-eye in his fucking bath*, she thought.

Though truth be told, she wasn't even sure if he had a bath to do it in. All she'd seen when she'd visited the loo was a shower as big as her entire bedroom. And the floor of it had been completely flat, too, so it wasn't like it doubled up. Which really only left her with one choice.

That he was absolutely not happy with.

"You can't seriously think I'm gonna let you take the floor," he said the second he clocked her trying to gather up whatever she could to make a nest. Though honestly, she didn't know what else he thought was going to happen. The bed she'd just pinched these pillows from wasn't even enormous the way she'd hoped.

It was inexplicably the size of a postage stamp.

Like minimalism also meant you were not allowed more than six inches of space to lie down in. So now she had to make things real clear. "Well, I can't sleep with you in that after the whole business in the car," she said, then pointed at his practically child-sized cot.

Much to his very obvious irritation.

His eyes pretty much blazed, briefly.

Before he shook his head in this oddly weary manner and looked away. "I wasn't suggesting you do. But good to know how you feel about what we just did."

"Hang on a minute. I didn't say how I felt about it."

"You said *whole business* like people say *shitshow*."

"Well, that's not what I meant. I just . . . it was . . ."

Come on, she urged herself. Find your words.

But she couldn't. She had to just hope he got it.

And thankfully, when he looked back at her, he appeared to have.

He wasn't annoyed or weary anymore. He was just resigned, it seemed.

"Yeah, I know," he said. "It's all right. I know it was a lot."

So now she was free to lose it just a little bit.

Which she did. Her face blazed so red she had to briefly cover it with one of the pillows she was holding. And she talked into said pillow, too, when she could finally speak. "Oh *god*, it was so much. I can't believe I said those things," she said, then dropped it just in time to see him looking—thankfully—just as embarrassed as she was.

"I wouldn't worry. Your things have nothing on my things."

"Even though I told you about my—"

"*Christ*, don't repeat any of it." His voice went high on the word *Christ*. And his eyes went to the ceiling, like he was searching for that very dude to come save him. Because, it seemed, it was as she had suspected—he was just as disturbed by the whole thing as she was, despite his protests to the contrary. A fact that he then confirmed. "And especially if we want to avoid accidentally talking me into doing anything like that ever again. Which judging by your reaction right now, I'm guessing is definitely your preference."

*No*, her body yelled.

But her body was being a dipshit.

It was just thinking of how good it had felt.

And not about whether it was advisable to fuck a man who was almost certainly only doing all this because he had a massive kink for horny women. After all, he definitely didn't seem keen on doing it again, now that the horniness had briefly abated. He seemed as normal as he had on the couch when she'd come out of the bathroom. Which meant that she had to be normal, too.

Completely normal and unmoved by all this.

"One hundred percent it is," she said.

And he nodded, firmly, in response.

"Right. Good. Same here."

"So then we're sorted."

"Totally we are."

They stared at each other.

Weirdly, it seemed to her.

And when the staring broke, it wasn't for a good reason.

"Unless you count the fact that we haven't settled the sleeping arrangements," he burst out. Like he'd been holding it in to try to maintain some semblance of normalcy. But couldn't in the face of the one particular problem they hadn't yet dealt with. "Which is still not going to be you out there on the fucking floor, no matter how many pillows you pinch. It's gonna be me, and that's the end of it."

*Ah*, she thought. *So that's what he'd been trying to argue for.* Which made a lot more sense in a way she should have immediately guessed, considering how fraught everything now was. But a lot less in a way he clearly hadn't. "Okay, but why? I'm far better equipped to do it than you are," she pointed out.

Only to have him look at her like she was bananas.

"How the fuck do you figure that one?"

"Well, for starters, I don't have a fucked back."

He held up his hands. "Hang about, *fucked* is just a little bit strong there."

"Okay. Then how about the fact that I've got more natural padding."

"Mate, you're not gonna win this by bragging about how hot your tits and arse are. In fact, if anything that's just going to make me more furious. Because now I said *hot tits* and *arse* to you when we only vowed about ten second ago to never be disgusting about each other ever again."

He shook his head at the end of that little tirade.

As if he couldn't believe what he'd just done.

And to be fair, she kind of felt the same about what he'd said. The words *hot tits* and *arse* were now swirling around inside her head, like a tornado designed to strip her of all good sense. She actually almost asked him if he really felt that way about her body, and only managed to hold on by digging her nails into her palms until the pain made her normal enough to say something reassuring instead.

"That wasn't disgusting. And we hardly vowed," she went with.

To which he shoved out an exasperated noise and looked at the ceiling again.

"Fine, then. It was weird, and we decided. How does that sound?"

"More like the truth. But I'm still not completely happy with it."

"So tell me what you would be happy with."

"Getting some bloody sleep, Alfie."

"Then get in the bed, you awkward little shit."

God, she even liked him calling her an awkward little shit. He said it, and her stomach actually did a weird flip. As if it were the equivalent of complimenting her butt and boobs, when of course it wasn't. It was rude and he was being a big jerk and she was supposed to be annoyed. So she did her best to be.

"No," she said. "I'm taking the floor. And you can't stop me."

"I can. Because I swear to god if you try to I'm just going to lie down on it, too. And I'm going to do it right next to you, as well. To completely invalidate your whole reason for making such an annoying, stubborn, silly choice."

She shook her head at him. "You wouldn't. You're bluffing."

"Yeah. If by bluffing you mean sandwiching myself so tight against your body we have to get a doctor to separate us in the morning." He took a step toward her. And dropped his voice by what felt like about seventy octaves. "Is that what you want, Mabel? You want surgery because you spent all night with my abs glued to your hip?"

"Not your abs. Alfie, say you would never do that with your abs."

"I'd do worse. In the middle of the night, I'll *breathe* in your *ear*."

He leaned in on the last word. Just to really drive it home.

Because he was an arsehole, a really annoying arsehole.

Whom she now had to concede to.

"Okay, you sod. Fine. I will sleep in the bed," she said. But the problem was she couldn't leave it at that. Of course she couldn't—there was no way she'd ever let someone who really would suffer on the floor actually sleep on it. He'd hardly be able to walk tomorrow if she did, so what else was she supposed to do? She had to add: "But you're going to have to come with me."

Even though she knew what kind of response she was going to get.

"Oh yeah," he said. "And how are you gonna make that happen? Magic?"

He was being pretty ridiculous, however. The answer was obvious.

"By threatening you with all the body parts I might glue to you if you don't."

"You bloody bastard. Using my own tactics against me."

"Like you're not proud of me for doing it."

"Honestly I sort of want to shed a tear."

He mimed it when he said it.

And she laughed, she did laugh. She tried to make things light.

Even though it was now fully dawning on her what she had just persuaded him into. She was going to be trapped on a mattress that didn't look fit to hold a hamster, with a man she had barely survived being opposite to inside a car. While wearing even fewer clothes than she had during that whole ordeal.

Considering she could hardly get into bed with her coat on.

A fact that she learned when she actually tried.

Then got a look so withering, she almost died.

"I'll get you something to wear, you great prawn," he said.

And he did, too. He disappeared for what felt like an age into what looked like a walk-in wardrobe, and returned with what could loosely be described as clothes you could wear in bed. But as the clothes were just a shirt of his and a pair of boxer shorts, she wasn't entirely confident that they were going to do the job she needed them to. In fact, she sort of suspected they were going to be much too short and far too tight and probably too thin to boot, considering whom they belonged to.

Though she didn't really appreciate by how much, until she

started putting them on in the bathroom. Because yeah, the shirt did button pretty easily. And okay, the shorts were mysteriously a size her butt could cope with. But neither of those things really mattered when she checked herself in the full-length mirror, before exiting, and discovered that she now looked like picture one in a porn mag spread.

"Fucking hell," she actually gasped out loud.

And it was fully warranted, too.

The shirt material was pretty much transparent. She could actually see the exact shape and size of her tits through it. Someone could have guessed her bra size with one look. And even though it wasn't as short as she'd feared, it didn't really matter. Because it was just a little bit tight around her butt.

So everything she had was pretty clear, anyway—even with the shorts.

In fact, if she was being honest the shorts were kind of making things worse.

They clung, and made everything look round and bouncy. Not to mention rude, the moment she did anything but gingerly walk a few steps. Because she tried—she lifted her arms, to see what it looked like when she did—and oh god oh god.

The shorts pulled real tight against her bits.

As in: *you can make out the shape of everything* tight.

And now she had to go in there, looking like this, with him probably waiting in bed for her like the husband she'd never had. Or probably would never have, considering he was amazing and hilarious and hot and actually made her desperately want to fuck him, instead of whatever she usually felt with men. Which was pretty much nothing. *It must be just what happens when someone is good at kissing and talking dirty*, she told herself. And that made sense, it did.

But it didn't really help her with this.

It just made her remember it all, in technicolor detail.

So now that hot ache was back, a second before she had to step out of the bathroom. And it didn't abate once she was out there. In fact, if anything, it got significantly worse. Because he wasn't in the bed, like she'd thought. No—he was still getting changed. He was tugging a jersey over his head, and slow enough that she got a long look at things she didn't really want to see.

Like his bare back: broad and heavy-boned, with a curve to it that she just had to follow with her eyes. Even though it made her go just a little bit funny. And especially when she took in where that curve ended. It hit the waistband of what looked like the most low-slung sweatpants known to man, and left her with nothing but that juicy ass of his. Just right there, with that worn material barely doing any work to cover him at all.

*One good tug*, she thought.

Then forced herself to look up before things got any worse.

Only to have him turn, and face her, and make it all worse anyway.

Because god, he'd brushed his hair out of the side part. Now it was all thick and curly and soft looking, exactly the way she apparently liked. And he was just standing there, staring at her through the semidarkness, with eyes that seemed just a little bit vulnerable. Like he too knew what they were going to do and wasn't exactly certain that they should do it.

Or able to believe that she thought it was a good idea.

Though it still shocked her when he voiced that very thing.

"Are you sure you want to do this?" he asked. Like she could read his mind now, somehow. And maybe he could read hers, just a little bit. Because god knew, she was having doubts. Lots of them. Starting with how the fuck she was supposed to cope with *that* laid next to her all night.

But of course she couldn't tell him that.

She had to be light, and reassuring, and not like someone who was trying her damnedest not to notice the heavy shape of a cock through a pair of sweatpants. "Absolutely I am," she said. "I mean, it's not like anything is going to happen."

"Right. Because we are rational adults. Who have made the choice to not."

"Exactly. We've said that things went too far. That we just got swept up by good kissing. And the fallout from good kissing. Now we can be sensible and describe exactly what our boundaries are and then easily maintain each one."

"My thoughts exactly. The boundaries are there, and we will abide by them."

"We will. We totally will. I can already feel how much we're going to."

*Lies*, her brain hissed at her.

But she didn't know how right it was, until she was in bed, and he lifted the covers. Until she felt that slight exposure, with just a hint of his gaze briefly on her. Then the dip of the mattress, usually so mundane and routine and *now I guess we get some sleep*. Only not here, no, not here, oh here it felt so strangely portentous.

And then she felt him.

Just a little, just the barest brush of his thigh, his forearm, his shoulder.

But even the barest brush seemed agonizing now. It was fat with the promise of more. Of his breath, ghosting against the nape of her neck or the curve of her shoulder. Of an accidental touch in the night, maybe slick with perspiration and almost too hot to stand. Definitely *too hot to stand*, she thought, considering contact was already like this.

Because she could feel the heat from him, no question.

It rolled off him in a wave and ran right over her.

She was practically suffocating, before she'd even tried to sleep.

Not to mention all the other stuff that was apparently going on with her.

Christ, it felt as if her whole body were one big nerve. Like he could just blow on her, and she'd do some very inadvisable things. Things that she didn't even know if he would welcome. Because sometimes it seemed like he did and would. But other times he just seemed furious about the whole business. Like she was triggering something in him, some *kink for horny women* issue, and it made him lose all the control he clearly wanted to hold on to.

So it seemed best to make sure he did actually hold on to it.

Or at the very least, that she didn't do anything that meant he couldn't.

Even if saying it was kind of embarrassing. "You know, maybe we should put something between us. Just in case," she blurted out, into the dark, stifling air. Then got exactly what she expected: the sound and feel of his head turning sharply.

"In case of what? I roll over and accidentally put my dick somewhere?"

"You say *somewhere* like it might end up in my armpit."

"Well, maybe it would. I don't know how you like to sleep."

"Then let me be the first to tell you I never do it halfway down the bed, with my arms inexplicably raised above my head," she said, and kind of expected that to be the end of it. Mostly because she could feel him trying not to laugh.

He got ahold of himself in the end, however.

"Even if you don't, it could still happen," he said.

And now somehow it was her turn to be on the back foot.

"How, exactly?" She snorted.

"Maybe I love to sleep really far up."

"Right. But you'd never be able to get in when my arms are at my sides."

"You never know. I'm good at finding my way into tight spaces."

*What the fuck*, she thought. For about twelve different reasons.

But could really only go with the most pressing one:

"Did you honestly just say the words *tight* and *spaces*?"

"Yeah, I did. But honestly I have no idea how that happened, considering I started out by debunking that as a possibility and am now fully onboard and somehow in the middle of warning you away from the very real danger."

He sighed at the end of that.

Heavily, it seemed to her.

Like he was having just as many problems as she was.

Even though that was preposterous. Everything he'd just said was preposterous. She wasn't the one in any danger. He was, if anything. So what exactly was it that he meant? "But why would you feel like you might accidentally do anything to me? I mean, it's not as if you're riled up by anything right now."

"What the fuck are you talking about? Of course I'm riled up right now."

"Even though you're just laid here. In the dark. Next to a friend."

"Yeah, a friend who got me off an hour ago, and is now nearly naked, about a millimeter away from me. Oh, and who also seems to be squirming around like an absolute maniac for no good reason that I can think of."

*Fuck*, she thought.

Because he was right, of course he was right.

She didn't want him to be right, but he was.

Somehow, she'd started doing exactly what he'd said.

And she didn't have a good reason for it, either.

So really her only choice left was denial.

"I'm not squirming. In fact, I'm completely still," she said.

But it came out too mulish and weak, and she knew it.

It took him almost no effort to pull apart her nonargument.

"The bed is practically rocking. I feel like I'm being fucked by a ghost," he said, and all right, now she had to concede. She had no choice at all.

In part because she was laughing too hard to do anything else. "Well, you were the one who mentioned your dick. What did you expect?" she asked, between giggles.

"That you would laugh. I said it to be funny. I didn't mean to be dirty."

"But everything we do seems dirty now."

"I know. I don't know what's going on with me," he groaned,

and okay, here it was now. The question she wanted the answer to. The reason he was losing it like this, repeatedly. Because deep down, she knew it couldn't just be some kink.

It had to be more. It had to be other factors.

And she had some guesses as to what they were.

Or at least one guess that sounded the most reasonable.

"Maybe it's just that you're having way less sex than usual," she tried.

Because of course she knew that had to be the case. He was with her all the time. It wasn't as if he could just nip out for the thousand one-night stands he probably usually had. Though somehow, it still felt shocking when he agreed.

When he more than agreed, in fact.

"Way less sex? Mabel, I'm not having *any* sex. And haven't for months," he pretty much scoffed. As if it was outrageous that she'd imagined anything else. Even though she'd barely been able to believe in far less. Some part had thought maybe he was, somehow. But no, no. He wasn't.

At all, apparently.

So no wonder he was a mess, really.

She was a mess just hearing about it.

It took her a full thirty seconds just to answer like a normal person.

"Well, there's your problem then. You inexplicably not fucking anybody," she said. With a little laugh on the end that she knew sounded false. Though thankfully, he didn't make her feel it.

She just felt him shrug.

"It's not inexplicable. I just, you know. Can't at the moment."

And then of course she had to ask.

No matter how much she didn't want to.

"Why not, though?"

"Because reasons."

"Yeah, and now tell me what the reasons are."

She heard him take in a breath there. The way people did when they were about to say something. But the something didn't come right away. It seemed to take him a while to get out the words, and when he finally did he sounded strange.

Hollow, she thought. Or like he was having to force it all out.

"Well, it would look like I was cheating on you, wouldn't it," he explained.

And okay, yeah. She could understand then why it had taken some effort.

Because it was silly. Surely, he could see how silly it was. "But you could be really discreet. Slip away to some hotel, sneak her in the back. Then get her into your room, and slowly, slowly undress her. Maybe with your teeth, yeah, do it with your teeth, and then just as she—" she said, and honestly didn't even think much about where she was going with this or what exactly it meant.

Until he cut her off, mid-sentence.

"What in the fucking fuck are you *doing*?" he said.

At which point, she realized exactly what path she'd been going down.

And covered her face with her hands.

"Oh god, I don't know. It just came out of me."

"And yet you told me off for saying the word *dick*."

"I'm not proud of myself, okay."

"Good, because you shouldn't be. Now *I'm* bloody squirming."

"Yeah, I know. I can feel you doing it. It *is* like being fucked by a ghost."

It was, too. Every shake of the bed felt as if something was pounding away between her legs. Once or twice she actually found herself rocking back into it—which made his next words a) justified and b) absolutely correct. "Told you so. But you didn't listen, did you, and now we're gonna be the only people in history who manage to make each other come by lying side by side, in a bed for toddlers, humping nothing but this fucking four-hundred-quid duvet," he said.

So what else could she do but agree?

"I'd argue, but to be honest I think I'm about thirty seconds away."

"Same. Maybe less if you keep accidentally saying horny things to me."

"Well, I won't. I'm going to stop now. I have a handle on myself, okay."

"No, you don't. And I don't, either. So you know what we're gonna do?"

*Fuck*, she answered for him in her head. But thankfully, he did not listen to her apparently batshit brain on that one. He just grabbed some pillows and shoved them between their bodies. Like she'd wanted to at the start, like she'd told him to do, like they should have done immediately. Because when you really broke it down, it was the only sensible course of action. It was the right thing to do.

And if all she did was stare at the ceiling for an hour after he did it, sleepless and feeling strange and stressed, well. That didn't mean anything. Everything was fine now. It was fine. She was safe from all the sex she definitely did not want.

Group Chat, April 8, 2022

**connieisstillreadytofightyou**

Hey baby mabie how was the concert?
I'm going to guess by your absence from
everywhere for the last god knows that you
don't know how the concert was but do
have a detailed knowledge of the insides of
Alfie's pants. Yes, I am dying to know how
good he is. No, I'm not going to press you.

**berrylicious**

No, she's not going to press you. She's
just going to press me to press you until
I go round the twist. Honestly Connie
he's good, okay? He's clearly very good.
Otherwise why would our little chatterbox
be so suddenly quiet?

Now, I know a Rug-Making Conference
isn't quite as glamorous as dating a sexy
beard who was in whole movies, but can
someone please help me decide which
outfit to wear in the event that I actually
win this thing?

**mabiebabie**

Oh my god lovey, I completely
forgot! Your National Award thingie
is coming up! Forget my sex-drunk
self, we must immediately find you
the perfect clothes. Now, do you still
have that gorgeous velvet thing?
Because my vote is that. Oh, you're
going to be so perfect, and win,
and I'm going to be screaming from
our table like an absolutely bonkers
stan. I even have a sign all designed
to bring along.

**berrylicious**

I KNEW THAT WOULD GET HER TO
APPEAR, QUICK CONNIE, YOU
HOLD HER DOWN I SHALL EXTRACT
ALL THE FILTHY DETAILS!!!

# Twenty-Three

## It Would Star the Other
## Hemsworth Nobody Remembers

*S*he knew things were very much not safe the second she woke up.

But she pretended, for a little while, that they were. She lay there with her eyes closed, trying to make everything all just a really lucid dream she had somehow started having. And it worked for about a minute or so. It really felt like this was not reality. Her leg wasn't truly jammed between his legs. She hadn't shoved her face into the crook of his neck, so deep that she was practically eating his expensive scent for breakfast. And she didn't have a hand underneath his jersey at the back.

No no no, none of that was happening.

Then she made the mistake of trying to move, just a little bit. She shifted her hips in a way that seemed like almost nothing.

Only it wasn't nothing, it wasn't at all, because the second she did she made accidental contact with whatever was between her legs. His thigh, she suspected it was, but couldn't say for sure. Mainly because she was too busy trying not to gasp over the wave of intense pleasure that simply rolled all the way through her body.

And what was she supposed to tell herself then?

This was definitely a real thing.

There was no way around it.

She just had to live with the fact that she had somehow dissolved the pillows between them in the night. Then pressed herself so tightly to his body that she could actually feel the pulse at his throat, thudding away against her cheek. She could feel him breathing, like a great pair of mechanical bellows.

And with almost no good way out of any of it.

Because she couldn't stay where she was. If she did, he would wake and find her surrounding him like some lusty octopus. But she also couldn't get away. Or at least, she couldn't get away without repeating what had just happened. And god, she did not want to repeat what had just happened.

It was still making her tingle ten minutes later.

If it happened again she was almost certainly going to make a sound.

Or worse: what if next time, she simply couldn't stop? What if she kept going and going, until she actually went ahead and made herself come? No, that was abominable. She couldn't possibly let such a thing happen. She'd have to arrest herself. Not to mention the fact that he would wake up and be appalled.

She knew he would be.

Even if he also apparently wanted to rut right back at her.

Because he did. He was. She could feel his hips moving. Just a little, but a little felt like so much when what she was talking about was someone slowly working his cock against her hip and belly. It made her flush hot all over; her clit seemed to swell against the small contact it had with him.

And though she tried to stick to staying still, she knew she moved.

Because now it was his turn to stifle a sound.

Only he didn't stifle it at all. He just full-on groaned in her ear. Followed by words, whole words, oh god, he was saying things right in her ear. "Is this what you want?" he said. And what was she supposed to say? *No, that sounds terrible?* She'd have sooner asked someone to lop off an arm than go with that.

Because damn, did it feel incredible.

She could make out the exact shape of him now.

How thick he felt, how obviously swollen and slick and oh so much better than she'd imagined. She could almost feel what it would be like to be fucked by him. To have him working inside her. And doubly so when he slid a hand over the curve of her arse. Like the night before, like he wanted to feel her there. Only better, because he didn't just stop at a squeeze.

He used that contact to urge her against him.

Slowly, softly, at first. Like a bit of light encouragement.

But then when she couldn't help letting out a sound, he went further. He worked her over him, in so good and firm a way it made her wild. It made her shake, and squirm, and get so slick she could actually feel it. Everything was suddenly slippery— and of course that only made things better, hotter, sweeter.

Now she was pretty much gliding over that thick muscle.

And it seemed he liked that just as much as she did.

"Oh, you're wet, you're so wet," he groaned.

Then to cap it off, he tugged her harder against him. He practically ground her spread pussy into him—and she didn't think it was really over his thigh anymore, either. No, it felt more like something else, now, like he'd shifted her and tilted her hips until she was almost right up against his cock.

And that was pretty much all it took. Just the thought of her clit against that big, stiff thing, of him actually using her like that to get himself off—it was enough. It was more than enough. "Oh god, I'm gonna come," she gasped.

But she didn't worry about it.

Because he was doing it, too. She knew he was. She felt him go rigid against her and groan loud and long—though even if he hadn't she would have understood. His cock was so close and so tight to her that it was impossible to miss it swelling and jerking as he went over. As he did it just as hard as her.

Like he didn't care about anything in that moment.

Not what they'd talked about, not what they'd said no to.

It was just pure pleasure, endless and perfect.

Until said pleasure dissipated, and left them with this:

Heavy breathing, and mess, and what felt like a stunned silence.

And finally him, puncturing it.

"Did we really just dry hump each other?" he asked in so incredulous and appalled a tone it honestly made her face heat. She almost wanted to answer *No, it was all a dream*. But managed to pull herself back from that absurd brink.

"Yeah, I think that's what we might have done," she said instead.

While trying not to let it show that she was cringing.

After all, what would she be cringing for?

He had done it, too. It wasn't just her fault.

He'd grabbed her butt and made her ride his cock.

Though somehow, the fact that he had didn't seem to make things any less weird—as he apparently well knew. "Even though that's a completely bonkers thing for two grown adults to do," he said, and okay, he was right. He was right.

But they had reasons, didn't they? Good reasons that he should take into account. "To be fair to us, it is really difficult to be rational and great at making normal decisions when you've accidentally jammed your leg between someone else's, while half nude and in bed. Not to mention the fact that we made the incredibly questionable decision to tell each other we were not allowed to do something again, then we described exactly how we would avoid doing it in a situation where doing it becomes a ludicrously easy thing to accidentally do."

"So basically we made it forbidden, then jinxed ourselves."

"That sounds about right, yeah. As batshit as it sounds."

He sighed then. And so heavily she felt it more than she heard it.

His chest rose and fell against the cheek she inexplicably still had wedged there. Although maybe it wasn't that inexplicable when she really thought about it. After all, if she moved she'd have to look at him. And he'd have to look at her. And this conversation was excruciating enough as it was, without throwing eye contact into the mix.

*No*, she thought.

*Better to stay jammed together for this.*

"So what do we do now?" he asked, somewhere over her head.

And she answered into his left pectoral muscle with as much rue as she could muster. "Probably never try to sleep in the same bed again, for starters."

"Yeah, that was absolutely mad of us. Honestly I don't know how we ever even came up with such a ridiculous idea. Or what made us actually agree to do it, and then just go the fuck ahead like nothing could ever possibly go wrong."

"I think it had something to do with your back. And only having one bed."

*Or at least that's what we told ourselves*, her mind chimed in.

And knew he was thinking the same, just by the derisive sound he let out.

"Christ, that wouldn't pass muster in a movie starring Channing Tatum."

"Yeah, even Channing would be too smart to fall for that old trick."

"He would. So now we're thicker than the thickest rom-com hero there is."

"Neither of us are Sandra Bullock. Both of us are the himbo. And apparently said himbos have absolutely no control over their own bodies."

"But I do have control over mine. I've never been ruled on the sly by my dick," he protested. Then seemed to realize how that sounded in light of what had just happened and corrected himself. "Or at least I'm not usually. In normal circumstances. When I don't have a half-naked you glued to my body, writhing and moaning and being all wet and oh fucking hell I'm starting to feel it again we have to get up, let's get up and get showered and dressed and have breakfast and be normal, come on. Come on, we can do this."

He clapped his hands together on that last word. Probably like he once had in locker rooms while trying to convince his teammates at halftime that they absolutely could come back from seventeen-nil. *We just have to put our backs into it, lads*, she imagined him saying. And the thing was—it did actually feel sort of possible, once he had. He was good at rallying the troops, it seemed.

Or at least, good enough that they managed everything he'd suggested.

She showered and put on clothes that he gave her. Good clothes, which covered everything she had. And he did the same. Then they ate slices of toast while standing across the kitchen from each other in almost matching ensembles. Massive jumpers, thick trousers, woolly socks—like two people about to go skiing in weather they were convinced was going to be incredibly horny.

And after that, there was just one more hurdle.

Saying goodbye once the car was there to take her home.

But it was okay—he had it covered. "Probably we should just shake hands," he said at the door, and honestly she was so grateful for his good sense and all the ways things almost seemed normal now that she didn't even think twice about it. She stuck out her own for him to do just what he'd suggested.

Then he did.

He took her hand in his.

And she felt her world narrow down to nothing but desire, just like that.

As if they had never left the bed. Or the car. Or that kiss at the concert. All these things were there inside them both now, forever an inch from the surface, and so intense that even something as nothing as this could make them burst right through. She knew it could. Because as she walked away she was still shaking almost everywhere, with that violent need to drag his body to hers.

And do every one of the things they shouldn't have done.

All.

Over.

Again.

Daily **Mail** Online, April 9, 2022

## Lady Love Seen Leaving Alfie Harding's 5-Million-Pound Home After Steamy Night Spent Together

**Footballing hero Harding invites his new love into his home**

**He tenderly caresses her cheek at the door**

**Willicker, 33, appeared flushed**

**"It's the real thing" a source claims**

After years of keeping his home closed to his string of flings and casual model girlfriends, Alfie Harding, 38, appears to have finally found the one.

The Manchester United legend was spotted bidding farewell to the new woman in his life, possible lifestyle guru Mabel Willicker, 33. He stopped to gently caress her cheek as she left early on Sunday morning.

Harding was casually dressed in a cable-knit jumper, his hair tousled in a way that suggested the night was a steamy one. Willicker sported a similar look, her own bulky sweater hiding her abundant curves, and her thick, dark hair styled messily over one shoulder.

A source told the *Daily Mail,* "It's the real thing, he's completely smitten," though when asked his assistant informed us that we should "Kindly go jump in a lake, you hateful vultures."

## Twenty-Four

### An Even Worse Classic Romance Mistake
### than the Last One

$\mathcal{S}$he decided the best course of action was just to be super professional. So she wore an actual suit to their next work session. Or at least, she wore the closest thing she had to a suit. Which was basically a jacket that for some reason was about two sizes too small, the only blouse she had that wasn't inexplicably completely see through, and the longest and sturdiest skirt she could find.

It went just past her knees and didn't swish when she walked.

So hopefully that passed for a sedate and serious working woman.

And not a sex maniac who was constantly on the verge of jumping him.

*You don't even like sex that much*, she told herself as she exited the car he'd sent—but very unsurprisingly not ridden to meet her in—and made her way up to his front door. And that felt true, right then and there. But less true once he was in front of her. Even though he'd done all the same sorts of things she had.

He was wearing a jumper again.

A big cable-knit one that hid just about everything he had.

Like he suspected his shoulders and chest were the things that drove her round the twist—and to be fair, he wasn't far wrong. She could still see the way they'd looked as he'd slipped that jersey on the night before. And feel that muscle against her cheek. And both memories were pretty fucking maddening.

But not really as maddening as him looking like he lived in a mountain lodge.

Because that was exactly the impression he gave in that fucking thick knit.

And especially when it was coupled with that beard.

His big, tangled beard that he'd obviously left even wilder than usual on purpose. As if the wildness was the thing that put her off, instead of just making her want to breathlessly ask whether he was about to split a log with his bare hands.

Though thankfully, she managed to be cool.

She just said something normal, like hello.

And yes, her voice went up and down in the middle when she did.

But if he noticed, he didn't say. He told her they should get started on some work instead. Then he pointed to her chair, and sat on what she now thought of as his step, and they got down to business. The good, correct, professional kind of business, which mostly just involved him telling her things that were okay to include, and her drafting them very roughly out. Or her slyly persuading him to draft things out by muddling things up or including things he didn't want, until he gave an exasperated sigh and started scribbling.

Though she noticed that he had a notebook of his own now to do that very thing. A nice one, with what looked like a suede cover in black. And he wasn't using a biro, either—it was a fountain pen, of the sort you chose when you enjoyed writing, or wanted to feel good while you wrote, or maybe some combination of both.

Plus, he really seemed engrossed in it in a way he hadn't been before. Prior to this he'd been reluctant and only done a little. Then he'd stopped, and paced, or gone off to make a cup of tea. But he didn't here. He kept going.

So much so that she started to think they could actually get through this. The sex stuff had just been a blip, brought on by all that fake-relationship madness. Now maybe they could be free to be things like friends and work colleagues.

Who did things like smile at each other.

Like the way he was smiling at her now.

Right before he did a perfectly normal thing like ask her to come to him, so she could see what she thought of what he'd written. "I feel like it's kind of disjointed and not really getting to the point," he said, as she walked over.

And then she sat next to him.

And tried to take his notebook from him.

And immediately knew that this had been the wrong choice.

She could feel it straightaway, like a drop in cabin pressure.

Or a sudden siren blaring, somewhere off in the distance.

Though it was still somehow shocking when he suddenly burst out with this:

"Okay, so here's the thing: I'm gonna need you to go sit back over there."

Because god, he sounded desperate. Even though a second ago, he'd sounded frigging fine. They'd been fine. Couldn't he just go back to being fine? "But you just said you wanted me to take a look," she tried. But he wasn't having it.

In fact, he seemed even shakier than he had a second ago.

"I know what I said. And it was a big mistake."

"In what way was it?"

"You know what way. Don't make me say it."

She wanted to look at him then.

Mostly to see if he was actually shaking as hard as she could make out through the tiny contact of his jumper sleeve against her jacket. But in the end, she couldn't do it. What she needed to say was hard enough without factoring in the sight of him.

*Bet he looks absolutely lust-fucked*, her brain suggested.

And her brain sounded bonkers.

But she couldn't risk that it might be right.

Not when she needed to spell out exactly why this was all confusing to her.

"Yeah, I think you're going to have to say it. Because most of the time I have no idea what is going on here. And I definitely have no idea what you're thinking about it all, at any given moment. I mean, sometimes it seems like I'm just making you do this, and not that you actually would like to on any level whatsoever. And others it seems as if you just want it, desperately, no matter what I happen to be doing at the time," she said, and did it all while staring straight ahead.

Only to get him turning her face with his hands.

So she had to see him looking exactly as she'd imagined:

Flushed, and foggy-eyed, and fucking *hungry*. Oh god, he looked hungry.

And when he spoke, his voice just sounded so hot and hoarse and low.

"Then you should probably know: you never make me, and I always like to, and right now I definitely desperately want it, even though all you happen to be doing is taking my notebook, while sitting next to me in a frankly ridiculous outfit," he said, and honestly she wanted to respond with calm dignity. She wanted to act like it was no big deal. But he was still holding her and still looking at her and he'd used the words *always* and *desperately* and *want*, and so instead of doing anything remotely reasonable, she just sort of lost her fucking mind. Like he'd lifted the only thing that had been holding her back, the only fence she had around her desire, and now all that was left was this:

"Then maybe we should do something about it."

But the worst part was: she could tell it thrilled him to hear it.

She saw it flash through those midnight eyes like a lightning strike.

So when he said:

"Yeah. Like you moving away from me."

It didn't help. It didn't put the brakes on things.

Because there were no brakes at this point.

He'd removed them by making things clear.

Now they were in a car careening out of control.

And even wilder: she was kind of enjoying it.

"Or, and hear me out now, I could stay right here."

"If you stay right here I'm gonna try it on. You get that, right?"

"I do. And honestly I feel like it might be a good idea."

"Explain to me how it would, exactly."

*Because I apparently want to crash and burn*, she thought in response. But of course, she couldn't say that. She had to come up with something more reasonable. More rational. Less governed by the fact that two seconds ago he'd told her he was going to try it on with her, like she was just that irresistible.

And she had something, too.

Something that felt right to her.

Even if it was also just a little bit bonkers.

"Well, it might get it out of our systems," she said. Only weirdly, once she had, it didn't sound quite as bonkers as she'd thought. In fact, it didn't sound bonkers at all. It just seemed like a chance to get whatever she was needing, without ending up exploding at the bottom of a cliff. It was all the hot sex, but with a handy exit strategy that could occur before they got to the tortured *but you could never really be my actual girlfriend* part. And even better:

He didn't seem immediately adverse.

He just looked briefly shocked.

Then curious.

"So your system is also experiencing a high volume of lust traffic right now?" he asked. As if he had no more clue about the state she was in than she had about the state of him. They were both apparently just fumbling in the dark, trying to find a way through whatever all this nonsense was.

And it could be that she had just uncovered a viable path.

"Okay, first of all, seriously, you need to stop doubting yourself because you have such a way with words it's ridiculous. Just absolutely first-rate, don't shake your head at me. And second of all, yes, of course it is, how could it not be when yesterday you dirty talked me into dying of orgasms? I would have to be made of concrete from the neck down to not still be feeling that."

"Honestly I wish I *was* made of concrete from the neck down right now."

"But you're not." She shook her head. "And neither am I. So

we should probably look at options other than wishing desperately that we were, while writhing in agony over something we could probably resolve really easily."

"You say *resolve* and *easily* as if it won't take much."

"Well, wouldn't it? It hasn't the last two times."

"The last two times have led us to this batshit place."

He scribbled in the air as he spoke. As if to illustrate said batshit place.

Though somehow, she suspected he wasn't quite as furious as he seemed when he did it. Because then he looked at her in this expectant sort of manner. Like he just waiting for her to come up with a way around what he'd just said.

And thankfully, she had a good idea how to do it:

She was just going to get him to do it for her.

"So then tell me what you think will clear the decks," she said.

Then got just the slightest flash of eagerness in his eyes.

Before he managed to smuggle it down and respond rationally.

"And by that I'm assuming you mean work this sexual tension out."

"That's exactly what I mean. So come on. Let's hear it."

"I don't think you actually want to know."

"You're saying that like you didn't tell me all about putting your cock in my mouth barely twenty-four hours ago. I'm pretty sure I can handle whatever you have in mind," she said, and knew what it sounded like when she did.

A challenge, of some sort.

Or maybe like she was goading him.

*You can't shock me, Alfie Harding*, she had told him.

And it made his eyes blaze the moment she did.

Then he straightened and met her gaze dead on, and oh, she knew it was going to be intense. She felt it barreling down the pike at her before he'd said a word. And now here it was, like a shotgun blast:

"All right. What I have in mind is you standing up, and

sliding your knickers down your legs. Slowly, slowly, so it drives me just about out of my mind. And then when they're finally off and you've got absolutely nothing on underneath that absurd skirt, you get it by the hem and just lift it all the way up for me. So I can see, you know. So I can look my fill at something I've heard and felt against me, but never actually glimpsed with my own two eyes," he said, then seemed to pause. As if to make sure she had fully processed that hot mess and was now sufficiently reeling.

Before he hit her even harder with the rest.

"And after I've taken that hot, probably wet pussy in, after I've seen as much as I can stand without going round the twist, I'd just lean forward, and lick the whole length of your slick little slit. Over and over, until you're trembling. Until you can hardly stay on your feet. Until you're begging me to finish you off. And I would, you know. I would let you have it. But not courtesy of my mouth, oh no. No, no—I'd get you up against that wall, get your legs around me, and fuck your orgasm out of you."

He paused again after that. Though this one was mercifully short.

It was just to give him a chance to sit back, satisfied.

Before he added smugly:

"So now tell me. How does that sound to you?"

Though honestly, she had no idea what he thought he was doing.

She wasn't about to run away in horror, the way he seemed to expect.

And mostly because she had never heard anyone say anything that she wanted more than that. "Like we should do it *immediately*," she said, without even blinking about it. Then got the exact shock from him that he'd been expecting from her.

"You can't be serious."

"Well, I'm not if you aren't."

"Oh no, I definitely am." He shook his head dazedly. "I just can't believe you are."

"Even though you almost made me come just talking about it?"

"You never did. Mabel, tell me you never."

"I can't. Because I absolutely did."

"But it was even more filthy than the other night."

God, she loved how high his voice went for that.

*Like a scandalized old lady,* she thought.

Then just wanted to press on him even harder.

"And yet at the same time, nowhere near filthy enough."

"You expected *worse* than that? Worse than me tonguing your cunt and then fucking you until you come all over my cock?"

"Well, you *are* a famous footballer."

"Yeah, but not all of us are having orgies nine to five. Some of us like a bit of hot dirty talk, a good couple or three fucks after some pretty fucking intense foreplay, followed by passing out in each other's arms and then making them breakfast in the morning. So now I gotta know what exactly you had in mind."

He looked away as he explained.

Then back at her when he was done.

And she knew why, too. Now it was her turn to be challenged.

But that was okay. In her current state, she felt up to the task.

"At the very least, you fucking my face," she said—as matter-of-factly as he had done. With, quite surprisingly, about the same level of impact. His eyes actually briefly stuttered closed; he couldn't seem to stop himself biting his lip.

And his voice when it finally came out was almost a growl.

"Oh, fuck me sideways, the mouth on you," he said.

She didn't know why, however.

She had so much more than that inside her, ready to go.

"Honestly that wasn't even as much as my mouth could do."

"So you had filthier in there but went with the tamer version."

"I did. I can still go with the unedited edition, though, if you'd like."

"Jesus Christ, yes. Go on. Let's have it."

"Well, I was thinking you could come all over my tits."

"Your bare tits, you mean. So you've got no clothes on."

"Of course. I mean, I'm imagining you unbuttoning most of what I'm wearing. Probably so you can fondle me while I suck your cock. But if you wouldn't be bothered about doing that, I could easily keep everything on."

"Yeah, no, that's very much not what I want."

"Tell me then, what you do want. Tell me, and I will."

"Take it off. Take your clothes off for me, right now."

But here was the best part: she actually wanted to. Somehow, against all the usual odds, he made her want to. Not just feel comfortable with it, not just feel okay, but want to, in a way she didn't even feel capable of fighting. She just stood as soon as he said it and started doing it. She started unbuttoning that jacket.

And sure, her hands were shaking a little.

Yes, it made her cheeks heat to just be here in the middle of his daylight-bright living room, right in front of him, peeling off her completely unsexy outfit. But it also weirdly felt good. Like this kind of thing could be a whole turn-on, under the right circumstances and with the right person.

Though she didn't know how this was either of those two things.

They'd just talked, rather mechanically, about getting it out of their systems.

And he was still the incredibly handsome, incredibly fit, incredibly funny and charming famous ex-footballer that he had been before. Really, any of those factors should have sent her into a tailspin of trying to stay fully clothed at all times. She'd been with men half as attractive and in demand as him, and still felt too nervous to completely strip down. To do anything other than pick lingerie that made her look perfect, and pretty colors that made her feel confident.

Because no matter how much you loved your curves, there was always a chance whoever you were with wouldn't. And yet somehow, those same feelings didn't seem to be happening here.

It was inexplicable.

Until she got to the zipper on her skirt.

Because she struggled, for just a second. She couldn't quite get it down—it snagged, and she cursed at it. And then she felt his hand on her leg. Gentle as anything, just stroking there in a way that was good, that was hot, that did it for her no question about it. But it did something else, too.

It showed her how much he loved what he saw.

And so did the heated look in his eyes.

And what he said as she let her skirt drop.

"That's it, that's my gorgeous good girl," he murmured.

After which, she had to admit, her state of mind wasn't just easy about everything. It was ready to sink right down into his arms. She had to force herself to stay on her feet—and she was glad she managed, too. Because this way she got to see the look on his face as she slid her knickers down:

All wondering eyes and parted lips.

Like part of him had known she would.

But couldn't quite believe she had, anyway.

He'd thought she would stop before she got to this:

Her very bare and very slick cunt, just there for him to drink in. And he *did* drink it in. He devoured every inch of that swollen seam and sparse black hair and the glistening mess she'd already made of herself. Then just as she thought she couldn't take another second of this intense scrutiny, he leaned forward.

He leaned forward, and he *licked*.

Like he had said he would, like he had told her.

Only somehow a million times more arousing than he had made it sound. Because he'd made it seem hot, that was true. But he hadn't really gone into details. He hadn't been specific about how he would go about it. And how he went about it was just beyond the fucking beyond.

He didn't do it fast and sure.

He did it in slow, almost hesitant stages. Like he wanted to weigh each step before he took another, she thought, and couldn't for the life of her think why that sent her through the ceiling.

She only knew that it did. That she watched him flick the tip of his tongue over the seam of her sex, and felt it sing all the way through her body. She had to bite back a moan.

But couldn't help letting it out when he looked up at her.

*To see how you like that*, her mind informed her.

And she was right because he did it again.

He watched and licked and watched and licked until she was trembling, until she was gasping his name and so overloaded with pleasure it almost felt as if she were doing it already. She felt as if she were already coming, just like that, before he'd even really paid a lot of attention to the parts of her that usually got her there. However, she knew she hadn't.

Because when he stood, abruptly, she almost cursed.

And for a brief moment had to wonder if it was possible to die of sexual frustration. "Alfie, please," she actually found herself saying. Even though she should have known. He'd told her this part, too. He'd said that he wanted her to do it on his cock. But now that it was here and it was happening, she felt thrown.

And not just because she was on the edge of all this.

No, it was the way he was, too.

He looked shaken.

Heated.

And so single-minded suddenly it was almost unsettling. She kind of wanted to say to him *Are you still there*, but at the same time knew why she didn't. It was obvious, the moment he scooped her into his arms and carried her to the bedroom and spread her out on the bed. Then even more so, even clearer, when he started stripping out of his clothes. She saw that stripe of black fur she'd glimpsed the night before, in full. The curve of his shoulders, the slight thickness at his hips.

And those thighs, god, those thighs.

They made her *squirm*.

She had to stop herself sliding a hand over them once he was there, between her legs. So it made sense that she couldn't say anything at all. That she simply let him cover her body with his and press his lips against hers. Then he groaned into her mouth that *she was delicious,* that he *loved every inch of her,* that he *just wanted to have her.* And all she could do was rub herself against him in response. Mindlessly, helplessly, as if she were beyond her own control before he'd even gotten to the best bit:

Him, sliding those shorts of his down.

So she could see what he'd inadvertently promised.

And he hadn't been exaggerating, either. Nobody who'd ever talked about his cock had been exaggerating. It was long and thick and so steeply curved she could almost feel it before he'd done a thing. She just got this delicious hot pulse arcing out from that sweet spot inside her, like an echo of what was to come.

And had to warn him before it got any more intense.

"If you want me to do it on your cock, I'd hurry," she moaned.

Though he didn't seem inclined to listen. He just put two of his fingers to his lips and licked. Slowly, so she could really see what he was doing. Then just as she was starting to really feel that, too, he slipped a hand between her legs. He found her slick, eager hole.

And slid all the way in, as deep as he could go.

Like he wanted to give her a taste, she suspected, of what was about to happen.

To get her ready, in a way that made her even more beside herself than she'd been before. She actually found herself rocking against his hand, before he even started moving. And harder when she saw his expression. His eyes drifted closed the moment he felt her wet heat.

Then she tightened around him, automatically.

As if she were trying to pull him more deeply inside.

And now she got a low, rumbling sigh.

"Gonna last about thirty seconds in this eager little pussy," he said. And honestly, she thought he was lying, she really did. Then she watched him put on a condom with what looked like actually shaking hands. In fact, they shook so much he had to start again with a new one. And when he finally covered her, when he got right between her legs and kissed the tip of his cock to her cunt, she could feel what this was doing to him.

It almost seemed like he was vibrating all over. Like something was going on inside him that was too much for him to reasonably contain. And when he finally, finally sank in, god. The sound he made. She'd never heard a man do anything like it. And certainly not a man as stoic as he was.

He didn't even like yelling when something injured him.

But oh, he gave it to her here.

He gasped and groaned and murmured in her ear that she was so fucking good. Then just as she felt as if she couldn't take another sound—or even the simple sensation of his heated breath against her skin—he spoke into the stifling near silence. "Cover my eyes," he said, and before she could ask, before she could even wonder, he blurted out the explanation. "I just can't look at your lust-fucked face and your luscious body and not come my fucking brains out."

And that was . . . she didn't even know what that was. She'd never even remotely had anyone express such a thing. The last guy she'd been with hadn't even enjoyed her moaning in bed. But apparently, Alfie found even the sight of her and the slightest hint that she was into this so completely overwhelming that it took him to the edge. It made him shudder and get all uncoordinated and sloppy, and then he gasped out a *please*.

And so she did it. She put a hand over his eyes. Though honestly, she didn't think it made things any better. Now they were fucking feverishly, with him sort of fucking *blindfolded*. Like they were playing some very strange kinky sex game of the sort that definitely did not cool things down. It made things hotter, quite obviously. It got him groaning her name as he all but shoved into her, over and over. And she couldn't help giving the same back. She lifted her hips to meet every one of his wild thrusts—and didn't regret a single moment of it. How could she when it felt this incredible?

*I'm going to come just like this*, she thought.

*Without so much as a single stroke over my clit.*

Though somehow, it still shocked her when that pleasure hit. When the excitement and the pressure of that delicious cock combined and formed a tight fist between her legs. Then it simply unfurled the second he spilled words into her ear. "Ohhh god are you coming?" he gasped, and she was, she was. She was arching up into him and making sounds that she'd probably be ashamed of later and most of all—losing all control of what she was doing. Because somehow, her hands were on his back. Like she needed to hang on, maybe.

But of course that meant there was no blindfold anymore.

And the moment that happened—the moment he saw her saying his name, eyes searching for his amid this soul-shaking pleasure—he seemed to lose it himself. The sharp focus in his gaze sank down into something soft and hazy and vulnerable. As if he didn't want to give in, but doing anything else wasn't an option. Not when she was trembling and clinging to him and saying the things she was.

"God, nobody makes me feel the way you do," she gasped out.

And that was it.

That was all it took.

Just the sense that he'd done this to her.

He'd made her this helpless, this beside herself with pleasure. And to the point where she'd confess something like that. Something that she should have held back but couldn't with him over her and inside her and holding her, those eyes so full of feeling she didn't know what to do with it all.

She just had to hold on as he went over.

So hard it almost looked like it hurt.

He seemed to actually grit his teeth against it.

His hands made fists in the sheets, in her hair.

And god, it just went on and on and on. In fact, he came so long and so hard she almost felt like she might go again. Those thick bursts of pleasure just seemed to bloom anew, from that place he was still rubbing over and against and god, god. She'd never known anything like this. It was almost too much.

Then somehow, somehow not enough, at the same time.

Because as she lay there by his side, in the aftermath, shell-shocked and breathless and still buzzing, he suddenly turned his head her way. Lazily, she thought, still drunk with it. But with a strangely determined gleam in his eyes. And then he just came out with it.

"Ready for more?" he murmured.

At which point, she realized: all this wasn't her, having fun.

Or finally getting free of whatever was happening between them.

It was just dragging her down deeper, and deeper, until finally she knew:

She was definitely, 100 percent, going to fucking *drown*.

All right Mabel, so how about I talk about the 2010 World Cup? Because see the thing about this is, everybody just knows about the goals and when I ripped my shirt off and revealed exactly how hairy I am and how I was the one who bollocked Gordon for being hungover that time. But what people DON'T know is that all I remember about that time was pain.

Grinding, constant pain.

Mostly in the ankle, but other stuff was already starting to go by that point, too. And I suppose you might think—but you were still just a lad then, Alfie. You can't possibly have been that bad then. Or maybe you see all the glory and think: you looked fine enough to me. But that's the trick, you see. That's the thing about the game. You have to operate at such a high level for such long stretches of time, and never let any weaknesses show, that the cracks start appearing long before they should. Long before what anyone would think was a normal time for it to happen.

And before you know it, you're a wreck.

A shambling mess.

Holding everything together with spit and a grimace.

And no one can know, because you're the boss, aren't you?

You're Alfie fucking Harding, nothing can ever put a hole in you.

But it can, and it does, and when that time comes, well.

You look around and find you've got nothing to lean on.

# Twenty-Five

## When You Only Think You're Waving

She did her best to not put too much credence into that whole drowning thing. After all, she did feel quite a bit better about things once she'd gotten a good night's sleep. And spent a bit of time doing normal things at home. She made breakfast and watched some daytime TV, and Connie stopped round to see how she was doing.

She breezed in looking as cool as she usually did. Currently blue hair still in the shape it had probably gotten into the night before, pale cheeks perfectly highlighted with something pink and something slightly sparkly and something shadowy. Favorite armchair in Mabel's flat already commandeered, so she could regale her with her latest escapades.

". . . and then it turned out, he was *trying to flee the country*," she finished breathlessly, while Mabel was still trying to catch up with the first part of the story. She had questions, and Connie was already moving on—to the actually exciting thing that was supposedly happening to her.

Even though it wasn't exciting in the way Connie thought.

And so she couldn't actually say anything much about it all.

In fact, even the stuff she thought she could say seemed impossibly difficult.

"So," Connie said. "Is he as hot in the sack as I always told you he would be?"

And she had to actually think about it. She had to go over what was okay to say and what wasn't, what was a lie and what was truth, and for so long that Connie started to look puzzled. "Hey, did you break?" she asked.

Then Mabel had to scramble.

"No, no," she said. "I was just thinking about how hot it was."

And thankfully that got a throaty cackle out of Connie.

"I knew it. I knew that lass wasn't lying. He can go for hours, right?"

*Well, he probably can when a fake relationship and my inexplicable horniness and us making things forbidden isn't ratcheting up the ridiculous sexual tension to levels neither of us can cope with,* she thought. But of course she couldn't say that. So now she was split right down the middle, between the person she was and the person she needed to be for Connie.

And it wasn't just difficult.

It was gross. It felt gross to do this to her best friend.

"Oh yeah," she gasped, in an even more exaggerated version of her usual bubbliness. And for the first time it didn't just feel like armor, or a kind of secondary part of her, but actively fake. Silly and dishonest. *You should be telling her about how stressful and exciting and awful and amazing all this is right now,* a little voice whispered to her. *She'd be able to help you with it, at the very least.*

But instead, she exclaimed over how sexy he was.

How good he made her feel.

Without ever letting on that her heart was breaking a little bit over the idea that he'd never be able to make her feel that way forever. All she could manage was a little hint of worry on the end. "Of course I know it's not going to last," she said.

But even that didn't help her.

"I wouldn't bank on it. He looks smitten in every picture I see of you both," Connie said. So now she had to somehow temper her friend's expectations. Brace her for what was undoubtedly going to be some kind of horrible fallout.

"He probably just had a flash in his eyes."

"How can he have a flash in his eyes when he's always looking at you?"

"Oh come on, he's not always looking at me."

"No, sometimes he's staring at your boobs."

"Well, to be fair to him they are my best feature."

Connie shook her head and laughed.

"Your best feature is that smile, and he clearly knows it," she said as Mabel's heart simultaneously sank and started to believe too much. *Maybe it is, maybe he does feel this way*, she thought.

And honestly, she could almost believe it when she saw him next. After Connie had zipped off to her next calamity, and she'd gotten the car over to his, she just walked in the door, and saw him, and all kinds of feelings swallowed her whole. And when she tried to fight back with the usual thoughts—like *Maybe he isn't that interested, maybe it's already all out of his system like you supposedly wanted*—her brain actually scoffed. It scoffed at her. *Look at him*, it said. *He's completely gone.*

And it was right. He was.

He looked simply ravenous.

Like a wolf that hadn't eaten for a week.

In fact, she honestly thought she heard him growl low in his throat when she slipped out of her coat and revealed the flimsy, flowery dress she had on underneath. And when she suggested they do something ordinary, like make cups of tea, he listened. He followed her into the kitchen. But he didn't act like a normal person, watching a friend put the kettle on.

He stood too close, for starters.

Really close.

As in, she could feel his breath on the nape of her neck. And the air stirring between their bodies. Not to mention the hands she could sense, almost but not quite touching her. Like he wanted to, he wanted to grab her by the hips and haul her into the curve of his body, but couldn't quite bring himself to just go for it. *Because he's still trying to be a gentleman*, she thought. And it was this that made her do what she did, in the end. Just the idea of him still holding back, still waiting for her to give the okay.

It sent her over the edge. It made her rub back against him

before she could even think about it. And as soon as she did, he responded in kind. More than in kind, really—he made another sound, low in his throat. Only this one was louder, and more obvious, and it ended with a string of guttural words. "Can't even wait five minutes for it, huh," he said, and though she flushed red when he did she couldn't deny it.

Or even say anything at all, really.

Because now he did have his hands on her hips.

And he wasn't using them to keep her still, or make things go at some leisurely, normal sort of pace. No, he was fully pulling her back against him, over and over, until she couldn't fail to understand what he was doing. He was working her over his cock. He was getting himself off, in a way that made her even more mindless than she'd felt before. She went to say his name, and only sounds came out; after a second of it she could hardly stay on her feet. Suddenly, her legs were liquid.

And not even holding on to the countertop truly helped.

She spread her hands over it, and still felt as if she were about to collapse.

But it was fine, it was good, because he apparently knew. He saw, or felt it, and just put an arm across her body. Like a seat belt, keeping her in this ride—which sounded ridiculous. But was definitely needed when she realized the other thing he was doing. He had started pushing up her dress, somewhere in the middle of saving her from sinking to the ground. And now he was pulling at her underwear, desperately enough that it made her gasp and squirm against him.

Though even that didn't make him pause.

"Tell me if you want me to stop," he gruffed out against the side of her face.

As if she were ever going to do that. Honestly it was all she could do not to actively hurry him on. To yank her own underwear down, and spread her legs, and bend the exact way he needed her. But she was glad she managed to be patient, to wait, to let him. Because god, the feel of him doing it all. He actually put a hand on her inner thigh, to get them apart. And when he pushed her over the counter, he put his free hand between her legs. To check if she was wet enough, she thought.

Then moaned when he proved her right.

He slid two fingers into her cunt and groaned over what he found there. "Fucking hell, I can't believe how much you want it," he said. "Getting this wet over me doing nothing but rut up against you."

And she didn't want to say anything in response, she really didn't. But the trouble with being this turned on wasn't just what it did to *his* mouth. It was what it did to *hers*. It seemed to disconnect said mouth from any safety rails she'd set up.

So suddenly she was nothing but a truth machine, willing to let out all kinds of things she usually wouldn't. "I got this wet just looking at you at the door," she said without even really thinking about it. Though thankfully, he didn't seem to mind. Quite the contrary—the second she said it she felt him press his mouth against the nape of her neck, in this maddeningly hungry sort of way.

And as he did, she heard the sound of his zipper.

Loud, even over the sounds of their harsh breathing.

Like a siren blaring out *He is going to fuck you now, he is going to fuck you now, just like that he's going to fuck you.* And he was. He did. The next sound she heard was the snap of a condom, and then it was just that long, slow, slide of his thick cock. First over and through her slick folds, stroking and teasing and waiting until she was practically pushing back against him.

And then, and then.

Oh then.

He just sank into her, all good and easy. Like on the bed, only even better somehow, here. Because there it had made sense that it had been so smooth and delicious. But here there had been nothing before it. And no time to relax and lie back. This was much more frantic and feverish, to the point where it almost felt rough. His fingers were digging into her hips; the counter was pressing into her.

Yet it sent her, all the same.

It made her gasp his name.

And she couldn't help being that way back.

She moved a hand to his hair before she'd even thought about it, and she knew she was pulling just a little bit. That she had a fistful of those curls and was squeezing too tightly. And when he went just a little too slowly for her, she couldn't help it. She pushed back against him, hard hard hard. She fucked herself on him, until all she could feel was this pleasure, this mindless near brutal pleasure.

Of the sort he seemed to be enjoying, too.

"Oh yeah, go on, go on, get what you need," he groaned, the second he felt what she was doing. So she did. She went faster, and harder, as if all that mattered was getting off. There was nothing more to this, nothing at all—just fucking each other and feeling good and being as filthy as humanly possible.

*I don't want anything else*, she told herself as her pleasure crested.

Then he spoke against the side of her face.

"Tell me you love it," he said.

And she went to do it.

The words were there, rising through her alongside the heated bloom of her orgasm. Then they hit her lips, and somehow, they weren't the same. They started out right, with the *I* and the *love*. But after that she somehow couldn't finish. She couldn't end the sentence. And oh god, she knew why.

Because she didn't want to say *it*.

She wanted to say *you*.

And so urgently that she almost didn't manage to stop herself in time.

The starting letter was actually on her lips. She felt them circle around it, ready to push it out. She had to jam her fist into her mouth to keep the word in, and even then she didn't feel safe. She couldn't feel safe, because that sentence was now racing around inside her head. Over and over, like a litany.

Like a taunt.

*I love you.*

*I love you, Alfie.*

And after that, she knew she wasn't just drowning.

She was already underwater, and far, far beyond being saved.

Text Messages, April 10, 2022

**Connie 12:32 p.m.**
Hey babe, is everything okay? I
know we were joking around the
other day but you seemed off. I
dunno, maybe I'm just being mad.
Just wanted you to know you
can tell us if it's not all hearts and
flowers.

# Twenty-Six

## When You Smile All the Time, Confessing You Can't Goes Like This

$S$he told herself that it had just been a mistake.

And that made sense when she thought about it. They'd been in the middle of a very heated, passionate, pleasurable thing. It was only natural that this had kicked up a lot of feelings. But especially for someone like her, with so little experience of this kind of intensity between two people. She was used to things like going on a date that ended with the person disappearing in the middle. Or maybe they made it to the bedroom with her, but then everything was so tepid and boring to her it barely felt like fucking at all.

Or at least, it barely felt like that compared to whatever this was.

So it made sense that she was all overwhelmed.

That she was ready to blurt out bonkers things at a moment's notice.

Actually hot sex had turned her into some other sort of person—one with no emotional guardrails and not a lick of sense in her head. And if she removed said hot sex, then everything would go back to the way it was. They could have those great conversations again. Or watch movies. Or go to concerts together.

Everything would be okay, she told herself.

Then she saw him, framed in her doorway.

Just there to pick her up, looking plain as could be.

That suit, just like any of the other suits he'd worn back at the beginning.

His hair parted, his beard trimmed, his gaze clear of any kind of heat. He even said something dull to her, like *Come on we need to get off if we're going to beat traffic.* Same as many people had said to her before. Nothing sexy, no sign that he wanted to fuck. No thread of desire thrumming through his words.

And it just happened anyway.

It popped it into her head.

Plain and simple.

*I love you.*

Though thank god, thank god, it didn't seem to show. He didn't look at her like it was there, behind her eyes. Or even notice that she'd briefly frozen, like her own thoughts had fucking shot her. He just reached out and took her hand, and led her past what was, by this point, only one lone photographer. *Smile,* he said, as they passed him. And she did, automatically.

But god, she couldn't help wondering what said smile looked like.

*I bet I seem like a corpse that someone forced with their fingers into grinning,* she thought. *Like* Weekend at Bernie's, *only about a woman who doesn't understand the first thing about her own feelings.* Because that was the thing, wasn't it? She didn't. She hadn't, at any point. Even though it was increasingly seeming like she'd been growing these emotions for quite some time.

*You felt like this before he even kissed you,* her mind said.

Only it didn't feel like it was just saying.

It felt like it was taunting her.

Like it was telling her how big a fool she was.

And at the same time, giving her absolutely no outs. Because if it was just sex that was doing this, well. She could escape, then. She could dismiss it. But if it was there now, when nothing was happening . . . if it had been there all along, lurking inside her like a second beat of a heart she didn't even know she had . . .

Then there was nothing she could do.

She just had to feel this.

And oh god, she did.

She did.

It happened again, once they were in the car. He reached

forward and touched her hair. Then just as she was half panicking and half wondering why, she grasped the reason. She had something caught in the tangles. Just a bit of fluff, no big deal. But he'd seen it, and sorted it, and done so almost absentmindedly.

Like it was pure instinct now to care about her.

And make contact.

And turn her inside fucking out.

Because Lord, did it turn her inside fucking out.

It hit her harder than the sex had. Than the kissing had. Than all the times he'd done similar things prior. As if her eyes had been forced open, and now all she could see was how much he meant to her.

And how desperate she was to tell him so.

*I love you*, she thought again.

But this time it wasn't just for herself.

It was aimed at him. It tried to shine out of her face and push past her lips, and only the last shreds of her sense kept the words inside. They clung on, with just the tips of their fingers. But even as they did, she could feel them losing their grip. Give it another thing like that, another touch of his hand, another hint of his soft feelings toward her, and it would be done.

And she knew it.

It was obvious now.

Though she tried to deny it just a little longer.

She let him take her hand again as they left the car.

And say that she looked lovely on the way in.

Then he closed the door behind them, and he turned to her, and she thought blankly: *He is going to lean in to kiss me, and when he does I will simply let it out.* Like someone realizing they were about to killed by an oncoming car. So just before it could hit, she swapped the words she couldn't help saying.

For ones that would stop all this before it could.

"Alfie, please no, I can't," she gasped out.

And to his credit, he immediately backed up.

That kiss he'd been about to give her turned into hesitation. Then concern when he saw how she looked. Because she knew the way it must seem: like she was suddenly falling apart. Her hands were in her own hair before she could control them; her forehead felt like it had been split down the middle. And even though she was fighting hard to breathe slowly and evenly, it wasn't working. She sounded close to hyperventilating.

So of course the first thing he said was:

"Oh god, what did I do wrong?"

As if he'd punched her, somehow, without knowing it. Which was good in one way, because it had immediately given her the space she needed. But terrible in another, considering he hadn't done anything of the sort. It wasn't his fault that she was inexplicably falling in love with him and frantically trying to hide it. He was just here minding his fucking business.

And that meant reassuring him. Right now.

In a way that didn't somehow make things worse.

"You didn't do anything wrong, Alfie," she tried.

But she could tell it hadn't worked before he even replied.

"I clearly did. So just tell me what it was that you didn't like."

*Being in love with you when we're supposed to be casually fucking our way out of nuclear-level lust*, she thought at him. Then thankfully managed to say something much more reasonable. "You didn't do anything that I didn't like. You never do anything that I don't like. That's kind of the entire problem."

"So then you want to hate it. You're upset that it wasn't awful enough."

"Yes. No. I don't know. I just feel a bit overwhelmed right now."

"Well, that's all right. Let's just have a nice cup of tea so you—"

She held up her hands before he could finish that thought. She had to, before he got her back to the scene of the last sexy thing they'd done. And then made her want to do it all over again. "No, god *no*, I don't want to do that, either."

"Why? What did Tetley's do?"

"Nothing. It just sat there while you railed me over the kitchen counter."

"So the kitchen counter railing is the problem. Damn, you know I felt when I was doing it that I was going too far. That I was getting too out of control," he said. Then shook his head at himself wearily. Like *he* was still the problem.

Even though he wasn't, he wasn't at all.

It was just that explaining that was really difficult without the ability to tell the whole truth. It meant she had to keep saying what was wrong without really saying what was wrong, and oh god, it was hard. Like conversational algebra.

"It's not you who's getting out of control. It's me. I don't like how this is making me feel," she managed to get out, but then of course there was the question of what exactly it was that she felt, hanging in the air like a big sign that said *I love you I love you I am pathetically and ridiculously in love with you*. So she had to try to clarify. "It's like I'm helpless. Like I can't stop doing this. Even though doing this is way beyond what I ever imagined. I thought it would just be a couple of fucks and then everything would be the way it was. But instead, it's like something has taken hold of me, and I just can't cope with it, Alfie. I think it might be killing me, just a little bit. Which sounds mad, I know, I can see how mad it is, but I—"

He stopped her before she could go any further.

Most likely because she was babbling by that point.

And somewhere in the middle, she'd started flapping her hands.

Quite clearly, because he took hold of them as he cut in. "No, no, it doesn't sound mad. It's okay, it's okay," he said. Soothingly, too. Though of course nothing could ever be soothing now. For several reasons, starting with this one:

"But it isn't. This whole thing was my bloody idea."

He kept trying, however. He squeezed her hands.

And said more things in an attempt to make it all be okay.

"Yeah, and sometimes ideas go places you didn't imagine. They do stuff you didn't really want. You think things are gonna be one way and then next thing you know it's the opposite. I get that, love, you don't have to explain."

"I want to, though. I just . . . I can't. And I can't just smile and—"

"You don't have to. And you don't have to just smile with me, neither. I don't mind what you're like, sad or sunny or panicking or whatever else. It's all right. You can just be whatever you need to be and only tell me whatever you want to."

She dared to meet his eyes on the end of that.

But when she did she kind of wished she hadn't.

Because they were so soft and so kind, and now he was speaking, in that low, grave voice of his. "You go home, and rest easy, and tomorrow we'll just pretend all this never happened," he said. And that was good, it was so good of him, he was pure goodness through and through.

There was just one problem with that:

It made her love him even more than she had before.

And in a way she knew she would never now escape from.

Draft Unsent Messages, April 15, 2022

**Mabel 6:36 a.m.**
Alfie, here's the thing

**Mabel 6:42 a.m.**
Alfie, I'm really struggli

**Mabel 7:47 a.m.**
Okay so I'm just going to say it.
I love you, and I know you could
never

**Mabel 7:53 a.m.**
I mean I think that you could never

**Mabel 8:02 a.m.**
I wish that you could

**Mabel 8:10 a.m.**
No, I wish I could be certain that
you might, one day.
But I don't think I'm built like that.

**Mabel 8:12 a.m.**
I don't think you're built like that.
So it's better this way.

# Twenty-Seven

## Reddit Would Have Definitely
## Come up with a Better Answer

$S$he thought that *maybe* she would feel better about things the next day.

Like there was a way out of her feelings, if she just focused really hard.

But then she discovered he had texted, asking her if she was okay. At six in the morning, no less—as if he couldn't even wait until a normal time to find out. He had to do it at the crack of dawn, and in the tenderest possible way she could imagine. Just let me know that you're all right, the message said.

So it wasn't a surprise that she burst into tears over it.

Or that she couldn't quite bring herself to reply.

Because of course she knew if she did that she was going to end up saying something really daft. Something that was apparently always on the tip of her tongue now, no matter how much distance she got from it. She separated herself from him, and let a whole night pass, and only made contact with him via text on a screen. And still, there it was. That urge to tell him how she was feeling.

And yeah, said feeling was less intense now.

It wasn't a straight *Oh my god I love you.*

But she knew it was dangerous, nonetheless. Maybe even more dangerous, truth be told, because it was so sly and insidious. *He wouldn't be disgusted if you said you were having mild affectionate feelings for him,* her brain suggested, in one particularly precarious moment. Then more terribly, it added on the end: *It could well be that he has them for you, too.*

And the worst part was: she almost felt herself buying into it.

For a second, it really seemed like something that could be the case.

After all, he'd said he enjoyed her company. And that he didn't find her hideous. And he obviously felt something like desire for her—even if the desire was mostly just his kink and a little less sex than he usually had. So wasn't it possible that this was enough? That if she said *Hey, do you think we could maybe do this for real*, he would say yes?

God, she thought. It was.

In fact, it sounded more reasonable than whatever she was doing right now—and so much so that she almost texted it to him. She came literally within a hair's breadth of tapping out the words, any words, just something that properly explained what she was going through.

But just before she could, another message popped up.

Like a word shield, deflecting the bullet she'd just aimed at her own head.

Maybe we should stop doing this altogether, it said.

And oh god, the sound of mingled pain and relief she let out. Because yes, sure, it was pretty devastating to know for certain that he wasn't feeling the same things. It made her heart briefly fall out of her body before she could get ahold of herself. But at the same time, it was far and away better than the humiliation she would have felt if she'd confessed, and then gotten an answer like that.

After all, one of those things was simply like swallowing bitter medicine of the sort she was very used to. Horrible, true, but in the end she'd survive. Whereas the other option, well. That was closer to having her heart cut out. And she knew that there was no real way to survive anything of the sort.

It would kill her, unquestionably.

And even though living like this wasn't great, she did kind of want to keep doing it. So she typed without even thinking about it:

That's probably for the best.

Then hit send.

*  *  *

$\mathcal{S}$he didn't hear from him for a little while after that. But that didn't exactly feel like a bad thing. This way, she had time to get herself straightened out. To build up guardrails around her emotions, so she wouldn't be weird when she did see him. After all, the last thing she wanted was to start blubbering in front of him. He'd have questions, then.

And what was she supposed to say? *I (33F annoying weird neurotic gremlin) fell in love with him (38M gorgeous wonderful famous rich hilarious caring superstar) and was really upset that he unsurprisingly wasn't that into it?* No, god no, that sounded absolutely batshit. She had to be better than that.

And by day three, she was.

She knew she was, because when Beck called her, her voice almost sounded normal again. It didn't shake or seem thick with tears. And when he suggested she come in for a meeting, she didn't even hesitate to say yes. In fact, that seemed like a good practice run of contact before she had to see Alfie again.

"I can be there in an hour," she told him.

Though it didn't even take her that. She simply threw on some clothes, got herself into an Uber, then breezed into his office, like nothing had ever gone wrong a day in her life. Smile wide, eyes bright, bubbliness firmly in place. *I am emotional Teflon,* she told herself, as she sat down in the seat across his desk from him. And honestly everything in front of her only helped with that.

He'd transformed Greg's old drab haunt into the coziest, warmest little nook she'd ever seen in her life. It now looked like the area of a library where kids got to read charming stuff. Every available corner was crammed with either soft furnishings, shelves overflowing with the most delightful books, or framed pictures of inspiring things. Or all three at the same time. She spied a whole beanbag sandwiched between two bookcases, with a photograph of him excitedly shaking Mister Rogers's hand above it. And a sofa similarly situated beneath a cross-stitched aphorism. Or not an aphorism, exactly.

Just a tweet she recognized.

*Everything happens so much,* someone had neatly sewn.

And she suspected the someone responsible was him.

He definitely looked like the kind of man who would never be above doing a bit of needlepoint, she felt. And not just because he was wearing an actual bow tie with the shirt and V-neck jumper he'd chosen to wear today. No, it was his expression that really sold the idea. Because however cheery and sweet she'd thought he'd be, from his company headshot and his delightful phone manner, the man in person was ten times that and then some.

He actually looked excited to see her.

And offered to *make* her a coffee once she was sitting down.

"I have this fancy doodad right here in my office, so I can, you know, play a bit of the host and kind of set people at ease," he said. Though he had to know his manner had already done just that. She felt more relaxed within five minutes of meeting him than she had in the entire time she'd spent in this building with anybody else. She almost wanted to thank him for being so much kinder than she was used to.

And that was before he got down to business.

"So I just want to start out by saying what a terrific, terrific job you've done," he said the moment he'd finished making her a caramel latte with extra foam. "Honest to goodness, if you had told me that somebody was about to persuade Alfie Harding into actually telling them personal things about himself, and then letting them put it all into a book, I would have thought you were plain nuts. But here you come along, bright as a button, and damn if he doesn't just give it all over to you."

Then he shook his head, like it was just that wild.

Even though it was pretty simple, really.

*Just gradually fall for him without your own permission or aware-ness, until you're a desperate mess of a person unable even to control your own emotions in a cheery meeting*, she answered him in her head. Then had to clench her teeth to stop said emotions from happening. *Things have to get better sometime*, she read, from the cross-stitch above his head.

And weirdly, it did kind of help.

As did him doing all the talking.

Even if the talking was about things she didn't want to think about.

"Not to mention the fact that you did it all while navigating the wilds of a relationship. I mean, if that's not a magical pairing of professionalism and things that make me all teary, I don't know what is. Truly you've got a gift, I tell you what."

*You've no idea, Beck*, she thought at him.

But before she could stress about that, he was on to something else.

"So I guess the question is now: What do you want to do next? Because your agent has just been chomping at the bit ever since you two kids got together, and now that you're free to talk about something new we absolutely should," he said, and so casually she almost didn't grasp it. She went to answer, almost gratefully, thinking about the last emails her agent had sent her, and only stopped when she fully realized what he'd done. He'd spoken as if this job were over.

Which made no sense at all.

It wasn't.

She hadn't even handed it in yet.

"I don't know what you mean."

"Well, now that this is all done."

"But it isn't all done. I've not finished."

"Oh, you're just being modest. This here thing Alfie sent over is as complete as I can imagine anything being. Though he did say you might fuss, so I'm to reassure you that everything is in order and there's no need for you to do a single other thing. In fact, he was quite adamant on that point. *She needs some peace, so you just let her be* were his exact words," Beck said. Then he shook his head, like wasn't that just the darnedest thing. Before adding, in that same *aw-shucks* casual-as-can-be kind of way, "Boy, is he ever protective of you. I about swooned myself."

And after that, she didn't quite know what to do with herself.

She sort of wanted to yell at him that none of this could be true.

But he'd said it so breezily, so matter-of-factly, so like she already knew, that there was no way to do it without seeming utterly mad. Or even worse: like she needed relationship counseling for a relationship she'd never actually had. He might try to console her, and oh god, that would just be so horrible when she barely even understood what he'd be consoling her over.

Because seriously, what had happened here?

She hadn't written nearly enough to make a three-hundred-page book.

Heck, she wasn't even sure if there was enough to make a one-hundred-page book. *Maybe he cleaned up your notes and filled in a few more blanks and got it to a number they were willing to accept,* her mind patiently explained. But her mind was a fool if it thought that helped. There was no way it could help when all it did was tell her he'd decided to cut all contact with her dead. He'd drawn a line under it.

And not even in a way she could be mad at.

Because how could you be mad when it made so much sense?

When it had gone the easiest it could possibly go for her? He'd even framed it like it was mostly done to protect her peace. And she could well believe that he believed that, too. So what on earth could she possibly do? There was nothing to say. Nothing that could be changed. If she tried to go back on it now it would only be worse.

But god, the way it hit her to know that.

How it stung her anyway, no matter how much she tried to see the good in it.

And she knew why, too. She understood fully, in that moment, sitting in Beck's cheery office while trying not to fall apart, what was destroying her inside. It wasn't just that she could never be with the man she loved. It was knowing that she'd lost her friend. Her good, good friend—one of the best she'd ever had.

He was gone. He was just gone.

She could never now have even that little thing.

And oh, that was just too devastating to bear.

But especially in front of Beck.

"You know, I just remembered I have to go," she said, and even as she did she could feel the tears in her voice. If she waited even one second more he was going to hear them, or see them, and she couldn't deal with that. There was no way to explain to him, and even if there had been she wasn't sure she would have wanted to.

It was always better if nobody knew you were in pain.

Or saw the real insides of you.

Because the moment they did, things like this happened.

You had a nervous breakdown in someone's office.

And would then spend the rest of your life never being the same again.

Group Chat, April 22, 2022

**mabiebabieisnotokay**
You guys, I think there's some stuff I
really need to talk to you about.

Post from the **Reddit** Sub r/hardingsarmy, January 3, 2023
u/alfredlover

I don't know you guys, I'm starting to feel weird about stuff. After that blind item that said no woman measures up to his last girlfriend and that's why he's never dating now, and those weird rumors about the memoir and then that picture on the mountain when he just looked gutted . . . what does it all mean?

I mean *I* don't think we went too far with the theories but a lot of people are turning on the theories and getting on her side and saying mistakes were made. Maybe he did like her? I mean she wasn't that bad. She was really nice to them girls who were upset about him being sad.

She didn't even get all up herself about the idea. She said they were wrong, that it had to be something else—then she said to send him a nice fan mail when his memoir comes out so he can feel good about his writing!

That's pretty lovely of her considering the theory that said they broke up because he realized she was hideous and awful.

So I dunno.

Were we the baddies??

One Year Later

There were twenty-seven reasons to not go to the party.

She listed them all in a notebook she'd been saving, because it was too beautiful to actually use. You know, just to really underline how massively important these points were. They were fancy-paper-you-don't-want-to-write-on important. And they definitely looked it, too, once they were all laid out. In fact, most of them were just general rules she'd abided by all her life, like: *It's a bad idea to spend time with a lot of posh people.*

And the rest were, if anything, even more vital.

Because they were practically a handbook on how to avoid embarrassment.

Even though most of them were just variations on *Alfie will be there.*

*He will see you with his eyes*, she'd written as her number-three reason to not go. Then underneath it, in lettering that looked just a little bit more wobbly but no less thickly and firmly written: *and he doesn't want that, he doesn't want it, if he did he would have texted you sometime in the last year.*

But that was the thing, wasn't it:

He hadn't.

Last she'd heard, he had been on extended vacation. Someone had taken a selfie with him on some mountain in New Zealand, of all places. Them beaming and astonished in the best hiking getup she'd ever seen, him in just his old duffel coat—which she'd long suspected he'd had since school—looking like . . . well. Not as angry as she had predicted when she'd clicked on the story.

In fact, if anything he'd seemed strangely calm, or neutral, or something else that she couldn't really understand but could sort of put a name to all the same. It seemed like his eyes were reaching for something, just a little bit.

*Solitude*, her mind supplied.

*Some relief from your constant squawking and trying to persuade him to do things.*

And that felt right. It felt really right. It made all the sense in the world.

So she wrote it down as number twelve on her list of reasons to not attend his book launch. Then she added: *All you did was annoy the shit out of him*. Which pained her a little more than she expected it to, after all this time. But in the end it felt better to do it. It felt bracing, like plunging into an icy ocean.

And she came out on the other side feeling stronger.

More resolved, it seemed like, to her.

So it was a real kick in the teeth to get a message from Beck, about ten minutes after she'd decided. Because the thing about Beck was—he had a real talent for talking her into things she didn't think she could do. Like when he'd suggested she could absolutely write a novel about her recent experiences. That in fact, they were very interested in a Cinderella story like that, with the kind of happy ending real life never had. And especially as she had a little fan base now.

Then when she'd still been skeptical, he'd wielded Alfie against her, like a lethal weapon. *He said that you would doubt yourself. But that you only did because you are so afraid of everything turning out terrible, even though it never possibly could when it was anything to do with you*, Beck had told her. Then she'd had to spend the next five hours trying not to cry in between hashing out a proposal for him with her agent. A proposal for a novel that he had then contracted.

And that she was now writing.

As if maybe things *could* turn out okay.

It was all right, sometimes, to have some hope.

Which was what she was thinking as he texted her: Why,

you not coming to this would be like me not going to my own birthday party. So it was pretty much a lost cause at that point. And doubly so when she texted Connie about it. Because Connie had been furious about the whole thing ever since Mabel confessed. First at Mabel for not telling her about everything while it was happening. Then when Mabel had apologized and explained exactly why she had felt she couldn't tell her, at Alfie for clearly being responsible for all the things that went wrong.

In fact, she felt it an incredible outrage that Alfie had roped Mabel into a scheme from a romance novel, then not fallen madly in love with her. Which, while completely unfair to him, did lead to absolutely hilarious messages like this: Yes you must go so we can swan in looking fabulous and tell everyone about your mega luxury amazing book deal while totally pretending he doesn't exist. Then two seconds later, another ping: That's the secret publishing code for your deal right, mega luxury amazing?

And so that was how she found herself in an unapologetically pink dress and ridiculously fluffy cardigan, with Connie on one side of her in that stylish purple thing of hers, Berinder on the other in the green velvet that perfectly set off her warm brown skin and sleek black hair, and finally Beck bringing up the rear in his blue tuxedo. *Like bookends*, she thought. *Or the nicest armed guards in the world.*

Then felt as if maybe this was actually going to be okay.

And that feeling continued, even after they got inside. Mainly because the place itself didn't seem half as intimidating as she'd thought it would be. It wasn't a big ballroom in some fancy house, like it had been for the last book launch she'd attended. It was more like a large but pleasant cottage of the kind she could imagine someone really living in.

And apparently, this was exactly what it was.

Beck accidentally confessed to her as she was busy delighting in the many comfy chairs and the collection of romantic movies all along one wall and the cozy little nooks that would just be the best to write in. *Yeah*, he said. *Alfie sure does have it set up nice here.*

Then he looked a little sheepish. Like he hadn't been supposed to say. But god, she was glad he'd gone ahead and done it anyway.

It felt good in ways she couldn't quite explain.

And right after that emotional whammy, she got a bunch of people being inexplicably nice. They were warm and welcoming, even when she babbled and smiled too much at them. And it didn't even seem to matter who they were. She met several footballers' wives, and someone who said he was a friend of Vinnie Jones. Then there was some sort of television producer, who wanted to tell her that it was a pleasure to make her acquaintance. Not to mention all the journalists.

Though she supposed that made the most sense.

They seemed to have questions for her, of the type that they couldn't quite ask. *You know any time you want to talk about you-know-what*, one of them said, and tried to slip her his card. But Beck and Connie and Berinder whisked her away before things could go any further, so that was okay. Or at least, better than having to chat about what they obviously wanted to chat about.

*So what was it like dating Alfie Harding*, she imagined them eventually saying. Or worse: *Confess, it was all a big put-on, wasn't it.* Because yes, it had been, but also no, it hadn't been at all. And sometimes, she wasn't really sure which she was going to blurt out. It was the reason she blocked accounts and numbers that tried to press her on it. And why she'd told Beck never to ask her about the specifics, beyond the things she was comfortable turning into fiction for this story.

Which he had abided by, bless him.

Even though she could tell, sometimes, that he desperately wanted to say something. To ask her things. *Are you really sure*, he'd once started with, and she'd known there was an end to that sentence. A pointed end that she probably wouldn't like. Because then he'd trailed away into nothing.

*Sometimes things just don't work out*, he'd said eventually. *I know that better than anyone.* Then they had sat in companionable silence, drinking warm cups of soup that he weirdly favored over tea or coffee. And he hadn't raised it again—not even when she suspected he needed to know something about Alfie's memoir.

No, when it came to that he'd just asked Alfie.

And Alfie must have answered.

Of course he had, because here the thing was. Arranged in a pyramid of hardbacks, in the glowing golden little room most people were milling around in. And thankfully, it didn't have his face on the cover. There was just the title, in a strangely pastel-colored font. *Like a romance novel*, she found herself thinking, then wanted to laugh.

But she couldn't. Because now she was processing what it was actually called. It wasn't *My Life in Football* anymore, for some unaccountable reason. Even though it still had been, last she'd looked. She'd checked online once in a moment of weakness and seen it there for preorder on Amazon.

Yet somehow that wasn't the case now.

No, now it was *The Only Other Person at the School Assembly.*

Which struck her as extremely odd for a memoir about footballing. But maybe just a little bit less so, in some terrified part of her brain. Because suddenly it was screaming really loudly at her about quite a lot of things that she'd pretended she didn't know. But now had to kind of think about a bit.

In a way that was making her feel quite sweaty.

And sort of like she wanted to run away immediately.

Instead of what she was actually doing, which was picking up a copy of the book. The one she hadn't finished writing—*You didn't even get a quarter through in any kind of reasonable shape* her brain yelled—but that nobody had ever asked her to so much as tweak in the event that things weren't quite right.

So she kind of knew what she would see when she opened it.

And yet somehow it still completely stunned her at the same time.

She read what was in there and let out a sound like the wind dying. The man next to her actually asked her if she was feeling okay, and suggested that it was probably the crab cakes if she wasn't. "I've felt iffy ever since I had one," he said, but she couldn't answer him. She was too busy having her brain blown out the back of her head by a book she was supposed to have at least partially ghostwritten. Or that someone else should have mostly ghostwritten.

But that Alfie Harding had almost fully written himself instead.

Nearly everything in it, every word—it was all him. And more than that:

It was all the truth, the whole truth, and nothing but the truth, so help her god.

Chapter one was actually titled: *If You Love Footie You're Going To Hate Hearing This*. And then it just plunged right in, completely unapologetically with: *Right, so if you're reading this thinking oh, this is gonna be a grand little trip down footballing memory lane, let me just stop you right there, mate. Because the first thing you should know about me is: I actually fucking hate football. And grand little trips. And, to be honest, memory lane. So what this here memoir is about to be I do not know. But I do know that's it not going to be close to whatever you might be thinking. So let's just all strap in and hope for the best.*

And it did not get less wild from there.

In fact, it got significantly more wild.

In about ten thousand different ways.

Chapter two was all about his childhood. But it wasn't her sanitized notes turned into something sort of accurate. Or even some of the mechanical-sounding passages she'd crafted to fit the brief. It was the kind of thing she would have written if she'd been let loose. If she'd been free to write as herself, with love for him.

Only *he* was the who had done it.

He described the childhood he'd actually told her about. That he'd sometimes even written about, before telling her it couldn't be included. Peeling the backs off cardboard coasters in pubs, so he could write little stories on them with the stubby pencils usually used to note down darts scores. Or hiding behind the sofa with a pack of Post-its, so nobody would catch him filling them with thousands of words.

And then just as she was feeling knocked for six by this, she flipped forward. Far beyond anything she'd ever even taken notes on, far past whatever she might have said.

And got to the chapter on how much he fucking loved romcoms.

*My favorites were the ones with Sandra Bullock in them,* he'd written. *But really, any would do. I wanted what they promised: soft-focus lives lived in enormous houses while wearing massive jumpers and having big feelings. Because it seemed almost constantly like my own feelings were meant to be small, compressed, like a lump of coal that someone was trying to turn into a diamond.*

*Only the diamond never emerged.*

*It was just hard, dusty rock all the way down.*

*And I hated that about myself as much as everybody else seemed to like it.*

*In fact, that's the real reason I actually stopped going on shit like* A Question of Sport. *It wasn't that I had a fistfight with David Weathers—although I did because frankly, he's a complete doorknob who can't keep his hands to himself—or that I didn't like how they did my hair, even though they fucking did do it wrong every time no matter how much I fucking told them the side part goes on the right. No, fuck no, that wasn't it. It's because I would see myself on whatever and find that man so far from the one I wanted to be that it would make me physically ill.*

*So now you're thinking, fuck's sake, this is depressing, isn't it? Is this all just going to be a dark descent into one man's disgust with himself and his inability to ever change? Well, it's gonna be a bit of that, I'm not going to lie. But if you bear with me a minute, it'll pay off, I swear. Because we're only a chapter or two of self-loathing away from meeting the woman I'm talking about in that title you were absolutely baffled by when you clocked this book on the shelf.*

At which point she almost put the thing down.

It felt like she had to, because her hands were sweating so much.

Somehow, she was shivering and yet boiling hot at the same time.

Which was probably just a natural consequence of being the most foolish, blinkered, oblivious person in the world. *You should have known,* her brain was telling her, over and over. *You should have guessed all this, you should have guessed he would do it himself and that he would do it honestly and rightly and it would be about you.* And it was true, she knew it was true, she knew she should have.

But she also understood why she hadn't.

It was because things never turned out all right where she was from.

Instead, your dad pissed away the money you were saving up for the Scholastic Book Fair. Kids made fun of you because you bought your clothes from Oxfam. Boys you liked thought you were strange, then later men you'd learned not to like too much thought the same. And if they called the next day?

It was only to say they'd never liked you anyway.

So you put your dreams aside and learned to live small.

To not write what you wanted, or be openhearted with friends.

Or believe that someone lovely might love you, against all the odds.

Even if they loved you so much they put it down in their books.

Because there it was, on page ninety-nine:

*Now here's the thing: I can't tell you anything specific about the person. You're not getting her name, so you can just put that from your minds right the fuck now. All you really need to be aware of is that she is, indisputably, the love of my life.*

*I know. Spoiler alert.*

And what was she supposed to do now?

How was she meant to cope, being all crushed down inside while this huge thing unfurled before her? She didn't know. All she could do was read on feverishly. She saw a million things from a completely different angle—like the restaurant, all the way back at the beginning, when he'd hidden behind the plant. And he'd told her it was just coincidence, but it hadn't been, it hadn't been. He'd done it on purpose, and not for any reason she would ever have been able to fathom.

*Her bloody bastard of an editor told me he'd gotten rid of her and that she was useless and they'd find me someone better. And all right, maybe I shouldn't have reacted to this news by being furious and following him to dinner to make sure he listened when I said I wanted her treated right. But in my defense, I was already so far gone on her it made me fucking fume the moment anyone tried to do her wrong. So yes, it's my fault he fled the country. And to be honest, I'd do it again.*

*I'd fight God if he got in her way.*

And that wasn't even the most extreme example.

No, the most was all the ways he'd carefully tried to describe the performance they'd put on, without really giving it all away. *I told the truth about the extent of my feelings to everybody else, and then hid it all from her. Because it felt like I had to, to save face. Because it seemed like too much. Too loud for where we were—like a man yelling about his love before you're even sure you're friends*, she read. Then thought of him bellowing at the paparazzi.

*She's my true love*, he'd said.

And now had to contend with the fact that he'd just been honest.

In a moment of high tension, they'd forced him into saying his real feelings.

All of which he'd then tried to explain away and turn into something small. Just a game to cover up all the ways it was real. Because it had been real, of course it had. It was there on page 119—*I wanted her so much I couldn't speak about it*—and 212—*she kept trying to make her desire smaller, I could see it, and yet couldn't stress to her just how little I wanted her to be smaller, how much I wanted her to be more, more, as much as she could stand*—and finally there she was, just flipping as far forward as the book went, to see the end of her own fucking story.

Her own *love* story. Her own *romantic comedy*.

*They say if you love something, let it go. Like letting go is as easy as opening your hands, so a thing that's hardly there can leave them. Instead of what it really is: sawing off your own arm, one millimeter at a time, with a wooden spoon. Then just standing there and watching yourself bleed, because you're too full of despair to do anything about it. Better, you think, that you let it happen.*

*Or at least, that was my thinking.*

*If I kept bleeding, I told myself, I could get all that useless love out of me.*

*But I realize now that the problem was and is: I don't want it out of me. I don't want to let out all the best parts and leave only the pain. To have the pressure, and not the diamond. It's not even the pressure that makes you a diamond. It's what she gave me: her seeing, her tenderness, her acceptance of everything everybody else finds foolish. And all the ways she helped me understand that it isn't.*

*It's not foolish to be who you truly are.*

*To not let yourself be crushed down into nothing.*

*Because it hurts when you try. But it's also the very, very best.*

*I promise you, I promise. My dearest one, I promise—because you probably know I'm writing this all for you, by now—it's better to be completely you, to dare and risk and take those chances, then to dwell in darkness. Go on, my love, and live your best life. Let it be beautiful, let it be glorious, let it be with someone who's all the good things that you deserve. You know that you deserve them.*

*Don't ever tell me otherwise.*

And after she'd read those last lines, she couldn't stop herself.

She just plunged into the party like a woman possessed. She searched for him in all the places she suspected he would be. And it didn't take her long to do it. Of course it didn't—she knew him well enough to know this, at least. He would be somewhere quiet, somewhere away from all these people, same as she would have been. So when she saw the closed curtains around what had to be doors out to the balcony attached to the master bedroom, she knew.

He was out there.

And he was.

She pushed the curtains aside and he was just standing there. Obvious fizzy apple juice in his hand, his back to all the festivities, every bit of him looking just as good as he had before. That curly hair, the curve of his cheek, the hint of those deep dark eyes, *god*. Then he turned, he turned.

And didn't even have the decency to look abashed to see her. The minute she came into view actual happiness washed over his face in a great wave. Like there was nothing else he could do. She pulled a string in him and out popped joy, no matter what the circumstances happened to be.

And these circumstances sure were something.

They felt like a fucking volcano inside her.

She came very, very close to just flinging herself at him.

But managed to settle for just shaking his fucking book in his face.

And possibly yelling at him, just a little bit.

"Alfie, what in the flipping flip is this?" she went with. But even then he didn't seem like a man who'd just told someone he loved them via his own memoir. And certainly not like one who'd said it in that absolutely overwhelming way.

He just seemed mystified.

"Think you'll find that's my memoir," he said.

Then he pointed. Like she wasn't quite clear on that part.

Even though she absolutely bloody well was.

"Yeah, I grasped that part."

"Then what are you struggling with?"

"You can't be seriously asking me that. Mate, this is supposed to be a boiled-down bunch of ghostwritten nothingness. To be about that time you had a dull footballing conversation with Terry Venables, written in a boring version of my writing. Or somebody else's writing. And instead, it's this. It's you. It's exactly how you feel, laid down perfectly on paper."

She flicked through the pages in front of him, occasionally pausing at ones she'd turned down the corners on. You know, to really give him the strongest examples of his many, many attempts at turning her heart inside out. Though she could see he still wasn't getting it.

And in ways she knew were not going to make any sense at all.

He was going to be absolutely weird about this, quite obviously.

Then sure enough:

"Yeah, but in my defense I didn't think you'd mind me not going with the dull conversations in the boring version of your writing. I mean you kept telling me it wasn't what you really wanted to do. And that I should just do it myself. So I did, without really thinking you'd feel like I erased your hard work," he said.

As if *that* was what she was talking about.

As if that fucking *mattered*.

And was not something so irrelevant she almost couldn't speak for a second.

Every word she wanted to say just tried to get out all at once, and created some kind of logjam. And when she finally managed, it wasn't with anything that got the point across. It was just outrage.

"For goodness' sake, Alfie, I'm not talking about my hard work."

"So what are you talking about, then?"

"Me being blooming *staggered*."

He at least had the decency to nod for that.

And agree with her in words, too. "Yeah, to be fair, you do look it."

"Well, can you blame me? I mean honestly, why are you looking at me like *I'm* being the weird one here? You're the one who named your hecking memoir after me."

"I never did. I kept your name fully out of it."

"Yeah, but *I'm the girl in assembly, Alfie*. I'm the bloody *girl*."

"Well, of course you are. It's just you and me that know that, though," he said. And then he laughed. He laughed, like she was being absurd. Or the only points of contention here were minor quibbles about whether or not he'd written down the words *Mabel* and *Willicker*. When of course they were not.

How could he not know they were not?

"Which is the only thing that matters. It's all I'm talking about here. I don't give a good gosh that people know it's me, you weirdo. I give a good gosh that I mean so bloody much to you that you did this absolutely wild thing. That you remembered this one little conversation we had, and that it affected you so strongly you gave it the most importance in a book about your *life*," she tried to explain.

And by that point she was really going for it, too.

She practically had hold of his lapels.

Or at least her hands were close to doing that very thing.

Only all she got in response was him, putting down his glass.

So he could take those hands in his.

*And try to soothe her.*

Even after everything, all he wanted to do was soothe her.

"Right. But I did that because it *is* the most important thing to me," he said.

Patiently, gently—like this was a thing that would ease her mind, too.

Despite how absolutely wild it was. Could he not see how wild it was?

"Oh my god. Oh my god, how are you saying this so matter-of-factly?"

"I don't know. Probably because it is one. A matter of fact, I mean."

"Maybe to you. To me it's like someone opened the Ark of the fricking Covenant right in my flabbergasted face. I swear to god, my eyeballs are about ten seconds from melting out of their sockets."

"Well, I've no idea why. I mean, I only wrote what you must already have some idea about. Because if you didn't, if you weren't bothered by the thought of me loving you and wanting more from you, why on earth did you run away?"

She took a second then. She had to, because she felt pretty sure her heart had just stopped. It simply ran to a standstill on the words *bothered* and *by* and *me loving you*, and then couldn't seem to get going again. She almost smacked herself in the chest, the phantom sensation was that intense.

And it didn't get any better once it faded.

Because now it was clear that she hadn't just fucked up.

He had, too. Of course he had, too. Somehow, he had, too.

So now she was the one who had to explain.

"Alfie, I ran away because I thought that things were really seriously going down a path that *you* didn't want. That you were just knee-jerking into it all and I was making you somehow and any second you were going to be disgusted," she said. Then wondered if his sudden expression was the one she had felt on her face on reading those passages. Like he had just found a door at the back of a wardrobe, and had the terrifying but incredible feeling that there was fucking *Narnia* on the other side.

Though like her, he tried to fight it. He tried to fight it really, really badly.

"That's not possible," he said. "I was so bad at covering it up. You must have suspected, at least."

"I didn't, though."

"Even though I told you in about twenty different ways."

"But you weren't specific. You didn't spell anything out. And Alfie, you have to know by now that I'm the sort of person who needs things spelled out."

"But I said all that about how lovely you are."

He raised an eyebrow then.

Like he thought he was onto something now.

Even though he completely fucking wasn't.

"That just meant that you were being nice."

"Nice. Is that what you told yourself?" He shook his head. "Phew, your self sure is gullible."

"It isn't gullible. It's just scared of making a fool of itself over a famous fucking footballer who probably says that sort of thing to every person he meets."

"But you know I don't say it to every person I meet, is the thing."

Okay, *now* he had a point. And so much of one that it made her cheeks heat.

She had to look away, embarrassed by how much she'd missed such easy things. Things she knew about him, things she understood, but had bypassed anyway in favor of what she always thought: that she was nothing. That she was not enough.

Even though she clearly was.

She absolutely was, and not just when it came to love.

When it came to other things, too.

Lots of things that she'd gone far too long without.

For almost no reason at all. *I don't know why I let things be this way for almost no reason at all,* she wanted to say. Yet somehow, she still found herself pressing him about it. "All right, I'll give you that. But the thing is, I needed more than that. I couldn't have gotten it with that one thing."

"So what about when I held your hand?"

"That was just for show," she protested. "It was pretend."

"Yeah. But the look I gave you after I brushed your hair wasn't."

"I didn't even know what that look meant. I thought I just startled you."

She glanced back at him then. Just to see how ridiculous he was finding her now. Only somehow, that wasn't what she saw when she took in his expression. It was all softness, all understanding, in a way that made her ache.

And that was *before* he spoke.

"You did. Because for a second your face was so full of unabashed affection for me that I didn't know how to deal with it," he said. Then more, there was more, oh, there was so much. "Honestly, do you have any idea what it was like for me, to see you look at me like I'd touched your heart? Like I meant something to you, like you could see softness in me, like you liked it, like you loved it, like all you wanted to do was ask me for more?"

*Because I did*, she thought.

*All along I did, even if I didn't know it.*

Though the more remarkable thing to her was that he had, too.

"I can't believe you felt that for me all the way back then. All that time ago."

"I felt something for you before that, Mabel. I felt it when you cradled my face in your hands. When you first talked to me like you enjoyed all the strange things I had to say. Even all the way back to when I first saw you in that office, so soft and earnest and lovely. Like everything I'd always longed for, but never been worthy of." He looked away, like he was remembering. And what he saw was so much more than she could ever have known. "Only you *did* think I was worthy of you—even if it was just for a little while, even if it was all just half pretend. And I want you to know, love, that I will always, always be so grateful to you for that. Because I swear, one second of whatever that was with you is worth a thousand years of anything I've ever known, from anyone else."

And then there was just silence.

A long, long silence.

That was only broken when he looked back and saw why she wasn't saying anything at all. "What are you crying for? Oh love, I don't want you to cry."

"I'm crying because I didn't know, Alfie. Don't you get it? I didn't know any of this. I didn't understand, not even deep down, I didn't, I just didn't. It seemed too mad, too impossible, too like something that happens in a bloody movie. And not just because I thought I was everything you didn't want—not just because I'm fluffy and silly, and you're serious and practical. Because I'm just so ordinary, and you're this beloved handsome rich icon. Who is also somehow funny and charismatic and interesting, god, you're the most interesting person I've ever met. Yet somehow, I'm supposed to believe you love me? It's absurd."

"Well yeah, if you put it like that."

"What other way would you put it?"

"That the love of my life might like me more than I thought."

He said it like he thought it would stop her being upset.

But of course all it did was just make it worse.

Because now it wasn't just words on a page.

It was right there, spilling out of him.

And the second it did she had to put her face in her hands.

Then somehow try to say her own version of everything he'd just done, through her fingers. In a voice that sounded cracked right down the center.

"Oh Jesus, of course I like you more. I don't even just like you. I love you, Alfie. I love you, I've always loved you. That look when you did my hair, that wasn't just me being touched. That was me *loving* you. I cradled your face because I couldn't not. And when I ran from you, when I was so hurt, it wasn't because you were rude. It was because I had read a thousand things about you and hoped for just a second that you were the sort of different I could already see. That you were like me on the inside. And you weren't in that moment." She caught her breath thinking of it. Of that crushing despair—and everything that followed. Before she finished: "But then you were. You are. You're the best man I've ever known."

And oh, she wanted to die once she had.

Because she'd admitted it all now.

Anything could happen, from that point on.

Like him taking the hands she still had over her face, and gently urging them down. So she could see him, looking the same as she had probably looked when she read those blasted words, and heard him say these blasted things: like his world had turned on its head, and every second of that upending was complete and utter bliss.

Even if it made him as ridiculous as she had been.

"Also, probably the most foolish man, though, I'm thinking now," he said, after a moment of deep and somehow incredibly satisfying silence. And he was holding her hands as he did it, too. He didn't let go. She was starting to think he might never let go now. In fact, she couldn't even think how he ever had.

Because she'd had her reasons.

But what had his been?

"Why were you that foolish, though? How didn't you know?" she asked.

And now it was his turn to look sheepish. He scrunched his face up on one side, hard enough that it almost closed his left eye. Then it seemed to take him a lot of effort to get the words out. Like it was the most embarrassing thing in the world.

Even though actually, it was this:

"Because you kept telling me that I wasn't your type. And when I told you what I thought your type was, you didn't disagree. And even though that became pretty ridiculous, after a while, I dunno. I just believed it. It made sense, given everything I felt about myself. I thought I was too brutish for you. Too much of a lad. Then even after I felt like less of one, in your eyes, even after I was honest about myself and you seemed to like it and then you were greedy for me the way you were . . . you said you just wanted me out of your system," he said.

After which, she had to very unfortunately concede:

He hadn't been that ridiculous at all.

Because she had told him at least some of those things.

And now she had to correct them all. Fiercely, so he'd never forget.

"But I never meant any of it. I never thought of you that way. You aren't that way to me. I was just so afraid, it seemed like giving you an out was the best option. It seemed like the best thing to do—to tell you that we could have this thing, then just stop," she said.

Then watched him glance, briefly, at the heavens.

"And then I agreed. I said sure, yeah, let's do that."

"To be fair to you, I did make it sound reasonable."

"You did. It seemed like the most sensible thing in the world at the time."

She shook her head. "Even though it was the silliest, really."

"Oh god, it was all so silly I could kick myself."

He laughed, then. And shook his head.

But he was squeezing her hands so tight as he did it.

Like it was so ridiculous, it was. But somehow at the same time it was all the ways people almost lost each other, over everything they couldn't say. *This is the way the world ends,* she thought. *Not with a fight, but with a single word left unsaid.*

Then felt like crying again.

She *was* crying again.

It was the reason he stroked his thumb over her cheek as she spoke.

"I shouldn't have told you it was killing me. I can see that now," she said.

"And I can see that I shouldn't have listened. I shouldn't have let you go."

"You thought you were doing the right thing. That you were helping me."

"I did. But now I wonder how on earth I didn't know."

He sighed and closed his eyes briefly.

Before he put the pieces together for himself.

"It was loving me that was killing you, wasn't it," he said. "Loving me and thinking I didn't love you. Even though I did, god, I did, Lord, I've never loved anyone in my life the way I love you. And I want you to know that now. I want you to feel it. I want it to be real for you, instead of whatever pretend scraps we fed ourselves because we thought that was all we could get."

"So that's why you wanted to do it. You thought it was all you could get."

"Of course it is. Of course it was. Even if I didn't always know it. Even though I told myself that we were doing it for the right reasons. That I was doing it for the right reasons. Deep down, I think I really just hoped that you would start to see what life with me could be like," he said, so wistfully she couldn't stop herself touching his face, the way he had touched hers. She didn't *want* to stop herself. She didn't need to. It was okay, now, to just be as affectionate as she'd always wanted to be with him.

And say all the things she'd kept inside for so long.

"Love, I knew what life with you could be like before a single second of the pretending. You told me when you were sorry, without ever actually doing anything wrong. When you made sure I was safe and comfortable, and defended me, at every opportunity you got. When you shared yourself with me, over and over, even when it scared you to do it." She took a breath. A hitching, emotional breath, just thinking of it all. Before she finished the last and most difficult bit. "I just wish I'd done even one tenth of the same for you. Because I would. I would make sure you were safe and defended with the last breath in me."

Then she dared to meet his gaze, and oh.

Oh, the many emotions now in it.

And the hitch in *his* voice when he answered her.

"But you already did. You already have," he said.

Which was baffling, it was, but only for a moment.

Because when she said:

"Against what? Against who?"

He answered like this:

"Against myself, love."

Softly, softly, so she could fully take it in, before he continued. "You made me see that all the parts of me I hated and hid— they are the best things about me. My greatest strengths, the qualities I should be the most proud of. And I am proud of them now, thanks to you. You can see I am. I put them all in a book, in my own words, for everybody to see. I am wholly myself now. Wholly the man I want to be."

And after that she couldn't help it.

She kissed him. She kissed him. She kissed him.

Hard, and as desperate about it as she'd never let herself be.

She hadn't allowed it before, but couldn't see why now. Because oh, the way he responded. It was like feeling someone fall and catching them in your arms. Like he'd been lost somewhere, and now finally someone was showing him the way home. And when finally, finally they pulled apart, he didn't let her go. He held her tight as she whispered up at him.

"So what do we do now, then?"

And he answered, eyes still full of her kiss and her love.

"Oh, I don't know. I was thinking we'd just live the lives we've always dreamt of, together."

So she responded in kind. With all her heart, and all her mind.

"Yeah, that sounds good to me. God, does that ever sound good to me."

## Inside Alfie Harding's Secret Wedding to Author Mabel Willicker

**Friends all sworn to secrecy**

**Not even his manager knew**

**Wedding dress rumored to have been made out of award-winning rugs**

**Bridesmaids all wore famed "telephone shoes"**

**Reddit group vows to debunk as conspiracy theory**

**Fans of the ship #Alfabel said to be "ecstatic"**

Anonymous sources claim that footballing legend Alfie Harding married his girlfriend of the last year, author Mabel Willicker, over the weekend.

Rumor has it the ceremony was held in an undisclosed location with a number of guests, and a possible buffet or dinner service, with either a string quartet or a brass band, depending on which tweeted account of the proceedings is to be believed.

In attendance were friends of the bride and groom, and some close family members. Tender glances and heartfelt vows were no doubt exchanged. Harding, 39, is said to have worn a dapper suit, while Willicker, 34, looked stunning in an outfit of some kind designed possibly by award-winning rug creator Berinder Sutanpal.

Our source told us, "See, I told you all they'd live happily ever after! Alfie Harding and Mabel Willicker FIVEVER!!"

# Acknowledgments

When I was a teenager, I daydreamed pretty intensely of being an author. But the way it went in my daydreams was usually ridiculously and impossibly fabulous. I imagined that I would have a wonderful and supportive agent who I went out to dinner with, and major publishers would bid for my novel, and then I would get a beautiful cover and a box full of glossy books, instead of the reality getting published showed me. Because it was fun and wonderful and I felt so lucky, but it wasn't any of that.

That was all pie in the sky. Something that could never really happen for little old me.

So imagine my total shock when it did, after fifteen years in this business.

All of that became a real thing.

Which is why the first person I'm going to thank is little me, for believing when I didn't. I'm glad I could finally give you something like those daydreams.

And then after that, there's a list as long as your arm, because I couldn't have done any of this without an army of people supporting me. My thanks to my agent, Courtney, for scooping me up and holding my hand and sticking by me when I stopped believing. My editor, Eileen, for that email three days after I subbed that made me sob with the realization that I was maybe more well-known and -liked than I had ever dreamt. It meant more to me than I can ever say. As have all of your support and your kindness and your thoughtful work on this book.

To everyone else at St. Martin's Griffin who had a hand in whipping this book into shape, including Lisa Bonvissuto for late-night genius Word doc help, Kejana Ayala and Hannah Tarro and everybody on the marketing/publicity teams who had a hand in such wonders as a whole pie made for my cover reveal, and Olga Grlic and Kelly Too for their beautiful design work.

And oh, to Leni Kauffman for her stunning illustration! Fifteen years, and this is the first time I've had a gorgeous fat woman on a cover of mine. Amazing.

Then, of course, there are all my buds and their endless patience with my spiraling. Lizzie, who started all of this. My Borg besties, Suleikha and Mel, who understand everything about it and talk me down frequently, interspersed with unhinged but very necessary tangents on everything from how okay it is to love a himbo to what is cursed about that fandom over there. Kylie Scott for making this even more special. Talia Hibbert, Olivia Dade, and Rosie Danan, for their forever smart advice and words that made my heart burst. Dahl! I miss you. Rebecca, thank you for saving my website bacon.

You're all the best. Also, I can hardly believe there are so many of you—whenever I read acknowledgments I always think, *Wow, that person is SO popular,* and here I am with an endless list of pals. If I've missed anyone, I am so sorry. Know that I adore you.

And finally, my family. My lovely mum, whom I also would never have made it without. You never once made me feel like this wasn't for the likes of me. The opposite, always. And my beloved husband, who made a force field around me. The one I used to imagine as a kid, to protect me from the monsters under the bed.

I love you, my one in particular.

You did and do so right by me.

Elizabeth Baker Photography

CHARLOTTE STEIN is the RT and DABWAHA–nominated author of more than fifty short stories, novellas, and novels. When not writing hilarious, deeply emotional, and intensely sexy books, she can be found eating jelly turtles, watching space wizards fight zombies, and occasionally lusting after hunks. For more on Charlotte, visit www.charlottestein.net.